Also by Jude Fawley

Novels
Bear Maze!
Karma Decay
Karma Ronin
Karma Mars *(Forthcoming)*

Novellas
The Car
Maligned
Mad Cow *(Forthcoming)*

BEAR MAZE!

JUDE FAWLEY

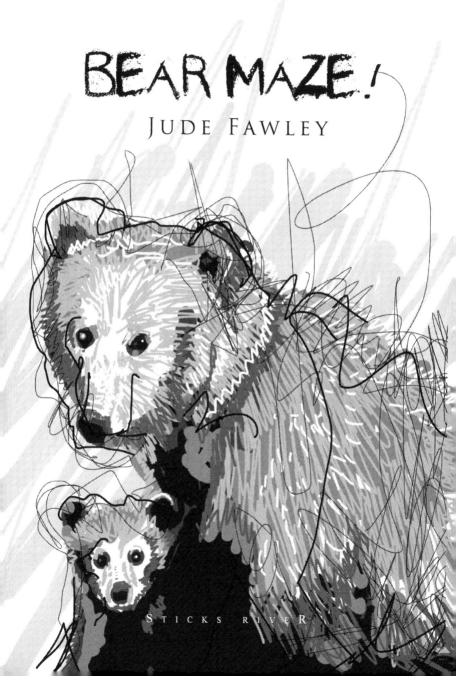

STICKS RIVER

STICKS RIVER

This book is a work of fiction. Names, characters, places, and incidents
either are products of the author's imagination or are used fictitiously.
Any resemblance to actual events or locales or persons,
living or dead, is entirely coincidental.

BEAR MAZE!

Copyright © 2015 Jude Fawley

DESIGNED BY KARL PFEIFFER

Selections of Chapter 4 by Forrest Heller

Text set in the Garamond family

Produced in the United States of America

ISBN-13: 978-1515179122
ISBN-10: 1515179125
Fiction

EXPANDED EDITION

To my Northern Star—
not shining as brightly these days, but I think I know the reasons why.
Light pollution is getting to us all

BEAR MAZE!

DER ERSTE TEIL: DER EINTRITT

KAPITEL EINS: BEAR AID

HE WAS A man of simple passions. As an eternal and abiding principle of his life, that was always true. His wife would have said that he was complex, so would all of the people that had once been his friends or colleagues, and most certainly his children, who were still too young to understand that he was a person. But he knew that they were all wrong. When he sat in his work chair, like he was that evening, there was nothing complex about his motivations. He was simply a man trying to do work. The work was complicated, but that was beside the point.

It was his misfortune that his spiritual simplicity was mirrored in his physical health. He envied the physically complex man, who could fall apart in stages, the type of man that aged in a probabilistic manner—for example, in that man's forties, his body would decide it had no affinity for physical exertion, later his head would randomly and independently go bald without consulting anybody, and his knees would retire in their fifties, even though his feet had aspirations yet. Such a man could have, in his nineties, a brain entirely in its youth, perhaps twelve years old, saved from ever experiencing the travails of puberty when his heart would suddenly fail and take everything down with it. That man was lucky. When the body of Daedalus decided to become old it did so collectively, it made a simple, unitary assertion—'we will be old!' All at once his back hurt, his sight and hearing evaporated, wrinkles appeared under his eyes, and a pallid grey asserted itself all over his body, to the point where he looked dead when he was sleeping.

He was a man trying to do work, he reminded himself. He started to wonder whether having a table in front of him would have positively altered his life in a meaningful way, if it would have made the difference between a successful night and slowly becoming a human plateau. Instead of on a table, his workbook lay in his lap, which was very lacking as far as level wooden surfaces went. The open pages of his workbook were slowly becoming black, but not because he had written or drawn anything in them. It was getting late. As if night was a satisfactory response to the demands of the empty page, he tenderly closed the book. His mind had become useless to him several hours before, and although he distinctly knew that to be the case he sat there anyway, lamenting its loss. Distracted and thinking about tables.

The book was a leather-bound collection of artifices, of alchemy and sadism, of formulas and carpentry. At least insofar as any of those things could be represented on paper. He found that sadism was easy to depict, and carpentry was much harder. After years of practicing technical drawing, he was still dissatisfied with every two-dimensional blueprint that he made, even for the simplest things. Carpentry needed to be embodied to do it any justice, he felt. But he didn't have tools anymore, so he tried to let it go.

Lately he had been conspicuously occupied by mazes, an obsession which mentally took him back to the time and place he had built his house. Then too he had been utterly fascinated with mazes, not merely with their construction but also with the worldview of a maze, their maxims, assumptions, their ethics, viabilities.

It had cost his wife a great deal of persuasion to get him not to build their house as a maze. He gave her a very long list of good reasons why a maze was the best place to live, but she wasn't convinced by any of them. His wife preferred the life of a castle, or at least the feeling of one, so would settle for nothing less than the most austere, practical, regal house that he could make. That was one of the first indications he was given, that he and his wife were two entirely different people. He hated ostentation. He would have much preferred to live in the dungeon of her fantastical castle, he would have preferred to build a house that extracted a castle's subterranean, its dark recesses and disjointedness, its loneliness. A house that celebrated obscurity. Like a real dungeon, it would have had the magnificent and suffocating presence of a castle on top of it, but nothing his wife would have been able to live in. He merely would have conveyed the essence of a castle above, with lumber and geometry. A real castle would have been unnecessary. He tried to think about how he would have accomplished the effect, but even his thoughts didn't do justice to carpentry either—he knew he could have built what he had in mind, but he would never be able to mentally possess it unless he built it. But it was in the past. Conjugal commitments said no.

Still the spectral taste of his maze lingered on his tongue, taunted him. He would have found solace in its abstruse core, in the miles of unlit obscurity that would have separated him from the world. In its actual form, the way he finally ended up building their house, he had difficulty finding peace. A man could simply stroll from the entrance to the master bedroom, if he had a mind to. If he *didn't* have a mind, he could probably have done the same. The aftertaste turned bitter and he desperately needed to stand up.

Already the night was impressively dark, and so was the room he was in, since he hadn't lit any candles. His workroom was the parlor of the house, which adjoined the foyer. From the foyer there was a staircase, or a short hallway to either the kitchen or his bedroom. The parlor contained bookcases, his chair, and a grand window that opened to the night sky, which was currently the object of salutary neglect by a new moon and a weak display of stars. He fumbled to put the book on a bookshelf, and he turned over again an hourglass on the window sill as he gazed outward at nothing at all.

He did the best he could to put mazes out of his head, but they wouldn't leave. Giving up, he decided it would be best to retire for the night. Through the absolute darkness of his house he easily, to his distaste, navigated to the door of his bedroom, where he paused. On the other side he could hear the light but audible breathing of his wife as she slept.

He loved his wife dearly, but he could not sleep next to her. He wasn't sure if it even had anything to do with her. For the past several months he had been having the worst of nightmares. They were worse than normal nightmares, worse than confronting his fears in the depths of unconsciousness, because at least such dreams would have been restful, if unsettling. His type of nightmares were half waking, they denied him the rest of sleep but also the presence of mind of waking. They were seeds of slumber that germinated into impostors of conscious thought, and so were creatures of purgatory. Whether waking life was heaven or hell he didn't know, but purgatory remained the same. For instance, a dream-thought would suddenly occur to him that all shapes had a unique and exact number associated with them. And, to understand any spatial thing at all, those numbers had to be added together. That was the seed. He would then dream of encountering a person. He wanted to know them. What innumerable problems he ran into, right away! Into what shapes was a person to be decomposed? The face was an oval, sure, but it was also more than that. And even if it was just an oval, what was the number associated with it? It was not the length of the semimajor axis, not its circumference—it was something much deeper and more intrinsic than that, so that he couldn't be satisfied with any obvious answer. Thus even his simplifications were incapable of being resolved, and yet his feverish mind considered not just the oval of the face, but everything at once. The strain would wake him up, but even then he struggled with the problem, and drifted back. Another example was trying to divide a sentence by the word *the*. He would formulate all the rules of division, maybe, and would break himself for an entire night trying to apply them in his sleep. It was oddly out of his control, and strangely lacking in the visual aspects of dreams as he knew them, so was driving him insane.

Standing at the doorway of his bedroom, he changed his mind. He turned back around, and walked away from the door and the vague confusion that the night would have brought him. Thoughts of mazes resurfaced—he couldn't help but feeling like he was in one, even in his simple house, and that within ten steps of the entrance he had already run into a deadend. He felt that if he returned to his work chair, he would at least have the benefit of being at the start again, with no progress made but the potential of a correct solution ahead of him.

Slowly, he returned to the beginning. He sat down. The chair was leather—he had killed the cow himself, had analyzed the personalities of a whole herd of cows until he knew he had found a tender, longsuffering cow with doleful eyes, which he considered at the time to be good qualities in a chair. There had been a complication involved, he remembered, killing the cow. The knife he used had been too small. It had been embarrassing for him, as a scientist, to underestimate the thickness of a cow's neck. But even a small knife worked in the end, when wielded by pride.

From the vantage of his chair he looked once more outward. If not for the three lamps visible from where he was, surrogate celestial bodies maintained by the city of Gibeah, he would have been able to see nothing of the outside world.

They emitted a slow river of light, on the banks of which would be one of the roads that led out of Gibeah. The light farthest to his right was very near one of the gates that monitored the exchange between civilization and wilderness, and the other two went toward the city.

As he watched, the light by the gate gave up its dissembling of a river, by acting in a way a river never could—it simply disappeared. He had been ready to dismiss it, to write it off as the consequence of an overzealous breeze, since the lamps were well protected from the whims of the wind but were by no means infallible, when two minutes later the middle light went out as well. Something was happening. A tree by the only remaining light, its foliage close around it, indicated with its stillness that no torrential wind existed outside. The agent must have been something else. He sat up straight, he stared piercingly into the darkness, as if his sight hadn't been failing him.

Something in him knew, with a power beyond conviction, that he was at the last crucial juncture of his life. That if he went back to his room and prayed for a good night's sleep, there was possibly a way back to simplicity again, pure and forgiving. That if he went outside, where his heart pulled, the way back would forever be cut off from him. That he really did stand at the beginning of the maze that he envisioned before, but he had misjudged its nature. The hourglass had not yet emptied, but he turned it over once more, and went to the foyer. There he opened the front door and, feeling the visceral cold of the air, reconsidered. He closed the door and went to his closet, where he put on a heavy coat. In the kitchen he found a candle and some matches. Once more in the parlor he felt much less confident than he had just seconds before—the candle seemed entirely inadequate to him, too reminiscent of all the lamps he had just seen fail. So he set it on a shelf and searched out his dictionary, where he kept his most valuable things. Between pages, a quarter of the way through the book, were four strands of hair, long and golden. He tied them in a loop, and placed them on top of his head like a halo. It also occurred to him to take a long straightedge ruler that he used on the rare occasion that his mazes utilized straight lines. He placed his head against the door of his bedroom one last time, listening to the breathing of his wife—then he was off.

The night was like the dreams he hadn't been having lately. It was unconsciousness, disclosed in the shape of a world—everything dark, everything cold. And just as he would have welcomed sleep, he welcomed the world and the challenge it brought, since he really couldn't see that much of anything. The third and final lamplight was still lit, far off in the distance, and he set off in its direction. It was the only stable object in his otherwise defunct vision. All the other things around him, the trees, the rocks, and a few statues he had made, were only selectively highlighted by the faraway light. They were unstable, they flickered and changed, they disappeared and reappeared in front of him like ghosts. Still, it was enough light that he could move forward.

Then the final light was taken from him, even as he watched. It went the way of the two lights before it, and there was a horrendous darkness surrounding him, the likes of which he had never experienced, and likely never would again. But it wasn't enough to entirely discomfit him as it might have some other person, because his environment had become remarkably reminiscent of the dungeons he had just been longing for, not minutes prior. The only thing betraying the illusion was the mercilessly fresh breeze that would have been much danker in a dungeon, after being filtered through the sediment of deep earth and decrepit bodies. Also, even an ephemeral light was more the essence of a dungeon, at least by Daedalus' conception; the light of faint hope, of the outside world, which made its ever-so-seductive trip inward—that was more befitting of a dungeon, to Daedalus.

So his spirit didn't entirely leave him—he came to a stop, and tried his hand at listening. Nothing but dead branches scraping, with the last clinging dead leaves of a bygone florid time, were to be heard. Truly a blind man, he did the best he could to conjure an internal map of his yard as he remembered it. It was a complexity he warmly received, in contrast as it was to the earlier simplicity of his house. Theoretically he could have used his ruler to probe about in front of him in further imitation of a blind man, but he didn't consider that an option, since it was his favorite ruler and he did not want to compromise its straightness by any misdirected swinging. So he held it under his right armpit and extended his hands forward slightly, at the very least not wishing to sacrifice his face in the ordeal. Reassured by the thorough silence around him, minus the trees, he took his first step since the loss of the final lamp. He immediately tripped over what must have been a wire, which resolutely deposited him on its other side. He chose not to react with his arms, nor to attempt to recover with his feet, and so ended up lying entirely prostrate on the ground, face down, with the ruler extending heavenward like an arrow from his back.

Accompanying his fall had been laughter. Partly, his inadequate response to falling had been sheer indifference, but it was also partly that he had been arrested by the sound of the laughter, so synchronous to his fall. As much as it would have been in his nature to do so, the wire was not put in the yard by his hand. He could also think of nothing that should have been laughing at him falling.

It had been a light, melodic laughter, the kind that left nothing in the air after it was gone. Very near.

He took advantage of his position—already reminiscent of supplication—to pray, there on top of the somewhat gravelly turf of his yard. The first and last words were holy and unchangeable, repeated ever since his childhood. Everything in between allowed for invention. "*Ich bin verrucht.* Apollo, protector of order and progenitor of all things lawful, thy humble servant beseeches thee, to be my guide in this, my time of need, to mortify those that would stand in opposition. *Immer sein Kind.*" With the last words a soft glow began to radiate from his head, from where he had placed the four strands of hair. It wasn't nearly enough to illuminate the world, but he could see his hands if he held them to his face, and they were a welcome sight.

Rising to his feet, he proceeded just as deliberately as before, one short blind step after another. With his hands he brandished the ruler in somewhat of an offensive manner, relying on the providential light from his head to forewarn immediate collisions. Still, his sides were too removed from its sphere of influence to prevent him from bumping into a tree with his right shoulder, which provoked another series of laughter. Recovering quickly he took a single strand of hair into the curve of his left index finger, and broke it from its place atop his head by pulling outward. An intense burst of light emitted coarsely through his yard, interrupting the laughter mid-flight and illuminating everything, albeit only for a second. Enough for him to realize he had been wrong about where he was, and to correct to his left a fair degree. Again he brushed a tree, again the laughter, but it had become more frantic, and he broke another strand to silence it.

His yard suddenly ended under his feet, giving way meekly into the cobblestone road that began at the east gate. Further along to the west, the road branched into two directions, one branch leading mostly to the cemetery, but with further divisions to accommodate other subsidiary destinations. The other branch led to the town proper. The third lamp, the last one to be extinguished, was situated where the two branches diverged. He increased his pace proportionately to the surety gained by being on a road, and came quickly upon the intersection.

Sounds of movement were ahead of him, footsteps of several people hurrying away. A bit of theatricality entered Daedalus' head. Loudly, with a confidence that startled even himself for its inexplicable appearance, he said, "Someone explain to me at once what is going on here!" He broke another strand, both to make an impression and to see anything at all, especially their reaction. The meandering light of a distant fourth lamp was slowly making things visible in a diffuse way, but it wasn't enough for him to make out any details.

Whatever their initial reaction to his voice was, when the light hit them it was to show a group of people running away, although two of them were largely inhibited by a ladder. The two seemed to refuse to drop their burden, but couldn't coordinate well enough between themselves to go fast with it. They were arguing in whispers, when Daedalus overtook them with his measuring stick.

"You'll explain yourselves!" he shouted. And, to the end of making a convincing argument, he lashed out at the nearest one. The stick caught the man flat across the top of his head, and probably didn't hurt so much, but it did inspire more conversation from the group. Daedalus was finally close enough to hear the exchange, and repeated the lashing motion throughout the course of it.

"And now there's an angel with a stick here, making inquiries," one said to the other, still in an only barely restrained whisper. "As if I didn't already feel uneasy about the whole affair. Should we—ah—explain to him?" He grunted when Daedalus hit him again.

"What do you mean, 'should we explain to him?' Of course not. This is all a secret, angel or no angel."

"Well that's easy for you to say, seeing as he's over here whaling away at me, and not you, like I was some sort of threshing needing done." At that point they entirely dropped their load, in order to more fully engage in debate.

"There wasn't supposed to be any witnesses! But now that there is, we're just going to have to make the best of it! What do you expect me to do?"

Daedalus struck again, even though it didn't seem to affect

much. The one man continued, "Ah! Now that one really hurt! The least you could do is trade me, then I wouldn't mind much going on our merry way and all." And they did. The man Daedalus had been physically remonstrating switched sides with the other, and they resumed their burden, along with their old pace. The multitude of stores that now lined the street provided a small amount of light here and there, with the cumulative effect that the scene was finally readily apparent.

Daedalus wasn't to be deterred by such a strange yet egalitarian turn around, but rather picked up where he left off as well. That time as he struck, he caught the fresh man with the edge of the ruler, instead of the flat side. If the lighting was sufficient, and had one cared to know, it could have been observed by the markings on the ruler that it was embedded a solid 1/16 of a cubit into the man's right shoulder, at its deepest point.

"Aghh!" the previous whisper was finally abandoned in the expression of pain. "No, I won't be having any of this!" he yelled, and dropped his side of the burden to run headlong after the others, who were a considerable distance ahead, the ruler making a fleshy suction sound as he pulled away from it.

The remaining man must have felt some strong obligation to carry the ladder to its destination anyway, with or without aid. He did not join the others in fleeing, but instead made his best effort at dragging the ladder, since it was too unwieldy for easy conveyance by one person.

Daedalus switched tactics. "I'll help you carry it, if you can tell me exactly what it is you've been up to?" The man remaining had already shown willingness to cooperate with him, to escape from the beating, if the other man hadn't insisted on the secrecy of their mission. So the approach seemed plausible.

He could see the man warring inside of his head, and it seemed he might concede to Daedalus' offer, but when he finally answered, it was to say, "No, that one there was likely

right, I've been sworn to secrecy, and this really isn't so bad after all. I'm moving along just fine, if you can see."

Daedalus' motivation to pursue was waning quickly, although he still had a fair amount of curiosity as to what was
happening. In the end, though, the waning got the better of
him. As suspicious as all of it was, it seemed as though he'd
done more harm than they had, him with his bloody ruler. He
bid the man farewell, and went to investigate one more thing
before retiring to his house.

The city wall, and the east gate where the road intersected
it, was only a quarter of a mile past his house.

His property was far removed from the norm of the city,
the land he was allotted being a good ten times larger than
that of anyone but the King himself. Daedalus was granted
the land back when he had favor—his allotment was propor-
tionate to the respect he had commanded. That was a general
principle, which was the reason that every other inhabitant of
the city—one hundred thousand by some estimates, considered lowlifes all—had hardly enough to exist on. At certain
times of diffidence he would consider apportioning out pieces
of his land to those that would make better use of it, but he
realized that it was never a reasonable thought. If he gave everything he had, it would have only helped a limited amount
of people, and it would have been just as easy and much more
effective to extend the city wall, to relieve some of the bulging that the population did against it. Quite possibly it was
just how conspicuous his house was that troubled Daedalus
at night. He didn't need the insight of his occupation to know
the problems of being conspicuous.

Familiarity told him that he had neared the gate, nothing
else. The last strand of hair on his head had nearly faded, and,
in the resumed darkness of the vicinity of his house, most of
what Daedalus could see was only afterimages burned into his
retina from the bursts of light. Only a small light, escaping
through the cracks of the guard shack's door in what seemed

to him ominously portentous ways, indicated that he had found the right place. He passed the guard shack and walked up to inspect the gate first.

He could only imagine that, years from then, the portcullis would be rusty and real, real in the way of things that decayed over time. But the bars still wore the veneer of artifice, were still unmistakably *made*. At least that was the impression he got by touching them, which was all he had to go by at the moment. Their artificial feeling could be explained by the fact that the gate and the wall that housed it were new additions to the city. Only some five years before—it hadn't been necessary until then. When it did become necessary, though, the job was given to some inadequate fool that vastly underestimated the human proclivity to procreate, most likely because he was so gawkily inadequate that he was universally excluded from that rite of procreation himself. That lack of foresight had caused the Gibeahn housing problem, at such a pitch just five years later! The houses were already built all the way into the walls themselves, welling up to extreme heights where they met its resistance, throughout the entire circumference of the city. Minus one conspicuous point.

The portcullis was firmly closed, and reassuringly locked. The only way to release the lock was in the guard shack itself, which was why Daedalus feared for the safety of the sentry. Due to Daedalus' living so close to one of the city's entrances—there were only three in all—he had made the acquaintance of most anyone that would ever operate the gate. Just by proximity. On some nights he would make extended conversation with the usual night guard, Wallace. He was the one who Daedalus feared for.

"Wallace?" he said, as he soundly knocked on the door. A startled noise ensued from inside, and the sound of feet rapidly hitting the floor. Daedalus knew it by intuition to be the sound of a man caught sleeping when he shouldn't. The same thing that made Wallace so amicable to Daedalus made him occupationally defective, and that was Wallace's advanced age. In a dire situation, it was likely that Wallace could not actually perform any of the duties that would then be incumbent on him. But since he'd had the job so long, either no one remembered to reevaluate his worthiness, or no one had the heart to fire him, hoping instead that his death would come before the next emergency, and they could then quietly replace him with a clean conscience. There was a great likelihood that they were experiencing that next emergency, Daedalus thought, and also a great likelihood that the sound behind the door was Wallace not being dead and quietly replaced.

The door opened from the inside, and a warm, wrinkled face presented itself, amidst a light that nearly blinded Daedalus after being in so much darkness. "Is that you, Marcus?" Wallace asked. "I recognized by the voice, come in! It is deathly cold out there."

Daedalus, often fondly and mistakenly called Marcus by the old man, was more than happy to oblige.

A hearth, large in relation to the size of the room, was intensely ablaze, radiating an excess of warmth. The fire, the quaint wooden furniture that furnished the place, and the compact size that concentrated all of those elements potently, lent such a coziness to the place that Daedalus could easily forgive Wallace for being put to sleep by it. It was unfair to sing lullabies to a child, then chastise it for falling asleep, Daedalus thought. Unless it was expedient to do so—Daedalus waved away all the pleasantries that usually accompanied his visits, to get to the heart of the matter. "You haven't seen any unusual activity lately, have you Wallace? Did you open the gate for anyone?" The likely answer would be that Wallace hadn't done either of those things, for being insensate in sleep. The group of men would have been there only fifteen minutes before, which wouldn't have left Wallace much time between dealing with them and going to bed. Unless he had the extraordinary ability of instantly dozing off at work, the envy of an insomniac like Daedalus.

"Speaking of all that," Wallace replied, "there was a time… oh, it couldn't have been but twenty years ago—my, what strange things time does, what errantry!—none other than King Gideon himself I believe, or was it Jerubbaal? rode up to these very gates. Demanding bread, or something like that—"

"This happens to be an exceptionally pressing matter, if you could just please—"

"A pressing matter! If you think this is pressing, then you haven't seen anything! How old were you when Abimelech took the city? You would have been just a lad, if I'm not mistaken, so you most likely wouldn't recall—"

"Excuse me." Daedalus had never tried *not* reminiscing with the man, and now that he had, he recognized the impossibility. "As it turns out, I have other things to attend to. I bid you farewell, Wallace. And we will speak again soon."

"So soon, you're leaving? Do come back, if you get the opportunity… no one listens like you do."

Daedalus hesitated for a second in departing, to look Wallace once more in the face, after the unexpected, pleading admission by the old man. The wrinkles of Wallace's face somehow worked together to conjure the epitome of piteous expression, and Daedalus realized that he wasn't truly looking at Wallace then, but only his soul, exposed perhaps for the first time ever in the most vulnerable of places, the human face.

"I…" Daedalus didn't know how to walk away from that expression. "Don't have the time right now." He left anyway. The cold outside seemed even harsher than before, and Daedalus felt like he was breathing in the essence of life itself, the way it stung so badly. In a good way.

He investigated the gate one more time, the best he could with his hands. He couldn't think of what the telltale signs might have been, if it was recently opened—but definite was the fact that it was closed again. He made his way tactilely back to his house.

An inexplicable amount of lights were on in his house, which was apparent very early in his return. They shone out of the great window from the room he had just recently been in, where he had looked inquisitively out toward where he was then approaching from. No one in his house should have been awake, or lighting lights. The revelation caused him to make haste in his return.

His front door was ajar. He'd spent long hours just sitting in his parlor, slowly and subconsciously memorizing the habitual place of everything that surrounded him, so that he immediately recognized that certain things of his had been unusually disturbed. Namely his hourglass, which had been turned over again, a grain of sand stubbornly stopping the vortex, and his chair, which had been rotated a few degrees. He was growing more agitated by the minute until he heard voices in his kitchen that were familiar, and perhaps capable of explaining what had happened. He laid the last depleted strand of hair around the hourglass, before cautiously making the simple way between the parlor and the kitchen.

His wife came into view first, leaning tensely against one of the counters that graced three sides of the kitchen. She was already looking in his direction, in anticipation of his arrival. The cabinets around her were in complete disarray, to a much larger degree than his parlor had been, with doors torn off and mud on the floor. Daedalus took the damage all in stride. Next to appear was David, whose shoulders were erect with the self-aware confidence of a protector, as he stood on the opposite side of the room as Bathsheba, Daedalus' wife. He was not visible until Daedalus had fully entered the room. Normally a bitter rage would have momentarily incapacitated Daedalus at the point of sudden discovery, but from hearing the voices he had had a suspicion, and was therefore able to surmount a much easier to manage, slowly gathering, contemplative rage. The two of them stared mutely at him, as if he had interrupted just by being there, and was therefore obligated to make amends to the conversation. "David, what brings you here, at an hour like this?" he tried.

The man replied, "There's been a Bear Raid, Daedalus. While you were out, gods know where, neglecting your household, the half of your foodstuffs has been taken."

"I was making investigations—"

"Yes, that is something you do often enough. Looks like you were measuring something, wonderful." The ruler was still in Daedalus' hands, in case of an emergency. "But what you have to realize, my good friend, is that your family needs providing for, and this takes precedence over your experiments.

"But anyway," he said, before resuming what he must have been saying before Daedalus had intervened, "there I was, lying my children to sleep, and about to go to bed myself, when I heard bears roaring from somewhere in the distance. Immediately it occurred to me that Bathsheba might be in danger, as the sounds were from this general direction, so I made all haste to get here as soon as possible. By the time I arrived, the damage was already done. The bears had taken all they could manage to carry away, which you are very fortunate did not include your wife, Daedalus. It's a shame, really—had bears still been here, I would have been more than willing to fend them off. This, what I'm expressing, is a noble feeling, and one you should really emulate yourself, Daedalus"

The fact that David, from where he lived a far distance off, had heard the rioting sounds of bears that Daedalus had not, struck him as entirely improbable and odd. But the evidence of the kitchen was undeniable, since the pantry door was completely absent, along with most everything formerly inside of it. Yet Daedalus wasn't looking at David, or his destroyed furniture, or his own remaining foodstuffs, as all of those things were accounted for and easily replaceable. Instead he looked constantly at his wife, so was able to witness the gradual forming of a warm smile that only employed the corners of her mouth. It was very subtle, although discernible to the keen eye. Daedalus generally had a keen eye, when he was close enough to see, but that didn't explain everything—a keen eye for fish-ing dried away to nothing on firm land, as the proverb went. As for the current sharpness of his eye, it had been made keen by certain experiments he'd done in ornithology. His wife's smile was the same smile he had seen in the corner of a baby bird's mouth, right before its mother vomited sustenance into it, which he had been polite enough to wait out before taking the babies away for dissection. Thus, Daedalus' mind slightly wandered as he imagined his wife, mouth agape and all excitement, waiting for vomit to be poured into her maw from above. The only thing that bothered him about the image was that it was David perched above her, slowly regurgitating all of the disgusting, half-digested things inside of him.

"Did you hear me, Daedalus? This is important advice that I'm telling you as a friend." David wore a concerned look, because he was good at that.

Daedalus snapped out of his reverie. "Oh, yes, yes. Quite. Where are the children? Safe?"

Bathsheba's gaze momentarily went blank. She hadn't checked. David very cheerfully made the admission for her, he said, "Haven't had the time to look into that one. Anyway, the gods have blessed us, that no one was harmed. And I suppose I could be on my way now."

Prior to leaving, he hugged Bathsheba and gave Daedalus a reaffirming pat on the back, and then he meandered out into the night. David did not live anywhere nearby—the visit hadn't been any kind of casual "Oh, I'll check on the wellbeing of my neighbors, as it is hardly an inconvenience." David had to walk a good three miles through sometimes treacherous terrain, all the more so for the lack of light to help safely circumvent its pitfalls. Then David had to face the same journey again, in reverse.

After watching the enemy disappear, Daedalus realized that his right hand had gone entirely white, turned into the hand of a cadaver, from clenching his ruler so tightly. The pure whiteness of his hand was disrupted by a vein of dark red that ran from where he'd drawn his own blood, from the pressure he had exerted against its sharp edges. He took a moment to look closely at his improvised weapon. The end that was stained with the blood of another, the offensive end, was still the model of exactitude. His own grip, the defensive end, had considerably warped.

Daedalus said, "I'll go upstairs and see how the kids are doing."

"Well, if you'll do that, I'm going back to sleep," his wife said, immediately becoming much more tired in appearance and demeanor. But still smiling. And not because of him.

KAPITEL ZWEI:
HUMAN COUNSEL

SUBSEQUENT TO EVERY Bear Raid, an Emergency Council was held to establish facts and blame of the ordeal, and to accordingly outline further preventative measures that could be taken for the future. The location was the Chamber of Divine Justice, nearby to Castle Horeb but in a building quite distinct in more ways than one. The Castle was ornate, an advanced architectural *tour de force* with buttresses, ramparts, and porticos as intricate as they were superfluous. The Chamber, on the other hand, looked as if it could have been hewn of one stone, just a complete obdurate mass of a thing. If a person was desperately fleeing from some massacre, hypothetically, and took the grand flagstone road that led to the Central Plaza, where they would then be confronted by both buildings, side by side as they were, it was difficult for Daedalus to imagine that person choosing the supposed fortress over the Chamber.

Whenever Daedalus had any business at the Castle, which was only accessible through the Central Plaza, he was forced to see the two side by side, just like his hypothetical person. It was always extremely difficult for him to go into the Castle while the Chamber sat just across the way. Perhaps something sub-conscious in him was always fleeing from a massacre. Going into the Chamber, and being able to give the Castle a resolutely cold shoulder was, conversely, an extremely gratifying feeling to him, and one that he had the pleasure of experiencing as he made his way to the Emergency Council.

He was not one of the Magisters that comprised the mem-bership of the Council, at least not anymore. He used to be the Magister of Science, but that was a long time prior, and reasons had been contrived to render him lawfully unsuitable for the position. A Magister was the foremost position of a Ministry—there were many Ministries, but of their number the more important ones, and therefore better represented, were: The Ministry of the King; of Apollo; of Science; of Economics; of Resources; of Education; and of Public Safe-ty. The offices of the Ministries were highly prestigious, and were appointed directly by the King for life service, or until the King saw fit to make a change. The other, lesser Ministries were largely ignored, so were a lot less politicized, and took the shape of interest groups more than anything else. The Mag-isters all convened not only for Emergency Councils, but on holidays, and other occasions specially designated by the King, such as coronations or funerals.

So Daedalus didn't appear that day in the capacity of a Ma-gister, but as a Witness. Direct Witnesses were allowed to par-ticipate in the Emergency Council, provided they only spoke when spoken to by the Council. Everyone else that wanted to listen was only an Audience Member, and was relegated to the numerous seats that filled the back of the Chamber, all a good, safe distance away from the dais of the Council. The Witness-es were honored with a privileged position in between the two.

Had Daedalus not been a Witness, he still would have come as an Audience Member, because the Bear Raids were a mat-ter that affected him deeply. In all technicality, he wasn't sure he really qualified as a Witness, since he had not seen or heard a single bear. It was a large risk he was taking, then—chances were, he could be accused of Contempt of the Council—but he felt that he had valuable information to present, so long as the events along the road with the lamps were to be in any way related to the Bear Raid. Daedalus had a feeling that they were.

There was a surprising amount of people in attendance. Daedalus had to wade through a large group of people just milling about the stairs leading up to the Chamber, and, once through the imposingly large oaken double doors, found that every seat of the Audience was occupied. The last Emergency Council had been nowhere near as popular—Daedalus sidled his way through the crowd, to the seats of the Witnesses.

Among other people that Daedalus recognized in the Witness section was Wallace, who was in a seat that bordered the outermost aisle of the Chamber, fast asleep. Daedalus could think of no other reason for his presence than that he was summoned, because surely he hadn't Witnessed anything in his slumber. If that was the case, it was potentially disastrous news for the future of Wallace's career as a sentry. It seemed he was taking the matter none too seriously though, but rather perpetrating the very crime that brought him there in the first place. Once again Daedalus couldn't blame him, since having the night shift meant that the early afternoon was most likely Wallace's usual time of rest—that was, if every time weren't Wallace's usual time of rest. Daedalus hoped that all his speculation was wrong—maybe Wallace had born Witness to important events after Daedalus' brief visit, and was to be commended for the excellent performance of his sentry duties. Daedalus could only hope.

A sharp, reverberating echo filled the Chamber. The Gavel of Justice had spoken, with all the might of Apollo himself lying behind the propagation of its sound. "Hear ye, hear ye, the Emergency Council is now in session. We begin with the invocation of Apollo."

The honor of reciting the invocation went to the current

Magister of Apollo, a short, balding man clad in many odd articles of religious import, which would have been impressive for their gold, if they hadn't been muddled in so much religious imagery and symbolism as they were. The Magister of Apollo spoke in a voice that would not have been audible, except that a stringent law forbade any sound emitted by the Audience as the Council was held. Thus, a life-fearful silence usually pervaded the Chamber from the moment the Gavel struck until the very end. "*Ich bin verrucht.* May Apollo see fit to lay his blessings upon this Council of divine moment. May He uphold justice and truth in this, the Chamber of Divine Justice. May curses fall upon the saboteur of this sanctity, until the third and fourth generation of their children. Oh Apollo, we are humbly at thy service. *Immer sein Kind.*" Immediately following those words was the only time the Audience was allowed to use sound for the whole duration, to affirm how humble they were. The sound of their humble affirmation roared from the sheer multitude of the Audience.

"Now see here, the following order of dealings is to unfold, in no other order, under the penalty of heresy," the Magister of the King said, who presided over the Council. "First will be a description of the event, as has already been ascertained by the Ministries, by the King, and by Apollo himself. Following this, the Witnesses will then have the opportunity to adduce further information, and then the Council will prescribe a course of action that shall have the weight of divine law." One of those selfsame prescriptions had stripped Daedalus of his title, three years before.

"Last night, at roughly three hours past vespers, it is believed that a troop of twenty bears entered from the east gate. This number is derived from the amount of reported foodstuffs gone, divided by the average carrying capacity of a bear." While he spoke, his eyes locked with the Magister of Science, as if he had been describing a complex formula that needed confirmation by an authority of the field. The Magis-

ter of Science seemed to realize his desire for approval, and
gave the man a barely perceptible nod, which nonetheless sufficed. The east gate was the gate by Daedalus' house. They
were going to pin it on Wallace after all.

"This theory is supported by Witnesses at both the north
and west gates, as well as the sentries of those gates, who all
reported no unusual activity in those sectors. Also, the damage was mainly limited to the eastern part of the city, increas-
ing the likelihood that this was the point of entry. The sentry
at the east gate, one Wallace Seyer, was reportedly asleep and
shirking duties when the bears made their entrance and exit.
Now, for testimony from the Witnesses. We would first like to
hear from Censor Magnate Foster."

There were many Censors, represented by the Magnate
Censor. It was their job to gather all information that would
potentially become necessary through the course of the proceedings. A man of their number had come by Daedalus'
house earlier that morning, to assess damage. With a piece
of parchment and quill in hand, he had followed Daedalus
around as Daedalus showed him all of his broken cabinets,
and tried to recall all of the food that was taken. Like everyone
else, Daedalus was compelled to overestimate.

Censor Magnate Foster, as their leader, compiled and analyzed the numbers. Foster had probably risen to such a noteworthy position due to his exceptional servility—his posture
was always slouched forward in a desultory inquisitive manner, diminishing his already minimal stature. He was the kind
of half-person that people could very naturally describe their
losses to. Even standing on the Chamber's enormous dais did
nothing to make him seem more important. "*Ich verspreche*," he
pronounced. "And thank you, Magister.

"The amount and location of the damage was determined
by the Censors through surveys made by way of carefully selected cross-sections, which were then generalized. Most victims went entirely unaware of their substantial loss until we in-

formed them that it likely happened, based on our predictions of the area affected. Ten Witnesses exist that either saw, or saw and were personally affected by, the Bear Raid—amongst these was a Sezurus, who captured two bears. Four further Witnesses exist that noted the entrance of the bears, along with the negligence of the sentry at the east gate. There are four Witnesses each that testify to the integrity of the north and south gates, but none that attest the same of the east, reporting instead an atypical darkness surrounding the area. *Es ist.*"

"Thank you, Censor Magnate Foster," said the Magister of the King. "Now, if the four Witnesses of the negligence of the east gate's sentry would please speak."

At that moment they stood—they were on the complete opposite end of the row as Daedalus, mockingly close to Wallace, who was still unconscious of everything—and Daedalus could see a blood-stained bandage on one, directly above his right scapula, bulging out from under his clothing. It was immediately apparent to Daedalus that they were the men he had confronted the previous night, while they were going about secret activities and carrying a ladder, audacious enough to testify against Wallace for negligence of their own actions. In the light afforded by the Chamber of Divine Justice, Daedalus recognized one of them that he didn't before. The Magister of the King continued, "Seraph, Petulah, Moran, and Demitr." They each bowed as their name was spoken—Moran was the one that Daedalus knew, but couldn't remember how.

For a moment they hesitated, forgetting who among them they had chosen to speak. Eventually the one called Petulah began. "*Ich verpsreche*, your Honors. Yes, we were just having an . innocent stroll, just three hours after vespers, as your Honors had the wisdom to discover. A strong breeze blew, and all of the lights were put out around us, all in one go. Which was already none too good for our nerves, but then we saw the bears after they entered, and then we were sorely afraid, and our nerves were in no condition to speak of at all. Just horrible. It must have been the work of Dionysus himself, all of it. And there they came, charging toward us, as if they saw us. Now, we did take all the measures so thoughtfully recommended by the wise Council—we did the Bear Shoo, followed by Playing Dead when the Shoo didn't work as well as we'd have liked. We really did give it our best, but we were much afeared for our lives… but this wisdom, which I can only speak so highly of, surely spared us our lives." The Bear Shoo and Playing Dead were both methods suggested by the Emergency Council several Bear Raids before, after the method they had previously suggested, the Bear Taunt, proved to be fatal in most cases. "The bears saw fit to move on. After this we went to the east guard shack, worried about the condition of the sentry. But there he was, fast asleep, and must have incidentally fallen asleep on the lever operating the gate. *Es ist.*"

The Magister of the King nodded sagely, and the four men took their seats again. He then said, "And this will be the entire testimony, unless other Witnesses wish to expound further."

Wallace didn't look like he was about to defend himself, so Daedalus stood up. Demitr and Seraph instantly went a ghastly white, with one of them looking as if they might pass out—Daedalus had already forgotten which was which. There was a moment of shuffling as the Audience moved to try and see who it was that might speak, followed by an entirely uncommon thing, a violation of the rules of the Council—certain members of the Audience booed loudly, and others groaned. Daedalus had thought that standing up was a foolish move on his part, but he was committed. "*Ich verspreche*, your Honors. I was making investigations of my own last night."

"Yeah, we all know how those turn out!" was a reply by someone behind him, the voice of which he did not recognize. He wondered if the man would be castigated—most likely the Council would absolve anyone that spoke against Daedalus, just because of who Daedalus was, even though the Audience speaking was strictly against the rules.

"Nothing of a scientific nature, my friends," Daedalus continued. Muttering by the Audience still accompanied everything he said. "Could you tell me, any of you four Witnesses," and he indicated them by turning in their direction, just in case the number didn't make those referred to clear enough, "what you could have been doing with a ladder, on this stroll of yours?" He would finally get his answer, even if it wasn't a direct truth. He had been listening with a careful ear to Petulah's testimony, and even though the cumulative effect of his words was misleading, it was obvious that he was very careful not to lie outright, which was an offense taken seriously even by the most dissolute of people when in the Chamber. The lights were in fact extinguished 'all in one go', and it was very possible that a strong breeze may have blown at some point or another. What was omitted was the role their group had played with the lights, and the irrelevance of the breeze.

"That's still a secret," Moran quickly replied, before consulting his friends. Petulah and one of the others quietly reprimanded him¬—Daedalus heard one of them whisper that he should never speak again. The last of their group, either Seraph or Demitr, the one with the bandage on his shoulder, looked like he was no longer in any condition to actively engage in his surroundings. He was a ghastly white, never regaining his color from when he had made eye contact with Daedalus.

"No, this time it isn't." The statement was more directed at Moran than anyone else, as Petulah resumed his duties of the rhetorician. "Some of the places we like to stroll along are hard to access." When all of the Emergency Council proceedings were said and done, some time later, and the deceit of the four was revealed, Petulah's excuse was looked upon laughingly by the general public, whence came the expression, 'they seem the type that would stroll with a ladder near vespers.'

For the moment, though, Daedalus had to fight an uphill

battle. "I watched this group put out the aforementioned lights themselves, one by one, with the use of a ladder. Furthermore, their actions were not directly accompanied by bears coming from the east gate—I was on that road all the while after their extinguishing of the lights, and at no point did a troop of twenty bears come across it. I also paid a visit to Wallace, who… was in no way sleeping 'incidentally' on top of the release lever for the gate. I am of the personal opinion that the bears entered from somewhere else entirely. *Es ist.*"

After he had spoken, the reaction from the audience was much more than just isolated noises—it was a full uproar. In their eyes, someone had violated the Oath by lying, what they held to be a necessary consequence of two opposing testimonies. The Gavel sounded itself twice, until silence was restored. The Magister of the King asked, "What say ye to these accusations?"

'We say," Petulah started. "… Was there any need to attack Seraph here? He really isn't doing well," he said, as an aside to Daedalus.

"So you did in fact confront Daedalus here, during your stroll?" the Magister of the King asked.

"Yes, your Honor."

"And was it before or after the Bear Raid, that he attacked you?"

"It was… these are hard questions."

"Hard questions? It was either before, or after. Possibly during."

"Well, during. Yes, it must have been during."

"And why was this not included in your original testimony?"

"Didn't seem important at the time."

"So, while you were performing the Bear Shoo, or Playing Dead, Daedalus was assaulting your party? Perhaps this is what interfered with the efficacy of your Bear Shoo?"

"Why… yes, yes that sounds very plausible."

"Your Honor," Daedalus summoned the audacity to reenter the discussion. "If I was truly assaulting these Witnesses here, during the mortal danger presented by the Bear Raid that they attest to, wouldn't I have fallen victim to the bears myself?" It was a generally known fact that bears would not go far out of their way to attack a person, yet the story was different when that person was placed conveniently in their path.

"And what say ye once more?" the Magister asked again to the Witnesses.

"The bears most likely considered him an accomplice at that point, and—"

"Excuse me your Honor, but when have the bears ever taken a human as an accomplice? This is unheard of. Of all the iniquity I've been accused, this is the most absurd, that somehow the bears would change their eternal ways in the wake of my putative depravity."

An obvious glint of hatred existed in the eyes of the Magister of the King, for Daedalus alone. But something inside of him still adhered to the dictates of Apollo, no matter what. "This does seem fairly suspicious. Do you four have anything to add that might increase the likelihood of what you claim?"

They visually consulted themselves, one last time, before saying, "Fine, our cover is blown. We were told to put the lights out."

"By who?"

"By the Lepers."

A righteous fury overtook the Audience, just like all other occasions in which Leper involvement was discovered. But what Petulah was suggesting was something unheard of—it was true that the Lepers were behind a myriad of subversive programs toward the city of Gibeah, but never simultaneously with a Bear Raid. Daedalus' mind raced ahead to think of what their involvement might have meant in a legal sense.

They would invoke the writ of Forced Witnesses. They would go and find a Leper that could fairly be assumed to represent and be knowledgeable of the interests of the Lepers, and force them to participate in the Council. They would bring in Korah.

The Magisters used the general noise as a cover to have heated discussion of their own. When it seemed as if they had decided on something, with some of their number in obvious opposition to that decision, the Magister of the King resumed his position at the forefront to deliver a verdict. "We will have a Forced Witness. Korah of the Lepers."

To most everyone else, the Magisters' decision came as a complete surprise. Not everyone was as well versed in the laws of Gibeah as Daedalus, who had prior experience as a Magister. Numerous times in his former career, he'd had occasion to seriously consider the use of the writ of Forced Witnesses. But he'd never seen it happen.

The Audience's reaction was qualitatively different than before—they got up en masse to leave, for fear of proximity to the Lepers. There were a few brave members that were going to wait the whole Council out, come rain or shine, Leper or no Leper. But they were almost denied the opportunity by the simple fact that they were nearly trampled to death, by the far larger number of the fainthearted.

"We will adjourn this Council until a time that all Witnesses are accounted for, this including Korah the Leper," The Magister of the King stated. There was no telling how long the intermission would take, considering the fact that the weeding process to find out who remained that was willing to retrieve Korah would be very similar to the process that just took place in the Chamber. Even amongst the soldiers of Gibeah, most people would opt to run for their lives instead of interacting with a Leper, potentially trampling on their way out the only suitable people the government had at their disposal. In which case, the worst case scenario, new men would have to be trained. Perhaps even *bred*.

An hour was passing. Daedalus' stomach was sending him

confused signals, most likely with hunger as their underlying cause. He had left early in the morning, before breakfast had sufficient time to be prepared. If there was even food left in his house for a breakfast. The bears were probably having a feast at his expense at that very moment, and not even being thankful. There had been a cured ham that Daedalus had been looking forward to in particular. Gone now.

So he spent the time meditating over food forever in the past, and then, when the thoughts became too painful, he contemplated the internal architecture of the Chamber for a while. All of its spaciousness was vastly underutilized, especially the upper reaches—it was as if the architect didn't want anything in the Chamber to be out of arms reach, but had an excess of stone he didn't quite know what to do with, so went a hundred feet up with the walls anyway. Expanses of nothing but gray, intersecting perpendicularly with gray, all beautifully pointless.

He heard Korah being brought in before he saw it. People gasped as he was brought by, even those, the people who were brave enough to stay. Korah was not, as with most Forced Witnesses, escorted into the Chamber. At least not escorted in a meaningful sense of the word, since it would have implied some sort of measure of supervision. No one, not even the guards that they did find to bring him, would stand within twenty feet of the Leper, and it was likely that he could have just walked away if the mood struck him. But he was compliant anyway, practically entering of his own free will. And he was whistling, sort of.

Moreover, he had a dignified walk that was extremely at odds with his position, not to mention the extrusions that covered every visible inch of him, and, one could only assume, the inches hidden under his entirely white raiment as well. The man was an unearthly white himself, with none of the connotations of cleanliness that white usually brought with it. Instead, it was a dim white. An adust white. The white of ashes instead of light.

Korah was lightly deposited directly to the left of Daedalus. From so close, Daedalus could just barely make out all the subtleties of facial expression that were all the more difficult to perceive given the inhospitable terrain that they worked upon, making the man's mood impossible to read at a distance. Some people's faces were steppes, their individual flora or fauna visible from miles. Korah's was a tropical rainforest.

Somewhere beneath all of that protuberance, Korah was affecting regality—Daedalus could see it. His chin was decidedly jutted out, and granted even a few more inches by a fortunately contiguous lump to complete the effect. He wore a headdress typical of the Lepers, emblazoned with their insignia. It was an insignia that Korah had designed and instated himself, when he had taken command of the Lepers. Korah had done a lot of things.

"The Council is hereby resumed, with all Witnesses present," The Magister of the King began. There were a few people that would have preferred not to be present—the Audience had a choice to stay or leave, but the Witnesses and the Council were committed once they started, and some were unsettled by the unforeseen turn of events. "Korah of the Lepers, you are now entreated to have born Witness to the events of last night, and whatever other events that may have directly contributed to their unfolding. Do you acknowledge this?

"Certainly."

"If you could describe, exactly, the Leper involvement in those events?" The Magister of the King officiated his office unflinchingly—everyone else around him seemed to be choking on putrefaction, yet he alone continued with a tenacity that Daedalus couldn't help but respect. From his pulpit, spatially distinguished from the other Magisters, the Magister of the King stared boldly down at Korah below him, some twenty feet removed. Korah returned the same look.

"*Ich spreche.* I would love to describe events to you, exactly as they unfolded." Korah's omission of 'your Honors', and mispronunciation of the holy words, did not go unnoticed by anyone in the assembly. Such flouting of conventions was expected, though, by those that brought him there. "Last night... oh yes, last night the force of the Lepers was split into two, with half on the usual Reconnaissance duties, and the other half on special operations. I am not disposed to disclose any of the information that was gathered—that is all highly sensitive material. But of the special operations, I can tell you whatever you want to know. Thanks to us, four tombstones in the graveyard have been exchanged with four others, similarly situated and of similar appearance, so that the effect is almost unnoticeable. Also, a number of street signs have been dealt with in a like fashion. The price of wheat has been raised by collusion to thirty shekels an ephah, make a note of that. The entire cattle population of Gibeah has been individually fed twice their weight in red beets, so expect all glasses of milk produced in the next week to be indistinguishable from glasses of blood that may be placed next to them. And we dropped a rabbit into the Bear Maze."

The last statement elicited a protracted 'eep' from the Magister of Apollo. Every member of the Council's eyebrow raised a fraction with each admitted infraction listed nonchalantly off by Korah, and Daedalus was amused by the collective ascent in their collective faces.

The Magister of the King responded with a thinly veiled righteous fury. "The leprotic influence of you and your people won't just continue to be tolerated. One day, the magistral and the leprotic will be put in proper relation, do you hear me? But that is beside the point. In all the things you described, I did not hear the offense you were brought here to be a Witness of. There were four men, who allegedly put lights out under your directive—do you recall this?" Lepers never directly did anything themselves, which was the reason that Korah phrased his sentences in the passive voice. They never touched anything— they just found a random Gibeahnite, and exhorted them to do it. The problem the government faced was that nothing the Lepers advised was legal, and even though the general public had been told as much by the government, multiple times, people still felt compelled to do whatever they were told by the Lepers. The four Witnesses were just four out of many.

"Oh, right, that," Korah said. "I forgot to mention that, since it was a trivial thing, really, and was widely deemed a failure among the Lepers. But I suppose we are responsible nonetheless, yes."

Nobody was surprised by the information, least of all the Magister of the King, who said, "Then that will be all the testimony required, unless someone wishes to add further?" Nobody objected. "Now for a discussion amongst the Magisters concerning prescriptions for the future." Henceforth, the Witnesses were forbidden to interject. No matter how absurdly the Council chose to handle a problem, no matter what kind of blatant misinformation they used to inform their decisions, the rest of the Council was theirs alone. An opportunity for the other Magisters to speak was finally at hand—so far only the Magister of the King and the Magister of Apollo, during the brief statement demanded by his office, had spoken.

Daedalus always thought it was a funny transition. Everything that preceded that moment, which had the same basic formula for every Emergency Council, was redolent of austerity, had the pureness of rote tradition. The Council recalled divinity, in its reaffirming of longstanding dictates and its passive listening. But everything after that point stank horribly of reintroduced humanity, as every Magister worked only to advance his own agenda in an open forum.

The Magisters' qualifications, before they were promoted to the position, were based largely on their volubility and ardor. Of course, the King had the final say on who was elected, but the Ministries could manipulate the pool beforehand by promoting only the candidates they liked, and stifling all the rest. The downside of that *modus operandi* was that a lot of the same people that were voluble and ardent were also egocentric and unreliable, Daedalus found, with the exception of the Magister of the King. Yet the Ministries desired the loudmouthed type of representative anyway, because only they could compete with the equally loudmouthed representatives of the other Ministries to advance their interests at every Council, including the Emergency Council. It was an arms race that resulted in a shouting match, every time the Magister of the King let them speak. And the floor was open.

Magister of
    Economics: There's nothing else for it. We are reducing the money supply to combat inflation.
    Education: There are several other things 'for it,' like—
    Economics: Not that I know of. Not that I care about.
    Public Safety: We need several more sentries at each gate, nightly patrols, the same kind of thing I've been advising for years now.
    The King: Simon?
    Resources: No.
    Philosophy (not considered a major Ministry, but still managed to get an occasional word in anyway): The real problem here is the impressionability of the public, as evinced by these four Witnesses. Impressionability is lethal when you have a dangerous force like the Lepers in circulation—the public needs a more definite code of conduct to abide by—aren't kids being parented correctly these days?
    Education: We're parenting them just fine.
    Philosophy: That was rhetorical. You wouldn't know how everyone is parented, you don't do it yourself.
    Education: Yes I do. And you know, Socrates, it would be a lot easier if you weren't always corrupting the youth. We do a great job, before your subversions. I do a great job. You, on the other hand, are just like a damn Leper.
    Philosophy: Your blind insistence on calumnies that I've

been absolved of truly amazes me, Meletus. So shut up.

Luxury: I think more yachts will mitigate the problems in our society, or at least mitigate how much a decent percentage of our populace cares about those problems. And every decent percentage counts.

Apollo: Maybe we could stand to provide a better upbringing for—

Education: My Ministry would need more resources for that.

The King: Simon?

Resources: No. We thought that the considerable drunkard demographic, decided to be viable in our last Council, would be more forthcoming with teacher material, but that was less successful than anticipated. And we haven't found a proper substitute.

Education: I didn't mean just teachers. Books would be nice.

The King: Simon?

Resources: No.

Apollo (who had been trying to intercede for a while now, but his atypical meekness for a Magister found him at a distinct disadvantage): I didn't mean an upbringing in school, I meant stricter adherence to the Faith.

(Everyone who wasn't the Magister of Apollo laughed)

Public Safety: I'm personally concerned about the red milk. Milk is a staple of a large percent of the population, but not many would be willing to run the risk of accidentally drinking a glass of blood, since they'll look the same. Now, I know I've heard tell that the King has a large stash of safeguarded cows, who couldn't possibly have been affected. Couldn't they—

The King: Treyshka, I'd stop right there, if you don't want to be accused of treason.

Public Safety: At least tell me something that can be done about the Lepers. No one seems to acknowledge how much of a threat their influence poses.

The King: The Lepers are just a trivial matter.

And then something unprecedented occurred. The last statement stirred something deep in Korah, and he rose roughly to his feet saying, "No, no. None of this." At that point he paused. And when he continued, it was with twice the amount of air propelling the words of an invective, his chest grossly bulging out to achieve sufficient airflow. "We, the Lepers, will not idly listen as you gallivant about, pretending to hold the cards. Dionysus has dealt especially kind with us. Tomorrow, when you go to mourn your dead, it will be someone else's dead, and the display will be entirely in vain. You'll be walking to the same marketplace you have gone to for years, but turn on the wrong street, and be entirely at a loss, and probably go hungry for a while. Your currency will inflate by an unexpected amount. You'll drink the blood, the life force of another, instead of nourishment. And Apollo will punish you, not us, for debasing the sanctity of the Bear Maze with a rabbit. How could you feign that this is trivial? And what could you retaliate with, when you realize that it is not? Dionysus laughingly accepts all retaliation, welcomes it. I swear."

When he was finished, Korah looked about triumphantly, as if he was expecting to be consumed in a laudatory backwash from the Audience. He quickly remembered that everyone around him was the enemy, and would make no such concessions to his rhetoric. Quickly he searched his mind for a proper substitute for his lack of partisan support. What he settled on was to slowly, a few well-placed steps at a time, approach random people of import, arms slightly raised, ablaze with leprosy, until those people became so uncomfortable they either stood up and left their seat, or closed their eyes and pretended they were somewhere else. It took him through the Witnesses, briefly and noisily through the Audience, and finally onto the sanctimonious dais itself, where he took the vacated seat of the Magister of Education. Not to misuse the chair, his face took on a scholarly tone, to its abilities, as he observed the effects of his procession from on high.

The Magister of the King continued unabashedly, "These prescriptions are seen fit by the Council, by the King, and by Apollo himself, thus having the force of divine law. The four Witnesses, Petulah et al, will be assigned menial work until they recant their trespasses. The Magister of Science is charged with finding a cure for red beets. There are no royal cows. I repeat, there are no royal cows. The wheat stores of the King, though, which do exist, will be opened for sale to the general public at a reasonable price for the indefinite future. Wallace is to maintain his position as sentry of the east gate. Daedalus has been cleared of all recent charges. And as for the Lepers—further sanctions than have ever existed before will take effect. Your impertinence won't go without consequence, Korah. All Lepers are to be killed on sight, and this charge falls even on the general public. Collusion with the Lepers will be punishable by death. *Ich verspreche.* Adjourned."

As the Magister of the King left the dais, followed very enthusiastically by everyone else, he was looking quite pleased. He patted himself on the back.

KAPITEL DREI:
BEAR INTERMENT

IT WAS A rule that whoever was a Witness to the Emergency Council was then a Witness to the Bear Interment, because of the paperwork it was found to save. The names of the first group could be filed under 'Witnesses', and then the job was done, instead of the much more complicated option, in which case a whole new group would have required filing. Having a group of Witnesses was just as necessary for a Bear Interment as it was for an Emergency Council. Many of the Witnesses would have gone to the Interment even had it not been required of them—not to satisfy the ritualistic import of the presence of Witnesses, but because, depending on their individual circumstances, to some it was cathartic to watch the bears be put away. That was because many people were Witnesses insofar as they had Witnessed a bear mauling a loved one, or, like Daedalus, carrying off a much desired meal, so that retribution was practically a demand. Most forms of retribution sanctioned by the government were a lot more satisfying than the Interment, though, which often led to disappointment for the Witnesses. It was readily apparent to anyone who chose to watch them, standing in a circle of stifling impotence, instead of the ritual as it was performed. The populace's expectations were conditioned by such conventions as the creditor's right over debtors—creditors were personally allowed to delimb any debtor who failed to meet the conditions of their contract. No harm was allowed to come to the bears.

Such social progress to the benefit of the bears was made possible by an activist group that eventually maintained the status of a Ministry, due to its popularity. The Ministry of the Bear didn't participate in the Councils because their platform was as simple as "Don't hurt the bears," and its Magisters started feeling redundant saying that and that alone all the time, so stopped showing up. Everyone else did them the favor of saying "Don't hurt the bears" if the need arose in their absence. The Ministry of the Bear was the first to decide that the bears should be lowered into the Bear Maze. There was an interim period, between when the bears started attacking and when the Ministry of the Bear started asserting itself, when no one was quite sure what to do with the bears once they were captured. Some were unceremoniously stoned, and others let go outside of the city gates. It depended on the clemency of the group that managed to catch them.

Six years before, there had been a sea change in the lives of the Gibeahnites. Six years before, the bears started attacking out of the blue, then the Ministry of the Bear arose, then the city wall, the Sezuri, the Emergency Councils, the use of the Bear Maze. Daedalus used to wake up early for the sole purpose of watching the splendor of the sunrise from his front porch, but then everything changed, and the grandeur of its eternal rebirth was mostly lost by the time it cleared the height of the city wall. That was the largest and most disquieting change for Daedalus. None of the other changes affected him so personally. He stopped waking up early in the morning. Life behind a wall was different.

The Sezuri were a group of people specially trained to capture bears, whenever a Bear Raid occurred. The bears were better organized, more powerful, and had better resources than the city of Gibeah, thus precluding any large-scale operation that Gibeah would have otherwise enacted to counter bear activity. The best that could be done was done—a wall that everyone hoped would prove mostly impermeable, and the Sezuri, who laid traps at the personal discretion of its members. None of their traps were allowed to be harmful, which was a hard-won argument by the Ministry of the Bear— and the only reason the Ministry eventually had its way was not because of the persuasiveness of its argument, which was, naturally, "Don't hurt the bears," but rather because unsuspecting civilians often fell into the bear traps, and didn't want to die in them. A lot of the Sezuri's traps, then, had to rely on ropes, falling cages, or strong persuasion.

The members of the Sezuri were highly trained, extremely intelligent, and had a higher mortality rate than the newborn infants of Gibeah (an interesting statistic graciously provided by the Ministry of Statistics, a Ministry whose main platform was to make sure everything stayed average). Their leader was Sezurus Magnate Stairwell, a giant of a man, whose claim to fame was having subdued a bear with his bare hands¬—on the night of a Bear Raid, while walking alone, he was attacked by a bear, which he managed to wrestle to the ground. Since no one who passed by was willing to help him, though, he was forced to lay on top of that bear in the middle of the street until morning, before his fellow Sezuri found him.

He had instantly been promoted. The civil branches of the government were different like that—people with talent had the opportunity of advancing, and of being in charge. But also crazy people.

The group gathered around the entrance to the Bear Maze was exceptionally awkward that day. The Witness system failed to accommodate for possible discrepancies between the Witnesses in the Emergency Council, the result being that Daedalus, the four strollers, Wallace, and Korah himself were all there. Daedalus took the rare opportunity to speak to Korah personally.

Korah was the most tone-deaf whistler that Daedalus had ever heard in his entire life, and yet was whistling every time he'd seen him, loudly. Never once was it an identifiable melody or song, never did it progress or resolve. It was so anti-musical that somehow it became musical again, at the other end of the spectrum. There was no form to it—it was as if he took the essence of whistling, the vibrations and the rushing wind, the dynamics and the act of breathing that constrained and defined it, and emitted those elements alone, reveled in them. It was one of those outbursts of noise that Daedalus interrupted when he said, "Kind of a rough state of affairs, that you and your people are to be killed on sight, isn't it? Perhaps you didn't have to push the Magister of the King so far."

"Excuse me, but you are?"

"Daedalus."

"Oh, right! I recognize you now. I had thought to turn you away, when I didn't know who you were, that is, but on second thought…" Korah had been standing off on his own along the edge of the Bear Maze, just staring into the abyss with a nonplussed look on his face that occasionally bordered on despair, yet whistling fervently. Into the Bear Maze—for the longest time it had been merely a thing to threaten disobedient kids and free spirited lovers with, a gaping hole atop of a mound situated in close proximity to the cemetery. The growths of houses surrounding the two were more wary of the Maze than the cemetery, making the Maze entrance the most open of spaces in all of the city. Along the edges to the entrance the earth just ended—there was nothing ornate commemorating where it began and the relatively straightforward world above it ended. The hole of the entrance had a ten cubit diameter, and was sheer blackness. But if someone could see down, furthermore, if they were to *go down* into it, they would find an ancient maze consisting of worn, subterranean stone walls winding out in concentric circles, with many false paths and one true that let out just six hundred yards away, in the middle of the cemetery. That was *if* someone went down into it—no one *did*, at least intentionally, except bears under coercion. And so it derived its name.

For all that the Ministry of the Bear exhorted that no harm be done to the bears, there was the one thing that they did condone, and even did it themselves—they took the bears to the edge of the Bear Maze, performed their rites, then threw the bears down, one by one. It was not known whether the bears died on impact, or days later of starvation, or whatever it might be. What satisfied the moral obligations of the people of Gibeah in their way of handling the bears, as far as the Ministry of the Bear was concerned, was that whatever happened to the bears after being pushed over the edge, even if it was just three seconds later, was not really their fault, since they were unaware, and thus they didn't technically harm the bears. And that was that.

"I said what I had to say," Korah affirmed. "We the Lepers do what we have to." He pulled lightly at the headdress atop his head as he spoke. "There's a new time coming, when we'll be recognized for who we are and what we do."

"You were never in danger of not being recognized. Speaking of what you do, I'm having a hard time interpreting the statement made by, say for instance, feeding cows beets. Strange way to 'Subvert' a people."

"If you saw how they treated the animals, you would understand. Did you know they feed cows to cows? And not even the good parts. Those beets were probably the best thing they've been fed since the day they were born. And if the milk turns red, if it disgusts them for what it looks and feels like, it serves them right."

"And changing street signs?"

"I can't just tell you everything." It almost looked like Korah smiled, but smiling seemed to be the one expression that his face was entirely incapable of performing, because of his horrendous skin.

Daedalus said, "Well, you may have your reasons, and this is just my opinion, but it's all folly—hundreds of your people are in jeopardy, and you've gained nothing by it."

"Gained nothing... gained nothing by it? Do you see how we are treated? We are expelled from the city, forced to live in the wilderness, amongst the bears and everything else. And why? Because of some cruel fate that decided to punish us twice instead of once—first, to be disfigured, and then to be ostracized for it. No, we will all risk jeopardy, would give our lives even, until justice is had and the human decency we've been denied for so long recognizes us once again."

"You're equivocating two forms of recognition. The recognition that earns you a noose is different than the recognition that earns you empathy. They are distant cousins at best. The things you're doing, you're only getting that first kind of recognition. But what do I know? I suppose the Lepers chose a leader that best suited their view on things."

"No one chooses a leader, a leader chooses them."

The conversation was cut short by the procession arriving, consisting of the Magister of the Bear, some Acolytes, and three bears in the flesh, chained together in a manner conducive to obedience. It was probably good that their conversation was interrupted, since collusion with the Lepers had recently become punishable by death, and the people gathered together at the ledge of the Bear Maze were glancing at Daedalus with more suspicion than usual.

The procession of bears halted on a patch of turf well worn by countless Interments, so that it was more brown than green along that particular arc of the chasm. They spread to their ordained positions, with the bears placed in the center. Two Acolytes held the chains on either side of the bears, and another was at their rear. The Magister stood off to one side, as he began reciting the traditional words of the Bear Interment.

Not many people understood the Ancient Tongue that all ceremonies were conducted in, they just knew the random phrase that they were sometimes called upon to say in response, and often didn't even know what it meant, just when and how to say it. Daedalus, on the other hand, did know the Ancient Tongue, and could therefore enjoy something he found humorous at every Bear Interment he attended—it used to be that the Magister of Apollo would lead sacrifices, at a temple not far removed from the Chamber and the Castle. That part of the city contained most of the buildings of civic and religious import. At the Temple of Apollo the Magister would eviscerate a number of animals in very specific ways, and then burn them at the altar. As one could imagine, it was a lot of work and none too sanitary, eviscerating animals, and the custom only continued out of religious necessity. After the bears started attacking, though, and after they were captured alive, it was reasoned that they could replace the bulls and lambs that the people preferred to use for their own purposes anyway, and the Magister of Apollo preferred not to play butcher upon. And the bears roughly filled the bill— they were animals. So everything that was once done at the old sacrifice was instead done at the Bear Interment, to satisfy religious duty, minus the bears being cut or burned. What was funny to Daedalus was that none of the words used at the old ritual were changed for the new version—they were just unheedingly transplanted, so that the priest would still recite "I cut out its still beating heart, and offer its requisite blood to the Lord." The bears perfectly fine all the while, as he did no such thing, the requisite blood nowhere to be seen, as everyone just stood around nervous at the presence of bears.

Also funny to Daedalus was when, every so often, there was a new Acolyte holding on to the bears. They had been trained on what to do, told time and again, "All you have to do is hold on firmly to the chain," but most of them had never even seen a bear until the day they were assigned to hold onto it, and nothing they could be trained or told prepared them for the real thing—the new Acolytes trembled heavily, and the bears were prone to roaring every once in a while without warning. In those moments, even the simplest of directives were easily forgotten, and the chains were dropped—that very thing had happened once, and the poor fellow had, on his very first day, been so startled that he stumbled backwards and fell into the Bear Maze. It had been a long time until they could fill his position again. It had also rained brimstone for a full week, since the purity of the Bear Maze had been violated by a foreign element that wasn't a bear—one of the things that Apollo always punished the Gibeahnites mercilessly for. Daedalus wondered what kind of punishment a rabbit warranted, that they could look forward to in the week to come. Thanks to the Lepers.

So the Magister repeated more nonsense about how he was cutting the fat from the entrails, now burning it, and what a heavenly savor! to which everyone knowingly nodded because they didn't understand. Korah was enraptured by a process he'd never seen before. He said aloud, to no one in particular, "Marvelous creatures."

Then the fatal moment in which the bears were given a light kick in the ass by the Magister, and the Acolytes let go of their chains, and the bears went over the edge, not forgoing to make a lot of noise as they did. And then it was over, with a few words in summation (translated "they are ashes now"), and everyone was allowed to go their own merry way.

"So long, Daedalus," Korah said in departing.

"Try not to get killed on your way out, Korah," was his reply.

The walk back to his house was surprisingly refreshing. There were three places in the entire city that trees were allowed to grow freely in: there was Daedalus' own yard, but the novelty of his own trees had entirely worn off for him from familiarity; there was the Central Plaza, but those trees were far too overwhelmed by the grand scale of the adjacent buildings to be enjoyable; and finally there was the cemetery, the one place left to him that Daedalus was just unfamiliar enough with that he could feel surprised by the subtleties of nature again. People were permitted to leave the city, and much new and exciting wilderness abounded just outside the walls, but a special occasion was required by the city, a reason. Daedalus thought that it was a sign of the horrible trajectory of the future, that a special occasion was necessary to enjoy nature.

But he had an occasionless joy of his own that afternoon, as he submerged himself under the laurel trees, heeding their canopies instead of the path. They were a little sickly of late due to the atypically harsh winter, but as the wind blew and they gently swayed in response, he was reminded of the life that never really left the world, but lay dormant until a more seasonable time was theirs to dominate. Daedalus had often felt like that himself, like he was being subjected to some infinitely long winter, and so he empathized strongly with the trees.

And then there was an abrupt transition—the world became buildings again, as soon as the houses felt themselves a proper distance from the dead and the Maze. Daedalus was reminded of what he held to be the essential distinction between men and every other living thing in the world, and it was evident even in the buildings, of all places—people changed their minds. What was once a shop became a home, what was once a stable became a shop, and in all their effort at efficiency with resources, or perhaps just from laziness, what the building used to be was often just as apparent as what it changed into. Often, people still had horses stabled in their new pottery shops, or a forge in their nursery. In contrast, there was no hint of the butterfly in the caterpillar.

When one floor was once thought to suffice, another was tacked on with the most shoddy of workmanship, and even that was deemed adequate foundation for yet another floor.

The houses swayed more than the trees in the wind, but reminded Daedalus of far different things. People changed their minds, changed everything about and around them. Everything else died with the same goal it started with, to thrive, to be closer to the sun—and the singularity of their goal manifested itself in their construction, just as much as people's multifaceted confusion manifested in theirs. Thus, Daedalus looked to the trees for his conception of purpose and unity, and as far away as he could from humanity.

Amidst all his reflections he almost missed arriving home, so lost was he in reverie. He was getting easier to distract every day, he noticed. Soon he would be too easily distracted to notice even that. It almost didn't sound too bad to him, a constant bleeding of his consciousness into the world around him—his current scruples still maintained too many firm boundaries for that to be possible.

The outside of his house really was a beautiful sight to behold. He enjoyed his house more from without than within, since his entire pride was wrought amongst all its facets. While he was building it, he literally consulted every angle possible for him to consult, to verify that it met both the mental vision he had built it from and his standards of aesthetic integrity from each. Adjustments had been made that would have defied most conventions of architecture and prudence. He extended one corner in the upper reaches of his roof several feet, and the resulting hollow between the original roof and the new one was of absolutely no internal utility, was not accessible by any door, was not an addition to the spaciousness of any rooms. It served merely to be a façade worthy of Daedalus' artistry. He had been an ambitious man at the time. He didn't know which he was reflecting on as he approached, the beauty he had coalesced into a wooden edifice, or the kind of man he'd been when he did it. Perhaps the two weren't as distinct as he thought.

Then there was what the house contained, constantly a

disappointment to Daedalus. Such as David, he soon found out. Once again. Daedalus found him in Daedalus' own leisure chair, working on something. "Good day to you, David. What's all of that you have there?"

"Paperwork."

"For what exactly?"

"Well… you see, last night my wife placed my two youngest by the pantry while she went about some other chore. Intending to come back for them, she assures me. But then the Bear Raid happened, and the bears must have mistaken the kids for food, being so close to the pantry as they were, so they took them. It was an honest mistake on their part. Kind of funny, really. Anyway, I have to do some paperwork that involves their death certificates, and so on. Tedious stuff."

"Sounds annoying." The only thing Daedalus regretted about the potential death of David's children was that their father hadn't died instead. His hatred ran deep.

"What's up with this thing, by the way?" David asked, indicating the hourglass where it stood, as always, on the window sill.

"It's an hourglass."

"I know that. But it doesn't work right."

"That's why I keep it around, it's the one thing I couldn't make right," Daedalus said. It was a very personal truth to confide to an enemy, but since he was sure that David wouldn't understand, he confided it anyway.

"Strange reason to keep something around."

"I know. Well, make yourself at home." He heard his wife bustling somewhere in or beyond the kitchen, and cared more to investigate that than to pretend to make idle conversation with David. "Bathsheba, darling? What are you doing?"

She yelled something about how he would have to come to her to talk, so Daedalus made his way through the kitchen and into the next room, where his wife was busy with clothes. She explained, "David's wife was too preoccupied with things, with mourning and all, to care for David's laundry. So I thought I could do the charitable thing and help him out. Them, help them out."

"Very considerate." There were many loving things Daedalus had in his heart for his wife, but also very few things he had to say to her. His hands didn't know what to do whenever he was around her—he surely looked the fool to her, waving them about indeterminately. Inside, he knew all the confused volitions that sent them conflicting orders, so that they did both, therefore neither. To embrace her? No, to maintain a distance—there were many reasons he wanted to maintain a distance, but was never persuaded by any of them when he saw her at a moment like that, dutifully scrubbing someone else's laundry clean. A lot of the things she did didn't help. It wasn't that his love for her was confused, or conflicted—his love was a very simple thing of unconditional warmth. But the nature and the expression of that love were two different things entirely.

Daedalus was at a loss for what to do in other ways as well. He'd envisioned the rest of his day as leisure, but David was sitting in his leisure chair, and if he asked him to move it would rapidly escalate out of proportion from there. Daedalus just couldn't be leisurely outside of his leisure chair. Conditioning quickly became his worst enemy, when things changed. He paced disconcertedly back into the kitchen, where he found his older son, Ephraim, drawing in a book.

It was Daedalus' workbook. "Bathsheba, who gave Ephraim my workbook! Ephraim, how did you get that? You know you aren't supposed to touch it." Ephraim was six and not yet sufficiently human enough to directly answer Daedalus. Instead, he babbled incoherently in expectant fear of reprisal.

"I gave it to him," came the reply from the opposite room than Daedalus had expected, from behind him, from David. "He was being rambunctious, and I couldn't concentrate on my paperwork. Couldn't even think of my youngest's name. So

I gave it to him to calm him down. Works pretty well, actually."

"David is remarkably good at parenting." Finally from the direction of his wife.

Daedalus was completely at a loss. He snatched the book from his son, perhaps a little too roughly, he thought afterwards, and was tempted to throw it at something, or tear it apart with his bare hands. He felt the need to commit some act of violence, right there where he stood, towering over his child.

The book was his only consolation in life, of late. He'd given up on actualizing any of his thoughts, on working with tools, on actually making anything. Instead, he would draw diagrams of things that could be made. Also included in its pages were puzzles he'd devised, traps, and mazes. It was all he had, almost everything he cared about, all in a book. After spending as much time as Daedalus had, working on that book, it had become a part of him.

So it was lucky that Daedalus didn't act as precipitously as he'd initially thought to, and tear up an integral part of himself, before even assessing the damage that the kid had done. Ephraim had a fairly new-looking charcoal stick in his hand, and had only been awake for a couple of hours, not all of which time could have been dedicated to Daedalus' ruination—Daedalus doubted that the damage could be more extensive than a couple of pages scribbled in, as kids were apt to do.

He flipped slowly through the pages as he stood there at the dinner table, still towering over the trembling child. The first quantity of pages weren't even touched—the book had been opened at random and handed to Ephraim, or something to that effect. Eventually Daedalus found that page. It was blueprints for a device that would effectively remove all the organs not absolutely necessary for bodily functioning, one by one. It started with the appendix, then the gallbladder, a kidney, and so on. To be used as a torture device, something he had thought of back when he had been slightly depressed, and so was stuck in a vein of designing torture devices for quite a few pages. Daedalus had drawn in some people, mostly just to demonstrate how they and the torture device related, but in accordance with his depression they all had excruciated faces. Their contortion varied in intensity, in proportion to the cruelty of the machine, all of which Ephraim had dutifully shaded gray. Then the kid had apparently grown bored or sated of all of that, and moved on to…

What Daedalus saw next caused him a long, silent period of introspection. The page was the blueprints to the Bear Maze, transcribed from a much more ancient document that Daedalus had found deep in the records kept at Castle Horeb. At the time, Daedalus had been especially interested in ancient architecture, and didn't really expect to come across the Bear Maze as he searched through all of those documents in their dusty eternal home, on shelves deeply repressed in the bowels of the Castle. But when he did find it, it piqued his curiosity tremendously, so he copied it into his book.

And there it was—many dark, sure lines, with one thick, childish charcoal line that hesitated in density, with many vacuoles of white amongst its gray, but never hesitated in direction. Just a line of absolute progress from the beginning to the end. The line matched all the other lines the kid had used to color in the foregoing pages, but Daedalus felt compelled to ask the question anyway: "Ephraim, did you do this?"

The kid, thinking he was still being admonished, gave one of the most tepid nods in recorded history. Daedalus asked no further questions, but walked away in a lost daze, meandering out to his front porch, passing David as he went, but not seeing him.

There were so many things that could possibly be explained by what he had just seen. A six-year-old kid could solve the Bear Maze, as easy as that. First try, no difficulty. He had to think—how far removed was his kid's intelligence from that of a bear? He'd seen embarrassing things out of his progeny, and impressive things out of the animals, and was bound to conclude that they were about on par with each other. So wouldn't it be just as easy for one of the bears to solve the Maze? Granted, they didn't have the advantage of an aerial view. Also, there was still the potential that they didn't survive the ritual fall. But if the fall was in fact fatal, there would be a mound of dead bears that would be more massive and gushy with each progressive ceremony, almost guaranteeing that one would eventually make it through the ordeal, as traumatic as it might have be for the creature.

And what that line of reasoning did a good job of explaining was a Bear Raid that did not enter nor leave through the gates. In the last Emergency Council it was never settled where the bears had actually come from—the Magisters dismissed Wallace of charges of negligence, but failed to follow up the investigation with the next logical question, "Where did the bears come from, then?"

The government didn't deem it important to keep guards on the exit of the Bear Maze. First of all, they couldn't spare the few trustworthy people they had for anything other than what they already did—the rest of the populace's work ethic was such that they would probably do a better job of guarding the exit to the Bear Maze if it *wasn't* their job, they were so insufferably ignorant and recalcitrant. The second reason was that their trepidation for the Bear Maze precluded any of them from believing in its survivability, even if it were demonstrably proven to them that the Maze only consisted of a nicely cushioned landing followed by a straight passage to the exit. Fear made monsters of things, and demons of monsters. So, even if they had the people to spare, still they wouldn't believe a guard was warranted anyway. Which made a large-scale Raid, staged from the Bear Maze, an exceedingly viable possibility.

The question that was left to Daedalus was what to do about it all. His welcome had been worn out with nearly everyone, but he really believed in the exigency of the matter. There was someone that needed to be told, someone who could be told that could actually do something about fixing the problem. There was the Council—Daedalus had had some recent success with them, against the four with a ladder, but he felt like he had more substantial evidence for that occasion. And the consequences of his argument had been much less far-reaching, so it didn't inconvenience anyone to believe him. If he was right about the Bear Maze, though, it would be a large inconvenience for many people, and they would find any excuse they could to discredit him, to save themselves the effort caused if he were right. Also, he didn't want to push his current luck too far, and hoped instead for a less fallible way of accomplishing persuasion.

Talking directly with the King sounded like his best option—although, it had been years since they last spoke, and the last time they did was a time better forgotten. Perhaps if Daedalus brought a gift with him, like a cake, amends would be easier to make, he thought.

Daedalus didn't bother to say goodbye to his family before leaving, he just returned to take a cake from the tattered remains of his kitchen, a cake most likely meant for their dinner that night, or David, and left. With all haste he made his way to Castle Horeb. He experienced a bout of indigestion as, this time, he was forced to choose the Castle over the Chamber.

There was a lot about Castle Horeb that disgusted Daedalus. And it wasn't just the fact that the castle Daedalus had designed himself was demolished in the wake of a very thoroughgoing purge of Daedalus' mark upon the city, although that did bruise his ego a little. Mainly it was how the Castle was rebuilt—Daedalus could have forgiven, if improvements had been made. That was not the case. They, the King among them, had made it explicitly clear to Daedalus that they'd rather live in a substandard Castle than one that was associated with Daedalus in any way. After those thoughts entered his head, as he approached the Castle, he decided that they were a poor rendition of his feelings, since they were biased—he was just indignant that the Castle, representative of the prowess of Gibeah, wasn't as excellent as it could have been. That was it.

One of its failings more pertinent to recent events was that the building looked the part of a castle more than it actually performed the duties of a castle. It was as if the architect, Newton, who Daedalus hated to no end, had thought his job was more to pay homage to a castle than to actually make one. To that end, there was a moat that looked the part of a moat, and a drawbridge, and ramparts, and so on. But they were like the pockets of some pseudo-fancy shirt, only a hair's width deep and sewn just to *look* like a pocket, as if a functioning pocket itself were inferior or required so much more work. In the same way, the ramparts looked protective but weren't accessible, since no door let out to them. The drawbridge couldn't be drawn, the moat was perfectly diaphanous, and looked more refreshing than dissuading. Those were only a few examples of a problem that recurred so often throughout the Castle that Daedalus couldn't look around as he walked through it, nor would he let his eyes entirely focus in front of him either, lest he saw some architectural abomination that made him instantaneously vomit.

There were two guards that manned the portcullis facsimile. They needed a name, and a stated purpose from Daedalus as to why he wanted to enter the Castle. "I want to speak to the King," Daedalus offered them.

"The King's Conference was yesterday. That was the only opportunity for the plebeians to interact with royalty. And that was only one of the questions, that you answered. I said, 'Name and purpose.'"

"The name is Daedalus."

"Oh ho! The King will want to hear about this!"

"The King will see me, then?" Daedalus couldn't help but betray his enthusiasm that things would go so favorably for him.

"I didn't say that, I just said he'll want to know. One can easily guess your intentions for coming here. He'll want to know that Daedalus is plotting treachery again. It's an assassination you've come here for, isn't it? An attempt on the King's life? Your posture betrays you, and this, this that you have in your hand."

"It's a cake," Daedalus responded. He held it up so that they could get a better look at it, just in case they didn't believe him.

"Well, then, I'll tell the King." The other guard had remained silent until that moment, but finally spoke as he saw some opportunity.

"As if! I'll be the one that they record in history textbooks as the man that saved the King from this conniving Daedalus' assassination attempt. What claim do you think you have to that honor, Mark, when all you did was stand there like a log? The effort was entirely mine."

"All of that might be, but…" The second guard broke off, and seemed to be straining to find an argument dumb enough to supersede the first's, but then started running without warning, into the Castle. "The credit will go to he who tells the King first, you fool!" he shouted in disappearing. The other guard was taken aback for a moment, and then took off after him. Daedalus was left to simply enter. And thus Daedalus infiltrated Castle Horeb.

There were things Daedalus couldn't help but see, even while simultaneously crossing his eyes and squinting. The stairs were uneven, he could have seen it from a mile away. The marble was ineptly hewn, atrociously fitted. All the affectation of grandeur fell flat. The atrium was supposed to be some mesmerizing display, and was designed with the concomitant confidence, but… it was hard for Daedalus to say where it failed, exactly. He was more of a holistic designer, never thinking of the parts, but directly channeling the whole, so that something he designed was entirely finished in his head before he even started with the physical materials, and as such he didn't have much practice with fixing parts. But if he had to guess, the best he could say about its particular failings was that it was hollow—Daedalus could see right through it, which wasn't just an illusion produced by the crossing of his eyes. The magnitude of a castle was too large for Newton, he didn't have enough good ideas to fill it. There were conceited people and geniuses, pretentious buildings and works of art. The new Castle was no work of art.

It was a long winding way to the Throne Room, the better to show off the splendor of royalty with. Visitors were forced to confront, forced to be impressed by, the Great Hall, a muse-um in miniature of tapestries and armor, the Theater, the Ball Room, and many more equally pointless displays of luxury. Fi-nally, he reached the anteroom. Daedalus could hear, through the closed doors that separated the anteroom and the Throne Room, two men bickering loudly, ostensibly the two guards that had accosted Daedalus at the entrance. On his way to that point, Daedalus had only seen people from a distance, mostly handmaids hustling about cleaning things.

Daedalus chose a room directly adjacent to the anteroom, which appeared to be a bedroom, most likely of a servant. There he waited until he heard the guards sonorously move their quarrel from the Throne Room back towards their posts. By the sound of it, nothing had been resolved between them. As soon as the coast was clear, Daedalus vacated the bedroom and carefully approached the doors to the Throne Room.

All the obnoxious, overweening forces of the Castle con-centrated themselves there, a deadly convergence—of all the things packed inside, that fact wasn't truer about anything more so than the people that populated it. The amount of gold in the room would have been deemed lavish by a Pharaoh. The amount of ostentation in the room would have suffocated an adult whale. And the King was situated right in the middle of it, trying his best not to be dwarfed by all the ornamentation that was made expressly to dwarf. To his right and left stood his Court, many of whom were recognizable as Magisters from the Council. The Magister of the King was making an announcement as Daedalus stood with his eye in the slit of the door. He said, "I present to you, Court of the King, the very estimable Magister of Health, with a presentation 'On the Noble Properties of Blood'." Since childhood, the rudeness of interrupting such presentations had thoroughly been imparted to Daedalus, so he decided to wait it out, standing outside the door.

The Magister of Health had the floor. "As commissioned by the ever prudent and generous King, I and several scientists of great renown have made certain investigations involving the noble properties of blood.

"Surely everyone present has bled at some time or another. The simple act of keeping a clean-shaven face practically demands it, and we are all gentleman here. Certain sicknesses have also been found to respond most favorably to the letting of blood, and even clean-shaven gentlemen such as ourselves are susceptible to disease, however contrary to intuition that may seem to the well-educated. It would be expedient, therefore, to know the consequence of such bleedings, whether the benefits of smoothness and health are worth the associated costs, whatever these might be. To properly make such a judgment, we analyzed. Many experiments were performed, much evidence was gathered—all parties interested in reviewing that information should be referred to my colleagues at the Ministry of Health, where such records are kept. This is our final conclusion, a conclusion we deem edifying to men of our society and, most importantly, for our providential King.

"It is commonplace knowledge that nobility is passed from generation to generation through the medium of blood. In this way a gentleman, even if he through extraordinary circumstance be abandoned and raised by peasantry, could always be distinguished from the plebs like wheat from the chaff. And, contrariwise, a pauper disguised in the guise of the blessed, the nobility, will always be discovered for the lesser being he inherently is. Everyone remembers Marcus."

Everyone remembered Marcus.

"The question presents itself, then, as to the extent to which nobility is contained in blood, whether it is entirely represented, or owes itself to other supplemental material, whatever that might be. We envisioned two ways of making a definitive answer to this particular question—first, to take blood samples of both classes and to analyze the difference; secondly, to study the effects on one given person of having different kinds of blood. The first turned out to be easier to implement, but even through our hardships with the second many instructive things were discovered.

"Noble blood is in general darker and more viscous than that of the commoner. Though the reasons might not be readily apparent, it is surely because the blood of the noble is in higher concentration, in much the same way that paints will gradually become more opaque, the more diluted they become. It would thus seem to be the case that the benefits derived from noble blood are from its concentration—to provide another analogy, from a truism of my field, medicines are much more potent when they've been distilled from their source and concentrated. The best comparison that can be made is that a noble's blood is like a fine wine—it shouldn't be watered down, unless it is given to the commoners. These properties of noble blood are easily verified through touch and sight.

"There also exists a tendency for the noble blood to coagulate faster. Being of relatively higher value, the body therefore more strongly exerts its capacities for retention, after an incision is made. An interesting case exists as proof, where a commoner was found to have lost, in the same interval during which a very gracious bourgeois took very minor losses, nearly half a cubic cubit of blood with no signs of abating. Naturally our conclusions are not based on this one case, though. It is just very demonstrative of a general trend. We find it of extraordinary interest that the body of the commoner itself seems to be aware of its value, or lack thereof, and will respond accordingly. This suggests a level of social awareness to the physical body, completely divorced from active consciousness, that we had never yet supposed. It is well known that the body, of its own volition, can maintain breathing and the pumping of the heart, along with reflexive motions in response to specific stimuli. But what we propose is much more, so that even we are still grappling with the consequences—that the body is not merely capable of preordained responses to stimuli, and habitual actions, but even *value judgment*. The capacity for judgment was long thought to be the distinguishing characteristic between man and animal. With our findings, slowly it seems the case that, in the hierarchy of creation, while man may still be of the very highest order, he is followed very closely by his body, given our current criteria. We recommend either a redefinition of humanity or an attempt to repress these characteristics of the body, so that our superiority remains well defined.

"But, for all of its importance, that is a digression. More to the point—naturally a man will want to know if an animal, take a horse for instance, can be brought to the level of humanity through the infusion of blood. What would have been extremely of interest would be whether the horse could be brought to nobility itself—can you imagine the consequences?—but of course noble blood is in short order, and it would be just as impressive if the horse could be brought to commonality, a commoner's level. Enough to demonstrate the soundness of the principles involved, if not the scope. And sadly the most that can be said about this is that we are actively pursuing its completion, this was the aforementioned—I wouldn't say failure, no—hardship. A horse contains a surprising amount of its own blood, and the highest attained ratio thus far of human-to-horse blood has been one to four, which is apparently still below the threshold of exhibiting human traits. The difficulties have naturally been the excessive bleeding of the horse, and the surprising difficulty of putting large volumes of blood back into a creature. I will be happy to report when these obstacles are resolved.

"And now for what everyone wants to hear, something of true explanatory value—it has been our discovery that the effects of noble blood extend far beyond greatness of character. We've observed the bleeding of a large quantity of men—what we can say, now, is that the weakness associated with the bleeding of any creature at all is the loss of nobility from the body, pure and simple. It is thus easily explained why men of nobility will never be weak, while it is common among the peasantry. The lethargy, lightheadedness, and loss of consciousness, even death itself, are due to becoming more and more ignoble, the emptier you are of nobility's vitalizing effects. The reason that bloodletting is useful in treatment is that certain diseases attack not the body, but the nobility of mind—and instantly you recognize this as true, as diseases cause weakness and a lowering of mental faculties. For this reason a horse will never succumb to a human's disease, because it possesses none of the requisite nobility. And for this reason it is profitable, though debasing, for a sick gentleman to occasionally fall below his vocation, to become healthy again by essentially evading the standard of the disease. What remains to be seen is if a horse can be cured of a horse's disease by a transfusion of humanity, basically the same principle in reverse, the results of which are promised in the future.

"As an addendum, the general inferiority of women can be explained through their monthly bleeding, which never allows them to maintain the concentration of blood found in men. No experiments were conducted for this, and no future experiments really present themselves as edifying to humanity—it is just an aside easily deducible from the principles already laid out, a solvable curiosity of sorts.

"Other obvious next steps would be, once a proper method is found, to inject the blood of a horse into a human, and to observe the effect, although by now I'm sure everyone could guess the outcome. What is most substantial in everything I've said, what I want to be taken away, is the self-evident superiority of noble blood—everything else has been a mere consequence of this fact. Thus it can be guaranteed that we, estimable gentlemen, have a bright future ahead of us, guaranteed in our veins, and that our progeny will be just as illustrious as we—not a hope, but a scientific fact."

General applause. The King was looking sadly down at his blood-red glass of milk, when he said, "Why can't we use the milk from the royal cows?" For time immemorial the King's Court had shared an afternoon glass of milk, but after the Magister of Health's speech the King was finding his tolerance low for bloody-looking things.

One of the Magisters responded, "The Lepers got to them too. This is it."

"And can't we drink something else?" was the unexpected reply for the King, who had quite the strong disposition for tradition and the habitual.

"There's wine."

Only then, only when the Magisters seemed to all be talking amongst themselves again, did Daedalus slip in as silently as he could. His caution was futile, though, as the door was directly facing the King and it was only a matter of seconds before he was discovered. The King's surprise at seeing Daedalus was most likely compounded by the fact that he had, only minutes before, been vehemently reported to that an assassination attempt by Daedalus had just been averted.

"Daedalus… why… why?"

"I have something important to tell you. And I brought cake." Daedalus carefully approached the King, cake extended.

"I don't think I can trust your cake right now."

"I wasn't offering it to you, I was offering it to the King,"

Daedalus told the man who had answered in place of the King, to express his distrust in the cake. It was the Magister of the King, and he had rushed up to intercept Daedalus as soon as he recognized who Daedalus was. "Will you hear me out?" he asked, once again addressing the King.

"I don't have a successor, Daedalus." Tears instantly started brimming in the eyes of the King. The dialogue of noble blood and progeny had clearly gotten to him. He turned abruptly to his right, to stare at a portrait of himself, which the King preferred over the use of a mirror whenever consulting his looks. He even fussed his hair, as if the portrait's gentle tousle, artistically rendered to invoke nonchalance, was actually his own hair misbehaving. The absurdity of which lay mostly in the fact that the King had balded considerably since having the portrait done.

"Nonsense, your Majesty, you have two beautiful children, Eric and Sebastian," said the Magister of the King, who apparently saw fit to intercede on both Daedalus and the King's behalf. The Magister of the King was so used to representing the interests of the King, at all of the numerous Councils, that he seemed to be losing the ability to differentiate his own identity from the King's.

"Those are your children, Oliver, not mine" the King reminded his Magister. "Don't you see? Don't all of you see? I'm the only one in that picture," he said, gesturing toward a mirror. "Not a single person that might take my place."

Daedalus wanted to console him. "Richard, Sofia didn't—"

"Don't! call me Richard. I am King Richard. And don't bring up the Queen." Once again it was the Magister of the King responding, instead of King Richard. Behind him, wrath had rashly possessed every feature of the King, down to the reddening of his head.

Even though Oliver was being exceptionally annoying, Daedalus knew that he was the one who had offended the King, not the Magister. Richard might have said exactly what Oliver have said, if he wasn't beaten to it. "I'm sorry. Please don't let any of our history cloud your present judgment. Please believe how earnest my reasons are for risking this, and coming here. I have to tell you, to tell all of you, about—"

"It's your fault!" cried suddenly the Magister of Public Safety, from his position to the right of the King. "We should have exiled you, or had you executed. Apollo is punishing us yet for your dissoluteness. We could have fixed it, if we could have fixed you."

The King had another outburst of his own: "I bet you anything—how much do you want to bet?—that if Sofia was still here, she would be barren, that Apollo would still deny me the consolation of an heir? Magister Treyshka is right, it's all your fault. Can we still exile you? Can we still exile him? You weren't pardoned, were you?"

"Richard!" Daedalus let his anger get the best of him, and was immediately afraid of himself. "If you really cared so much about Sofia, and about the longevity of your Kingdom, you'll listen now." Daedalus was veritably shouting by then, to overwhelm all of those that rose to protest. They were pushing him out, they were all talking at once to the King, they were pushing the King, they were all loudly berating Daedalus. "I know where the bears are coming from, why they can circumvent our defenses. They're coming from the Bear Maze. They're using the Bear Maze!"

"No," said the Magister of the Bear, who did occasionally show up to the King's Court, even if he didn't go to the Emergency Councils. "The job we do is much too good for that to be possible."

The King retreated higher into his throne like a spider whose honor had been wounded. He scowled the kind of scowl that denied the possibility of light. "I won't believe it. I don't believe any of it."

"You won't help me out? You won't help Gibeah? Only you could override the sanctions against me. I can't be a Magister anymore, none of these people would let me. So I can't litigate. If I can't litigate, I can't affect any of the necessary changes to the Bear Maze. Nor would anyone in the Ministries trust me enough to collaborate. Only you could say otherwise, could make all of this possible. Can I call on you as a friend, as I once did? It would be retribution against the bears."

It became dead quiet through the course of Daedalus' implorations, although there was still half-hearted pushing from the Magisters. Before anyone had a chance to respond, a thoroughly turbaned mass of a being barged into the room, carrying with it a straw broom. It began making aimless sweeping strokes that didn't clean anything in particular, as it windingly made its way around the circumference of the room, weaving through people. Everyone present turned to watch it make its way.

"What are you doing?" the Magister of the King finally asked.

"I sweep," was its muffled and androgynous response.

"No, you aren't really. Nor are you wearing your uniform correctly, might I add." The Magister of the King was a strict disciplinarian when it came to uniforms.

Above an entirely random mass of clothing, the standard uniform had been added like an afterthought, and was furthermore put on backwards. "I make improvement to uniform."

"No! No! There are reasons you have to use the uniform correctly! I like the uniform! Who are you? Oliver! Get me the Keeper of the Grounds. I will have this resolved immediately."

Even though he had technically given the order to himself, the other Magisters knew what he meant, and one of them sent their retainer off to summon the Keeper of the Grounds. It took several minutes, during which time the intruder continued to sort of sweep, as if its authority on the matter was not being challenged. A slight, wearied man was finally brought in and situated before the King, who took on an officiating demeanor. "If you could tell me, Keeper, who it is sweeping my floor here, and why it was scheduled during a King's Court?"

The Keeper murmured a few indecipherable things.

"One more time?"

"I said 'It's not my authority, King.'"

"How do you mean, it's not your authority? You are Keeper of the Grounds, by Apollo's name!"

"Certain duties were redistributed to make it more even. The Mistress of the Chamber Pots sees over those kind of things now, not me."

"Are you absolutely serious? Why wasn't I told! Please, get this man out of here, and bring me… bring me the Mistress of the Chamber Pots." Though he had a perfectly acceptable reason to make the demand, it had still embarrassed him to say it with so many respectable people around. Several more minutes elapsed before the Mistress of the Chamber Pots was present.

"I'm going to ask this again," said the King to the Mistress, who hadn't been asked anything yet, "who is this sweeping my Throne Room and why now?"

The Mistress said, very coolly, "Your Majesty, I have no idea who that is. And furthermore they are wearing the uniform incorrectly."

The King had had quite enough, trying to talk to the staffing to resolve the matter. Though it was below his station, he attempted to speak to the intruder directly, yelling loudly "Hey, you!"

Instead of heeding, it tried running away, but its stride was hindered by the tightly wound cloth about its legs. It insisted on a full stride anyway, though, and the result was that it tripped on a loose fold and crumpled awkwardly onto the floor. In the process it unraveled a bit, revealing its leprotic contents.

"A Leper! In the Castle? Kill it everyone, kill it!"

Daedalus had never been called on to kill anything before. He looked about for what weapons might be at hand. The only plausible things were priceless artifacts, everything in the room being gilded as it was, down to the chamber pot. There was also the broomstick the Leper had brought with it as an attempted disguise, which had been dropped amid the tumult. Daedalus doubted he could do much killing with a broomstick, but picked it up anyway. Next he had to consider which end would be most effective—the bristles seemed more annoying than lethal, so he tried using that end as a haft while he swung what was normally the handle as a blade. He wasn't nearly quick enough, though, nor was he much interested in actually harming anyone, so the Leper was able to scramble away before it was ever in any real danger. The one swing he did attempt met the floor without intercession. Everyone else had been just as slow as Daedalus to react.

Daedalus commenced to give chase, to appease the King, and was joined by other members of the Court, but he was out of breath a shameful twenty paces later, and the Leper was far sprightlier than was fair without the impedance of the turban. All the other Magisters were just as old as Daedalus, and just as likely never to catch up with the Leper, but they trundled along anyway. They were either still in denial about their age, or far more disposed to obey the orders of the King than he was, no matter how implausible they were. Daedalus left them to pursue, while he returned to the Throne Room and the King.

"There was nothing I personally could do, although it looks like others are on it. But back to the topic at hand." Daedalus thought that he could perhaps be more persuasive without the presence of the Court, which he believed harbored more resentment to Daedalus than the King did.

"No, no, I'm not helping you. You stay right there, until the rest come back, so we can deal with you properly. You've made a grave mistake this time, Daedalus."

As Daedalus waited, a few members came back as a small group. "We found a naked servant further down the hall, your Honor. She said that the Leper asked for her uniform, and was so nice about it all, that she just felt obliged to give it to him. The audacity of the thing, to come in here and try to gather information like that, in front of us all, as if we were stupid. Reconnaissance, I guess those damn Lepers call it."

While the King was preoccupied listening to their report, Daedalus silently made his way out. He wasn't too disappointed, since he'd never really expected to succeed anyway. He was already formulating his next move as he went.

KAPITEL VIER: HUMAN SYCOPHANCY

HOW QUEEN SOFIA was abducted from Castle Horeb, some three years prior, as told by Daedalus' son Ephraim to Daedalus' other son Manasseh (and with the exception of a few precociously learned words by Ephraim, also how any other child might have told the story):

The pitch black night shrouded the bears in secret mystery. Dad heard them coming and rang the Bear Alarm! But it wasn't enough—the Bear Alarm is not very loud. You need lots of people to ring it for it to work, and the Bear Alarm never makes it past Deaf Alley anyway. Of course the Bear Alarm was Newton's idea—what an idiot!

The bears galloped as fast as they could. I bet you didn't know, but the average bear can outpace even the fastest human. People were flung away or trampled by the bears, but they didn't mean to kill anyone—it was bad for Bear Business. "Don't kill any humans!" grunted the Bear King.

When the bears came to the Castle they were perplexed—they had expected a mighty fortress of impeccable danger. They believed that getting past the moat would require significant energy, and so trained for it. But the bears, more persuaded than dissuaded by the awesome moat, frolicked in it. They played Bear Games such as "Try Not to Barf" and "Try

Not to Poop," which can be played in both team and individual varieties. Hence, the moat was considerably dirtied.

But, after a short while, all of their bear games and frolicking, which required considerable noise, awoke the castle guards. They ran outside as fast as they could. The bears didn't care and kept frolicking. The guards became nervous and one EVEN threw a rock. The bears noticed but continued frolicking. But then one guard remembered what he was supposed to do, and shouted: "Go away you stupid bears!"

The rest of the guards caught on, and started taunting the bears too. "If you bears are so smart, why are you so dirty!?" added another.

It was the Bear Taunt technique from the Adult Council meetings. The bears would have none of it. They were very upset after being Bear Taunted. "That's very hurtful!" roared the Bear King. Some guards ran, some guards tried to wrestle the bears, and some guards tried to appeal to reason: "Why stop frolicking when you are having so much fun?" Other guards tried irrational reasoning, basically just screaming. Most of these guards were thrown into the disgusting poop moat. Gross, right?

The guards that ran away couldn't run into the Castle—the doors were locked. So the guards ran around the Castle, which was fine with the bears. The bears had other things to do, they had to penetrate the Castle. Luckily, Bear Scientists had it covered. They designed a system where bears stacked on top of one another to form a Bear Ladder. I don't know how it worked—the bears are really strong, that's all you've got to know.

Storming the castle, the filthy bears insidiously and diabolically undid the work that many servants had done to make the Castle clean and hospitable: Doors smashed! Glass shattered! Furniture broken! Food, carefully prepared, eaten! But the worst of all was the Carpet Dirtying— humans had not yet developed the technology for cleaning carpets and the ENTIRE CASTLE HAD BEEN CARPETED! Now the carpet had to be replaced. Yes, that's true!

The bears roamed deeper and deeper into the castle. Nobody knew what to do. So they woke up Sezurus Magnate Stairwell, who was amazingly still asleep. "Yes, what is it?"

"The bears have breached the Castle walls!"

"We'll stop them—follow me. We need to protect King Richard."

Stairwell donned his Sezurus gear, gathered a few servants and guards, and headed to the Royal Chamber. The Castle interior was illuminated by the dim glow of lamps. The soft carpet muffled their steps and made it easy to sneak around. Faint, distant roars and furniture breaking permeated the night air, through sound vibrations and stuff like that. It's physics.

"Wait!" Stairwell hissed at his posse. His posse was made of Wallace, Aether, and Pallace. "There's bears ahead in the Royal Meat Room." They knew the shortest route to the Royal Chamber was past the Royal Meat Room, which is normally kept unlocked. What do you mean, "Why didn't they go a different way?" You can't just go a different way! It wouldn't work! Every passage in the Castle goes by the Royal Meat Room. Just listen, and stop arguing.

"How many bears?" whispered Pallace.

"What do we do?!" panicked Aether.

Stairwell thought back on all his bear-prevention training. "The bears really enjoy meat. We can probably just sneak right past them."

The posse of four inched toward the Meat Room. The Meat Room entrance was perpendicular to the hallway, if you can imagine that. It was a door on the side of the hallway, not a hallway leading directly to the door. So the bears wouldn't necessarily see the posse coming, pretty much. Got it?

Pallace sweated nervously as her heart pumped faster. She had never faced bears before. Bears were known to steal human women. "Maybe the women are murdered and used as fish bait?" she thought. It reminded her of her cousin, who had been stolen by bears. Wallace thought about his wife, and wondered if she was in danger. Aether thought about his dog, and how stupid his dog was.

The door to the Royal Meat Room was open. The posse could hear the bears eating and chewing and grunting and rummaging. Huddled against the wall, Stairwell peaked through the half-open door. He held up his hand with three fingers in the air to indicate three bears. None of them saw Stairwell as he crept past the door, they were much too busy eating. Aether went next. Then Pallace, carefully tip-toeing. One of the bears turned to the door, sniffing with its big, wet nose. Growl growl. Pal-

lace could hardly breathe. The bear stepped toward the door, peaking out.
ROAR!

"Scatter! Scatter!" barked Stairwell.

ROAR! *The bears bounded out of the room. Jumping and shoving, quickly the bears pinned everyone but Stairwell. You can't outrun a bear! I already told you, not even the fastest human. Fine, Wallace made it out too, and followed Stairwell. Stairwell didn't look back as he ran to the Royal Chamber. He knew he would be no match for so many bears. As he made his way to the Royal Chamber, he could hear distant grunts and yelling from different directions. He tried to pinpoint the action, to understand the circumstances—how many, where, and who would win. But he couldn't. It was the Fog of War.*

Anyway, Stairwell tried rebuilding his posse, finding more and more people as he went. Stairwell was charismatic and that helps. Charismatic is when you can get girls to like you. Not like Dad, no.

Stairwell and his posse, now twenty strong, made their way to the entrance of the Royal Chamber. The entrance to the Royal Chamber is a big room, always lit with torches. The floor is carpeted with blue, and the walls are a dingy stone color. King Richard emerged from his Royal Chamber in full battle armor and gave a motivational speech. I don't remember the speech, it's not that important. "My King!" said Stairwell, "We are here to protect you!"

Distant bear grunting drew closer and closer. "Stand tall! The bears come for me!" said King Richard. Bears poured into the room and charged! There was no time to think.

The men and women only had sticks and swords, except for King Richard, who also had armor. The bears used their fierce paws and claws, and their black eyes were savage and wild. Elasus' eyes locked with the bear charging him. Elasus? Elasus is that one guy. Anyway, Elasus charged the bear. The bear leapt at Elasus. Elasus ducked and swung at the bear with his stick, catching its foot as it flew over him—
WHOOSH!*—in slow time. The bear groaned a little, and landed on all fours like this. Elasus turned and whacked the bear in the face with all his strength. Growl. Whack again. Grunt. The bear grabbed the stick. Elasus couldn't move the stick. "Help!" It raised its right claws, real dra-*

matically. Elasus got the feeling we all do when something terrible is about to happen but we are powerless to stop it. And not in a deep, thoughtful way, like the slow death of a family member, but in a physical way. Like when you run down a hill too fast and are bound to hit a large tree and can't stop. You just crash right into that tree. Slash, cut, blood!

Dad always tells this part of the story differently than Wallace, but I think Wallace's version is more historically accurate. Wallace wasn't going to just stand by and watch everyone get beaten, so he ran towards the bear and jumped as high as he could. Time slowed. Wallace kept his legs high. Tick. Tick. Tick. Bam! He landed on the bear like he was riding a horse! Wallace grabbed the bear's ears and held on tight. The bear's fur was wet with poop water, which made it hard for him to hold on, but he knew his life depended on it. The bear went into a furious rage! It ran and bucked, just like a horse, and Wallace kicked it to make it gallop faster. Wallace scanned the room. He saw a bear pinning a woman to the ground. Wallace pulled his bear's right ear as hard he could, which made it turn real sharply. He squinted his eyes, to focus. Bam! Roar! Groan! Wallace's bear collided with the other bear. The poopy fur was too hard to hold on to—Wallace flew off his bear, and landed on a vase. The bear, dazed and confused, ran away!

Stairwell clenched his stick—haha no not his dick, his STICK. His FIGHTING STICK. And his breathing became shallow. Like asthma. Out of the corner of his eye, he glimpsed a paw. WHAP! It felt like a hammer. He fell backward. The bear slowly stepped over him. It looked down at Stairwell, straight into his eyes. Stairwell, feeling better, punched the bear in the nose. To get him back, the bear thrust its paw downward at his head, trying to smoosh him. Stairwell dodged, pulled his legs back, and kicked the bear with all his strength. The bear was forced backwards. Stairwell stood up and charged it, and the bear got back on all fours and charged right back. Stairwell and the bear grabbed each other's shoulders with all their strength. Stairwell could feel his muscles burning. He wouldn't last long. The bear's grip weakened. It let go of his shoulder with one of its paws, to try to grab Stairwell's leg. Big mistake. Boom, the bear fell to the floor, with Stairwell on top. Stairwell grabbed the bear's right paw, twisting it. The bear groaned in agony! "Bad bears! Bad bears!" yelled Stairwell.

The largest bear headed straight for King Richard. This bear had some sort of leather case attached to its body. Richard swung his sword. The bear dodged. Richard swung again. The bear dodged. Richard swung again! The bear grabbed Richard's sword arm. Richard pushed as hard as he could, but this bear was the strongest! He's strongest because he's the Bear King. Did I not say that? The Bear King is the strongest bear, it's obvious. So the bear squeezed Richard's arm. "Agghh!" Richard dropped his sword, which made a muffled sword-on-carpet sound. The bear grabbed Richard by the waist and leg and pinned him on the ground. Richard played dead. Really!

As the battle raged on, the bears were definitely winning, overall. A couple of bears were busy breaking the door to the Royal Chamber. Queen Sofia, stick in hand, was waiting for them. When the door finally broke, she rushed at the largest bear. The bear didn't move. Sofia hit the bear a few times with the stick, but the bear didn't mind. It slapped the stick out of her hand. Two other bears restrained her as she screamed. The bears attached Queen Sofia to the largest bear, who still reeked of stinky, foul poop. Sofia ralphed! Ralphing is when you vomit. Because when you vomit you go "ralph". I didn't make it up, it's what people say. Just let me finish, it's almost over—this was a kidnapping! The bears, who knew the Castle pretty well by now, scurried away, taking Sofia with them. And they never brought her back.

Daedalus had to fix the Bear Maze himself. Worse, he had to explain to his wife that he had to. He called her Baths, because that was what he called her when he wanted to be endearing. He provided all the reasons he knew to provide, that it was for the good of the people, the good of their food, their children, for the good of her. The time he spent away wouldn't be so long, the neglect for his family wouldn't be so much. And the payoff would be worthwhile, would be worth it all. There would be safety and security, it would be like seven years before when the world was carefree and the walls that bound their city in weren't even conceived, wouldn't have been believed in. The sun and the moon alike lit a haven—and havens were capable of rebirth, Daedalus could be a midwife. He said all of those things, and more.

And she countered, hadn't he neglected his family enough, was more the best idea? Was the life they had so bad that he had to go about trying to construct all of his fantasies with a hammer and chisel? Would he love the world better if he had made it himself, was that why he didn't like her, didn't respect her, because he hadn't made her, and fondness for the workmanship of another was too much for his ego to handle? Could he possibly trust himself with tools again, after what he had done with them the last time that he had picked them up? She let him have his pen and paper, let him sit idle in his chair every day as she ran a household, was that not enough for him? Did his avarice demand more? Once sated with all the good things in life, would he press for more until the lining of his stomach burst from the sheer amount of selfishness he had?

Daedalus assured her that she was perfectly wrong on most accounts, and that he loved her dearly. He would probably require a lot of raw materials that he hoped to be able to salvage from the house, and that if there was anything she didn't want any more, anything at all, if she could please set it in a pile for him to use? That was when she stomped off, flustered as a woman could be.

An inventory of every material available to him had to be made, before he could decide what was in his capacity to make. It was the exact opposite of how he usually designed things, and made him uncomfortable, but he did it anyway. In the past he had faced no such restrictions—whatever he lacked he could go buy himself. Or, when his favor had been at its extreme, whatever he needed had just been provided for him, all he had to do was ask. But at the moment, the former was just as impossible as the latter. There was surely a warrant out for Daedalus' arrest, since he had not stayed to be dealt with back at the Castle. If not an arrest warrant, there was at least enough suspicion abounding in the city about "the subversive activities of Daedalus," that going anywhere to buy material, and interaction with anyone at all, was out of the question. Time was also of the essence—he had to complete whatever work he might be able to do as soon as possible, just in case he wasn't allowed to finish his modifications to the Bear Maze before being punished for whatever it was they might accuse him of. He knew all the risks associated with what he was doing, and had his doubts, but his sense of duty was strong enough to override them all.

Several hours of intense rummaging into every corner of his house yielded Daedalus a couple of blankets, one of his own chairs, and the superfluous wood from his roof that was his pride and joy, but not absolutely necessary to keep the rain out. There was no longer a useless hollow maintaining beauty over Daedalus' head. Also, there were toys he hadn't seen his boys play with for some time, trash that hadn't been thrown out of the city yet, and heirlooms that had been in Daedalus' family for generations, which would be useful for their metal. Those and other odds-and-ends made a massive pile that Daedalus then considered from the vantage point of his working chair, which he was using for its original purpose as a chair for the last time. It and everything else in front of him was being systematically incorporated into his ideas for the Bear Maze expansion, which he delineated in his work notebook, using the very same page that his son had drawn in just that morning.

His pen worked furiously. It had been a long time since he had worked with any passion—the foregoing years had been a torpid haze for him, and his pen had moved accordingly, with thick and deliberate strokes. Finally, everything was erratic for Daedalus again, there was the glory of creation once more—unlike all of his recent designs, he knew that that one was to be acted on, and the thought fueled his fervor.

Daedalus was forced to light a candle as his work extended

well into the night. He had never needed the use of a candle in the past years, either—usually his ideas had been exhausted long before the sun was. Reconsidering, Daedalus extinguished the candle. It was something he could use for the Bear Maze, and he didn't want to expend it yet. He continued in the dark, not worrying about the accuracy of his sketches, as the paper in his hand was more of an aid anyway to the master design that was formulating in his head.

A few hours before dawn, he had planned everything that it was possible to foresee, leaving the rest to be resolved in the process of creation. So he woke his horse up, who was not pleased to be disturbed at such an abject hour, and hitched his cart to her, whispering soothing words all the while, and stroking her back. Then he gathered everything he had into his cart, which was so full that he was forced to walk alongside her.

There was one last thing that he had nearly forgotten. His tools. His wife had hidden them from him some time before, but, fortunately for Daedalus, he had every single hiding place possible in his house ranked from most clever to least, something he had devised after years of long hours sitting bored in his chair. He gave her the benefit of the doubt and started at the most clever of hiding places, in a barely accessible nook on the second floor, and worked his way down the list, and was pleasantly surprised when he found his tools lying in the third most clever of spots. And then he was ready to go.

The way to the Bear Maze was dark and foreboding. Lanterns were not used in the cemetery, since it was a tacit understanding that no one was to be there, or at the Bear Maze for that matter, after dark. The trip there was uneventful nonetheless, the only thing of note being the disembodied sounds of birds that permeated the air. Upon arriving at the exit of the Bear Maze, Daedalus unloaded everything from the cart, turned his horse about, and gave her a resolute slap on the ass. He knew that she would find her way home, even though she would have to cope with the annoyance of being attached to a cart as she tried to live her normal life. Regrettable, but it was the best he could do for her.

His choice to annex to the end of the Bear Maze was an obvious one. Had he tried to work from the entrance, such difficulties as the initial plunge into the Maze and dealing with potential survivors from the last ceremony existed. Until that moment, in which he entered the absolute darkness of the end, he didn't realize that even he had been subject to the conditioning of fear for the Bear Maze, a fear which was extraordinarily common with everyone else. Sometimes the glaring commonality of everyone and everything asserted itself in that way, humbling him—Daedalus felt it then. But he fought it. He only went as deep as the first turn, before beginning his labor.

And there he worked until dawn, performing untold feats of construction. And when dawn came, he persisted yet, and dawn became afternoon, and afternoon evening, as Daedalus furtively and tirelessly worked deep within the confines of the Bear Maze. He entirely lost track of time, as it was always a perpetual twilight inside the Maze, once his eyes had adapted. He fell asleep mid-stroke, in some new passage that he was etching into the dank walls of the labyrinth.

He awoke some hours later with his face planted against the stone of the wall, slumped forward in a seated position that had devastated his spine. It wasn't nearly enough to deter him—he finished the stroke that he had begun before sleep's rude interruption, and followed it with many more.

After that went on a while, Daedalus came to the conclusion that he needed more materials, having used up all the ones he had. So he made his way back into blinding daylight, for the first time in what must have been two days, and stumbled his way back home. Physically and emotionally exhausted like never before, he couldn't focus on anything that didn't have to do with the Maze. When he got home, his wife was startled to see him. She asked him a lot of questions, but when he ignored them all she eventually left him alone.

He sifted once more through the entirety of their possessions, and drew more things out that could be of use, things
that he thought he couldn't live without before, but changed
his mind—he started to only think of things in terms of what
the Bear Maze needed. While he was home, he couldn't help
but fall asleep on his own bed, as inviting as it was.

Sadly, though, all of his new supplies could not be transported by the cart as they had before—he brought them all
out to his horse again, but found her keeled over in her stable.
Thinking that she was just fatigued, and that he could coax her
into action if he tried, he patted her chest, only to find a gold-
en arrow sticking out through one of her ribs. She had bled
to death after collapsing in her stable. The materials had to be
conveyed some other way. He carried them himself.

The process repeated itself multiple times, over days. There
was once when his wife told him, in one of his intermittent
stays at the house, "Daedalus, the government's been by, looking for you again. I told them I didn't know where you were,
but there are only so many times I can lie for you."

There was another occasion—though they were all blurred
together for Daedalus, he had a hard time differentiating anything from anything—when he had been standing in front of
the mirror. "Honey!" he yelled. "I'm taking your mirror."

"Seriously? For what."

"It's for the Maze."

"What could you possibly use a mirror for?"

"As a builder, as a deceiver, it is my job to find the uncommon in the everyday. There are so many things that you see
and use every day that would confuse and disturb you in a different light. My job is to create that different light. The mirror
would be perfect."

"Just because it disturbs you to look in the mirror, doesn't
mean the same applies to everyone. You haven't bathed yourself in a week, have you?" She was probably right. Daedalus'

face had recently grown new wrinkles, which housed itinerant dirt and grime, as if they had been built to meet the newfound demand made by all the dirt and grime of the Maze. He never looked his forty years more than he did at that time—he had always enjoyed a youthful face. His youthful face must not have been able to handle the Bear Maze.

"I'm taking it anyway."

Some other time, Daedalus had been sitting dazed on the ground—he had used both chairs after all, instead of just the one—and he was just contemplating Mazes as he sat there, left turns and right turns, backtracking and finding oneself. There had been a knock at the door, and Daedalus answered despite how little he understood what was actually going on in the world, and despite how unpresentable he really was. He was lucky it wasn't the government—it was David. "What do you want?" Daedalus asked.

"I'm here to take Bathsheba to dinner."

"What?"

"She's been through a lot lately, and she could use a nice night out." He attempted to enter, but Daedalus unintentionally barred his way by simply not moving.

Mentally lost in the Maze, it took Daedalus a moment to gather words. After a moment, he said, "You're going to leave now. I'm going to shut the door, and you're not going to be there anymore."

"Just a minute! I'll be right there!" Bathsheba called from upstairs. Daedalus had taken every other step from the staircase, since only half were vital for getting from top to bottom. Or bottom to top. It was good wood.

Because he didn't have the time to remain standing in the doorway, keeping the two apart, eventually he moved. His anger stayed. That day, as he worked, Daedalus tried to incorporate his feelings for David into the Bear Maze. Chisel and hammer poised in hand, he meditated solely on David's face, and such a rage possessed him that he drove the entire length of the chisel clear through the surface of the stone, so that it was no longer retrievable.

From the moment he closed his eyes, he had nightmares about the Bear Maze, about things not coming together right, about not having the sufficient tools for his purpose, especially considering that his chisel was embedded deeply into a wall somewhere, so that his waking life and his sleeping were one and the same practically, and sometimes he was shocked when he thought he had done something already but found it undone, because he had labored only in his dreams and couldn't differentiate the two. It was reminiscent of the nightmares he'd been having for months, but more real.

A lot of golden arrows had been surfacing lately, centered in the things Daedalus had brought to build with, ruining them all. Daedalus didn't ask questions, he merely considered it another challenge, and found ways to repurpose the ruined materials as he went. The arrows were useful themselves, as consequences for bad Maze-choices of bears to come, so that Daedalus was thankful more than anything for the sudden plethora.

He could think of so many uses for an hourglass in the Bear Maze, an astounding amount of possibilities, but the hourglass was so unforgivingly sentimental to him that he couldn't bring himself to do it. Just like he could think of an equivalent amount of uses for a severed hand, but that didn't mean he would cut his own off. Direct analogy.

Then they found him one day, hard at work. Bathsheba had been true to her word, she said she wouldn't lie anymore on his account. Dangerously armed with the truth of his whereabouts, they came in force, tackled him, pinned him down. And even though his thoughts had been entirely centered on his maze for longer than he could remember, when they cornered him Daedalus was only ranting about Bathsheba.

"Tell her that it was all for her. That she might be having dinner with another man, but she'll be doing it in safety, by my hand it is wrought that she will always be safe. Tell her that as much as I have nightmares about what I'm doing with my life, and what I'm doing here, I have nightmares about the way her eyes looked at me the day we first met. The two nightmares are one and the same. No, they're not nightmares, I really couldn't even tell you what a nightmare was anymore, but they haunt me so, they will never leave me. They were the most serene of heaven, the kind that you hope you'll end up in when you die but know that you don't deserve. Have you ever been haunted by serenity? Avert your eyes before you see it, serenity, or else you'll never let it go. I'm warning you. If she were to look deeply into what I've done here today, from that heaven of hers that I don't know how she made, she'll find her own eyes, or at least she'll find how much they mean to me. It's more than her eyes that I mean, but I keep going on about them, don't I, but what else am I supposed to say? I can't very well say anything about her soul, it is a thing too dear to me, I don't have the right. So let's just call it her eyes. I put them into everything I do, they mark my work, more surely than a signature ever could. I could write it with my blood but it wouldn't be closer to my heart. But that serene heaven is here most of all, the one I don't deserve but I will perish before I give up on. Don't you feel like you're sort of in a heaven as you stand here? Did I do a good job? Won't someone tell her? It would be such a shame, I just couldn't live with myself, if I went through all of this trouble and nobody told her."

Tears were streaming down his face, making rivulets through the coating of dirt and worry lines. He struggled violently as they tied him up, but the discerning eye would have realized that he wasn't struggling with his captors, but with some demon in his head. The two were easy to confuse, though, so the men sent to retrieve Daedalus beat him savagely, although he never let that deter the words that he seemed inhumanly bound to say, like some higher force, some puppeteer who didn't need the soundness of his puppet to relay his message, spoke through him.

"I never meant to kill Icarus. He was my son, he came from me, he came from us. Could something that came from us really die? I build walls, but I never meant to build walls between us. It's just that sometimes, in a mass of walls you've built, in a labyrinth, you can't always keep track of what's still with you and what's on the other side. I never meant to lose track of you. I would go back and make a map if I could, if someone just gave me the chance. I want the chance."

And they carried him away.

When he regained consciousness, he had no idea where he was. It was dark and humid, and smelled of human excrement. But very soon he recognized the place as his own creation—the dungeons of Castle Horeb. What a complete surprise to him it was—he had thought they demolished all of his castle before building anew, but didn't know any better because he hadn't been allowed near the construction site. They had kept the foundation, the dungeon being the foundation to every castle, perhaps deeming it too much work to rebuild that as well, only for a matter of principle.

It lightened Daedalus' heart in more ways than one. The first, that his own work was still holding the Castle aloft and secure, and that there was hope for its perseverance as a castle yet. The second was that he had wonderfully thick, wrought iron bars cradling him in their midst. They were smooth—Daedalus let his bruised and battered fingers travel up and down them all. The other three walls were of solid stone, precisely fit so that not a chink could enter the mind as some symbol of their frailty—they connoted only solidarity, only eternity.

It delighted him so, but his delight was not perfect—in the perfect paradigm of a prisoner, the prisoner knew nothing of what lay outside their cell. That added to the despair of being a prisoner, that they wouldn't have any idea where to go if they did manage to break free, which meant that they were more likely to get caught again than escape. But Daedalus knew every pathway by heart, the best route out, where all the guards were apt to be. Had he gleaned all of those things by years of acclimatization, of learning the idiosyncrasies of every guard and exploiting that information to formulate a way out, through petty bribes and sheer fortune of coincidence, that all would have been fine. But he knew enough about his situation already, and it bothered him to no end. Still, he felt better than he had in a long while.

Days went by, and food being brought to him became his measure of time. It wasn't a perfect system—sometimes he would be sleeping soundly when his food arrived, and by the time he woke up there would be rats devouring it. Other times he would wait for ten hours to be fed, before realizing that he had probably been up all night. He needed the sun to keep him honest. He subsisted on stale bread and water, with the occasional moldy cheese. And it was beautiful.

There was a day that someone was approaching at an unusual hour, at least by Daedalus' conception of time, and his curiosity brought him to the grating, in order to see the new visitor as they passed. They didn't pass—they came directly to Daedalus' cell.

It was a man, whose divine aura defied the darkness surrounding him, so that he glowed a warm golden. His features were immodestly handsome, with perfectly formed, high and proud cheekbones underlining the most piercing eyes that had ever punctured Daedalus' soul. He had flowing curly hair, wreathed in laurel. Apollo himself stood before Daedalus, expectantly.

Daedalus' first reaction was to prostrate himself on the floor, but Apollo forbade it. "I've not come for you to pray to me. I could get that anywhere, from anyone else. I come, of course, with quite another purpose."

Daedalus apologetically returned to his feet. "What is it you want of me, my Lord?"

"'My Lord,' you say? Could it be you truly mean these words? If I truly was your Lord, you would have done a better job following my will, I feel."

"When have I ever deviated?" Daedalus was honestly perplexed, his eyebrows became taut in questioning supplication.

"You really don't know, do you. Those were my arrows that impeded your path, the very arrows that brought down the mighty Python, all those years ago. You're an intelligent man, I would not have given you the hair from my head years ago if you were undeserving—you should have recognized my arrows. But you refused to consider them for a second, refused to take the second's consideration that would have identified them to you. It's a kind of ignorance. So, you haven't truly sinned on that account, but you haven't exactly followed my will either, have you? I did not want the Bear Maze amended. I am order—I am the one that ordered that you were stopped, one way or another."

"And now that I am stopped, have I found grace in your eyes again? I am punished for my transgressions, I am imprisoned." Daedalus' heart hung on the answer.

"Grace! Punished? What matters is not that you are punished, but that you are contrite. Contrition! And yet here you are, happy as you've ever been, in prison. This is some sick perversion that could never find grace in my eyes, prison means nothing if it isn't a breeding ground for the penitent, and you haven't repented, Daedalus."

"I apologize sincerely for the way I am, and also for trying to fix the Bear Maze. I thought that it would be better to serve its purpose?"

"'Serve its purpose,' he says, as if it had one."

"To keep the bears in."

"The bears are my punishment to the city of Gibeah, why would I want them contained? What happened to my real sacrifices, with slaughtered animals and burning flesh? I liked my sacrifices. But now, people sacrifice the bears, they sacrifice their punishment and expect a reward out of it. What kind of insane distortion of logic is that?"

A valid concern, or at least he thought so, was growing in Daedalus' mind as Apollo spoke, which he probably shouldn't have voiced, but his insistence on consistency overrode everything else: "If these bear sacrifices aren't appeasing to you, the Bear Interment and all of that, why do you enforce the sanctity of the Bear Maze? You punished for the man that fell in and you'll punish for the rabbit, if you haven't already while I've been locked up down here."

"As much as it pains me that the Bear Maze is the new form of religious observance, I have to hold people accountable to the one they choose. There are gradations of piety—someone who abandons my sacrifices but adheres to the new rules they choose is still sinful, yes, but better than the one who can't even abide by the rules they made themselves. I reward at least some semblance of order."

Daedalus let everything sink in for a while, as Apollo stood watchful over him. Finally, Daedalus added, "I really don't know what more I can say. I've had a hard time lately—"

"You're not the only one who has lost a son, Daedalus. I handed over the reins to my dear Phaethon's demise—"

From another cell adjoining Daedalus' came the feeble words of a fellow prisoner, the voice of whom Daedalus hadn't heard until, at that moment, he began a warbly recitation, "And the Sun-god, all this long while, remained in the deepest mourning, as in eclipse, and hates himself and daylight, gives way to grief, to grief adds rage, refusing his duty to the world."

"Do you hear this, do you hear this blasphemy?" Apollo was furious, glowing stronger and stronger until his connection to the sun was undeniable. "He recites the pinnacle of my shame word for word, as if it were flattering! Do you know what these pathetic fools, these prisoners, pray to me for, every night before they fall asleep and have pathetic dreams about fresher air? They pray for justice, as if justice wasn't the very reason they were here in the first place! They deserve to rot, every one of them, for their blatant omission to know that rotting is all they deserve. I will teach the world what order is yet. But I've become distracted—my point was, that even for a god it is difficult to be the cause of a son's death. But we must move on, duty must resume, and I still drive daily the same chariot that took the life of my own son. Duty continues. And for failing to recognize this, Daedalus, I condemn you here to rot as well."

Then the unthinkable happened. Without a sound, and entirely without warning, bears flooded into the dungeon from all sides, from every direction. Even Apollo was taken aback—he took two steps in retreat. They flowed in, dislodged the heavy iron door of Daedalus' cell in one fluid, easy motion. They swarmed over Daedalus, and then left just as suddenly as they came. Apollo had never seen anything like it, in all his long days of lighting the world.

DER ZWEITE TEIL: DER LABYRINTH

KAPITEL FÜNF: BEAR RETARDANT

EVERYONE WAS ABSOLUTELY baffled by the disappearance of Daedalus, especially King Richard. Daedalus had been perfectly disposed of as recently as four days before, and then a day later the door to his cell was just as missing as its former prisoner. Richard had always had his reservations about locking Daedalus in a prison that the man had designed himself—now he knew why.

They had interrogated prisoners who had putatively seen the whole ordeal, but they all spoke about the kind of fantasies that too much time in solitary confinement was apt to make a man say—one of them said they saw bears, the other said that he had seen Apollo even, walking amongst mortals, vouchsafing to talk to Daedalus, of all people. The prisoner that said he saw Apollo also said that he had impressed the godhead with some recitation he owed the education system for knowing, and requested that someone please thank the Magister of Education. He also requested, while they were at it and if no one minded, cursing the Magister of Public Safety, as he was of the opinion that there was nothing inherently dangerous about fire, it was everyone's reaction to fire, like having burns, that was dangerous.

Since that prisoner seemed so fond of education, the King made sure that someone was sent to teach him that even though Apollo was to be believed in, it was the *divinity* of Apollo, which prevented the god from coming down and associating with the sorry likes of humans, especially prisoners. The reformation of prisoners was taken quite seriously in Gibeah.

It was self-evident that Daedalus had escaped on his own. Only that could explain how he managed to elude the sight of every guard, and the Castle defenses. A 'wave of bears,' as the pathetic adulterer had called it, would have surely drawn the notice of *someone*. Someone whose sanity was not under suspicion, that was. Still, Richard was uneasy. One man being able to penetrate his defenses could be just as disastrous as an entire army—why had he expended so much money to have the Castle fixed, if it still wouldn't keep all the people he despised out and the people he was forced to associate with in? There had been many failures lately on that account. Daedalus had found his way both in and out, as well as Lepers. And bears, that fateful day years earlier. Sofia had found her way out… it continued to pain Richard excruciatingly, whenever thoughts of his Queen Sofia entered his head.

Was he not paying the guards enough? Maybe he was paying them too much—it would be wonderful, if the problem was as easy to fix as that would be. Or maybe if he provided incentive for guards seeing things, that would get results. But the last time he tried that, his ears had immediately been full of all kinds of sightings, from ghosts to chimeras and all manner of things between. The last thing he wanted to pay for was someone's rampant imagination.

If Daedalus had escaped, though, it was not clear who might have been harboring him, or where he might have hidden. Investigators were sent by the King to Daedalus' wife, Bathsheba, who assured them all that she would have sold him out again if she had the chance, but he wasn't at home and she had no idea where else he would have been. The King also sent investigators to the Bear Maze, to make sure that some obsessive impulse hadn't driven Daedalus to finish what he had heinously started. Daedalus was not where he belonged, nor was he in any of the other cells—perhaps he just preferred a corner cell and moved himself, someone reasoned—or anywhere else that anyone thought to look for him. The King wasn't sure that he had the best men on the job, since, due to lack of a better option, all of his criminologists were criminals—but what else could he have done? He had to make do with what he had, and everything he had seemed to indicate that Daedalus was no longer in Gibeah. Three days, they had searched.

Which may have been a blessing. Richard had thought before that the recent misfortunes of Gibeah all had Daedalus as their common source. Now that he was gone, maybe Apollo would be more forgiving, maybe everything was as it should be. The best way that Richard knew how to verify that things were the way they should be was by Augury, so he called the Magister of Apollo to him. The Magister of Apollo was only ten feet away, so it did not take long for him to arrive.

"Yes, your Majesty?"

"I was thinking that, because of recent circumstances, it might be prudent to make an Augury."

It used to be that the Magister of Apollo himself would decide whether it was prudent to make an Augury or not, which became a problem whenever Richard wanted to know something, but the Magister denied him because 'the window wasn't right,' or some other nonsensical religious jargon. Like when Richard had wanted to know when he would stop having nightmares, and the Magister at the time had told him to wait until a more decent hour, and he would see. So Richard found himself a newer, more pliable Magister, who didn't consult the hour of the day before he consulted Apollo like he was told.

Naturally, then, the Magister was quick to agree, just like Richard had picked him to be. "Y-y-yes, your Highness. Right away."

But the Magister of the King overheard, and said, "All in good time, my Majesty, but have you forgotten that we've scheduled a King's Court for this very moment? I was just about to make the announcement. Surely we must wait until the day's obligations have been met."

"Get on with it," said the King.

In his herald's voice, the Magister of the King said, "And now, gentlemen of the Court, we will listen to the Magister of Education and his exposition 'On the Benefits of Trauma in Education'."

The room became silent, and the Magister of Education made his way to the customary place for speeches to be delivered from. He daintily cleared his throat and began, "Thank you, your Majesty. Today I wish to speak about the advances in pedagogy recently being implemented in the more experimental of schools in Gibeah. These advances have been researched and put forward by my Ministry, and I feel it would be beneficial if everyone were to be aware of what they are and how they function.

"Practically the only limitation to the cognitive faculties of a man is his memory. It could be countered that critical thinking, for example, is somewhat distinct from memory, and is a common human limitation. But if a man with a perfect memory could be imagined, it would be hard also to imagine that he would be lacking in critical thinking. All of which suggests that the memory is the precursor to all other cognitive faculties, and thus if a good foundation is laid, everything else will follow.

"Being as it is my sole concern in life to further the educational capabilities of our fair city, to provide for it in any way I can, it would appear that my only real objective would then be to improve the memories of all our citizenry, by whatever means plausible. A few home-remedies of sorts have suggested themselves throughout the years—to get a full eight hour allotment of undisturbed sleep; to eat a nutritious breakfast, and other meals in healthful amounts and at regular points in the day; supposedly the omega-3 fatty acids found in seafood are very instrumental; regular exercise to promote blood circulation; the list could go on for quite a while. And while all of these may be helpful in ways, it must be admitted that they cannot be an integral part of the memory process—a man could do without any and all of them, and still have a perfectly functioning memory. What we are looking for, and trying to improve upon, must then be an even more basic operation.

"And the answer is probably more clear than you would realize. Think back to all of the things that you can remember in your own life—I bet I can enumerate them all for you. That is right—like a magician, I will reach behind your ear and bring forth the contents of your memory. What do we have—the death of a loved one, the biggest lie you ever told, the severest pain you've ever experienced, your first kiss, your favorite book, being shamed in public. What is the common factor in all of these things? I would maintain that it is a heightening of the senses, from the extremity of the human experience that these events represent. What can move a man more than his favorite book, and is he not much more aware when he is so moved? Never are the impulses of the body so confused as during a first kiss. Nothing is more tragic than the death of a loved one. They can all, everything I said, be considered *traumatic*. When people hear the word traumatic, they associate with it scarring. 'That scarred me for life,' etc. And even though this expression has a mostly a negative connotation to it, it must be admitted that a memory and a scar are practically one and the same. That a full memory, a perfect memory, would really be a perfectly scarred memory, a memory that retained an imprint of everything inflicted on it.

"As educators, we cannot make the memories of our students more susceptible to scars. But we can make what we teach more scarring. In this way teaching by the rod, the traditional way, is vindicated. For a long time we've been drifting away from it, since it is generally perceived as barbaric. What has to be remembered is that the human body itself is barbaric, that although we may idealize it, and call it a reflection of divinity, we cannot let this 'refined' system of values misinform the way we treat it. I've seen far too much of that, I've seen parents under the impression that their children already carry a worthwhile worldview and a fully developed faculty of judgment, and therefore allow their children 'freedom of expression,' and allow them to make decisions for themselves, and do not hit their children for the same reason they would not hit a grown man. I've seen no greater perversion of the truth than this lunatic's construction. It wouldn't bother me so much if these inordinately entitled children did not end up in my school system, and become my obligation, but they do and they are.

"From these obvious truths, how does one devise a better educational system? The rod is not perfect, it is just an indication of the right direction. We must make every moment that the child is learning traumatic to him. The problem is that the body quickly becomes desensitized to the same sort of trauma, and this is the failing of the rod—it is only one type of trauma, only one facet. There are only so many times you can hit a child before it stops caring. What other methods proffer themselves? You can teach a child his multiplication tables and then tell him his parents have died—he is likely to remember the day he learned multiplication. But this can only work once or twice, especially if you are lying. You can make a kid stand in the front of a classroom and undress in front of his peers, while reciting the Gibeahn Laws. But if you make a whole class do it, after they've all gone the particularity of their having been naked is diminished by sharing the experience with everyone else. That's a limitation.

"So what we've done is to come up with no less than thirty six ways to traumatize a child, and systematically spread them through the curriculum, so that all major educational milestones line up with one of these thirty six traumas. In this way the child never acclimates to the sort of trauma helping it to learn, and it is my belief that no better method could be devised to teach a child. I hope that in six years, when our first specimens emerge from the other end of our new program, I will have the kind of results to verify the assertions I made today. Thank you."

General applause.

Hardly two minutes after the Magister of Education had finished, the King proclaimed, "Everyone, everyone follow, we are having an Augury." The Throne Room went dead silent, when it had been full of private conversation just the moment before, from people congratulating the Magister of Education, and from others tending to personal affairs of their own.

There were so many Magisters around Richard. Before she was kidnapped, Sofia used to be the only person consistently with Richard in his Throne Room. He would have her stand facing the Throne, so he could look her over as he sat in his grandeur. Or occasionally he would have her hold a cup next to him, so that he might drink whenever he liked. Just the two of them. Then she was gone, and the Throne Room had been horribly empty without her, and he had been quite thirsty, so he established a 'King's Court,' for which all the Magisters were required to accompany him as he spent all his day on that Throne, that seat that he had come to identify with his lower half more than his own legs. Accordingly, he couldn't leave it longer than most people could leave their legs without longing for it back. As a result it was much livelier in the Throne Room, which slightly dulled the pain he felt. But his bedroom was still irrevocably empty—he would never think to take another wife, and he couldn't very well compel the Court to preside over his bed as he tried to sleep. Although, every now and then Oliver, the Magister of the King, would end up in Richard's bedroom anyway, would even crawl into the King's bed with him, saying afterwards that he had mistaken it for his own. In a way, and only in that one way, Richard was glad that his wife was no longer in Gibeah. He could vividly imagine Oliver making the same 'mistake' with her—but wherever she had ended up, it was surely out of his reach.

Before leaving to the Augury, Richard checked his appearance in the mirror that he'd installed on the wall to his right—he always liked to see himself to the right of himself, it comforted him—conveniently angled so that he didn't have to leave the solace of his Throne to fall within its domain. Once again, there was a stray hair on his head that no matter how he tended to—he could cover the thing with wax, something he had tried, and he thought he'd waved the thing triumphantly in the air after pulling it out—it would still stand in a bold state of recalcitrance, the likes of which a king rarely encountered in his own kingdom. Futilely he brushed it down, but, being content with the remainder of his appearance, he felt free to go.

There were only three rooms that constituted Richard's life. He'd long since grown tired of seeing his realm and the people that lived in it—those were all sights he found absolutely loathsome, for all that they used to please him in the beginning. Slowly, the feeling of power, of owning everything, so that seeing anything at all reminded him of his power—slowly that feeling had gone sour, and no matter how he would have liked to throw it out as one would do with any other trash, he couldn't let it go. The people couldn't very well govern themselves, after all. So his life was reduced one room at a time, until it settled on three: the Throne Room, where he held King's Conference and King's Court; his bedroom, where he held King's Anxieties, and King's Regret; and the Augury Room, a spacious place where birds could have room for flight, opened up to the sky and all its elements, but well-adorned nonetheless. A lot of artwork relevant to the function of the room decorated its walls, such as depictions of famous Auguries of the past, many of which involved the Oracle of Delphi. Those three rooms—the rest of his life was spent in the hallways that connected them.

Everyone followed obediently as Richard marched the distance between the Throne and Augury Room. The Magister of Apollo had an exceptionally difficult time keeping up. Once there, the whole company took a moment to gasp for air, as luxury had made their breaths shallow. Eventually the Magister of Apollo was composed enough to go about his preparations necessary for the rite. A bird cage rested in the corner of the room, and the pictures on the wall framing it had all taken on an interesting haze, a blurring of all their features, a side effect of the profuse bird droppings. Other implements included a smaller cage, a fount of water, dissection tools, bird food, and a pile of stones in the very center. Half of those things were considered sacred. Also, the bird food had an exorbitant amount of insect infestation, but the beauty of insect-infested bird food was that it was still bird food.

The Magister of Apollo, Aaron, took the smaller cage to the larger one, which was brimming with fowl. A small hole opened on its side, through which Aaron could stick his arm and individually grab birds to throw into the smaller cage. They would then be transferred to a table that was in the center of the room, near the pile of stones. The birds squawked a life-fearing squawk, a god-fearing squawk, perhaps having a notion that a god was the reason that a select few of them were about to die.

"Ah, little devils!" Aaron had his arm fully immersed in a cloud of birds, who had all learned to use pecking as a last measure of survival. Despite the pain, Aaron soon gathered enough birds to commence. He placed the newly full, smaller cage on the table, then made his way to the fount. Holy water was taken from the fount and sprinkled first on the birds, then on the stones, then on the tools of dissection. He whispered a few words over each as he poured the ablution on them, though the words were drowned out by the continued vocal adamancy of the birds. Finally, he took one bird from the smaller cage, rapped it sharply against the edge of the table to settle it down, then cut it in half with one of the tools. Its blood was poured over the stones after the holy water, and the words that accompanied the action were drowned out by one less voice than before. And so it was ready.

"Alright, prepare yourselves, everyone," Aaron said to the congregation, giving his work one last diffident, cursory look as he did. Preparing themselves involved each person picking up a few bloodstained stones, and a few of them tested the heft of their ammunition. "Are we good?" He got a nod from everyone, so he opened the sluice to the smaller cage. The birds, recognizing the opportunity for freedom, did not hesitate to take full flight.

The room *looked* like it was completely open to the world, since a sizeable chunk of the ceiling and the upper quarter of one of the walls were nonexistent. What did exist, though, in spite of all appearances, was a very fine net that let nothing more than a slight breeze and the idea of sky through. Its purpose was to discomfit all the birds in their escaping—and as they flapped about in the net, the men of the Court were then to throw stones one by one until all the birds were felled, at which point the waning vitality or death of each bird could be analyzed for portents.

The birds made a straight line for the sky, every one of them. The members of the Court held their fire—it was essential that the birds realize the error of their presumption before being stoned to death, for many reasons. But as soon as they hit the net, at the pinnacle of their confusion, the Court loosed a massive, lethal barrage of stones at them.

Every single stone missed. Not only that, there was an audible rending of material, and after only a moment's discomfort, the birds all successfully managed to leave the room entirely, out into the blue sky.

The men of the Court were bewildered even before the net

fell down on top of them, after which there was much tripping, yelling, profaning, and despair. The Magister of Apollo had to use the sacred implements of dissection to cut himself free. It was a blasphemy he absolutely loathed to commit, but only resorted to after everyone had struggled for over fifteen minutes just to become more entangled than before, with the net and each other, which became especially awkward for some. Another five minutes were required to cut away some very tenacious pieces of net and some especially entrenched Magisters.

It was nearly dark before they were well-enough disposed to talk about what had happened. "Does this count as an Augury? What does it mean?" asked the Magister of Public Safety in a very worried, beseeching manner.

Everyone turned to the only resource they had, the depictions of Auguries past that surrounded them all. "I don't think this has happened before," said one of the Magisters.

"There's the time over here, under the window, where one stone killed the entire flock," suggested one. "What did that end up portending, again?"

"I don't think it's similar at all. And I think they all caught malaria, after that Augury," answered another.

"Well, that's good news. I mean, if the two aren't similar at all, then our fate shouldn't be similar to everyone catching malaria. That's something," joined a third.

"That's what our fate *isn't*. What *is* our fate?" The Magister of Philosophy.

"Well, we'll start with a poll. How does everyone feel about the Augury we just made?"

All paused for a second, until one offered, "It was beautiful."

"There's nothing too horrible about beauty," a Magister said. Most agreed.

The King spoke for the first time since leaving his Throne Room. "Good enough. Let's go back." He was missing his legs.

Days went by after the Augury, days of worry for the King, days of wondering what that episode really might have meant. He had said "good enough" at the time, but that was mostly just a show of confidence. On the inside, he was burning with anxiety. His appetite was even more sparse than usual, and he'd taken to vomiting the few things he could stomach to eat.

He focused on sitting on his Throne, since he didn't know what else to do. He felt pallid, could sense the sickliness of his skin, yet his mirror assured him daily that he still had a healthy sheen, a rosiness even. He felt betrayed by his appearance, like it wasn't doing its part to represent the way he truly felt inside.

A couple days before, he had sent men to evaluate the damage that Daedalus might have done to the Bear Maze, to see if it was reversible. If it could be fixed, it was possible that it would appease Apollo to repair the damage, and the likelihood of the Augury being fortuitous would accordingly be increased. The men he sent had instantly developed severe rashes upon entering the exit of the Bear Maze, though, and refused to continue on account of discomfort. Whatever damage Daedalus might have done to the place, it looked as if it was Apollo's will that it stayed. Which perplexed the King all the more.

The King was in the process of trying to inconspicuously whiten his complexion—if the sickliness wouldn't show, he would disclose it himself, by whatever artifice necessary—when a Messenger of the King entered the Throne Room. It was often that one of their number came to inform the King and the Court on the state of Gibeah, since it wasn't often that any of them actually saw the city. Whenever the Messenger entered the room, a hushed silence took over, to allow that everyone might hear what was going on in the world about.

The Messenger cleared his voice harshly, rolled his eyes into his head to probe his memory a bit, and then started in a loud reporting voice: "Hail King Richard! You look… actually, you don't look too well. Anyway, breaking news! But first, the weather. The weather of Gibeah is fairly seasonable—a temperature of fifty degrees, with highs in the sixties expected throughout the early part of the week. The sun is out right now, actually. Preparations for the Festival of Good Humor are well underway, and the likely appeasement of the peasantry is forecasted to be high, with average riot levels lower than they have been in years."

The report was interrupted briefly for an applause by the Court, to commend what a good job they'd done. The Messenger respectfully waited their ovation out, before continuing. "But most important of all is a recent discovery with far-reaching consequences, something that the public has yet to be made privy to. A while ago, you the Court commissioned a group to research and develop possible counteractive weaponry against the bears." The Court slowly nodded, as some of them vaguely remembered having commissioned such a research group. "Well, finally you have your results. Deep in Samsonite territory, there is a flower which, once its components have been harvested, yields an extremely potent sedative, whose effects are virtually indistinguishable from death. This sedative, once incorporated into the military's standard issue blowgun, would actually make the blowgun useful. Within ten seconds the chemical agent takes full effect, fully incapacitating the bear."

"This is great news! Can you believe it?" exclaimed the Magister of Public Safety. And great merriment abounded amongst the other Magisters, with congratulatory handshakes circulating throughout the room.

The Magister of the Bear was hesitant. "Does it hurt the bear?"

"Absolutely not, sir. It just sedates them. Permanently."

Then he too, the Magister of the Bear, was fully convinced and merry.

"Great news indeed," said the King. "When will it be ready for use?"

The Messenger took on a fearful look, is if the adage of not killing him might be violated if he said what he had to say. "Well, there's a thing, you see. As I said, the flower is only endemic to Samsonite territory…"

"Continue."

"So we haven't harvested a nearly sufficient quantity to mass produce the agent, since the flower would be extremely hard for us to acquire, as you very well know. The one flower that they did have, to do the research and establish results, was taken from the beautification of one of the bear's suits of armor, in the last Raid. It was brought to us, more or less."

"So you need more."

The Messenger flinched. "Yes, and we wouldn't be able to get more without the Court's authorization of a military expedition to recover the flowers. None of the researchers are willing to go to Samsonite territory themselves." Having delivered the message, the Messenger waited worriedly for the response. Any kind of request for resources, such as people, was deemed egregious by the King, no matter the reason. And he often reacted violently. The reason for his adverse temperament wasn't quite known, but it was a reality that most people had adapted to.

Samsonite territory was the land occupied by the Samsonbear, a particular long-haired breed of bear that was extremely violent, but fortunately never saw fit to invade Gibeah. The bear that had the flower in its armor was surely not a Samsonbear, just a run-of-the-mill variety with the brazenness to enter Samsonite territory and pick flowers.

The King thought aloud. "Half of this is good news. The other half is the last thing I ever wanted to hear. Are they sure the flower exists nowhere else?"

"Absolutely sure, your Honor."

"And they want me to send my men, risk valuable lives, to get it for them? Although, it would be extremely practical…" This train of thought continued in Richard's head, since he didn't dare voice it aloud. He was having reemerging thoughts of Sofia, and all the feelings of hatred towards bears that were associated with them. He could finally avenge himself, avenge her. He could pay the bears back for all the damage they'd done to his psyche. He was envisioning the first successful offensive launched against the bears in over three years, the first offensive even imagined possible in a very long time. Up until that point, it would have been fatal to attack the bears—even if the Magister of the Bear allowed it—guaranteeing the death of whoever was sent against them. The bears were far too powerful, and could return the damage of even the most dangerous of human weapons, tenfold. Not only did the bears have their strength, they had their cunning—any stealth attack made against the bears was doomed to failure, was immediately discovered and thwarted, as the bears had their way of thwarting everything. Many stealth attacks had been executed while it was still deemed acceptable to kill bears. Literally executed—the bears had tracked them all somehow, captured them, then killed every person at a ceremony that was the bear's barbarous equivalent of the Bear Interment, which involved much dismemberment.

But with a new weapon, an amazingly strong sedative, stealth wouldn't be necessary. Overcoming the indomitable strength of the bears wouldn't be necessary. Just a simple shot, which would seem innocuous enough to the bears until it proved to be their downfall.

"As much as it pains me to say," Richard said to his Court, "risking the lives of a few will provide untold benefits to the rest. It has been too long that we've lived under the tyranny of fear for bears." It had been too long since he'd seen his wife. "And it is time that we take back our proper and rightful place in the world. Whatever steps are necessary. I promise you—and tell the group that sent you, Messenger boy—you will get your men. I will personally oversee that they are equipped and briefed, and that they realize the full import of the mission they will complete, that they realize what a milestone in human history that they themselves will be a part of. And as to whoever established this research group," a few Magisters tepidly thought to raise their hands, but none of them did, "I heartily thank. Let it be done."

With any luck, Richard thought, that was the meaning of the Augury. The freedom of the birds from the room, from death and suffering, would be like the freedom of the people, released from the walls of Gibeah at last, and the fear that kept them inside like a net.

The Messenger was exultant that he got off so easy.

By the next day, all preparations had been made. Sadly for Gibeah, the whole of the military had to be committed to the mission, since they were only fifteen in number. And when only half of those reported for duty, and the other half were nowhere to be found, their number had to be supplemented by the Sezuri, including Sezurus Magnate Stairwell, so that there would be fifteen again. Fifteen was deemed an appropriate and sufficient number by King Richard, who nevertheless hated to concentrate every single reliable person he had left in Gibeah on such an extremely dangerous mission—but he was so blinded by its importance, the sheer magnitude of the event, that he let it happen anyway, heralded it even.

He gave another brief, impromptu speech as they all stood at the city gate. It was the east gate. Its usual sentry, Wallace, was no longer in the guard shack, but included in the expedition itself, since he had 'proven his worth and capability' in the last Emergency Council, and during the Bear Raid that had prompted it. So he, along with everyone else, had been fitted with a dulled sword that was to be used as a last defense, as stealth was to be their *modus operandi*. They were also outfitted in a nice camouflage suit that the King had never seen, much less heard of, until one of his advisors recommended it for the purpose. And to complete the ensemble, everyone was given a sizeable backpack, to be stuffed with flowers. The flower had been described to them, at least as well as a flower could be described to a group of grown men.

Even though all Samsonite territory was considered dangerous, it wasn't exactly true, since the bears didn't occupy it fully—rather, they marauded within its boundaries. The hope was that they could be entirely avoided.

The King perorated, "Every single one of you is definitively changing the course of humanity today. Have no fear— Apollo will guide you, will be your breath and your sight, and will keep you in safety. Upon your return, you will be honored in a way befitting such great deeds. Now, the best of luck!"

With that, the King and the Court accompanying him gently herded the expedition out of the gate, some of whom were looking as if they were having second thoughts already. Then the gate was closed after them—the men could not return, and the King could do nothing but wait.

The mood of the expedition might have been foreboding indeed for its members, and some might have run away, had it not been for the distraction supplied by a conversation between Stairwell and Wallace. No one knew how it started, but, once it was in full swing, everyone was eventually listening and amused, almost forgetting that they were going deeper and deeper into the unforgiving wilderness.

Stairwell had been retelling his shining moment, that night he'd spent on top of a bear that made him everything he was. Wallace countered, "Oh yes, that reminds me of a similar time. It was quite a while ago, most likely before you were born, so there's a great chance you didn't hear about it. I was picnicking with my family—in the very place we're headed to, I'll show you when we get there—and I left my family for a moment to go pick some berries, as I was struck by a sudden craving, something fierce. Well, halfway through picking them I suddenly realized how tired I was, so I took a bit of a nap, there in the pleasant shade of the bush, when lo and behold! I get woke up by screaming. I run to see what's the matter, and it turns out a bear had been mauling my entire family while I was away! Couldn't believe it. So, I says, 'Hey bear, you better watch out,' and it must have taken this as a threat or something, because it charged. Now, I wasn't quite sure how to react, so I tried hitting the thing. I did, punched it three times, square in the jaw, but those bears are resilient fellows, take it from someone who knows. So you know what I did? I tackled it, and sat on it like you did. Until it died of boredom—took three days."

He then launched into a full-scale retelling of his childhood, which no one remembered, Wallace included. Its epic narrative took them all the way to their destination, the border of Samsonite territory, some four hours after they had left the city. They could tell they were there by the lack of anything intelligent in the vicinity. Samsonbears had a strict diet of unwitting creatures, because everything that knew better stayed the hell away. So the eternally inept squirrel and deer were present, and a multitude of insects, but that was all. Nor was it a subtle difference—the wilderness of Crete was very densely populated with a myriad of species, anywhere one went, with the exception of the city because that was all the city really was, not really a strict inclusion of humans but a strict exclusion of everything else.

"Tread quietly," Stairwell advised.

Wallace couldn't help but relate to the group the last time he had to be quiet, and how remarkably similar it was to the present. "I bet you if you went and got yourself a protractor, you'd find life goes in circles like that," he said while nodding his wizened head.

Not a flower was to be seen, even of the wrong variety. Stairwell motioned for them to continue deeper into the territory. Some of the men began shaking violently in apprehension, and Stairwell, who realized their fear, gave a few of them a reassuring pat on the shoulder, and nothing more.

"Well I'll be, there it is!" Wallace exclaimed, and trotted to a bush as fast as his haggard legs would let him. It wasn't often that he and objects of his memory were reunited, especially at his ripe age, when most of his friends were rotting in designated places, so he became very emotional with the bush. The bush bore berries of a deep shade, very overripe, but Wallace greedily ate them anyway, and not for the flavor. Some ancient, tarnished feeling in him demanded their consumption.

"We have to maintain unit cohesion, fool," Stairwell said, as he tried in vain to pry Wallace away from its thorny branches. Stairwell was at least twice the mass of Wallace, and clearly in better shape, yet as hard as he tried he couldn't budge the man from his engorging reverie. But while he was straining in the attempt, something caught his eye that made him forget all about Wallace. It was a flower with very tiny petals, bright yellow, that grew in thick clumps. "I found it," he informed the rest of the group. He let go of Wallace, forgetting entirely about him.

They followed Stairwell into a large clearing, full of all kinds of flowers. They took the bags from their backs and began stuffing them vigorously with the yellow ones, extremely relieved to have reached their goal without incident. Some laughed, some cried, everyone was merry. But their rejoicing was premature—a few elated shouts from the group that couldn't be repressed were answered by several roars from the forest.

Everyone in the group was so deathly still and quiet after hearing the roars that they literally all heard Marcus, one of the younger in the group, soil himself, and no one blamed him. Stairwell alone kept confident, and made an entirely superfluous hushing sign with his index finger, unnecessary because no one but him would have been capable of speaking at that moment even if they wanted to. Especially Devon, who, unbeknownst to anyone, had silently bit his own tongue off.

There were a couple very promising seconds of peace and

quiet before a group of three bears ruined the moment by tearing into the clearing and felling two trees, roots and all, in the process. They were Samsonbears, their strength inordinate, and their hair an unusual, flowing length, which might have been considered majestic-looking by some, as it blew languorously in the wind, if it wasn't for the fact that the wind was caused by the breakneck speed at which the bears were travelling in their direction to massacre them.

Of the many and diverse forms of panic, the group elicited a good variety.

Devon fainted, helped by the considerable blood loss from his severed tongue, blood that he'd just been swallowing in liters. As he fainted, then, he explosively vomited all of it back up at once, so that it looked to the rest as if his head had blown up. Which didn't help anyone's fear at all, as some then had the added concern that the bears were capable of head-detonating terror from a distance.

Marcus had a paralyzing fear, evinced earlier by the apoplexy of his sphincter. It quickly radiated from his ass to his whole body—his legs, his arms, even his heart. And since he didn't move, he was the first true victim of the bears, one of which actually clawed him in half in passing, while Marcus did nothing but stare.

Darius was a screamer, Evan was of the denial variety. "Nice, nice cuddly bears," he kept saying to himself. Jarvis was a self-mutilator, tearing at his hair and skin from some untold horror inside of him that was struggling to find expression. All those perfect specimens of the variety of panic died where they stood, the Samsonbears overtaking them easily.

The rest of the group had a more mobile panic, and put up a better chase than the others had. The bears were ready to oblige, even happily, it seemed—amidst their excessive roaring and noise making, a derisive laughter might have been discernible to someone well versed in bear behavior. They chased all of the humans down, one by one.

Stairwell, on the other hand, had an inventive panic. He began frolicking through the flower field, gathering handfuls of flowers as he went, as if he were just there to enjoy the beauty and the sunshine, and to have a generally fun time before returning home to take a nap. It possibly would have been completely convincing even, such was Stairwell's art, if it weren't for the fact that a great part of the flourish of his frolicking was lost amongst the bushes, on account of the camouflage he wore. The bears did hesitate, though, and it occurred to Stairwell that they weren't buying it wholesale. He even had the presence of mind, entirely surrounded by bears, to recognize that his camouflage was hindering his performance. He wondered quickly whether he could salvage his strategy by stripping and continuing, but upon consideration it didn't seem plausible to him. The bears would catch him with his pants down. "Fine!" he yelled, and threw down his fresh-picked bouquet with more disdain than a woman abandoned at the altar. "Have it your way!" And he drew his dulled sword.

There was a second, before the battle began, for which Stairwell was completely overpowered by the smell of flowers. It took him far away from the bears, to somewhere else entirely, somewhere deep within his thoughts. A place he hadn't been to in a very long time. The air was impossibly sweet, and it made him feel like genuinely frolicking, instead of just the feigned frolicking that he had been doing, moments and eternities before. But he repressed the impulse—he knew he shouldn't.

Another wave hit him. The smell reminded him of a house he'd been in, but could remember almost nothing about. He didn't know where it was, or who owned it, or even what it looked like. He only knew that he missed it.

KAPITELSECHS: HUMAN SUFFRAGE

KORAH WAS WRITING a letter to his wife. Like most simple things he attempted to write, it instantaneously became overly philosophical, a little historical, and much longer than anyone would have the patience to read:

Sweetest Miriam,

I'm going to try to make myself clear. It may take a lot of words, and a lot of random thoughts, but I hope I can at least explain myself a little in the process.

There are many thoughts in a human head. Naturally, some people have more thoughts than others—a broad spectrum wherein some heads are so retentive that the sheer presence of memories is enough to drive them crazy, while, on the other end, some heads are so porous that if you put your ear against their temple, you can literally hear a whistling sound as their stupidity breeds itself. Many thoughts are unimportant, many contradictory, and many are the core of their owner's identity. Often there is a large overlap of these three categories. And you wouldn't really know just how unimportant, contradictory, and vital each of your thoughts might be, unless you took the time to inventory them all, to pass them through a filter of sorts. What would that even look like? And is it even possible?

I am, as you are most likely aware, more introspective than any of the people I associate with. I'm not bragging, it's probably not a good thing. But I have many reasons to be the way I am. Unlike so many people who unquestioningly adhere to their strongest beliefs—often the strongest beliefs are the ones that people reflect on the least, refusing to entertain for a second that they could be wrong, or could ever possibly require a second thought—I consider daily what's important to me, as objectively as I can manage. At least I try to.

So if I had to say what's most peculiar about me, I would say it is the nature of my core beliefs, the beliefs that I identify myself with. With some people it is religion, with others it is family, or acquisition of wealth. For me there are two things, a person and an idea. The idea is both easily stated and impossible for me to work out—a definition of humanity. It constantly plagues my mind, it's what keeps me up at night and keeps me distracted on a beautiful day like today. The person is you.

Korah looked up from his letter for a moment, long enough to survey his surroundings. He was sitting at a leprotic sentry post, overlooking the city of Gibeah from outside of its walls. The Lepers were doing extra surveillance, after Gibeah had sent out a small army three days before. When nothing moved, he went back.

It's not so simple, my definition of humanity. The words people use the most are rarely easy to define. In what follows, I make the assumption that children would give the simplest, purest answers, unconditioned as they are by the confusion of the world. So we ask a child.

To begin with, we keep the question simple. Instead of asking the child about some abstract notion, we ask about the concrete form of humanity, its manifestation as a personality trait. And just assume with me that this isn't some stupid kid, because then what would be the point? We ask our ideal child, "How would you describe a man with humanity?"

"He is good," the child answers. But what is is*? or* good*? These questions were posed at the beginning of humanity, and are still in the*

process of being unsatisfactorily answered—what it might mean to be, and what irrefutable and discernible criteria could make certain things good, at the same time necessarily distinguishing them from what is bad. Concrete humanity—who would have thought it would be so hard to define? Because we are unsatisfied with the answer given, we will ask the larger question. Perhaps we'll be pleasantly surprised, and the harder question is easier to answer. We ask the child, "How would you describe the humanity of man?"

"It's what makes us what we all are," our child answers. But I, a grown man, have to stand here and think about how, even though most people want the same things, feel much the same way, eat the same, love the same, die the same—it's not the extensive similarities that people really care about. So that if "It's what makes us what we all are" was given as a definition of humanity, it would be a hollow answer, an answer that wasn't really believed in, in practice. All the minute differences have always mattered more—people are segregated according to gender, culture, race, age, ability, whether they are left or right handed, whether they eat with a fork and say please and thank you whenever it's proper. And what of the humanity of the annoying? The infant? The elderly? The sick? The humanity of the enemy? Maybe it isn't in all cases denied outright, but it's granted with reservations, with qualifications, with insincerity. Most pertinent to my thoughts are the differences that separate the Lepers. Our humanity.

It's a disease. The people who have it didn't choose to, are by and large innocent. If the case were put in front of an honest judge and jury, all propriety seems to indicate that those that suffer from leprosy would be acquitted of its guilt—but the conventions of real life will never be as fair as a court, otherwise there would be no need for courts. So I have to take the burden on myself, the redemption of all these marginalized, innocent people of the world. I live for them.

If any proof is required about the extent of the injustices done to us, there is a rich history of abuses against bygone Lepers that can be drawn from. I think I am literally the only person that knows this history, and I always make recourse to it, with every personal and political decision that I make. I spent months secretly immersed in the old records kept at Castle Horeb, records that were written and forgotten.

Daedalus didn't know it, but while he was sifting through old architectural blueprints, Korah had been down the hall all the while, trying to make sense of all the events that had preceded the present, and why the present had to be just the way it was.

Early on, I had thought to share what I had labored so hard to learn— the bounty was plenty, and I imagined to myself what wonderful benefits would arise from the sharing of that wealth, like the general enlightenment of our people. But nobody cared. At all. The Lepers are perfectly content to follow my directives, almost entirely without question. I had always attributed this blind obedience to an impressive and unconditional loyalty. Now I know that they were unquestioning because questions would require thinking, mental labor that they prefer to avoid entirely.

So while history provides so many good reasons for the Lepers to be vindictive—and all those reasons cycle infuriatingly in my head, like an immortal hurricane—whenever I speak publicly, I have to keep them all to myself. Whenever I say, "We should spy on Gibeah because," I witness an immediate loss of rhetorical effect, as soon as I use the subordinating conjunction. So I cut out all explanation. All my pretty modal variations of speech are reduced simply to the imperative. "Go do that. Go do this." And it's slowly eating away at my insides. I want to find at least one more person that shares my appreciation of the historicity of the moment. One person that identifies with the cause. I thought it could be you. I think that's why I'm writing this letter. I'm still hoping that it can be you.

I'll give you an example, of the kind of history I'm talking about. I'm going to tell you a story. And a brief disclaimer, before I begin— first of all, Gibeahnite hypotheses about the motivations and psychological makeup of the Lepers have always interested me, and secondly, this story was originally written from the perspective of the Gibeahnites, which, on account of my first disclaimer, I prefer not to alter. The amount of irrational bias contained in their version is enough to keep me motivated against them for the rest of my life:

A long time ago, and the exact date is not known, only that many generations have since passed, Apollo could boast of having the subservi-

ence of the entire human population of Crete. The bears were at the time unaffiliated, but that didn't bother Apollo in the least. It was a golden age of productivity, of wealth and excess, wherein one only had to throw seeds and crops would spring forth in response, without need of labor. No laws were required because everyone possessed a natural inclination to do right, all children were born healthy and lived to have children of their own, no crop failed, and no field was barren.

Those were the days that Apollo would walk the streets of Gibeah, because the sight pleased him so. Something about the straightness of the roads, the eternally promised growth of the vegetation and the people—the lawfulness of it all—was pleasing to a deity.

But then the fateful day arose when Apollo first set eyes on Daphne. To Apollo, her fairness was equaled by nothing—in his long days of toiling over the world, from dawn until evening, nothing he'd ever seen had awakened anything to equal the overwhelming feeling that he had for her. She was already married, but love knows no propriety.

Apollo began to repent of the laws and customs that made her someone else's—what had appealed so completely to him before, order, was now deathly acerbic in his mouth; it was the painful irony of having inadvertently built his deathbed in good humor, with all the astuteness of a master craftsmen. So he turned on everything he'd believed in, before that moment.

He waited until it was dark. He waited until she was alone. He would have waited forever for the opportune moment, even though every second his desire remained unsatisfied was a pain worse than death. The kind of pain only an immortal can suffer, because it would have driven a lesser being to kill himself long before. And when the time was right, he cornered her.

"Do not be frightened," he said, taking her by the arms. "It is I, the Sun God. The Sun's beauty has captivated countless souls, and you've captivated the soul of the Sun—what that must say about you!" She struggled violently—for a while, she had just stood there, spellbound, but then the gravity of the situation dawned on her and she ran with the might of every moral she had, out of the grip of Apollo and into the woods.

Even in marriage she had remained chaste, you see.

Apollo followed with all the energy he had. He still tried the method of persuasion. "Who can boast of a lineage like mine?" he asked her. "Who could possibly be as worthy? You know my great deeds, they are re-told time and time again at the temple you go to worship, this I know. To worship me! Now why can't you grant me the consummation of this worship, and just stop running?"

Even if she could hear him, nothing would have swayed her for a moment. But she was deaf to him—everything was drowned out by the dangerously intense beating of her heart, as she ran deeper and deeper into the woods. But the stamina of divinity will always outmatch that of a mortal, and though Apollo's heart was thoroughly polluted with lust for Daphne, it outdid hers as she collapsed in a sobbing heap, and he took her.

Months later her husband was furious. She told him that it was the child of a god, and that, more importantly, it wasn't her choice. She pined and pleaded in a way that would have broken the hardest of hearts, but her husband had become desensitized to her charms after long exposure. Beauty was replaced by familiarity, and since she betrayed this familiarity—she 'did' something he could never forgive—she became nothing to him. He made her take him to the place that it happened. She took him deep into the forest. He killed her there.

Only this would conceal his shame.

But the bears found her. And her beauty, still tearstained in death, was strong enough to draw even their sympathy. The murder had been an inhuman, grotesque act. Her husband had cut open her womb to expose the barely half-formed child, had cut it out and cast it aside. The bears found this and, understanding enough of what had happened, chose to sew it into the thigh of the Bear King, where it might continue to be nourished.

Apollo knew that Daphne had been murdered, knew the guilt was his own, but his true source of lamentation was the fact that he could look on her no more. He took a branch from the tree under which her husband had eviscerated her, to remember her by. It was a laurel tree. He planted a grove of it over her empty grave in Gibeah, and forbade that anyone cut it down as she had been cut down, so he could look upon its beauty when he couldn't look upon hers. It was to be the last personal touch that he added to the city.

For when the first leaves emerged above her grave, some seasons later, there was a boy who aimlessly wandered the streets of Gibeah. Apollo might not have ever taken notice, had the boy not happened upon the very same fountain that Apollo was in the habit of sitting by, where he could admire the intricacies of the water as it made its way down the fountain's height. The boy disturbed Apollo's quiet contemplation by climbing into the fountain, and splashing around in a very disruptive manner. Apollo was more perturbed than he could ever recall being, and didn't quite know why. He had to quell a divine impulse to smite the apparently joyful boy, who seemed to splash more from the clumsy way he tripped about the fountain than from playfulness.

Still, Apollo wasn't above ordering a passerby to remove the boy from the fountain, so that he could enjoy it again without the chaos that the boy instilled. The man who was ordered to move the boy, a good god-fearing man, stutteringly obliged to help. He climbed into the fountain and approached the boy, and grabbed him by the arm, but as soon as he was touched there was a change. The boy's face instantly went from a dazed look to piercingly serene—the effect of his eyes alone was so strong that Apollo nearly choked. In the next second, the man in the fountain was covered in protuberances from head to toe. There were many people that had stopped to witness the spectacle, as the traffic by the fountain was usually large. Universally, their mouths were agape, and they did not know what to do or to think, so unexpected was the transformation. But Apollo ordered them into action. He himself was in the throes of trepidation—everything that he held sacred as a god was in jeopardy, to him. He could feel it.

"Seize that boy! I command you all!" It was the last thing anyone wanted to do, but those were a dutiful folk, who obeyed nonetheless. Everyone who came near the boy was infected with leprosy. Anyone who thought to come near the boy was infected with leprosy. There were ordinary, healthy people who, three weeks after these events were all said and done, still thought to themselves, retrospectively, that they should have been there at the fountain to come near the boy—no sooner had the thought occurred to them, then they were instantly leprotic. Whence it is said, whenever one is horribly disfigured by some dutiful intention, that they 'thought

to come near the boy,' since this was thought to be pathologically bound to the disease.

In the following days, the remaining healthy populace, those fortunate enough not to be taking a stroll the day of the fountain ordeal, did not initially know what to do with their leprosy-ridden comrades. It became clearer and clearer that the Lepers were not fully human, though—it wasn't obvious enough when they were smiling, or when they were trying to be any kind of expressive. Also, the way the Lepers were constricted in movement, how they often rearranged their clothing, and how they hobbled about, and took especially long to bend over and pick up the things they occasionally dropped—all ostensibly due to the pain of their infliction—led to largely confusing body language, one of the cardinal sins of a social world. People that had been happily married before, but now had one half of their sacred union inhumanly bloated, couldn't maritally function. And it soon became apparent that the affliction was contagious, since a man that said he hadn't thought to come near the boy even once, nor had he thought about any other duty in quite some time, nevertheless contracted the disease.

His personal explanation was that 'he had to look at the damn things all the time,' and since looking at Lepers was therefore deemed dangerous, it was publicly accepted that the Lepers should be somewhere that normal people didn't have to look at them ever. And so the day came when the Lepers were given only the most vital of amenities, and were collectively ousted from the city. There were no loved ones present, since they didn't care to see the Lepers go. There was just a small delegation that had been commissioned to begrudgingly oversee the matter. Quietly the Lepers went, quietly they obeyed. The same proclivity for obedience that had earned them their affliction, when they listened to Apollo, guaranteed that they would be obedient to authority once again, this time to the demands of an officially commissioned delegation.

From that point on, the history became slightly less interesting to Korah. So he stopped writing the letter, but he didn't stop thinking about the past—how the Lepers had then formed a sort of loose confederation, and about the failures of the Roanoke and Jamestown Colonies, as the Lepers were completely unprepared for the realities of living in the wilderness. At that point in time the Lepers were still bound to molest Gibeah by way of Wandering Invasions, otherwise known in the literature as Tourism. That was back when Gibeah still had no walls—when they exiled the Lepers, it was considered by the Gibeahnites a matter of trust that the Lepers wouldn't come back. Tourism was when a moderate-sized group of Lepers would just wander through Gibeah, without any real purpose other than what could be attributed to the average sightseer, often with a Leper Tour Guide who would point out the fountain that was so monumental to their condition, on the off chance that they actually passed by it. Which, if they did, was only entirely by coincidence, due to their aimlessness.

The Gibeahnites, upon discovering the marauders, would beat the Lepers with sticks until they scattered and left the city in all directions. Many good sticks were sadly and irrevocably soiled in the process.

And finally entered history the man that Korah admired and emulated most, Friedrich of the Lepers. Friedrich was "a despicable and pretentious man, somehow born from the pus, refuse, and spoiled skin of a dissolute Leper Whore in some godforsaken mire of the wilderness of Crete." Korah knew the whole passage by rote memory. "Entirely without a purchase to hold on to, the cretin clung to life. It is universal knowledge that no domesticated animals, no agriculture, and no cooks and ovens are to be found amongst the Lepers, or anywhere in the wilderness for that matter, yet the Leper Miracle provided for the disgusting child, thus allowing this inchoate perfidy to mature into full-blown blasphemy." The Leper Miracle was a technical historical term denoting anything that somehow made it possible for the Lepers to survive without the means of a city, which was deemed impossible by the Gibeahnites, unless it was accounted for by the provision of some miracle.

Friedrich singlehandedly expanded the repertoire of Leper Activities from Tourism, where it started, to include, among other things, Suggestion (otherwise known as Subversion), Reconnaissance, Lowering of Standards, and the Bacchic Rites.

The Gibeahn historian went on, "Suggestion is the Leper's misleading term for outright sabotage. The Lepers will tell otherwise upright citizens of Gibeah to do something sinful, and the Gibeahnites, in their naïve and impressionable purity, will just go along with what they're told. In this way the Lepers continue to debase the society of Gibeah, which can no longer be golden and no longer pleases the eyes of Apollo. Apollo abandoned us because of the Suggestion of the Lepers." Thus Friedrich was accredited with a repulsiveness with the power to move deities.

"Reconnaissance is the Leper's attempt to try and understand civilized society, but as much as they study the mechanics of our higher order, its workings prove too complex for them to learn from. In their blind persistence, though, they continue to try and learn, by way of spies that they send into Gibeah, even into its most sacred of places." Korah's favorite instance of Reconnaissance was when Friedrich ordered Mandolin the Leper to Suggest to a priest that he 'go be a wolf for a while', which the priest blindly acquiesced to do, while Mandolin put on the priest's garb and ministered to the congregation for three whole years, to gather information about the religious principles of the Gibeahnites. The congregation itself never noticed—it was generally acknowledged that his sermons had seemed insightful and even enlightening at the time, but in retrospect his leprotic ways were obvious and sinful. It was the priest's wife that actually noticed, after three years, when, during intercourse, he accidentally yelled 'Clymanthine' instead of 'Clemander,' her name, while climaxing.

"Lowering of Standards is anything that allows the Leper to be satisfied with its life. Naturally, the life of a Leper is devoid of anything that would normally make a life worthwhile, such as beauty, a house, and monumental architecture. Both their women and their reflection must be disheartening sights to the Leper, and in order to cope with this state of affairs, one can deduce that the Lepers must Lower their Standards. The details on how this concept was first introduced into their 'society' are vague, but the effects were visible externally— Lepers that had tended to mope and be discontent before, as they should, were suddenly developing a sort of Leper Pride, a Leper Patriotism, and this was achieved solely through the leadership and 'wisdom' of Friedrich.

"Most appalling of all would be the Bacchic Rites, and it is absolutely fortunate that, unlike Suggestion and Reconnaissance, normal society is not subjected to these, as they involve only the Lepers. The god born of Apollo, Dionysus, is the god worshipped by the Lepers, who were originally his creation to begin with. The extent to which the deity interacts with his following is unknown—perhaps the Lepers only worship a god that created, then despised them. Such would be in keeping with the Luck of the Lepers. Regardless, at indeterminate times (the spontaneity of the holiday is its trademark) the Lepers will perform the greatest of debauches, only equal in depravity to the debauch preceding it. Somehow the Lepers procure enough wine to erase the night from their collective memory without the use of vineyards, or any other plausible resource that one could imagine would create wine. The deeds they then perform, at the Rite, are indescribable and best left at the scant level of detail provided."

What impressed Korah the most about Friedrich was his personal involvement with the Leper Mission. There had been many other leaders since him, but none had done anything similar to Friedrich's 'Graveyard Suggestion', for instance:

It used to be that every grave was provided with a bell attached to a string, in case the buried party was not fully dead, and wanted out. Friedrich had convinced a group of ten people, normal Gibeahn citizens, to let themselves be buried and furnished with bells, after finding out from Reconnaissance that the staff of the graveyard was obligated to promptly respond to any ringing grave. There was to be a funeral for the late King, with the entire upper caste of Gibeah in attendance. Friedrich installed himself in the tomb of the King, through Suggestions to the Royal Embalmer. His instruction to the group of buried people was to start ringing as soon as they heard the ceremonial trumpets, which accompanied the interment of the King's tomb in its privileged position in the graveyard. When all ten of the bells started ringing, then, the entire staff of the graveyard (which even for such a grandiose occasion was still only eight in number, the cause of much procedural confusion when confronted with ten graves that all required 'prompt response') had to all abandon the royal funeral to unearth the other tombs, as per the dictates of their occupation.

The attending crowd was already experiencing heavily stirred superstition at the advent of so many dead-bells ringing, when Friedrich proceeded to jump out of the royal tomb, emitting all sorts of guttural sounds, and bit the Queen through her mourning veil. And since Friedrich had been thoroughly mummified for the occasion, and what skin showed was of course decaying from his leprosy, he made a very convincing reanimated, bloodthirsty King. Then he ran away. He never explained the import of any of it, whether it was satirical or just for fun. That was the art of Friedrich. Only recently had the truth been discovered by the Gibeahnites—for years that king had been referred to as the Zombie King, until Friedrich's biography, written posthumously by a close friend, became available in the city and cleared up the details.

"And how did a thing like Friedrich become the leader of the Lepers?" the historian continued. "Democracy. Of all the insufferable inventions of the Lepers, the most insidious is Democracy. They *voted* Friedrich as their leader, as if leadership were not a divine gift, given only to the blessed few who are intercessors with the deities amongst mortals. The Lepers mock the divinity of royalty when any common, base person among them can be *voted* to leadership—for all intents and purposes, deified. The thought of which is blasphemous!"

Which would make Korah the offspring of a blasphemy. The vote to install Korah as the leader of the Lepers had been unanimous, something that he still couldn't make sense of. Surely he had made a few enemies, he thought. Surely he wasn't the unequivocal answer to everyone's prayers. And yet he was the head and voice of the Leper Colony, a Colony so steeped in Leper Tradition that he had nightmares about having even the slightest ideological divergence with his precursors. A Colony so ignorant of itself, that it didn't know what the term Leper Tradition even meant.

Korah couldn't help but think of the Bacchic Rite two days prior, as he stood overlooking Gibeah in all of its urban glory. The city really was a marvel, a masterpiece of human ingenuity. And like all masterpieces, it was poorly planned, poorly executed, and stank of raw sewage, but shined brilliantly whenever the sun hit it in just the right way. Two days before had been a similar kind of masterpiece, but the light that struck it had been the light of the moon.

"Tonight, we honor Dionysus," the Leper Priest had told Korah. The Rite happened whenever the large supply of wine was found—that time, it had been located in a tree. The sole purpose of the lives of half of the Lepers was to search the wilderness for the next supply, and the search was never in vain, a large supply of wine always disclosed itself to the persistent.

The information quickly circulated throughout the Colony, and the Leper Spies were recalled from Gibeah, so that everyone would be present. And when the sun went down, when Apollo took his last look at the world, they began to drink.

The location was always the same, a small clearing whose ground had been stamped barren by the consistency and fer-

vor of the Rite. In the middle were the vestiges of many bon-
fires past, and another pyre was already constructed on their
ashes, ready to burn. The area was decorated about as much as
one could decorate a forest.

Korah would just watch from the sideline, the edges, the
outside. He would brace himself against a tree whenever his
head felt heavy and he couldn't stand any more. It was hard for
him to watch the Rite, because he was in love with people's in-
hibitions, everything that held them back, made them proper.
The look on his face, then, must have closely resembled the
look of a man watching his loved ones drowned before his
very eyes, because that was practically what happened.

Those people would take the wine in like an answer to a
prayer, would forget their sorrow, would start calling each other by their first names. It had taken Korah years to glimpse
into the souls of many of those people, over many steep and
laborious paths, through all the obfuscation they used to cover
it. People he knew, people whose wellbeing he cared immense-
ly for—yet, as he watched, he recognized all those souls exposing themselves directly, the unscrupulous shrugging of their
heavy social veils. And nothing was more uncomfortable for
Korah than the unmitigated sight of a soul, standing vulnerable and naked outside of its fortifications. The fire raged incessantly, and the people raged incestuously, not caring whether
the object of their drunken affection was friend or acquaintance, immediate family or stranger. Korah liked to believe that
they all knew how disgusting they were, baring their souls—it
was just that none of them minded because everyone else was
doing the same, and deep down it was similar to something
that they really wanted, an intimate bond with their fellow human, everyone meeting halfway, naked outside their fortresses.
Even closer to the truth, since intimacy would imply boundaries—they wanted an unbounded bleeding into their fellow
man, a chaotic symbiosis.

They became a dangerous mixture of far too truthful and

far too apt to oversimplify. They would take all their complicated feelings that were derived from years of knowing each other, really knowing each other, and crush them into the all-too-restrictive words "I love you," just to use the same words again with someone they hardly knew, so that the meaning of the words was practically a vacuum inside of the physical shell of the utterance. They would tend to dance far too closely to one another, would heedlessly make close and personal physical contact with anyone they happened on, they didn't care at all and just moved on from one person to another because their drunkenness realized the drunken truth that everyone is basically interchangeable.

The drums beat heavily, many flutes filled the air, and people danced and touched and groped the whole night through. They made inappropriate contact, asked inappropriate questions, and were all greatly pleased with themselves. All was merriment. The Bacchic Rite was an orgy.

All of those things were more disquieting to Korah than the fact that everyone that partook in the festivities was a Leper, which added an element not found in any other kind of orgy. The hand that caressed the buttocks of some lustee was prone to leaving part of itself there, incriminating evidence for anyone that wanted it, whether in the form of pustules or mortified flesh. It was either that, or the hand took part of the buttocks with it, almost as a keepsake—but it had to be one or the other, there was a weaker element and a stronger, and the stronger always took leprotic traces of the weaker with it. In the mornings after the Bacchic Rites, there would be so much human residue shed on the ground that vultures would actually circle the clearing for a week, as if the remnants were corpses.

During the Rites, Korah would be attempting to think about nothing at all, the only healthy mode of thought he had recourse to at such times. He would try whistling instead, even though he was so out of sorts that the tune always failed him.

But every so often one of the revelers would notice Korah at the outskirts, break away, and ask so many tactless questions. A women whose shirt had recently been rent down the entire left side, her hair entirely in disarray and sweaty—their hair normally being the one feature still capable of beautification for the Lepers—meandered to Korah and said, "How are you? I hear Miriam gets better and better every day."

Korah's response might have been positive, had she simply left the question at 'how are you?' But what followed, a comment about his wife, didn't permit Korah to even feign that he was alright, since the subject of Miriam distraught him so much.

For over a week, Miriam had been getting better. It was something that had never happened in the entire history of the Leper Colony—Korah knew because he had voraciously devoured their entire written history in the attempt to find that very thing, a case like Miriam's, which would have at least been noted as an exceptional curiosity in history's annals. Her leprosy was going away. Day by day she looked more like a person, a Gibeahnite, which was the absurdist oddity Korah had ever seen. He never wanted to see her like that.

Perhaps it wouldn't have been so bad for him, her getting better, if not for the sentiment in her head that accompanied it. She wanted to move to Gibeah, and naturally it would have to be alone, since no Leper was allowed into the city. For a while, Miriam had still identified herself as a Leper, even as she got progressively better, and the thought of life in Gibeah was still inconceivable to her mind. But eventually her sentiment adapted to her health, and she felt entitled to go there. Korah's feelings as her lawful husband were overridden by the 'opportunity' for her to have a normal life. And so on. And Korah was mortally wounded by it.

He gave the woman the most dismissive of answers that he could find, that he was fine and Miriam was fine and that everything was fine, and she then did Korah the favor of leaving to rejoin the festive orgy. But others joyfully came to Korah, while he was knee-deep in sorrowful thoughts of his wife, to try to make idle conversation out of his other most painful concerns.

"The Leper Mission is going great, Korah," one said. A remark that seemed levity enough, but the identity of the speaker made it an extremely awkward comment, for Korah. It was Sybilis, whose son had just died while doing Reconnaissance in Gibeah. That morning. And the father knew it, yet still felt it warranted to compliment the Leper Mission.

Korah couldn't leave it alone, he had to respond just as forcefully, just as tactlessly, from the other direction. "The Leper Mission just cost you your son, Mr. Gauld. How could you say that it is going great?"

"It's for a good cause," was his simple, and apparently candid, response. Korah could smell the overwhelming amount of alcohol on the man's breath, and the profuse sweat from the man's body, mixed with a surprisingly pleasant lilac scent. Korah hated the problem that the man presented. It was a widespread problem—Sybilis was just a single manifestation of a larger trend that Korah couldn't understand. So many Lepers were dying, Korah was at fault, and nobody cared, nobody bore a grudge, everyone was very supportive.

He could try arguing his point with people like Sybilis, but he already knew how that argument would unfold. Korah would say, "It's my fault, all my fault, please blame me," and they would counter with, "You did what you had to do, it may have been a difficult set of decisions you've had to make, but they were all for the greater good, there was no way around it."

Couldn't Korah have done differently?

The answer would have been more clear-cut, if it weren't for the fact that, in spite of its losses, the Leper Mission was still performing very well by most measurements. Many successful Subversions, much intelligence gathered from Reconnaissance, and the economic benefits of Leper Tourism were unassailable. There were just so many *casualties*. Up until three years before, the Leper Mission was a paltry skeleton, subsisting on what it could. Korah had insisted on safety, on forgetting the Mission for a while, because of the lives that were spared by giving up—there had been a *reason* to scale back, a reason that Korah lacked now. The losses from a fully operative Leper Mission had become tremendous—the city of Gibeah had developed brutal weapons to counteract the Lepers, begun in response to the especial annoyance of Friedrich, and that art of weaponsmithing had been developed throughout the generations, until just three years before.

In fact, Korah could see a striking similarity between himself and Friedrich—the Gibeahn reprisal against Friedrich had been devastating, yet Friedrich was still considered a great man, a hero, a savior.

And then, in a single moment, everything changed. Daedalus was at the end of the chain of Gibeahn weaponry development, and when Daedalus was eradicated from the city's physical memory, instead of just disposing with the last link in that weaponry chain, the entire chain was disposed of—Gibeah took a two hundred year technological step backward on a matter of principle, went from some truly ingenious implements of devastation back to the use of sticks for defense. For the Lepers, it was as if a sluice gate had been opened— they could thrive again, flow and wash away everything that wasn't firmly rooted to the ground. They flooded Gibeah. In some places they encountered embankments, sandbags, fortifications against their tide, and those were the cause of many Leper casualties, but in the end the flood prevailed. Although death by sticks was annoying, it was not fatal to the Mission.

The present, then, the present—Korah could feel a great amount of erosion undermining all the things that made him okay. When King Richard declared that Lepers were to be killed on sight, it signaled a renewed effort to exterminate them, by the citizens of Gibeah. And his wife was willfully becoming one of those citizens. During the Bacchic Rites most of all, those were two matters that he wanted to think of least, the condition of his wife and the Leper Mission, yet he'd already been expressly reminded of both by the guileless revelers. He could abolish the whole affair, and end the Bacchic Rites—he knew he could. And the Lepers would deferentially bend to his will. But he couldn't do it. First of all, because of the Leper Tradition that strongly insisted on the Rites, a Tradition that he could never bring himself to modify or discontinue. And secondly, because it made all the Lepers so damn *happy*. He could see it in their eyes, glinting as they danced wildly around the bonfire. Korah was suffering the sight of everyone else's blithe happiness when someone caught Korah's eye.

Korah's inner turmoil became so forceful that he collapsed against a tree—all the problems he'd had before suddenly seemed so limpid, in comparison. There was a little boy dancing around the fire. Which was nothing peculiar in itself—the kids weren't discriminated from the orgy. But the little boy was not a Leper. His skin was of absolute paleness and fairness, his profile slender. Others took notice too—one man broke away from the frenzied conglomeration to take the little boy by the hand, to marvel at him and share the marvel with the others. "Look at this... thing, here! What a treat we have!" Some stopped to take notice of the boy, but no one noticed when the man holding him instantaneously became a boar.

"Yes, he's right, a treat indeed. I want him for myself," said another man. He too became a boar. The dancing suddenly reached a fever pitch. Or maybe it was just the disoriented blur in Korah's eyes, as the weight of disbelief drove him to the ground. The dancers became wilder, flailing, symbiotic, visceral. They all blurred together, for Korah, bled into each other, everything was blurring together and they were one, the fire was one, the trees, nature, everything entered his vision the same, together—its only defined piece a small, smirking child that had vines twined into his long hair, deliberately making his way to Korah one step at a time. People that stumbled upon the boy in their raucous excess may have been transformed similarly, but Korah couldn't tell anymore, everything was blurred together and the change was indiscernible, because the whole was still the whole and this was the one and its parts were somehow the same, had to be the same, even if they changed, because the whole never changed and it was confusing and he was drawing closer and closer to Korah and Korah couldn't retreat, couldn't leave the support of his tree, he could feel the bark pressed with a demented gravity into his left temple and it was his only comfort, even as it hurt like hell. Like hell. Korah could see hell, there was a fire and a little boy.

"Hello, Korah," Dionysus said. "It is good to finally meet you. You are the leader of my people, and I never met you." Korah had to struggle with the very essence of his being to make out any of the words that Dionysus was saying, and they were still confusing to him.

"I, I… Dionysus."

"Yes, we are Dionysus. You are very right. Why don't you join them? They are having fun. I gave them wine to have fun, and you aren't having fun with them."

Korah could hear his heart palpitating itself to death in the tree, his left ear was full of his dying heart's sound and his right was full of dementia, of Dionysus. "I have fun. I have my own fun. I'm having fun."

"You're not like them."

Korah heard the heart in the tree stop entirely, and he was immediately full of concern for the tree. "I'm trying," he said.

"You have to do more than that, Korah. You have to make them proud. You have to drink." And with those words, Korah's mouth was suddenly full of a dark liquid, and he didn't even have the sense to choke. It was all like sap, sapping in.

Korah couldn't decide whether the memory of that day, or the one after it, haunted him more. He awoke in the middle of the clearing, along with everyone else. Or most of everyone else, it should be said, since not everyone woke up again after the Bacchic Rites, and that was considered part of the fun. Korah had a throbbing headache and only vague memories of the night before. Visions of the kid slowly seeped into his head throughout the day, and he was never quite sure about their veracity.

A strongly reawakened sense of duty seemed to be the consequence of every debauch, as if the sentiment had been lying in wait as people partied, just to make its move in the morning when they were weak and incapacitated. Korah had a strong urge to visit his wife where she was being kept.

It was a considerable walk from the clearing to the Infirmary, because the Lepers kept absolutely nothing close together, for no better reason than that it had always been that way. For the sake of efficiency Korah had tried to introduce Close Living and Close Community, but there had been an outbreak of deaths by asphyxiation, and everyone had blamed the closeness of everything, so Korah was forced to recant all the changes and let everything be apart again.

The Infirmary was rarely used. The Lepers were a hardy folk, used to discomfort, and were more prone to dying of wounds and diseases than to getting them checked. But Miriam, Korah's wife, was a different story. She had a severe *comfort*, she was becoming more foreign by the minute and the Infirmary seemed the most appropriate place for her.

Korah let himself in through the front door, just a bunch of sticks bound together, the portal to a large tent. The Infirmary was one of the only buildings the Lepers tried to have, as no one lived in houses.

There was a small vestibule, a room to the left and one to the right, divided by a wall made of furs. Medical supplies, sundries, and a small kitchen were to the right, and all the patients were kept to the left. No one was manning the chair that faced the entrance, the usual spot of the patroness of the Infirmary.

As Korah continued into the tent, he realized it was because she was attending to Miriam.

"Miriam."

"Korah!"

He couldn't believe the tenderness in her voice. After all she put him through, after all the agony she had in store for him, she continued to be oppressively affectionate to Korah. Korah attempted a wistful smile in response to his name. "How are you?" he asked.

He was finally in a position to get a good look at her. Her features were surprisingly marred, and Korah didn't understand why that was until he glimpsed the contents of the patroness' hands. A bit of mud, mixed with small twigs and other detritus. Korah didn't know whether it was supposed to be a poultice or an aesthetic substitute to the leprosy that was fading from Miriam's figure.

"I… I'm fine. Actually, there's something we need to talk about." She didn't wait for Korah to protest against the necessity of what she wanted to say. "I'm finally ready to go. I don't care what they tell me here. They smear my face with soil and then bring me a mirror, and try to convince me that I'm still a Leper. I'm not fooled." She gave Selvia, the patroness, a very cross look. "I know that I am better."

She was right. Korah could see, through the façade of the makeup, a face that was startlingly beautiful. It disgusted him—he could feel something deep within himself wretch, something much deeper than his stomach. "Do you really have to do this, Miriam?"

"Korah," she said sweetly. "I love you," and his heart wept uncontrollably, "but I'm not passing up this opportunity. I have a chance to be normal, a chance to be among the fortunate, and it would be selfish of you to stop me. You have to let me go. I would do the same for you."

She would do the same thing for him. That's the last thing he ever wanted to hear. After so many years of being the rhetorician, he seemed to be failing at making convincing conversation of late. He didn't know in the least how to respond. "Miriam... really?" He literally racked his brain for every word he knew, tortured it until he had them all, to see if any of them were capable of changing her mind. But it was futile, and furthermore, as he spent time laboring over words, she slipped further and further all the while. "Is it really so bad here? I can give you almost anything."

"You can't give me a city, Korah. A city, and all its people, and all its possibilities. Don't pretend that you can do any of that. I promise... I promise you that everything will work out. That you'll be happier. Now won't you tell them to let me go? They won't let me go unless you tell them to. I could make it out on my own anyway, but I'd rather go peacefully."

Korah spent the last few moments of his sanity contemplating deeply. "Let her go, Selvia. I'll take her."

He couldn't remember the conversation they had on the way to Gibeah's gate. He was terribly distracted, and the sun was so beautiful, so mercilessly beautiful, and spring was coming again and the forest held so many rewards for the attentive eye and Korah couldn't really look at them, but he did anyway, and she was talking about all the lovely things she would do and the lovely people she would meet. There were birds and they made bird's nests and for the most part it seemed that the nests worked in every way the birds wanted them to.

Korah thought about kissing her one last time, to have something to remember her by. But he knew that his lips were the weaker element now, hers were far too composed, and his lips would go with her, the keepsake would be hers instead of his, and not the other way around like he needed, and she wouldn't want the reminder. So he refrained.

It only took a couple words from Korah to the Gibeahn sentry, to get Miriam through and to the other side. Korah could finally control his gaze long enough to memorize every minute detail as she walked away—he could have painted a picture, without missing a detail. He did just that, every night in his head.

Korah was letting the vividness of that picture dissolve as he stood at his own sentry post, a Leper's post, overlooking Gibeah. The picture contained a truth he couldn't believe. She was on the inside, and he was on the outside. To combat the picture he had a letter in his hand, written for her. It wasn't finished—looking it over, he knew that it needed an ending. The middle seemed questionable to him as well—he had spent a large majority of the paper ranting, and the rest retelling the rape of Daphne, which seemed slightly inappropriate. But there was a reason. He added:

When you go to the city because you're feeling normal, you're living by their rules. You're tacitly agreeing to their values, the values of a society that abandoned people in need to the wilderness. We're better than that.

I couldn't tell you not to go. You are your own person. But that doesn't mean that I can handle your absence. I've been separated at my core—humanity, and you.

If you ever decide to come back, half of me will be here waiting.

Your faithful Korah

He folded the letter up, and put it in his pocket. He looked at Gibeah again. He could see her in every house that presented itself to his vision, her on the inside, starting anew. Smiling. And he was on the outside.

KAPITEL SIEBEN: BEAR APER

NOT FOR THE first time lately, Daedalus had no idea how to feel. He went on feeling anyway though, in spite of his indecision—he couldn't just stop. For instance, there was a knot in his stomach and an extreme nausea in his head, which may have been caused by his conflicting emotions, just as easily as it could have been the meager prison food that was by then a large constituent of his mass. He had never been disavowed by a god before. He'd seen many people disavow gods, watched it as it happened, even—those people acted like it was the advent of some never discovered clarity, after the release of some long-suffered burden. But he'd never seen the inverse, a god disavow a man. Maybe the process was the exact inverse, he thought, and some large burden had been placed on Daedalus' shoulders. That made marginal sense to him. Still, he didn't know how to feel about any of it.

Daedalus attempted to resort to stoicism, an old friend of his. 'Whatever will be will be.' He had always thought of stoicism as a renunciation of feelings, as if living in accord with nature meant being just like nature, impassive and indifferent. But stoicism was a lot easier to live by when nothing happened to him. As soon as things started happening, things that simply refused to be ignored, Daedalus realized how untenable stoicism was. Some basic and inalienable aspect in the depths of his soul refused to pass off so many recent events simply as 'the course of things,' simply as fate. Such a passive mindset was bound to be stepped on, bound to be abused. Something in the human soul refused to tolerate abuse for any long period of time, he reasoned. Abuse was either redefined or ended.

Which was why Daedalus asked himself, as the bears bore him away from the prison that, as it turned out, he had made for himself, "Am I simply to sit here, while gods condemn me to rot, while bears carry me god knows where, to do god knows what—god knows, but since he abandoned me, he would never have cause nor decency to tell. Should I just sit here while little by little the influence I have over my governance is being taken away from me, all my contributions to the world are being deliberately erased, until all I have left is my own house, until I am confined to my own house, which, granted, could have been a sanctuary to me, if not for its contents, which now seem haphazardly and idiotically gathered?"

In other words, introspection and idleness alone soon seemed an exhausted course of action to Daedalus. His activity in the Bear Maze had already been a provisional reaction, but he finally felt ready to fully embrace his new course. Or at least half of him felt this way. The other half was confused and sentimental, and didn't know where it was going. So he asked, "Where are you bears taking me?"

Naturally, the bears didn't really respond. But Daedalus knew from experience that it was rare that a new method would have immediate and appreciable results—it was much more often the case that the first action taken after saying "I will now hold everyone accountable to my new paradigm, and make no exception," was to first ask questions of ineffable things, of bears. He asked anyway.

They did make a lot of grunting sounds, and the feel of

their rough fur was grating against Daedalus' back. Those were the things he had to work with. Also, the night sky was flowing uninterrupted over Daedalus' head. He was turned upright and couldn't rotate his neck enough to see down, only to the right and left, and even that small amount of mobility was impeded by unkempt tufts of fur everywhere. But they were outside, in the open, and there was a freshness in the air that Daedalus knew didn't belong to a city.

His thoughts went through the natural progression of a person strapped to the back of a bear. First and foremost thoughts of safety. Then the reevaluation of everything once held sacred, which he had just went through. Following those were thoughts of his family. Had he broken his promise? He probably had—it felt broken, from the vantage of a bear back. He'd promised that he wouldn't be negligent. Promised that what he did would be for the better, would fix so many problems. Obviously, though, he had failed in that endeavor. If his intention had been to discomfit the bears, his current circumstances were all the evidence needed to prove that failure. Bears continued to disrespect the honest effort that the human walls made to keep them out. Even the most heavily guarded of places in the city, the prison of Castle Horeb, was apparently easily accessible to the bears. Which meant that everything was accessible, that nothing was safe, that Daedalus' efforts had been in vain. He was reproaching himself harshly for that vanity.

"I want answers! Where am I being taken?" More grunting. The sound of feet splashing through a stream, then thudding on firm ground. Foliage brushing up against fast movement. These landscapes were filtered through to Daedalus by way of jarring motion and the occasional slap in the face by a branch, and other similar indications.

Finally everything came to a halt, all the frantic noises stopped, and slowly Daedalus' ears adapted to hear the relatively quiet ambient noise of a river somewhere in the near distance, and gentle shuffling. Then Daedalus was deposited, and allowed to stand for the first time in the three hours it had taken to arrive to that point. Daedalus felt unsteady at first—he hadn't done much walking in his cell—but he eventually regained with confidence that beautiful thing that made him human, the ability to be upright.

The bears had the same capability, but had a preference for being on all fours. Bears in all manner of posture were the first things Daedalus saw as he took in his surroundings. Their presence and their quantity were no surprise to Daedalus, as he had been mentally preparing for what had to be the case, namely that if he was captured by bears, he'd be dealing with bears. Most likely until his demise, whenever and however they chose to go about it. What was a surprise to him, since it was in no way associated with the conception he had of bears and the bear mode of life, was the number of dwellings that circumscribed his vision. The Lepers didn't even have houses—why should the bears? His question was soon answered.

A woman, a human woman, came to Daedalus as soon as he was put down. "Daedalus! It is so good to see you!"

If he was being perfectly honest with himself, he had never expected to hear his name again while he was alive, unless he himself chose to say it, just to foil that sad reality. What he expected even less was to ever see again the person who said it. "Sofia... what could you possibly be doing here?"

She dismissed the bears who had transported Daedalus, and had remained standing around him as if at attention. With her gesture they all hastily departed. "I'll explain everything, in due time, but it won't be out here. It may be warming up, but there's still a chill in the air, can you feel it? I know spring is on the way, but I'm not the type to pretend the weather's fair just because my heart wants it so. You see so many fools freezing to death for that very reason. No, we'll go inside. I have accommodations for you, and we can speak in warmth."

Daedalus didn't know what to say in response, so he just

followed as she led him toward a rather large, wooden construction. Out of professional interest, he carefully inspected the building as they approached. The first thing he noticed was that it was precariously balanced in a way that gave him cause for concern—although it was night, there was enough moonlight to clearly illuminate a fairly rugged terrain, with no truly flat ground to be seen. They were in the geographical penumbra to the several mountains of Crete, and the ground was disrupted by boulders and thick heath and carelessly sloping hills. His 'accommodations', and other buildings that he could see adjoining it, had been built in spite of, and not in accord with, the terrain. A moderate amount of leveling would have been the prescription of any carpenter, but the houses must have been relying solely on self-medication. Their geometrical lines clashed horribly with the unadulterated organic nature of the ground. It gave the impression that the houses had just landed there, instead of being built. Daedalus didn't trust the stability of his personal accommodation in the least, but entered it anyway, since it felt circumspect to do so, as Sofia led him in.

The inside proved to be far more comforting than the out. Whoever had designed the living apparatus had an aptitude that leaned far more toward interior decoration—the walls were a pleasant lavender color, the chairs were a plump leather, and the décor all adhered to a strict and sightly motif. He almost instantly felt at home. But when he moved too far to one corner of the inside, to get out of the way of the door shutting, the whole contraption visibly tilted under his weight, and he was disabused of the home illusion just as easily as he'd been beguiled by it.

"Please, have a seat," she said. Daedalus warily conceded. "You must have a few questions, yes?"

"Yes, I—"

Sofia blithely interrupted Daedalus, who must not have been keeping the desired pace of conversation well enough. "Like why I'm here? No, I suppose you know the answer to that, but everything following that must be a mystery to you. Ah, but we should start with some necessary preliminary things. If you really want to understand, I'll have to explain much about the bears that you Gibeahnites don't know."

The headlong pace that she dove into the conversation captivated Daedalus. His captivation was a godsend, because she spoke so fast that anything less than rapt attention would have only heard a blur of sound. She said, "For instance, I bet you weren't aware of this distinction. Common practice in Gibeah has it that there are two types of bears, the Samsonbear and the common variety. The only reason they can tell the difference is the obvious physical distinction between the long hair of the Samsonbear and the short hair of the rest. And of course, the 'perspicacity' of the Gibeahnites ends there, 'job well done, let's go home, boys.' All of the subtleties escape them entirely. Not you, I know that you have an eye for things, Daedalus, it's just that you never had a close association with bears, otherwise you would have set the Gibeahnites straight, shown them their errors, I know you would have. But they have people, whose *sole* job it is to study bears, in Gibeah. How could they go so awry, be so unperceptive? No, there are many varieties of bears, many tribes, and they all have their differences. There's a complex system at work that you know nothing about."

"Continue."

"Here's how it applies. Did you know that there are two different breeds of bears that invade Gibeah? In keeping with their blindness, the Gibeahnites thank Apollo that only the 'common' bear raids their city, and the Samsonbear minds its own business. This would be a gross, gross misstatement, oversimplifying the matter entirely. It's always been two types of bears, and these correspond to two different types of raid, or hadn't you noticed? One steals the food of Gibeah, the other steals the women."

The revelation was in fact surprising to Daedalus. She continued, "Obviously, I was taken by the tribe that deals in women, who we refer to as the Niederbear. A name we made up, truth be told, since there isn't really a Gibeahn word for it."

"Who do you mean by 'we'?"

"Did you not see any of them on your way in? The other women. I'm not the only one, not by far. But don't let me get distracted—I was saying, yes, there is the Niederbear, who takes your women, and then the Höherbear, taking all your food. These are just two of the many. There's other breeds, like the Intelektuellbear, but I doubt any Gibeahnite has ever come across any of those, as they keep mostly to themselves, up on the north coast. I'll keep the story simple, and focus only on the two that would interest you. Niederbear and Höherbear.

"So anyway, there is a huge feud between these two types in particular, which originated from territorial disputes, but eventually fleshed out into much more. Something you have to keep in mind, as I continue, is that bears have very addictive behavior. If they live in an area for a while, they develop an inextricable fondness for it. If they find food somewhere—in a city like Gibeah—they become dependent on it. Until they would rather die than forfeit the habitual. This should explain the initial bloodiness of the territory wars—both laid claim to a region not too far east from here, which has since been expropriated by the Höherbear from the Niederbear. The Niederbear is admittedly weaker than the Höherbear, they have a genetically perpetuated slighter stature, and they have a considerably less dire snout, among other things. These are realities that beings don't like to discuss around here, but are true nonetheless. So we lost the territory wars. But not without a fight, not without the largest amount of bear casualties in the history of bearkind. My König Scherzeherz especially, the leader of the Niederbear, had a very dashing role in the war. But I won't bore you with any of those details, since they aren't directly pertinent. "

She gesticulated wildly as she spoke, which Daedalus was

privately amused about, even as he was interested in the content of her dialogue. But he had a question, so he intervened, "I'm confused by your use of 'we' again. You said, 'we lost the territory wars.' You women lost it? I don't follow."

"Oh, no, all apologies. Over the years I've started identifying myself with the Niederbears. If I ever say 'we' like that, I'm referring to them. Us. Anyway, both of our populations were severely depleted, the Niederbear and the Höherbear both. The Höherbear, though, being victorious, took the victor's liberty of having all the females of the Niederbear. Every single one of them.

"There is some justice to the world, though. The Höherbear had the largest population explosion it had ever experienced, the female Niederbear being much more fertile than they were used to. They couldn't feed them all. They outstripped their food source, they wandered farther and farther from the territory they had expended so much energy to conquer, until they happened upon Gibeah. Yes, the Höherbear was the first to raid Gibeah, and once they started, they became entirely dependent in a matter of months, no longer really knowing how to use the wilderness to meet their nutritional requirements."

A look of dismay suddenly entered her face, and she hurriedly and abashedly added, "I feel like I'm leaving so much out. There's so many other factors, other details, I'm making so much of a mockery out of some really interesting events and things. Will you please excuse the imperfection of my account?"

She looked so pathetic and imploring when she asked, that Daedalus couldn't help but be sympathetic. "Sofia, I don't even want you to think like that. You're doing a great job. Please, keep going."

"It's just that there's no one here to talk to, so I'm all out of practice. The bears are a laconic bunch, and the women are talkative enough, but they get bored so easily of all the things I'd prefer to talk about. But where was I... oh yes, the new set of priorities for the Höherbear came with a new focus, and the Niederbear fell to the periphery of their concerns. This allowed the few surviving Niederbears to avoid the complete extinction of their kind—we embraced our unimportance, and it saved us. A few years later, when we were assured of our stability, we began to address the many exigencies we had, namely where to live and what to do about our own severe population problem, the exact opposite of the Höherbear's problem.

"The plan originally was to steal our own women back, but this was futile. The Höherbear esteemed their prize highly, and guarded them proportionately to their esteem. We were prudent—the lives we had were few and dear, and we didn't want to jeopardize them in futile efforts. So we got creative—we took Gibeahn women. The thought was that just any women would do. A woman's a woman's a woman. It must have been a surprise to us that this was not the case—the procuring of women from Gibeah was easy enough, Gibeah is a joke, but the plan was essentially flawed. No progeny came from this newly devised union. Women died in the process, couldn't *handle* the process, as it turned out. I'm sorry, I would be more thorough, but the details make me blush and I don't think it befitting of a lady to debase herself with such description."

"I forgive you. And I get the point."

"Good, good. Okay! And another important bit. While we couldn't get the female bears back from the Höherbear, their food was easy enough to take, isn't that funny? The Höherbear goes through all the trouble of getting it from Gibeah, just for us to take it right back off their hands. They value the protection of the women more than the food. It might be a platitude, and lame of me to say it, but only one thing can be closest to the heart. And everything further removed is easily removed."

She paused there with a firm finality, as if it were self-evident that her account was completely sufficient and in no need of addition. So she was genuinely surprised when Daedalus denied its totality by asking a few questions, as was his wont.

His methodology was to go in order of ascending importance, starting with the least. "How did you learn all of this?"

"Oh, we can talk to the bears."

"Talk to the…"

"You're right, that's a slight misstatement. We can understand what they say, and they can understand what we say. So be careful what you say around the bears, since they do understand you, and you wouldn't want to upset them."

"That's impressive."

"Not really, no. After you've lived long enough around something, you learn its ways. Not impressive, just natural. The course of things."

"And these names you use for the bears, you said you made them up yourself? What do they mean? Or how did you come up with them?"

"What the names are, actually, is the closest transliteration we could come up with for what the bears call themselves. They have a very guttural language, and it's hard to capture it exactly."

"Fair enough. And, I think the question that is most on my mind, why am I here? I am not a woman, and I hope they don't mean to try and procreate with me. You've explained the difference of our genders, haven't you?"

"Haha. No, they don't want to procreate with you, they want to procreate *through* you."

"Wh-what?"

"I'm sorry, that must sound just horrible. Let me explain. It really is silly of me that I didn't tell you why you're here, it slipped my mind entirely. It's just that we all know exactly what's going on, here in our lives, and it's hard to remember what the outsider wouldn't know. I told them that you're an inventor—the best there ever was." Daedalus took time from being dismayed to honestly blush, and he made to deny the assertion, but she insisted, "The bears are clever, they really are. They can do impressive things, things that the Gibeahnites wouldn't even dream of, this is true. But *you*, you're something else. I told them that you could solve our problem."

"Which problem is this, exactly?"

"That we can't procreate…"

Daedalus was aghast for a good minute or so, and she patiently waited until he had recovered. He said, "The possibility of it aside, you couldn't actually *want* it, could you? Are you just going along with their desires because you're captive? Because in that case, we should really be talking about what I could do to get you all out, instead of just complying with them."

"No, no, this is the way we want it to be. We love the bears. This is for all of us."

Sheer incredulity from Daedalus, followed by: "What about Richard? What about your husband? This surely goes in the face of many things, what is proper and scrupulous being the least of them. Your feelings for Richard? He misses you dearly, he still pines after you every day. You wouldn't believe—"

Daedalus was caught completely unaware by the wrath he inspired from Sofia: "Richard! Richard! He doesn't pine after me, he pines after his deficient conception of me. I don't think you realize, Daedalus, just how much history we don't share, me and him. We are two different people—I don't care what kind of lies they espouse at the altar, about being of one flesh, and all of that. Two differing people, with differing desires. I have a rich inner life of my own, or didn't you know? Things I want out of life, things I want to do, interests that conflict with his. Richard denies me all of these. He would make as if I lived to serve him half of the time, making me stand in certain places in certain ways because the sight pleased him so. The other half of the time he would pretend he realized that I was a human too, with all of the concomitant human complexity, and he would let me 'do my own thing.' But in his heart of hearts he was still selfish and delusional, he wanted 'my own thing' to still be serving him, under him, he would set me free but wholly expect that I turn around and willfully bend over again for him. Ah, but here I am, and I'm fully upright, Daedalus. Are you just as surprised as he would be? I bet he sits in his Castle all day and daydreams about how helpless I am, imagines that I am shamed and beaten, or worse. But look how proud I am! Would anyone imagine?

"And I love Scherzeherz. You just have to meet him. He's getting along in years—all of the Niederbear are, that's why it's so important to resolve our crisis now, before they get any more arthritic than they already are—but he's so *wise*, and understanding. I've never felt my humanity to be so completely respected, and by a bear, of all things! No, I don't wish to escape, this is my home, not a prison, no matter how it might look from the outside. And I will stay and help their cause, I will make all the babies they will ever need, whether or not you deign to help. But you will help, Daedalus, won't you? Tell me you will!"

She verily glided between her vehement rage and endearing pleading, seamlessly. It scared Daedalus. "I'll... do what I can?"

"Great! Better than great. We'll start on the morrow. Tonight there is to be a feast, in celebration of your arrival, and it would only be appropriate if you partook, being the guest of honor. Then we'll get to business tomorrow—tomorrow! I can hardly believe it, that it's finally happening! Take some time to yourself, the feast will begin in just an hour or so. Goodbye!" and she departed.

Daedalus soon found that time to himself was going to wreak havoc through the medium of his emotions, perhaps from then on. It was all well and good to find out that the bears didn't mean to maul him, or reproduce with him—only *through* him—but the positive relief of those thoughts was quickly overwhelmed once again by despairing over his family, a despair that never vacated the back of his mind, as he discovered. He envisioned his wife, lost, helpless, and with David. He envisioned his children having a homework question that would go unanswered. He envisioned many such tormenting things, and was glad when the hour of waiting finally expired, and he could carefully and creakily make his way out of the house.

Upon exiting, Daedalus found the scene that greeted him very comical. A very long, wooden table was set up in a clearing not too far removed from Daedalus' house. The table embraced the inconsistencies of the terrain much more suitably than the houses did, with shorter legs where the ground was raised, or no legs at all wherever the table could be braced on a boulder or a tree stump instead. He thought the efficiency of the whole affair quite laudable. One side was bordered with chairs all along its length, and the other had none—Daedalus presumed that the bears found the use of chairs cumbersome, and that the chaired side was for the women. If the table was representative of their respective populations, the bears had also done a very commendable job of stealing a number of women equal to their own.

But none of those things were what was comical to Daedalus—what was comical was that the food was being set, and the bears apparently had a hard time observing the human convention of waiting until preparations were complete before starting. They saw food, they wanted to eat, simple as that. Several women had to abandon their role in setting up, in order to concentrate on staving off the bears, as the bear's effort became more and more concerted.

A few of the women took notice of Daedalus, and guided him to one of two seats at the head of the table. He could tell just by the elaborateness of the other chair, really a work of art, that it was meant for Sofia.

Preparations were finished, a gong was rung, and everyone gathered en masse to the table. Sofia was soon at his side, and was quick to indicate that the magnificent bear at the other end of the table, some ninety cubits away, was the fabled König Scherzeherz. Daedalus surmised by the length of the table, and the average eating space requirement of a bear, that there must have been roughly fifty of the creatures left, no more.

Sofia made an announcement, although she had to fight sonically with a few bears—it seemed that a constant roar was the best that could be expected with the Niederbears, because she did not chide them, just said loudly, "We have the great honor of having Daedalus, the inventor, among our number. This is the beginning of the end, my brethren, and tonight we celebrate." Her words were greeted with much celebratory commotion, which, to Daedalus' untrained ears, sounded remarkably similar to a massacre in full swing, and he almost lost his appetite. Until he saw something that changed his life.

Halfway down the table, buried in a heap of wonderfully prepared entrées mixed with raw meat, was a cured ham in all of its salty glory. It caught Daedalus' eye like a fishhook, and wouldn't let go. It was *his* cured ham, the one that had been stolen in parallel with David's two children, who Daedalus now expected to be lying nearby in a dish of gravy, or something similar. First he was dumbfounded by the ham, then he was asking Sofia if it could be transferred from the center to him, before any of the bears got a hold of it. They graciously obliged, and it was set in front of him, the obese splendor of a full pig. And Daedalus ate the whole thing—he stopped heeding the world, the Queen to his right, the bears all around, until the last ounce of it was gone.

Tears were welling up in his eyes. Dreams came true. Things that were once thought lost forever came back. Every injustice the world could devise was rectifiable, and he ate the proof, he reveled in every savor of it, even as some basic components of his being, his stomach and his nerves, sent ignorant signals about how full he was and how much he needed to vomit. His higher faculties ignored all of them as irrelevant, and savored it all. Nothing in his life helped his faith more than that pig, that feast.

When he was finally in a condition to observe his whereabouts again, he found that the bears had practically demolished the table in his mental absence. Food was scattered in a nearly quarter mile radius, as much from the clumsy and raucous nature of the bears as from the fact that some bears were more reclusive, preferring to drag their food off to a lonely distance, and not all of the food made the transfer. Food debris was arrayed all about the table as well, and the bears that had eaten it were torpid and messy.

Which reminded Daedalus of something, so he turned to Sofia, who was still at his side, and then had an extended private conversation with her about all of the things that Daedalus was still curious about. "It just occurred to me that the bears didn't hibernate this season. Why is that?"

"Well observed. Mostly. Hibernation is a misnomer with bears, something I really wouldn't expect you to know. But you're kind of right anyway, a lot of the tribes forwent 'hibernation' this year. There's just too much going on, too many important things. Three months is a long time to sleep with so many things on the table. It actually really concerns me, their forgoing to sleep—it's like an insomnia, only magnified a hundred times. A lot of weird things are coming of it."

"Like what?"

"That's a long story. Maybe some other time I'll tell you about it. I still don't feel like I fully understand it myself."

"Okay. I was also wondering, so long as I have your attention—I know that we, the Gibeahnites, that is, occasionally capture bears during Bear Raids. But I didn't know until now that there were two different tribes at play, so I'm not sure how many we've captured have been Höherbears, and how many Niederbears. You said something about being prudent, and not risking the few precious lives you had left... has all of this worked?"

"Sadly," and she lowered her gaze, "some of ours have been captured, but we feel that the odds of our survival were much more in our favor this way. We took losses, but every option we had entailed loss, so we just had to grin and bear it."

What interested Daedalus most had been approached indirectly by his last question. Her answer to that question, the sorrow in her voice, implied an answer to his next question that puzzled him deeply, so he pursued: "So... they don't get out of the Bear Maze? I know we put them there, but I was under the impression that it was only a temporary setback for them."

"No. None that were captured have returned."

Daedalus took a while to think of everything that meant, about his original assumption of the ease by which the Bear Maze could be navigated, and the modifications that assumption had caused him to make. He thought about what it had cost him. He had been sure, *absolutely sure* that there was no reason the Bear Maze would be unsolvable. Perhaps the initial fall was still an active factor. He just didn't know anymore. That his efforts had been pointless didn't depress his spirits too much, though, as he was still elated from the pig.

Sofia caught his eye again. She was looking affectionately out at the bears, as they lazily rampaged about after the consumption of their meal. Daedalus didn't know what affection might look like, when coming from a bear, but nothing about the way they stampeded around all self-contentedly looked like they were grateful, or like they returned the affection of the women in any way.

So Daedalus broached the matter. "I know this might be a sensitive subject, or inappropriate of me to ask, but... do the bears really feel the same way about you as you seem to feel for them? I admit that my knowledge is lackluster on the subject—perhaps there is something that I am missing?"

She hesitated for a second in answering, then her lips looked as if they might form words, but she didn't make a sound, perhaps changing her mind. Then she said, "I can't believe I'm telling you this. It feels like a rather personal subject. But, for whatever reason, I feel comfortable around you. They actually—the bears—went back on the original plan, and it wasn't too long ago, not in my memory at least. They tried to get their own breed of females back again, even after they already had all of us, grouped here like we are. I couldn't tell you why they did it—maybe they were frustrated about the lack of our fruition? Sentimental? Desperate? Regardless, it was a rough spot for us. Thing was, we women already had the solution worked out, we were fortunate."

She had almost been close to tears, Daedalus could hear it in her voice, but then she smiled as she renewed her dialogue. "They were addicted to our cooking. While they were out, trying to reclaim what was lost for them, they got hungry, and remembered that we had food in the oven, back home." As she spoke, she had been looking distractedly out into the wilderness, but then she turned to meet Daedalus' eyes directly, and Daedalus thought there was something intensely wild in her look. "And now here we are again. And we can pretend like nothing happened. So, to answer your question. Maybe you can't see it—maybe even I can't see it—but there's something in their heads that brought them back to us. Yes."

He didn't respond, but rather looked at the bears anew from the perspective of everything that Sofia had said, and noticed something that he hadn't before. It was shameless the way the bears defecated, in the presence of everyone, out in the open. But it soon became apparent to Daedalus that they confined their defecation to one area in particular, and he recognized that prudence as being influenced by the women, who must have commanded what decency they could out of the bears. And the bears complied, they walked from relatively afar to defecate in that area alone. Maybe that was love.

The next time they spoke it was Sofia who initiated conversation, while Daedalus was lost in his bear reflections. "The more and more I think about what I'm asking you to do," she said, "the worse I feel about it. I know that we rescued you from prison, and prison couldn't possibly have been pleasant for you. But... I realized that helping us to procreate would have strong connotations for you with children, with... with Icarus, and I'm sorry how insensitive it was for me to ask something of you that was bound to awaken such bad memories."

Daedalus was just silent in response, which left her to awkwardly fumble further on the course she had chosen. "I really don't think you should be so hard on yourself, it wasn't really your fault... I mean, I can empathize, and I don't think you should be beating yourself up as much as you have."

He only returned an insipid stare—internally Daedalus was apologetic that a stare was all he could summon to his face, because he knew that she was trying, only trying to be considerate and caring and if she said the wrong things in the process he understood all too well.

"Anyway," she continued, "I would say that you should just forget all about helping us, but regrettably I can't be so selfless. We really need your help. Tomorrow, though. We'll talk about all of that tomorrow."

Never had Daedalus had such a strange admixture of dreams as that night—fantasies about pigs and nightmares about copulating bears, sometimes at the same time. He woke up in a cold sweat and was all too glad to sidle out of his house and into the fresh air.

There were many things that Daedalus thought, but didn't say. Sundry tools and materials were thrown at him unceremoniously, or was the previous night supposed to be enough to achieve ceremony, meant to win him over? He wondered how much of what he was going to do would be done willingly, and how much would be compulsion, if he was really a slave and if he tried walking away from all of it then they would chase him down and drag him back. The thought struck him as funny, that someone could be a slave their whole life and never know better, until they tried to do differently, tried to do something that didn't appease their captors, and suddenly found bars where they thought the boundless abounded.

A large part of him was willing. He honestly wanted to help Sofia, he had known her for so long and had never denied her anything in all that time. He also empathized strongly with anyone that had a cause they fought for, he empathized with people in their travails. So he gathered the tools that were thrown him, and visualized what exactly he needed to accomplish.

First he spoke to other women, who weren't as squeamish and ladylike as the Queen. They described to him all of the particulars of the failed copulation, which turned out to be twofold—the women's frames were too small and frail to resist breaking, which just wouldn't do, and also that the bears lost interest too quickly to finish their part of the mating, because the women weren't redolent enough of the females they were used to, which was a sore topic only begrudgingly addressed by the women, who valued the success of Daedalus' work more than they feared any soreness.

Daedalus' solution was simple. He had no idea if it was the solution expected by the women, but for the most part he didn't care, since he preferred to do things his way. "I need mahogany," he told the women, who relayed the message to the bears. He really would have liked to see how the bears felled trees, what sort of ingenuity they possessed in that respect, but he was far too busy arranging other things, and only saw the lattermost portion of their work, when they rolled the stripped logs back to camp.

Daedalus worked out in the open, under a tepid but warming sun. The bears had a vague interest in the proceedings, and would amble about Daedalus' vicinity for long lengths of time, would leave, and would often return. Or at least Daedalus thought that some bears would return—they all looked practically the same to him, although apparently the women had learned to differentiate, because he heard enough of them pining over so-and-so, who was so much more handsome than the other, and so on.

Thoughts of Icarus did eventually surface, and Daedalus couldn't tell if it was the nature of the work, if those thoughts were bound to surface while he contemplated how copulation between human and bear might be made possible, and what kind of offspring could possibly come from the union—he couldn't tell if it was all of that, or if Sofia's suggestion that he would be reminded was to blame, a self-fulfilling prophecy. She thought he would remember, so he did. How unwittingly callous of her that would be—regardless, there were many painful memories mixed with his calculations and measurements, and they made his hands falter more than once. But his proclivity for creation was stronger, it lifted him in its torrential swelling, and eventually had him flying around, making all sorts of cuts and arrangements. He was in the Maze again.

He couldn't finish it that day. He went to bed and had more dreams, this time about potential ideas he could implement in his creation, about solutions to problems that had discomfited him during the day. Relatively pleasant dreams. And when he awoke he went straight to work again, not because he was compelled but because he was obsessed by then—he had a mission. And by that evening he was done, and the entire population of the Niederbears, including the women, coalesced around it in awe.

There were murmurings: "Is that really... did he really?... I don't believe it, he couldn't have."

Daedalus' creation was a suit, in the likeness of a female bear, or at least his interpretation of one. There were none around to model by—he just assumed they were smaller, and inverted. It most likely offended many women of the audience, it and its two orifices—one for breathing, one for procreation. It opened like a treasure chest would, with latches on the side, so that the women would fit inside, face down in a prostrated position.

Daedalus couldn't help but be proud—he would demonstrate all of its features to any woman or bear that strayed close enough to be talked to. "See, they go in just like so, and then you would go in like so, and you can just imagine…"

Sofia was there. She eyed it, bemused. "Will it serve its purpose?" she asked.

"I can only hope," Daedalus said. "This isn't how I usually go about creating. For a number of obvious reasons, but the one I mean in particular is that I didn't make many empirical observations about the process of bear procreation. This was mostly out of necessity, though. It's analogous to a suicidal person devising a way to kill themselves—they don't have much opportunity to experiment with what works best. But I did what I could."

"So, what now?"

"That… that's as far as my expertise goes. I have nothing else to amend with my invention, and nothing to recommend with its use. All that's left is to try."

She turned to the congregation. "Who wants to be first?"

There was a veritable cacophony of screaming in response. Jubilant women, jumping up and down excitedly with their hands raised. "Pallas, it will be you." Everyone not chosen, everyone not Pallas, scowled bitterly at the chosen woman, but she was too elated to take notice. She shyly approached the contraption, then turned to Daedalus expectantly.

"Wait," Daedalus stammered. "You really don't mean to try it here, in front of everyone, just like this?"

"He's perfectly right." She ordered a couple people to retrieve candles, which were placed in seemly places around the suit, and then it was deemed ready by the women.

"So be it," Daedalus said. He gave Pallas the exact same tour that he'd been giving to everyone else. The process was excruciatingly simple, but he did it more to soothe her than anything, because he noticed, as he assisted her inside, how violently she was trembling. It appalled him that the voice he used to soothe her was the same voice he once affected to soothe his horse, back before Apollo shot her with arrows. But it calmed the woman nonetheless, so he closed the lid over her, which had amongst its features cute little ears and an adorable, poofy tail. Features that he had just been proudly displaying moments before, but, with a woman inside, he suddenly didn't feel too sure about. It was soon to be defiled. "Please just... just do it," he said, to no one in particular.

A bear was selected in the same fashion. Daedalus couldn't watch, he just looked at the audience as they observed in rapt attention. So he didn't see exactly what went wrong, just heard a reverberating snap and all of the erratic screaming of the women.

He finally turned to look, and the result wasn't pretty. The woman had been pulped, the suit was in no way salvageable, lying in pieces every which way, which was reminiscent to Daedalus of how the food was scattered about the feast just two days prior.

Sofia rushed up to him. "What happened?" Her voice was full of that womanly demandingness that Daedalus missed so dearly. "I... I wasn't watching. But I assume I underestimated the... intensity of the bears."

"So what's your solution? What would you change?"

"We're trying this again?"

"Absolutely."

"Well then, I hope the bears like their women fat."

Two days hence, they attempted once more. They brought out the suit, the crowd, the candles. Daedalus was completely incredulous that anyone could be convinced to climb into his deathtrap, so he was dumbfounded when it was the same jubilant, excited reaction as before. He assisted the eager, shaking woman into the now much larger, reinforced mating contraption.

Then they found out.

KAPITEL ACHT(UNG):
HUMANITIES

THE FOREST WAS unforgivingly dark, so much so that it seemed to penetrate all the way into the mind, so that they had to blindly grope through their thoughts just as much as through the treacherous and dense vegetation. Eerie and spectral sounds emanated from obscurity, just further confusing stimuli to be jumbled with the rest.

Wallace was undaunted, and he braced Sezurus Magnate Stairwell on his right shoulder as they jointly hobbled their way back to Gibeah. What failed to disconcert Wallace about the darkness was that he was already mostly blind himself, so the caprices of light didn't affect him much—it was practically all the same to him.

What did reach him, even through his blindness, was the surreal sound of his surroundings. As if to combat it, he droned on in his earthly way, to restore equipoise. "What happened back there reminds me of... no wait, that was different. I woke up when my family was being mauled, but I slept through all of what happened to you. Are you sure you guys made much noise? I must be a sounder sleeper than I used to be. Things change? Nope, this is an entirely new one on me, quite different."

Stairwell was mostly silent for his part, though he couldn't help but gasping from the exertion of every step that he made. Blood continuously flowed down his leg, but blended so quickly into the darkness behind that it could effectively be ignored. In the morning the trail he left would look like a celestial signature, made with dark ink on the world.

The stream could be traced up his leg to a gaping wound at his hip, for which the two had made the best compress they could extemporize. There were several other wounds, more elevated on his body, around his ribs and arms, but they were mere tributaries to the first wound.

For whatever reason, Stairwell felt the need to contribute to the conversation, although he could only cough out his words, it made him lightheaded to use his air for anything but forward motion, and he couldn't breathe any deeper than he already was. "You... you saved." That was enough for a first round. He then had to recompose himself, before adding, "My life. I appr... Thank. S."

"No trouble at all, really. I feel better rested than I have in a while, truth be told. I should get around like this more often, before all of that sitting I do becomes permanent."

And so they progressively neared the city, their pace so slow that they didn't reach it until dawn broke behind them. Stairwell had the strange sensation of feeling better and better as they went, loss of blood and all, and was carrying more and more of his weight. By the time they reached the gate he was fortified enough to stand on his own, as Wallace went to the small porthole used for communication between the sentry and the only selectively permitted outside world.

"What's wrong, is anybody there?" Stairwell asked, when he noticed Wallace's confusion as he peered through the porthole.

"You know what? I think I know what the matter is. I'm pretty sure I'm the one on sentry duty right now. Yup, that's it. We'll have to go to another gate."

The rumor spread quickly through Gibeah that the flower expedition had returned. The message was relayed straightaway to Richard, where he was holed up in his Throne Room as usual. He asked the messenger if the expedition had been a success, and the answer given was yes. The King ordered that the members of the expedition be sent up in their entirety to be commemorated. He was surely surprised when only Wallace and a severely wounded Stairwell were escorted in.

"What happened?" he finally uttered, when his stupefaction had subsided.

Stairwell took the liberty of retelling the story in his own terse style, ending with, "I owe my life to Wallace. Had he not been around, I would have bled to death in the wilderness."

Richard made an extremely important decision in the time it took to finish a sentence. "These are truly commendable things that I hear about you, Wallace, and if even half of them are true I feel justified in what I am about to do, and that is to promote you to the Mars Magnate."

"What is that?" Wallace asked, not ashamed of his ignorance.

"The highest military office, second only to me. And it is well deserved."

Wallace contemplated his good fortune, then realized, "Is there anyone left in the military?"

"You best attempt something a little closer to gratitude, before it becomes the shortest job you've ever had. Now, you say you do have the flowers? That the mission was still a success?" The King wanted his flowers.

"Yes, your Majesty, here they are," Stairwell said as he unshouldered the bag that he still had slung across his back, and surrendered it to a servant who had rushed up to take it.

"Then I dismiss you, Sezurus Magnate Stairwell. Mars Magnate Wallace, if you'll stay around to be briefed on what your job actually entails."

After the Sezurus Magnate had left, a general commotion broke out. One of the Magisters said, "This wouldn't have happened if we had weapons. And I don't mean any of this flower nonsense we've been getting into lately, I'm talking about the real weapons that we used to have. Why aren't those brought back? This could all easily be resolved. How many lives did we just waste for no good reason? Does the weight of those lives not trouble anyone else?"

Several other Magisters vocally assented to the Magister's opinion, and others roared back.

"Silence!" shouted the Magister of Public Safety. He made his way quickly to the Magister of the King, and continued, "Do I have your permission, Magister of the King, to address this situation before other damaging opinions have time to breed? I mean, of course, an Emergency King's Court."

The Magister of the King considered it briefly. "You'll have to allow that the opposition be allowed to speak after you," he said, to which the Magister of Public Safety warily assented. "And what will your presentation be called?" he asked.

"On the Inherent Value of Life."

Immediately the Magister of the King officiated. "Gentlemen of the Court, I now entreat you to listen to the Magister of Public Safety as he delivers to you his dialogue, 'On the Inherent Value of Life'."

"Thank you, your Majesty.

"These are tragic events that bring me here before you. Though there may be controversy in the way I choose to address it, I want to emphasize strongly that they affect no one deeper than me, who has nothing but the most profound respect for the lives given in service of our community. After I have spoken, another man will appeal to you. He will say that this tragedy could have been averted if we had been better armed, if we had been more lethal. It is very likely that no such appeal is needed, that you already feel that way yourselves. It is true that, had the victims been armed, the deaths we mourn today could have been averted. It may surprise some of you that I make this admission, as if I was arguing against that very fact, as if its validity could have been contradicted. As if I would be conceding everything to the man who will speak after me. But there is a subtle difference—I said that the deaths we mourn today would have been averted. I did not say that the tragedy would have been. What concerns me is that had we killed them all—the bears, the enemy—and everyone came home, we would be celebrating right now.

"I'm going to say the same things I said three years ago—they are still as relevant now as they were then. That, in situations like these, if anyone dies it is a tragedy, no matter who we may call innocent and who guilty. The common conception is that if a thief breaks into a house and kills its owner to take his possessions, he is deserving of death. For this reason, we would celebrate the occasion where the thief is thwarted, where he breaks in and is immediately disposed of by the owner. It is considered just, it makes a hero of the owner. What I challenge you to believe, what I truly believe myself, is that the life of the thief is just as sacred as that of the owner. That a violation of human worth exists in both instances that I provided, that they are exactly equivalent in tragedy, and yet we choose to evaluate them so disparately. Let me help you to come to my conclusion, though it shouldn't be necessary—say that the owner never would have amounted to much, was no one special. Say that, had the thief survived, he would have recanted his sins and, through works and deeds, would have become a saint. It is not impossible to believe. Say what you want about the nobility of blood, about the inherent and immutable traits of man. It is perfectly easy to believe that a man, no matter how sinful he has been in the past, can wake up every morning and treat everyone with simple human decency. And there is nothing more to it than that, when it comes to being a saint. So what would then be preferable, during the event we constructed—that the saint died, or the average man? Once again, the answer should be neither one nor the other. What does it matter if one was a thief and the other an innocent man?

"Three years ago you stood here with me and affirmed the basic value of all living life. You decided with me that weapons of destruction were fundamentally beneath our standards as a society. That pain and death were not to be willfully inflicted on our fellow brother, or any sentient being. That even though there might be people who would not adhere to our standard, whether they are our enemies or do not possess the moral or mental faculty to believe what we do, it should not make a difference. What is right is right, and wrong is wrong. And I cannot say how proud of all of you I was that day. It is beyond my capacity of expression. I can think of no cleaner, no purer evidence that we partook in divinity, than that one belief we upheld as a community. And so it saddens me that today we talk of going back, although I do understand that even the greatest of societies will lapse into ignominy. Whether you choose to listen to me or not, I will always be on the side that values all life as beautiful, as invaluable, and therefore above our right to arbitrate over, either in the court of law or in our houses as the thief breaks in.

"So three years ago we dismantled all our weapons. We didn't make equivocal definitions about what constituted a lethal weapon, as opposed to a necessary weapon. We did it to deter murders, whether they were the spontaneous kind found on the streets or those sanctioned by a government. Arguments that humans were the problem, and not the weapons, were dismissed as fallacious. It is true that humans are a problem, and were the problem, but human sanity, human intelligence, human decency, will always be a bell curve at best. That's not pessimism, that's statistics. It can't be hoped that the left half of the curve will start behaving better just because we really want it to. We can inform and instruct, we can advance as a society as far as we want, but it must be acknowledged that however far we get, some will be behind. Especially the farther we get. What can be amended, what we did amend, is the accessibility of destruction to society as a whole, which was a completely practicable and effective approach.

"Violent murders were significantly abated. People still occasionally strangle each other, but what's to be done about that, really? Not a single bear has been verifiably killed since its implementation. No better outcome could really be hoped for by a Magister of Public Safety.

"And I'd be lying by omission if I didn't say this, that a large concern of mine is that more might be expected of me in combating the rough future ahead of us if we go backwards, and bring destructive weapons back. As if it were my fault.

"Yeah, that's about all I have to say."

General applause.

It wasn't long before another man was in front of the Court, saying very artfully that, "those were a lot of wonderful, idyllic things we've just heard from the Magister of Public Safety, but unfortunately all wrong…"

The King had a torrent of thoughts wreaking havoc to his sanity. Where had the halcyon of his childhood gone? Flown away? He could have sworn he hadn't wandered far, and yet the way back was irrevocably lost to him.

Executive decisions had to be made. As a child he'd been given the best of educations, the humanities. Grammar, rhetoric, logic, arithmetic, geometry, astronomy and music, in a sun-soaked room with ancient, worn books and a private tutor that answered to the same description, and went into a violent fit of hacking whenever Richard answered a question incorrectly. And he'd been studious—of course, he'd had the same basic insouciance underlying all his interactions with the world as any child did. But whether it was to make his father proud—a bold, imposing figure—or because nothing better presented itself to fill the idleness of the days, or perhaps so his tutor wouldn't choke to death, he had listened, and he had learned.

So it was entirely beyond him, why none of it sufficed him as a king. He looked to the people that he had surrounded himself with, his Magisters. They seemed competent enough, they answered questions with pretty words and relevant-sounding confidence, and he wasn't blinded by their glaring impotence. How did they get along in life, and accomplish the things they accomplished? Or were they just so many King Richards, under a thick veneer of pretense? He couldn't tell. He would take them individually aside, and try to strip away their veneer by asking nonsensical questions, so he could finally witness the quaking and irresolute form underneath, and be content. But that never turned out the way that Richard wanted it to—for the most part, the Magisters were far too deviously adroit, and even when they were obviously confused Richard didn't blame them, not after all of the blathering he did to get them that way. No, he couldn't expect something coherent to be made out of his insoluble idiocies, it wasn't fair of him even to think so.

The flowers had been delivered to him, and it seemed that they were capable of curing all his maladies and wistfulness at the time—how elated and boyish he'd felt upon receiving them—but then some nervous harbinger had stepped up, told him that the flowers were not enough, that although one bag brought back was lovely, all fifteen bags had been necessary to make do. Mass production of the tranquilizer was still impossible unless more was gathered. For the time being, all that could be made of the materials at hand was twenty munitions, and experts were fairly sure that more than twenty bears existed in the wilderness.

Those things had been reported, and his Magisters, loudmouthed as they all were, had immediately given their opinions, to the last man. And so it was possible that Richard didn't have to do any thinking of his own, he could just defer to them. At least one decision, however arbitrary it might be, still had to be made by the King, though, and that was *who* to defer to. It would have been a lot more helpful to have all those highly educated experts around, if they ever all agreed. But, for all their education, for all the absolute truth they putatively held, they still differed on practically everything. The flower situation had yet to be resolved.

"We need to use the munitions we have to secure more flowers," a Magister said.

"We have enough to subsist off of, purely for self-defense. If we overcome the next Bear Raid entirely, it is more than likely that they'll give up on future excursions and we'll have accomplished everything we need to," said another.

"The bears aren't nearly that fictile. We'll have to resort to a much more aggressive deterrent against their future activity—scare tactics. We'll tranquilize all their leaders, and their organization will crumble."

And, of course, Richard had the constantly recurring thoughts of Sofia on his mind, and was wondering if twenty rounds would be sufficient to get her back. In the end, though, he somehow managed to be reasonable. It was extremely difficult for him—he had to wade through so many thoughts of 'why me,' but he announced to all: "We will get more flowers, and will avenge ourselves of the Samsonbear in the process. We'll show them that we're not to be trifled with. After we tranquilize them, we'll cut off their heads and parade them in front of the other bears—"

"Excuse me," inserted the Magister of the Bear.

"Fine, how effective would parading the limp body of a bear be, for morale? Unharmed, of course. We'll make it very comfortable for the bear."

"We would have to find someone capable of carrying the bear first."

"We'll have to find anybody at all, before that. The military needs replenishing."

"Stairwell could probably do it. We still have him."

"Stairwell looks like he can barely carry himself, at the moment."

"Isn't Terel filling him back up with horse blood? Other than that, he'll just need a bandage and some analgesics. He'll do fine."

"Still, having a military might be beneficial."

"There aren't really any eligible people left in Gibeah."

"We'll have to use the Draft, then."

"Will those people be capable of fighting?"

The Magister of Poetry took it upon himself to respond to the last concern, with a long harangue. "This is the beauty of the future of war. Don't you see the trend we've fallen into? It used to be the case that skill was required to fight. Well-trained, extremely fit men, who could withstand the burden of armor, the half-ton of metal that would be poured over them so that they could withstand this other angry protrusion, the even heavier and sharpened metal stick that they tacitly decided to hit each other with. You might argue that it isn't heavier, but the true weight of a thing is its ramifications, and a sword has more, I assure you. There was an art to wielding this stick, an art to dodging it, an art to staying sane under the weight of it all. But through the years we've been shedding all of this art, and along with it the weight—our newest weapon doesn't require any skill nor strength, just a breath that even the shallowest of lungs could summon. A kid could do it. I suggest that a kid do it. Perhaps I was guilty of understatement when I said that this was the future of war—this is the future of everything."

There was much mumbling after the Magister finished, but no one could find any particular point that they disagreed with.

"Then it's settled." King Richard picked up the thread, since he had to be sure to add the final monarchial touch to everything they thought of. "Conscript children, show them the basic functioning of the blowgun, enough to get them by. Shouldn't be hard, shouldn't take much. Spare Stairwell, since the carrying of the bear is an integral component to the master plan, and I wouldn't want him incapacitated and incapable of doing it. Mars Magnate Wallace, you'll be leading the mission this time around."

The Gibeahnites had strong reservations against being drafted, but were otherwise far too idle and lazy to resist. Their sons were taken from them. And after the King had seen off that group like he'd seen off the first, he waited with a great sense of foreboding.

Something was going to go wrong, had to go wrong. He could feel it like the loneliness he felt in bed every night, and there was nothing he knew the feel of better. Gibeah was exposed—it was almost the exact quantitative duplicate of the last exposure the King had risked of Gibeah, but he felt like there was something qualitatively different, qualitatively amiss the second time around. He expressed his concerns indirectly to his Court, namely the Magister of Resources, because he was standing the closest. "Simon, we need better defenses against the bears."

"That's why we're collecting flowers."

"I mean now, I mean for the interim. I can feel a breeze—a breeze shouldn't be able to get in here. Don't we close the doors around here?"

"Sorry, Chester left it open. We'll get right on that. As for our defenses, that city wall will have to do."

"The bears can scale it in a single bound."

"It will have to do."

"I can't stand for this. Where is Treyshka?" Treyshka was the Magister of Public Safety.

"He... he didn't show up," spurged the Magister of Apollo, who was also standing nearby.

"Didn't show up? Hasn't anyone looked into this?"

"We didn't think it was important."

"Everyone attends the King's Court, everyone! I want him

found!" His subjects might as well have been in the throes of *rigor mortis*, the way they continued to stand and stare at him blankly. "Now! Do it yourselves for once, by the Gods!"

"Oh, us," said the Magister of Education. "Now that you mention it, he was taking a strange route to the Castle this morning. I was on my way here with Deretius, you know the lad, and I saw him going off in the complete opposite direction."

"Strange route indeed," someone chided in.

"Where was this?" the King demanded.

"Southwest quadrant of the inner city, and he was going southward."

"Toward the Bear Maze? Or the cemetery? What could possibly concern him down there?"

"No idea."

"This is a lead enough, anyway. Go. I want you to go, all of you." They obediently filed out of the room, and left Richard to his solitude. He would make them useful, every last one of them, if it was the very last thing he did. He had a new resolution—things had to change, and presently, to combat the looming portent that Richard still couldn't discharge himself of.

They returned in an hour or so, one of them bearing a wrinkled parchment. That one, the Magister of Practical History, laboriously cleared his throat before beginning, "This paper was found in the Magister's—late Magister's, I should say—doublet that he was so fond of. It reads: 'My last will and testament. I leave to Simon, my dearest comrade, the most cherished of my possessions, my ever-loyal steed. He will be waiting in your stable.' Signed Treyshka Idanova."

"What's the import of that?" The King was flustered.

"Oh, we're quite sure he's dead. We found the doublet strewn on the ground, at the edge of the Bear Maze. It's very dangerous to be riding your horse, even your most loyal of steeds, near the Bear Maze like that. We're not sure what got into his head. But Simon here's very lucky. By the sound of it, the horse is a keeper."

Simon interjected, "I didn't even like the fellow."

"D-dead? You're absolutely sure—and *that* was the content of his will? Nothing about his estate, heirs?" the King asked.

"He does have a lovely situation up there on Briar Hill, but he has no family, no."

"No family? No heir? I'm not sure any of you know, but the Magistral Office is now hereditary. You have an obligation to have children."

"I personally did not know. That's not the curriculum we teach at Gymnasium," the Magister of Practical History said. "We teach that you hand-select each Magister, and thus impart your divinity. I would know, I wrote the textbook."

"No, it's been different for a while now. I picked you, you have kids, your kids are an extension of you, it's always you in the office. If the office were to change hands, if I were to pick another, it would suggest the fallibility of the regency for choosing wrong the first time around. I am not fallible."

"Then who is going to be the new Magister of Public Safety?" someone asked.

"No one. The office was just eliminated. Although next time, I'll make sure it is someone more fertile."

"Are you suggesting that you shouldn't have chosen Treyshka?"

"Silence! I would have you killed, Damascus, if I hadn't chosen you myself. And if I knew, with better certainty, whether you had an heir of your own."

The Court wisely kept silent about the fact that the King himself lacked an heir. The King was obviously not to be trifled with that day, his face was crimson red and truculent lines were accumulating over his brow.

"Now please, have children."

The next day, Simon was riding to the Castle with several other Magisters, on his new horse, and he couldn't help but gloat for his good fortune. So he would show off, encouraging his steed into feats of equine excellence, switching in rapid succession between a trot, a gallop, a canter, throwing in the intermittent spin, flourish, and so on.

"That really is a fine specimen you have there, Simon."

"Isn't it, Acaya? I'm fairly pleased with it, myself."

Another Magister said, "I wonder if that isn't one of those horses that Terel has been filling up with human blood. That would certainly make sense of its noble demeanor."

They all agreed, although none of them knew for sure.

Since Acaya had praised something about Simon, he also had to criticize, in order to maintain balance. "It does take a while to form that excellent bond, though, between man and horse. Even a noble horse, I imagine. You've never been much of a rider anyway, have you? It couldn't be expected that the two of you have a perfect affinity for each other already."

"Nonsense. This horse would follow me to the grave, I can feel it between my thighs. I would bet my life that if I let go of the reins, it would still follow my every will."

"Let's see it."

With so much affected reckless abandon, Simon tossed the reins aside. The horse almost immediately veered to the left, which was the cause of more than one guffaw from the rest. "So much for following your every will, eh Simon?"

"Don't be senseless—I just realized I have an errand this way. I'll meet up with the likes of you later, at the Castle."

"Must you run your errand now? The King hasn't had a tolerant disposition of late, if you hadn't noticed. And we're already nearly late. Your absence won't go unheeded, though it might go unheaded. I implore you, as a fr... frellow Magister."

"Please, don't worry yourselves!" By that time Simon was shouting, fading into the distance.

"I'd like to know what got into his head," they commented amongst themselves.

Simon on the horse:

"Desist! Desist, you blasted horse! I can't believe I praised you, I can't believe I got up fifteen minutes earlier than my wont this morning just to feed you oats by hand, I was so joyous and naïve! But you've proven me foolish now, haven't you! I just lied to all my companions back there, to save face. That's right, your deplorable, deplorable recalcitrance nearly effaced me, almost cost me my beautiful face, and I doubt you give a damn. Halt, in the name of Apollo! I want to see your teeth, I want to pry your bloody mouth open and inspect your gums. I bet they're rotten. I bet you have cavities, gingivitis, who knows! you might be rabid. I should have noticed as I fed you those oats—I sowed those oats myself, spared no labor in care for you, and this is how you repay your debt of gratitude? I've been foolish, I've been a fool. Where are you taking me?

"I hope you know, it's not just anyone mounted on you right now. Countless people fantasize about this very thing—most of them horses. I am the Magister of Resources. Speaking of which, since when have we had trees? Why did no one tell me about these? What are they, laurel? They feel thriving. Look at this branch, this is green and verdant on the inside, you wouldn't know unless you broke it like so. Maybe you would know, you're an animal, you all seem to have a sense for that kind of thing that I must have lost a long time ago. I can think of so many uses for these trees, just off the top of my head. But nobody let me know, and that's a problem. I feel like you're partially to blame—why haven't you taken me here before? I know we just met this morning, but is that really an excuse?

"And the sun up there! My God, is it radiant. So wasteful. If I could only harness the half of that. The wind—it's so refreshing, so stirring. Why is so much energy expended pointlessly? I can't even begin to describe how little I understand. The stars will make a full circle tonight—the whole celestial sphere, actually. A circle! And Venus is in retrograde. The moon begins filling again, have you heard of anything more absurd? Ever?

"And then there's the Bear Maze you're coming dangerously close to. Maybe human excess is the worst. It takes energy to sleep, even—I think this is one of the greatest atrocities the world has ever conjured out of its addled bowels. Otherwise useless people still want food so that they can continue to be useless. And rights, they want rights, and respect. What am I supposed to make these from? Where else am I supposed to pull from, to satisfy these 'God-given' rights? I dare not ask God for the material, that's for sure. He gives these rights, then no way to sustain them. No, instead we have bad humors—two kinds of bile, blood, phlegm, there isn't anything worthwhile in the whole lot—we have dyscrasia, avarice, limited resources, beautiful women, until it's practically a logical necessity that someone gets the short end of the stick and the capacity to whine about it. I didn't even know we had sticks—you really should have shown me earlier, you damn horse.

"It gets confusing. I don't even remember who built this Maze, or why. Better yet, it isn't important! Even if we knew its original purpose, we would use it wrong. When the outsider conquers, and on a whim decides to subject the people rather than kill them all outright, the first thing they do is demolish all of the temples. Break the spirit of the conquered. And do you know what they do with this piece of land that now has infinite possibilities, you stupid horse? They build another temple on it. Why? Continuity, appeasement, pure distillation of the human spirit? You tell me. I would believe in a heartbeat that the first Gibeahnites found the Maze right where it is, and destroyed every brick of it. Then built it again, because they knew how well a Maze fit into the Maze-shaped hole they had just opened up. Wouldn't surprise me in the least.

"What do you mean by this, you horse? You're really just going to deposit me into the Maze like this? What right do

you think you have, and who did you steal it from? I can hardly stand to look at the thing, it is such an affront to common
sense—at least let me close my eyes first. There will be too
much dust down there, dust from the broken stones of the
first Maze, pulverized until it's not recognizable, until it just
looks like your typical dirty floor. There are two Mazes down
there. Those bricks could have been used to make our walls
higher, then we wouldn't have even needed the Maze—isn't
that almost funny? No, I couldn't bear even the scent of that
wasted dust, best I not breathe at all, I shall close my airways
after my eyes. But before any of that, do you have pen and paper? Good, good. Give me time to write out my will. I want
someone else to suffer you, you vile thing. I'll give you to Alicx,
my 'dearest friend.' I suppose the King will be upset I don't
have an heir either. I have a wife I can't stand and an overabun-
dance of illegitimate children, isn't that good enough? But I
won't mention them, not in my will. Okay, I'm done. Have
your way with me."

He screamed all the way down. Whence came the expression and the game "Simon Says," originally utilized for the
training of horses so that they wouldn't disobediently kill their
masters.

There were certain decibels reserved for how loud the King
was being. "Where is Simon? I have questions I need to ask
him. I have an abundance of sticks that need people to wield
them. I have an abundance of city that needs more wall to en-
compass it. I have a lot of needs, but I need Simon first of all.
Now where is he?"

"He was running errands on his horse, last I saw him."

"What! What the—"

"But that isn't nearly the most pressing of matters. We have
Mars Magnate Wallace here—"

"Wallace? Mars? Flowers!"

"Yes, he's here, and… I'll let him tell you himself."

If Wallace had been accustomed to the conventions of the Court, he would have approached the Throne sheepishly, especially considering the news he was about to deliver. As it was, though, he knew nothing of decorum, and approached with a blunt ignorance that could easily have been misconstrued as temerity.

"What do you have to report, Mars Magnate Wallace? Can I finally rest at ease?"

"Everyone you sent with me died. Except for me, although since I don't think it could rightly be said that you sent me with myself I think that what I said first was technically true. I would tell you what happened, if you had the interest."

The King answered, between fumings, "Yes. Yes indeed."

"So, we had a right-fine sending off from the gates, great pomp and ceremony and all, and everyone was in high spirits enough. The kids were smiling, and probably meant it, didn't know any better. You could tell them all you want about how they were going to fight bears, and not everyone that left would come back, but they wouldn't have any of that. You could be telling them, and telling them true, and all the while they'd be competing over who could blow their dart the farthest. Lost a couple of tranquilizers that way, and I'm sure they would apologize to you 'bout that if they were 'live to do so, but sadly... Anyway, they'd be laughing, and I told them about how things wouldn't always be so funny, but then I got to thinking to myself—if things wouldn't always be so funny, shouldn't they laugh while they still had the chance? While they still had the heart? Just because it'd eventually fail them doesn't mean it'd be wrong while it came through... Anyway, I was silently reflecting about all this for a while so I could think of something better to say, because that's what I'm all about, and then they started saying various things themselves. We'll see what I can recall for you, but like I was saying I was kind of distracted, and am getting old, furthermore."

Everyone waited in silence, for a while. Wallace scratched his head.

"Ah, it's recurring to me now, like I'm hearing it for the first time, that phenomenon ever happened to you? One of them was talking about how much they loved the draft. Then they were saying something about how they finally reached their destination, some odd about them being larger than they would have imagined. Then one was very concerned, said that the tranquilizer was supposed to be effective in just a matter of seconds, but something was wrong. Another said it was just like school, just another trauma, and that they must have been learning something. Bunch of screaming. By the time I had figured out the right thing to say, the best of my wisdom to all of youth, they were all dead. I'd say it now but you're all fairly progressed in years, and the moment isn't right neither. So I was disappointed, if you can imagine, but I finished my job anyway, gathered some flowers, and here they are."

The King was utterly distressed. He had a confused admiration for Wallace, but the fact that they had exactly the same amount of flowers as before—the King assessed the volume of the pack from where he sat—and a massive loss of youth besides, were some of the last things he wanted to hear. He wasn't surprised—he had expected as much would happen all along, it was all part of his foreboding, but just because he expected it didn't mean that he wanted to hear about it. "The tranquilizers didn't work? What is the meaning of this? I saw them work myself, we tried it on that one guy, what was his name?"

"Eronius."

"Eronius, yes. Who can explain this to me?"

The Magister of Internal Wellness stepped forward. "We were prepared for that question—you must be just as surprised as we are—but…" Randomly, the Magister broke down. "Things are just so hard, lately….this used to be a fun job. I used to tell people, 'hey, guess what, I'm the Magister of Internal Wellness,' and they'd be like, 'oh, really, what kind of job is that? Never heard of it.' And I wouldn't answer and I wouldn't explain because I was content enough on my own. I started explaining what my job is to people, just the other day. Sorry, sorry," the Magister blushed deeply, "We have your explanation. We brought in an expert on the flowers. But we'd prefer, once again, that you, your Majesty, interview him yourself."

The man alluded to stepped forward to present himself. "Your Majesty, I am Jamal Williams, leader of the research and development of the Department of Biochemical Warfare."

"Yes, yes, get to the point. You know what went wrong?"

"I... I do. My field researcher—you have to understand, he's a sensitive fellow—he knew all along that... the Samsonbear, since they live around the flower, they actually eat the flower. It's a dietary staple to them. Which explains why your expeditions couldn't help but encounter the bears. Anyway, since they eat the flowers, daily, they've developed this sort of immunity to its psychotropic effects. Now, my field researcher knew this full well—I for one just learned all of this, just this morning, it's been a bad day for me—he knew it, but chose not to divulge the information because... because he was convinced that his work would go uncredited, unappreciated, and he could have his vengeance by letting things run their course, and letting you fail to tranquilize the Samsonbear. I would beg for you to forgive him his naïve, intellectual little mind."

"Have him executed, somebody. Immediately. I really need to find Simon, I have to replace these researchers with people that are less egotistical and selfish. I need to know where I can find some of those."

"While we were distracting you with all of this news, we looked into the matter. He's dead. Simon is dead. He is survived by his horse, the little trooper, who he graciously left for Alicx, his dearest friend."

"I didn't even like the fellow," Alicx said.

Day by day the number of the King's Court thinned. The King took Oliver, the Magister of the King, aside. "How many Magisters did we have, just a few weeks ago? It was forty seven, wasn't it? I just took a count and there's only nineteen left. Can it really be the doing of that infernal horse? Why do they keep riding it?" The King had, by then, lost all of his hair, and his skin had recently broken out into severe rashes, which were red and chafed jagged at points where his skin rubbed against itself. The damage was largely invisible to the casual bystander, but the way he scratched at it wasn't.

"If you saw the horse," Oliver said, "you wouldn't blame either party, it or them. It really is a gallant thing, a model specimen. And yes, it's true that the Magisters keep dying from riding the thing, but it's not that the animal is unruly, just that a certain mastery is required—so now it's almost a challenge, all the Magisters *want* to ride it, because they want to prove that they have a firm enough hand to be capable, to survive."

The King didn't care how firm any of his Magister's hands were. "They couldn't have picked a worse time to play at such charades, and only one of them had a son to replace themselves with. What is his name? Abrachius? And the Magister's garb doesn't even fit him properly, look how he nearly swims in it. I've noticed he doesn't move around much, for fear of tripping. See! Are you watching? The Magister of Pestilence Eradication is beckoning him over, probably to discuss the fulfillment of some very important duties, but the kid just shakes his head, refuses because he doesn't want to fall over. The productivity lost! I lament it so."

"You could probably regain some of that productivity, if you conceded to choose a few replacements for the Magisters we've lost. You should hear their grumbling against us. The ones left, they're mutinous—they despise the fact that they have to take over the responsibilities of their dead brethren. And should anyone blame them? Such consolidation was never meant to happen."

"I told you! I'm not going back on my policy. And furthermore, tell them what you just said, that this was never meant to happen. Them and their stupid horse! They're killing them-selves, and criticizing me for it. The fault is their own, I don't care if you say I shouldn't blame them."

The King had other concerns on his mind that he didn't let on about. For the past couple of days birds had been running into his window. He'd been peacefully surveying out the win-dow from his Throne Room, a large mosaic slab that was clear in its bottommost portion. The view was pleasant, kids could be seen gallivanting in the streets. Then a bird had startled the living daylights out of him, when it careened into the glass di-rectly in front of his face. It hit the window with such force that it splattered and stuck to the window, for long enough that he had time to get Aaron, the Magister of Apollo, to identify it.

"Aaron, I know you're somewhat of an ornithologist, will you look at this for me? What is this bird? I feel like I've seen it before."

"Yes, you have. It's a partridge."

"Doesn't ring a bell."

"The kind of bird we use for the Auguries."

There was another incident that nobody knew of at all. He'd woken up from his bed, which was all the more empty for its largeness, when he brushed up against something under the sheets. He lifted them to find a pile of birds, dead and de-caying next to him.

And every day, more would hit the window. He was para-noid to look at that side of the Throne Room, because every time he did there was a fatal avian collision, always right on cue.

"Dapper, I need to talk to you about renovations to the city."

"Why me, of all people?"

"Because you picked up all the duties of the Magister of Resources and Public Safety now, too."

"I have a hard enough time keeping up with Poetry. I'd like to know how you could fairly expect more than that."

"Are you serious? Damn the poetry. Now is not the time.

Things are falling apart, buildings and people are falling down, and we're doing nothing to replace them. That's nothing that poetry can fix."

"Well, then I have nothing to offer. Sorry."

And then they all were dead, every single one of the Magisters, all from trying to master a horse. With the exception of the Magister of the King. Richard said, after a long, awkward silence between them, "Why did you survive, of all people?

"I don't ever leave the Castle, so I have no need of a horse. Also, I wanted to discuss something with you."

"What? What could you possibly want?"

"I know you don't like talking about it, but I'm going to be perfectly candid with you. I know you don't have an heir—I want you to adopt me."

The King was taken aback for a while. "You can't just be my son like that."

"There's no good reason why not. Law can work miracles, these days—you wouldn't even believe it. All you have to do is sign a few papers and everyone would be under legal duress to call me, and to think of me, as your son."

"Get out of my sight. Right now. I can't stand to look at you."

Oliver was indignant, but obedient enough to do as he was told. Then the Throne Room was empty again, empty of everything except Richard, and he didn't do much to cure its emptiness. Just like it had been after Sofia was kidnapped, just as spacious, just as lonely. In fact, it was so reminiscent of that time that Richard swore he could smell her, smell her waning presence as if she had just been there the day before, had been stolen by a group of insidious bears just the day before.

All of the Magisters had fallen into the Bear Maze. Apollo would be upset. More than upset. Richard was so deep in all of his reflections that he was drowning in them, when the mosaic window shattered loudly into all of its composite pieces. A maelstrom of birds entered, screeching, fluttering, and filling the room. He let out a gargled scream.

KAPITEL NEUN:
BEAR NECESSITIES

KORAH HAD BEEN getting sicker and sicker by the day, ever since the Bacchic Rite. It manifested itself strangely—he'd been vomiting constantly, until he was a strange pallor, even by Leper Standards. He was incessantly dizzy, had a hard time concentrating, and was quite feverish. A lot of the Lepers were concerned—they tried to confine him to the Infirmary, but he would always escape when the moment was opportune, and continue his work.

It was the image of Dionysus that haunted him, childish and demonic. The words he had spoken kept echoing in Korah's head: "You have to make them proud, Korah." With the whole fear of his being, Korah took those words to heart, and his first measure in making everyone proud—he wasn't absolutely sure who 'them' denoted, so decided to make everyone proud, just in case—was to disappoint his fellow Lepers by not staying where they put him.

Plans were blizzarding in his head, so that he gave everyone the impression, whenever they talked to him, that he was lost in a world of low visibility. He would stare at nowhere in particular at all times, and would talk to people as one would talk to foes hidden and waiting in ambush.

Perhaps strangest of all, in everyone else's opinion, were the orders he'd been issuing lately.

"Reddleman, come here," Korah said to a strangely colored Leper. His real name was something else entirely, but he was always referred to as the Reddleman, until nobody could remember what his name had originally been, even the man himself.

"Yes, sir?"

"Have they found the next Wine Supply yet?"

"No, they haven't. Are the rumors true? Are we not using the next Wine Supply for a Bacchic Rite?"

"Yes, that's true," Korah said.

"In God's name, why? This is unheard of. Just like all the other things you've been doing lately. I hear you've been putting on a saddle and emulating a horse around in Gibeah lately. Please make sense of this. As it is, it sounds like blasphemy, like you've forgotten the Leper Mission."

"The wine is going toward one of the greatest Subversions in Leper History, and I assure you—"

"What about killing people? What about that, Korah? That's not a Subversion, or any other form of acceptable Leper Activity."

Korah's face became extremely agitated. "Now listen here. I won't have you going around making baseless accusations about my conduct. If you really want to know, listen, and keep your libel for afterward, if I still seem reproachable." If Korah were in any better state of mind, he would have noticed the peculiarity of a Leper, besides himself, asking *why*, for once. "I'm not killing anyone. Everything I do, from the most trivial of things to the gravest, is in strict accord with the Leper Mission. I promise that the Leper Mission is the last thing I would ever turn my back on. That being said, let me explain how the Magisters and the horse emulating all fit in.

"You can give a man a ride to a cliff, but you can't make

him jump. You should hear the way those men talk, you really should—they're all pompous and hollow, and they all talk to no end, even when there is no one else around to hear. No one but them and a horse, that is. They're the kind of men that are only words, and it is still beyond me whether they were using them to try to convince a horse, convince themselves, or just to hear the air full of all their own convictions. Proud men—I lead them to a ledge, and even though they might be perfectly safe from falling over it, they are so frustrated at being led so close to a cliff that they will jump off of it at the first opportunity, of their own will. And this is the Leper Mission in its most essential form—to punish people with their mortal sins, for their mortal sins. Their pride killed them. So, you must understand, it really pains me to hear a lecture about the Leper Mission and how I may or may not be in accord with it, when it's all I think about, it's all I do, and it's all I am."

The Reddleman appeared to furrow his brow, most likely probing his mind to find the extent to which Korah had provided him a satisfactory answer for his misgivings. He finally snapped to attention, as if awakened, and said, "What would you have me do, sir?"

"Where is Krenshaw?"

"By the Leering Pole, last I saw him. Still organizing operations."

"Thank you."

"Anything else?" the Reddleman asked.

"One more thing, yes. I don't care how many Lepers you need to conscript to do it—find me the next Wine Supply."

Krenshaw was right where the Reddleman had said he would be, issuing orders to a handful of Lepers that were gathered about him. Korah only caught the last portion of what was being said to the audience, but was able to put together that he was giving advice about the current most effective disguises to avoid recognition while on Reconnaissance. It was an art that changed dramatically with the times, and had to constantly be kept up to date. A very unstable circle kept Reconnaissance afloat, because the information used to inform what the best disguises were required diligent gathering of information by Reconnaissance of trends, fashions, and so on, while, on the other hand, Reconnaissance was only possible by already employing all of that information as a disguise. If Reconnaissance ever missed a step, it would be a fatal trip, and so Korah kept men as capable as Krenshaw on the job.

As the party dissolved, Korah approached the man. Krenshaw stated, before Korah could get a word in, "My, you don't look good at all, my friend. Shouldn't you be in the Infirmary?"

"Never mind any of that. Do you have that list I wanted?"

"Of all of the Magisters? Yes, it's right here. Although I've recently learned that a few of these names should be crossed off, and that it is your doing."

"You've heard correctly."

Krenshaw waited for a moment, as if waiting for Korah to add something, and when he didn't, Krenshaw asked, "Don't you want to hear the Casualty Report? You're usually all about that. I have all the numbers prepared for you."

"No, not today. I was actually wondering if you would help me put my saddle on, it's awfully tedious to do it by myself."

"Of course, right away, Korah. Still going as a Thoroughbred? That's still a good choice, although the trend is tending toward something a little less pure—the Gibeahn counterculture is on an upswing, and they'll be wanting a Quarter Horse. Just so you know."

"Appreciated, as always."

"Another thing I thought I would mention. You do know that Gibeah is sending out a large expedition to gather flowers, much like the last one?"

"I have heard mention of this, but it is good to have it verified through more than one source."

Korah led the man to an outpost very close to the Gibeahn outskirts, which he had chosen due to its unfrequented nature. Inside an occult, rickety structure, Korah had hidden his saddle and other materials for the purpose of disguising as a horse.

Krenshaw immediately set about saddling Korah up, with the expert eye of a man that had spent a lifetime making people undetectable in enemy territory. "Tell me, Korah. That list I gave you—why didn't you need it sooner? I know what it's for—all of those men are dying. But you made it quite a ways down that list without needing it. What changed?"

Korah laughed for the first time he had in a while. The effect wasn't cheerful, though, but rather crazed. "I had been going off of word of mouth—a lot of names I knew already, but others were extremely obscure. Like, there's a Magister of Interior Decoration. I'd never heard of the guy. Anyway, I listen as they ride me about, and sometimes they mention other people, who I then take mental note of. Others take care of my transition on their own, even. But my problem arises when they're so busy talking about themselves that they fail to mention anybody else. That's already happened a few times, and I've only barely been able to salvage the situation. I don't want to leave anything else to chance. Thanks for the list. And the help with the disguise. It looks suitable?"

"Like a dream."

"You know, to be a horse isn't so hard. But to be a horse that everyone is jealous about, that's another matter entirely."

Korah waited patiently in the stable of some Magister or another, trying his best to look like a horse at leisure. None too punctually, as the Magisters didn't take their timeliness very seriously—on more than one occasion, Korah had wasted an entire day waiting in the stable of Magisters who simply neglected to go to work¬—the main door lurched open, spilling morning light on all the hay strewn across the floor, and all the other decrepit animals that littered the stable. The Magisters would only tend to their animals when they were feeling particularly pastoral—other days, they used their affluence to have other people tend to them. Other days, they forgot entirely. The result of which was that Korah was housed next to the skinniest pig he'd ever seen—he'd never seen a pig's ribcage, outside of eating from it, but there it was, protruding from the unhappy creature like an inverted mortal wound. Before the Magister had arrived, Korah had dropped his equine pretenses long enough to get it some food that he found on a shelf. The food was only couple of beets, incidentally, and they probably weren't enough to save the pig's life, but he brought them back to their stall anyway. When the Magister finally arrived, the obese man had to kick the pig into a corner in order to have room to mount Korah from his favored side.

"I love it when the servants already have the horse saddled in the morning," he said, as he struggled to ascend. Wherein he looked, for a brief interlude, like a turtle stuck on its back. "Or did no one ever take it off of you last night? No matter."

Korah also struggled, trying not to grunt or otherwise complain as the full weight of the man came down on his back. But like the most proper of steeds he just grinned and bore it, and trotted his way out of the stable, initially in the direction of Castle Horeb.

Korah had a few reasons for why he let the Magisters get most of the way to Castle Horeb before turning, even though it was more work that way. First of all, the Magisters usually rode in groups, and he liked to let them convene so he could glean facts of current events in the Throne Room, which were hard to access through any other channel. The second reason was more psychological in nature—if he was disobedient from the start, coming out of the gate, the Magisters wouldn't blame themselves for his disobedience, they would just think that he was an insufferable horse and nothing could be done for it. But if he started out by letting them dominate him, they would take it personally as soon as he deviated—they would look at the dominance they'd had for the first fifteen minutes, think about how wonderful it had been, then search themselves scathingly for what had gone so suddenly lacking in their character, that their relationship with the horse would change. In other words, they would take it as a matter of pride.

"What a marvelous coat you have," said the Magister as he stroked Korah on top of his right shoulder. "In all my days, and with all my experience, I've never seen anything quite like it. And to think that you are mine."

Soon they had caught up to the main group, which would travel slowly until all its constituents were concentrated. Since they waited for everyone before they picked up the pace, on the days when a Magister chose not to go to work, most days, it would take the group nearly two hours to travel the two miles from the wealthier district, where the majority of them lived, to the Castle.

"Boraxis, what a pleasure to see you! And your horse, oh my! We hear tell that Alicx couldn't handle him, and here you are, the lucky successor."

"Yes, yes. Apollo truly smiles down on me." With those words, Korah felt a variety of pressures applied by the Magister's knees, and a tap to the left ear, which induced Korah into several quick movements that he knew to be indicated. It was difficult—the moves were easy enough for a horse, perhaps, but to reproduce them with the human body required an athleticism that Korah didn't think he had. And he might have despaired, if he wasn't so mentally distant. He was delusional, he began to think horse thoughts, which spared him the turmoil of understanding the human thoughts that might have been going through his head. Those thoughts just floated around without a receptacle, such as how sore all of his maladapted muscles were, how weak his joints, how much his skin burned where it chafed with the saddle, how the gravel impressed harshly into his hands and knees. He thought only of moving forward, with only the slight and distant reservation of human thought that soon he would have to divert to the Bear Maze.

Apparently the moves Korah had made sufficed, because they were greeted with general applause. They had been talking for some time before Korah remembered that he could understand them if he tried. "The King's been a crazed lunatic lately, don't you think?"

"I can hardly stand it, myself. All he talks about anymore are birds and tranquilizers. What about the feast we're supposed to be having on the morrow? I bet he doesn't even recall it, I bet it completely slipped his mind, because of all those other 'worries' he's got."

"If that's manifested divinity we have there with King Richard, you can count me out. Call me an atheist. I'd rather be accused of that than devotion anymore."

"Are we still going to have that rebellion we were talking about?"

"Oh yes, any day now. It's high time someone competent took the helm of this city. Someone that remembers feasts and isn't afraid of birds."

"How is power going to be split? Equally, if I'm not mistaken?"

"Equally? There's forty-nine of us, or at least there used to be. That would be horribly inefficient—there would be absolutely no way we could decide on anything."

"We'd be like those damn Lepers."

"Yes, the damn Lepers. I propose, therefore, that we install a leader of sorts, and the rest of us will all advise him. You know, so that things will finally get done, unlike those other past reigns by kings."

"Oh, and who do you propose fill that leader's seat? Yourself, I presume?"

"Well, I wouldn't be adverse—"

"Wouldn't be adverse! This is the Magister of Antiquation, talking like he's Prince Valladium, have you ever had such a laugh! You're out of touch with the present, Herodotus." A few of the Magisters obliged him with a laugh, and then Korah decided to make his move, as he realized that the Magisters wouldn't have any useful kind of conversation that day.

"Hey, where are you going there, Boraxis?"

"Forgot something."

Korah had to ignore all of the efforts by the Magister to resubjugate him—it almost happened that Korah fell forgetfully back into obedience, but he was just lucid enough to prevent that.

"As if! We all know that that horse is going to kill you. It's off to the Bear Maze with you! Guess you didn't have it in you to tame the thing."

"If I had half a mind to do it, I'd trample you to death with this steed," the Magister replied, obviously frustrated by his own impotence. Korah had to reflect quickly if that was something he should actually go along with, but he ended up deciding against it. "I'll be back to make you regret saying those words. Right after I retrieve this thing I forgot."

"Good luck!"

After Korah had disposed of the man into the Maze, he collapsed to the ground in great relief, right along its edge. A sudden image struck him, as he lay there, of the Bear Interment he'd witnessed just a couple of months before, though it seemed much more distant in his past. He wondered if the germ of the idea, of disposing men like he did, had come to him then—his mind was far from pellucid of late, so he couldn't tell for sure, but it seemed reasonable. He could imagine himself, those two months before, standing a bit more upright and introspecting a great deal more competently. He would have been laughing a sickened laughter, at the mendacity of the Gibeahnites. They had contrived a way for themselves to feel justified dropping an animal God knows where, and washing their hands of it, as if the way they killed an animal nullified the fact that they killed it. If the Gibeahnites would acknowledge that they were killing the animals, and at the same time maintain that those killings were morally justified, it wouldn't have been nearly so appalling to Korah. But they *contrived*, they used sleight of hand and smoke and mirrors until they killed without believing they were responsible.

So perhaps even two months before, Korah had formulated his response to them, the Leper response, the Leper Punishment. If the Gibeahnites believed that such disposing of animals was okay, then he would force the proposition to its logical conclusion—that humans were animals as well, and as animals it was okay to dispose of them identically. If they would willfully put animals into the Bear Maze, they would willfully put themselves there.

He made sure that the will he'd obtained from the Magister was readily visible to those that would come searching for him, before he shakily departed. He had other things to attend to.

Upon returning to the Leper Colony, he was immediately remitted to the Infirmary. Selvia admonished him sternly, but the creased brow of motherly worry belied her admonishments. "I'm going to petition for actual walls, if you're not going to respect the boundaries that the sticks around the Infirmary are supposed to represent. Just because it's easy for you to weasel your way under the fur curtain into the outside world doesn't mean you should. You're sick, Korah, and no matter how important you think your work is, it isn't worth you dying over. Now come over here so I can get a good look at what you've done to yourself this time."

She beckoned him over to one of the cots that lined the ward, but before he conceded to follow her, he asked, "Has anyone been over to see me in my absence?"

"You'd know the answer to that if you stuck around."

"Selvia, seriously."

"The Reddleman was here. But I don't know why because I refused to take a message, and you just get your leprotic ass

over here before I find more forceful means to do it myself."
Korah didn't feel like calling her bluff, so he sat down, and let
her strip him of his shirt. "My God, I can't believe this." Blood
was running all down Korah's back, there were severe abra-
sions, continents of unsettling discoloration, and flesh hanging in places that it wasn't meant to, even by Leper Standards.
"What have you been doing? How could this possibly be happening to you?"

"I've been carrying the weight of the fattest people in the
world on my back, all of it, all of them. If I look the worse
for it, it wouldn't surprise me. All of their excesses will come
out of my skin. It's difficult…" And Korah choked on his
words, as if he might cry, as if he really didn't want to do it—
then drily continued, "But I will do it. I will bear the sins of
the world."

"Now, Korah," Selvia said, "what's gotten into you lately?
I know you've had a little bit of a hard time, what with Miriam and all, but you've never taken anything this far. You never used to take anything so seriously—don't get me wrong,
you've done great things for the Lepers, but you always used to
take time to yourself, time for respite, time for recreation. You
could dearly use some of that time now. Take it from someone
who knows—you're going to kill yourself at this rate."

"I really appreciate everything you're saying, but if you'll
just bandage me up a little so I can be on my way. I need to
talk to the Reddleman."

Korah asked around until he found Lepers that knew where
the Reddleman was, and then found the Reddleman himself
shortly thereafter. "It is my understanding that you've been
looking for me, Reddleman. Any news?"

"Yes… we've found you your Wine Supply, and we're waiting for your orders on what to do with it. Already people have
been spreading the word that there's another Bacchic Rite in
order, so we've had to go around telling them that it isn't the

case, and everyone's in disbelief. You're going to have to make it clear what we're doing with it. You said something about a Subversion?"

"Yes, I did. Listen, there's to be an army of sorts leaving Gibeah tomorrow morning, to collect flowers."

"I've heard of it."

"Good. We'll need recruits from them. What I'm intending is a Subversion, so the Gibeahnites will have to do the deed themselves, and there's much work to be done. I needn't remind you what to say to them, do I? I'm entrusting the matter to you."

"I've got it under control."

In the morning, as Korah was galloping out to Gibeah, the Reddleman left the Leper Colony alone, decked out in patriotic Gibeahnite colors. He intercepted the army only minutes after it was out of sight from the city.

"Excuse me, good gentlemen, may I have your attention?" Nearly all of them turned to face him, curious of the apparition, with the exception of an elderly type that continued to meander forward, as if oblivious to the interference. "My God, they're all children," he said to himself before continuing. "It is my understanding that you've all been chosen to wage war for the city of Gibeah—congratulations!" There was a loud cheer from a young group of teenagers, boys that would probably be enthusiastic for anything. "You're about to die for that city. You'll go out in these high spirits you have, and you'll be cut down. But it is commendable that you die for a cause." The cheering took on a new quality—it was still loud and energetic, but was veering toward anger. "And how did all of this come about? Oh, you were drafted, that's right."

An individual then spoke loudly enough to be heard over the resulting uproar from the crowd. "It isn't fair!" Everyone then yelled in agreement.

"Now, now, I can't have you going on with a false impression like that, so allow me to correct you," the Reddleman replied. "It is absolutely fair that you've been drafted, and I won't let you think otherwise. All your life, you've been leaching off of the benefits that a government provides you, you've been accruing debt ever since you were born. If not before that, even. Don't forget this. And you've also been living under a government that has explicitly disclosed the possibility that one day it might call on you—this is what it asks for in return, that occasionally you fight for it, and you've done nothing through all your years to change the terms of your contract. So when they finally do call on you, I won't stand to hear anything about unfairness." The crowd became disconcerted, maybe even ashamed.

"This is the truth of your discontent—you've been hoping all this time that it wouldn't be you that was called on, to repay that debt. You've never wanted to be the great man, the magnanimous soul, the one that would take responsibility for the continuation of your government. When you desert your army, when you follow me, I want it to be with this understanding—that you're not rebelling against some great injustice that's been done to you, but rather, you're deserting because it doesn't suit your palate. Can I get an amen?"

He got an amen, but the turnout wasn't as great as the Reddleman had expected, after the cheering had died down—only half of the army split off to accompany him back to the Leper Colony.

It was extremely dangerous work to bring back an army to the Leper Colony, even an army of children, and he was surprised that Korah had asked it of him. He would have known that the move was unprecedented, if he knew anything about Leper History. Almost every step of the way he had to convince the army not to kill the Lepers that were bustling around them, Lepers who suffered a number of lashings before he could quell the children again. He had intended to take them straight to Korah, but learned that Korah was still in the city on some errand, which forced him to try and make small talk with a bunch of easily distractible teenagers with swords for nearly two hours, before Korah showed up.

Korah looked as if he was in no condition to even be standing, as he hobbled up to the group. The Reddleman walked to meet him. "You've done well, Reddleman," Korah said, as he sized the group up. "We're all going to go to the Wine Supply. Show us the way."

While they traveled the considerable distance, Korah collected every Leper that they came across, telling them that he had important things to tell the whole Colony. He also sent a couple Lepers out to gather the Lepers abroad, and to bring them back to the Wine Supply, where he would make his speech.

A lake opened up in front of the travelers, and Lepers were already standing around its circumference, apparently waiting for instruction. The Reddleman gestured to the middle of the lake, where a great brown mass was afloat.

"You mean you haven't brought it to shore yet?" Korah asked the Reddleman.

"You told me you wanted them to do all the work."

"So be it. And while they're out doing that, I can talk to all of you." Korah then turned to the young Gibeahnites, who seemed to be eagerly awaiting directions. "Strip down, boys. We have something that needs retrieving."

Almost the entire Colony was gathered before Korah—some couldn't be found, and a large quantity had died recently, a reality that Korah would have been disappointed about had he been in his right mind. But he wasn't, so he proceeded as if everything were normal. The Gibeahnites were splashing loudly in the background. "I want you to know," Korah started, "that I am proud of all of you. Better people couldn't be asked for—I don't care what the Gibeahnites say about you. They don't see people the way they should.

"I'm going to ask you to do things today that should never be expected from a person. This wine," and he gestured in its general direction, "is, by all rights, yours. But I'm taking it from you. And your lives," he waved his arm at all the Lepers, "your lives are your own, but in all likelihood I'm going to take them as well. I sincerely regret taking your wine, and your lives.

"But today, for all intents and purposes, we march on Gibeah. My recent actions have jeopardized your lives—this I know. And I know you know it too, and it breaks my heart when I look into your eyes and don't see blame. If this same loyal spirit still resides in you, I'm asking for all of it. I'm asking you to follow me to the end of what I've begun." Tears were streaming down his face, but no one could tell.

"We'll give them our wine, and our lives. We'll force it down their throat until they choke on it. We're going to wage war until they accept a definition of humanity that includes everyone, even us. We are making retribution, and I hope that when you walk the streets of Gibeah with me tonight, you feel it as strongly as I do." Everyone was dead silent, and Korah felt awkward as he was pouring his heart into such an unreflective void. But then he saw their faces, and his heart was lightened more than it had been in years. They were beaming.

"To Gibeah!"

The Wine Supply was in the largest oaken barrel that the Lepers had ever seen, its planks being at least six cubits in length, and its diameter at its widest point was about five cubits. The Gibeahnites all made a concerted effort on one side to roll it towards its destination, the barrel making a vitriolic sloshing sound with every push. The sheer size of the barrel forced the Lepers to take the least covert of paths, the main road to the north gate of Gibeah.

A merciless wind was ripping through the newly budding trees, sometimes tearing an entire limb off and casting it in the path, so that several Lepers constantly had to work to keep the path clear for the barrel to roll. Often the wind would take the wine on its own, and everyone was forced to run to keep up. It wasn't long before they were upon the gate.

"State your name and purpose," the Gibeahn sentry demanded.

"The Reddleman. And I have a wine delivery."

"Oh, then come right in."

Korah was whispering to the Reddleman as they marched through the streets, and the Reddleman would fervently whisper back. Korah hadn't told anyone their destination, he just gave directions for the barrel rollers as they became pertinent. Any Gibeahnite that they passed was gathered, in much the same way Lepers had been gathered not long before, which was an easy task due to the attention that the enormous barrel drew. Soon the Gibeahnites outnumbered the Lepers two to one.

Then they arrived at the Old Fountain, still thawing from the winter cold. "Reddleman, once again I'm leaving everything to you. I have other things that I need to tend to. Don't let me down."

The Reddleman was swift in delivering orders. "I need buckets from everyone that can provide one." Many Gibeahnites momentarily departed to retrieve their buckets, or anything that could serve the purpose. In the meantime he arranged that the barrel was abutting the Fountain, which was no mean feat for how large and cumbersome it was. By then, most of the other Gibeahnites had returned, and he had them empty the entire Fountain by hand, into the street around them. The volume of water was large, but they made quick work of it from all the hands they had.

Meanwhile, Korah found Krenshaw at the back of the procession, carrying out the logistics of the operation as he always did. He asked him, "Krenshaw, could you bring me Dee?"

"You couldn't possibly mean to—"

"Yes, I do."

"Right now doesn't seem to be the best of times."

"I don't see why not."

Krenshaw hesitated, but eventually passed the task on to another Leper. The Leper retrieved the small girl and took her to where Korah decided to wait, away from all the commotion of the ordeal and whistling to himself. Korah thanked the older Leper and took the young girl by the hand, leading her further away from the Fountain and into the quieter streets of Gibeah.

The Lepers were trained in the arts of Subversion from a very young age until well into their adulthood, due to the difficulty of the subject matter. It was a simple psychological fact that the younger children performed Subversion well, even with very little training, but for whatever reason the older children and teenagers generally did not. Instead of restricting their entire age group from Subversion, like some of his precursors had done, Korah preferred to personally evaluate every Leper as they came to that age threshold. If he thought that they could perform to standard with the other Lepers, they would be allowed to continue being an active member of the Leper Mission, even given their age. Those who failed had to wait until they were older, and had relearned.

For that reason, the little girl was nervous and shaking—she knew that she was being evaluated, and by no one less than the leader of the Lepers himself, who held her by the hand as they walked through the streets of a city entirely foreign to her. Korah tried to calm her nerves with a conversation, less for the content of what he had to say and more to break the tension of silence that was obviously getting to her.

"I think you'll find it helpful to think of Subversion as sewing. The analogy isn't perfect, but that's really beside the point. Imagine that God has sent you a shirt to be mended. He wears his clothes pretty roughly, and sometimes they're bound to tear." There was something very unsettling, even to Korah, about the delicate features of a child covered with leprosy, like the girl who looked up to him as he spoke.

"So you are a little seamstress, and I'm a seamster. We've got quite the task on our hands, don't we? Something really serious. Say that God has sent us one of his favorite sweaters, except that it's torn from the collar all the way down to the waist, and furthermore the elbow of the arm is missing, just gone. A few things to remember: first, this is God's favorite sweater, we're not just going to tell him he needs a new one, that's not our job. We work with we have. Second, we cannot add a patch to the sweater. I'm afraid we're going to get overwhelmed in numbers here, but there are two reasons why I say we can't add a patch. The first is that adding a patch would change the identity of the sweater. When God was happily wearing the sweater a week ago it didn't have a patch, so why should it now? It is very unlikely that we will find a fabric that will match the original, and even if we did, as soon as we add a patch we are really changing the dimensions of the sweater, right? Especially if we try to use a patch for the first tear I was talking about, the one from the neck down. There's more material, it's heavier. We make the sweater larger than it used to be, and we don't want God to be swimming around in the sweater we send back, don't you agree?

"The second reason we can't add a patch is that it is more likely to fall apart. Maybe not, you say, because you are the master seamstress. But we know for a fact that the original stitches of the sweater served God well, until they were torn, and that's the kind of performance that we are trying to copy. When we add a patch we have no way of knowing that the sweater will behave the same—it could start bending in ways it never has before when God holds his arms up, for example, and that could lead to something going terribly wrong. So we use only the needle and the thread. We do not provide any substantial material to the mended sweater. We could much more easily get away with sewing the hole for the hand to the hole for the head, and make a wonderful little loop, than adding any material of our own. The reason for that is where our analogy starts to get a little forced.

"The torn sweater I've been talking about, sent to us by God, is the people we Subvert. We're trying to mend them. What you'll have to really try imagining with me is that the sweater has a conscience of its own, that it will recognize when its identity has been changed, and will reject the changes. The sweater recognizes when it doesn't fit around God the way it used to, and it will blame the tailor. We are all the clothing of God. But we are also the seamstress and the seamster, you and I. So when we go talk to these people, like we are about to, what you have to remember is that you only have a needle and some thread. You will never successfully change their identity, it doesn't matter how persuasive you think you might be. But you might be surprised how easily you can sew their arm to their head without them ever noticing."

Korah indicated a little boy that was sitting on the dilapidated porch of a house, alone and contentedly playing with a stick. "He will be the one. What you need to convince him of is that he should come with us to our Fountain. I won't tell you how you should get him to do that, I just want you to remember everything you've been taught."

She smiled tepidly up at the leader, and made a few diffident steps in the playing child's direction.

"Go on," he said. "I believe in you very much, Dee."

He derived great personal amusement out of how assertive her tone was. She was a little Spartan, he could see it clearly. She said, "Hey kid!" and had the little thing off its guard from that second on. She continued, "What are you playing with that stick for, don't you have any better toys?"

"My mommy said I don't need toys," was the child's dutiful but bewildered response. He could think of no reason why a complete stranger would be blatantly challenging the worth of his playthings.

"You don't really agree with her, do you? I saw a kid down the street that was playing with a miniature horse. I bet you like his mom better, don't you? She lets him have more things."

"I love my mom," the boy passionately stated. The girl was taking a very harsh angle, challenging a lot of the boy's stronger emotions. She was going to have to become subtler very soon, or the Subversion would be lost. She looked back at Korah, and all he did was put his hand to the top of his head so that it made a circle.

"It's not really about toys," she said. "It's about being able to be like an adult. Adults can do stuff, and can have stuff. You want to be like an adult, don't you? You seem like a very mature young man."

He was more receptive to the praise, and nodded. So she went on, "An adult like you want to be, an adult like yourself pretty much, would love to do the things that we're about to go do. You should come with us. And an adult like you doesn't have to ask permission, no matter what your parents say. If he thinks it will be fun, he will just go do it. Will you come do it with us?"

For a second the kid looked back into the house, into the bondage of his childhood, and considered all the times he was told not to leave the porch, and not to talk to strangers. But he was feeling much more adult now, and could see in himself all the things a person needed to be an adult. He had the right to choose. So he said, "Yeah, that sounds fun."

When they were finally walking away, Dee looked up at Korah expectantly, and asked, "Well, how did I do?" with a sincere smile, yet trepidation. She added a light, melodic laughter, the kind that left nothing in the air after it was gone.

He said, without hesitating, "Very well. But we'll talk about it later. For right now we have to get him dressed up, my little seamstress."

Back at the Fountain, only one thing remained for the Reddleman that he'd been ordered to do. "Hearken, all you Gibeahnites! Gather around, gather around. Absolutely everyone." He gave them a moment to crowd in, until they were packed together stiflingly thick, and the wind pulsated violently around them. "Apollo is on his way. And I need you to hear me out before he gets here.

"He's going to ask things of you, and you may feel compelled to listen. This can't be the case. No matter what he says, I want you to just stand there, with the dullest expression you can manage. I wouldn't just ask you to do this for me, though—I'm going to explain why it's exactly what you'll want to do. Apollo—"

"Isn't real!" someone eccentric from the crowd yelled.

"No, he definitely is."

"He hasn't done anything for us!"

The Reddleman wasn't in a mood to be interrupted. He didn't have much time. "You people live under so many delusions, don't you. He is real, I repeat, and he's done many things for you. None of that's the point. He's done miracles—he is order, and you rely on the gifts he's given you daily. He is what makes the world predictable, and he guarantees that the same will be the case tomorrow. This is worth more than you could ever know. You owe him everything—but you will be petty. That is what I'm asking of you. You'll forget all the services he rendered you yesterday, and ask yourself what he's done for you *today*, or what he's done for *you in particular*. You'll despise his godliness. You'll laugh every time you hear that you were made in his likeness—an ironic laugh. Everything that is base in you will rebel against the noble—don't repress it any longer. Ask yourself why there is famine, why loved ones have to die, why so much suffering exists in the world—every impertinent question that you have in your head, ask it all. And ask it quickly, because here he comes."

The sky darkened into a pitch black almost instantly, when

it had been evening just seconds before. The wind stopped of a sudden, leaving the stillest of calms. Everything came to a rest, nobody moved—they just stood there in the complete silence, the only sound being the sound of the wine as the Fountain took it to its womb, and sent it cascading back down in waves. In those moments, everyone around was intensely aware of how different they were from everyone else, how each person was a separate entity that could never perfectly relate to another, no matter how hard it tried.

That was when Korah arrived, escorting by hand a little boy, whose long hair was intertwined with vines. He said, "Here is your Fountain I promised you, young sir. Climb in."

The atmosphere brightened ethereally, not from a celestial body, but from some emission much closer. "What is this treachery?" a voice boomed. "You violate the sanctity of the Bear Maze, you cast doubt and slander upon my name—I hear you on Sundays, and every ablution you make is done with a tepid hand, every prayer with a tepid voice. Don't think I don't see it, and don't think I don't hear it. And now you defy to face me with this bold impertinence?" Apollo was resplendent, his face as hot as a thousand Julys.

"A memory that I've spent hundreds of lifetimes forgetting, conjured from the past?" The kid was splashing gaily through the Fountain, oblivious to his surroundings. "It astounds me, my apostles, that you listen with such rapt attention to the leprotic influence. The Lepers are at your gates! And what are you doing? You're listening to them—you will always prefer to listen to the devil on your shoulder than to the God in the sky. Why? Is it because they're closer?

"I could give you so many things—I could give you everything, and you'd still find reason to be discontent. I've seen it happen before—the kings among you fall into perfidy and godlessness faster than anyone. And I'm getting tired of it.

"You have one more chance, Gibeahnites. You either seize that child now, and deal away with him, or face my fury forever."

214

It was a moment of truth. The Reddleman quickly took his eyes away from Apollo, to survey the faces of the Gibeahnites he had assembled and lectured. And to his great relief, not a single one of them waivered, not a single one budged in compliance with Apollo's ultimatum.

Apollo's expression was indescribable. He was reliving his half of the tragedy of Daphne, and the scene at the Fountain, and experiencing the pure defiance of everyone that he had chosen for himself to be worshipped by. It was anguish.

Korah saw it all, and knew that he had succeeded—the purest Subversion that had ever been accomplished. Even in his moment of triumph, though, he had one strong reservation—he couldn't decide if Friedrich would have done anything like it.

"I know where to aim, this time," Apollo said, while deftly drawing his bow. He notched an arrow and let it fly, before anyone had the time to react, and it went straight through Korah's chest. Mass confusion ensued.

Apollo's divinity was distorting his human features. With a calm fury he loosed arrow after arrow, through the head and heart of every Leper that presented itself. Gibeahnites and Lepers alike were scrambling to escape the vicinity—anything but face the wrath of Apollo. "No, no you don't," Apollo boomed. "Did you think such a betrayal would just go unanswered?" And everyone that tried to flee, Gibeahnite or Leper, was turned into a bird.

Apollo then turned his attention to the boy, who had abandoned his merrymaking out of terror and just stood in the center of the Fountain, stained red, dumbfounded, and shivering from the cold. Apollo gripped the kid by the neck, and the small mass let out a startled yelp in response. Apollo walked to the rim of the Fountain, a hard, granite border, and then beat the kid's head savagely against the stone until nothing remained in his hand to beat.

"Are you happy now, Lepers? Is this what you wanted? I'll

kill every last one of you." Broken bodies were crawling miserably on the ground, often times being trampled by people who still ran, only to become birds.

A small group of teenage Gibeahnites maintained a very admirable amount of composure through the din. They were originally taken from the army, and their cool-headedness might have proven invaluable to Wallace, had they kept allegiance with him. They looked at the blowguns that were still in their possession, their tranquilizers. Then they looked back at Apollo, and wondered what kind of effect it might have on a God. So they tried.

The darts entered Apollo's being in rapid succession. At first he was only startled, as if he'd been bitten by an insect, and he patted at the annoyance. Then he began to sway drowsily, and finally crumpled to the ground.

It was serene.

The Reddleman crawled, desperately and painfully, to the place he had last seen Korah. He found him by the edge of the Fountain, in a pool of blood that was indiscernible from the wine that pooled about him. The barrel had a larger capacity than the Fountain, and it was overflowing in dark rivulets.

"Korah! Korah! Oh no, no…"

Korah gasped, coughing up blood. The Reddleman seized him firmly by the shoulders. The arrow was protruding out from Korah's ribcage, its golden feathers scintillating in the light that Apollo continued to radiate, only duller now. The arrow must have been all the way through Korah's chest, but he was lying on his back, so the Reddleman couldn't tell.

"I'm sorry," the Reddleman said. "If I'd have known that this is what you were planning, if I had known that this is what things would come to, I would have talked you out of it. Who's going to lead us now?"

Korah's eyes looked as if they were adrift in the middle of some deep ocean, and hadn't seen land for days. But then he snapped out of it. "I'm not done yet. Not until this is fin-

ished." And with a strength that couldn't have come from his body, but somewhere beyond, he pushed himself upright. He had to catch himself against the Fountain when he nearly faltered. On the Fountain, his hand touched something with a strange texture. He looked at his hands to see that it was the gore of the child, splattered around everywhere. He wiped it off on what used to be a white cloak, but had recently taken on the color of blood and wine.

"Everyone that can stand, do it!" Korah yelled. There were mumblings, and a barely perceptible shuffling, but no one stood. "Now!" Slowly, they rose. Twenty people remained, twenty people stood out of the hundreds that they had brought with them. "Help me carry him."

Korah himself took Apollo's leg, and others stooped to help him. It took six of them to lift the deity, and then they slowly bore him forward. The rest just milled about the procession. Korah proceeded silently.

Every step came directly from a reserve in his soul. Being a horse had been incomparably easier. There were long tracts of time that he didn't breathe at all, because he couldn't. The feathers of the arrow in his chest led the way.

In an hour, they were at the Bear Maze. Three of them had died on the way. Korah stood on the very ledge, staring into the abyss. "This is a consummation. First it was bears, then it was humans, and now a God." He exerted his last energy casting Apollo down. "Now it is a new era. Dionysus is chaos."

KAPITEL ZEHN: HUMANITY (ICARUS)

PARTRIDGES HAD HAUNTED his way there. Through the thick of the forest he could hear their plaintive cry, always pursuing him, and he knew the greatest shame. Now Daedalus looked out over the ocean, a soul without comfort. Recent events, and a desolate view, were forcing him to recall the last time he'd ever left the city, some three years before. He did not retreat from it, which was perhaps due to his melancholic temperament, or maybe some other reason entirely. He stood there and took all of it in.

The ocean hadn't changed. It was still bleak at its horizons, and daunting everywhere between. The waves were constantly whitewashing the beach, like some timid writer who would never decide on a single thing to definitively say. Daedalus would make a horrible ocean, he thought to himself. He was always definitively saying too many things. And, like an ocean that would have to constantly recede in order not to wash away its imprint, he'd said so many things until he had nowhere to retreat to, backed all the way against the farthest lonely horizon. And many fish would die from that tendency of his.

A memory came to him: The first time that he had ever

seen her. He was a young man, and was an acolyte of the fashionable, so that for the first time he'd started caring for his image. He wore clothes of a more affected cut, and still sat awkward in them because he'd not yet adjusted. The world was simpler for him, then—he would just immerse himself in its mysteries, would suffocate himself in them until he had to surface, gasping for air. It was only when he tried to float, up and away from life's mysteries, that things became difficult for him. Sinking was easy. Drowning was easy.

He would go to the temple because he was a devout man. Apollo had never appeared to him, nor had he spoken to Apollo, and he didn't understand what anyone meant when they talked about their *relationship* with Apollo. But he believed. There was something about the dawn, the dawn he would watch every morning, that bespoke a divinity to him. It was as simple as that. For Daedalus, theology seemed to confuse too many issues, and to try too hard at something so simple—he hated the purity that was lost when people asked *why* He should exist, the purity lost when they had a relationship with him and they were touched by his grace and so became a healed people. He didn't hate that those relationships might exist, he wasn't jealous on account of his own lack on that front. No, he hated that 'healed' people still talked like broken people, and were shaming Apollo's good name every time they called themselves his miracle.

He kept most of those thoughts to himself.

Her, on the other hand, he knew nothing about. And maybe that was the intrigue. She would show up to the same temple, and sat several pews in front of him and one seat to the right, unerringly, so that she was always seeing the preacher from his left nostril, because his dais was moderately elevated from the rest of the building. She must have had reasons to be there, beliefs and motivations, but he knew nothing about them, only that she nodded more fervently to certain points the preacher made than to other points, which she would just receive with a passive, acknowledging look.

She wasn't as consistent as he was, as far as attendance was concerned. Some days he would hear a sermon better because he didn't have the added distraction that she provided. But there was also a certain disquieting emptiness in his stomach on those days, which he tried to dismiss as childish. He would wonder where she would be, instead of at the temple. Was he more devout than she, or was his constant attendance due to the fact that he was looking for every opportunity to look at her? She had a beautiful face, round with no particularly defined feature. At times when he would admonish himself—he was always strictest with himself most of all—his reproaches evolved to include her, because she was adulterating his piety. He didn't know the exact reason he went to the temple anymore, and that was a problem.

Then he found out her name. He had his own habitual seat, but he left it, approached hers at a rate of mere inches per week, like one might sneak up on a coral reef. Finally, he was in a position to impede her exit as she tried to escape to another lustrous Sunday afternoon, and she said 'excuse me,' and he said, 'to whom do I owe the pleasure,' or something ridiculous like that. But she answered, after she realized what he meant to unearth, 'Bathsheba.' He had said something about how strange of a name it was, in its exotic way. He said it was surely a sign of the times, that all these strange names were coming from an exotic impulse that must be at the heart of our consciousness. She had replied that no, it had come from her parents, and furthermore it wasn't strange, but was the name of many normal people, and she was one of them.

They had a kid, entirely unexpected. They had just barely figured each other's names out, and then they had to figure out one more—they called him Icarus. Actually, Daedalus had insisted on Aureliano, but Bathsheba had discredited it as an outlandish sort of name, too exotic, and her choice of Icarus had won.

During that time, the gestation, Daedalus also was more productive than he'd ever been in his life. On the strength of some of his inventions alone, he had been selected to be the Magister of Science, unheard of from the nepotism of the Gibeahn Magisters. The King himself made a large display of giving him a quaint parcel of land, on the eastern edge of the city, where he could build a house. He told Bathsheba that he'd always seen himself in a maze, and that he really wanted to make one for them to live in, but she easily dissuaded him of that. For her alone he built a modest house, consulting her at every step, which he would always refer to as his promissory of forever. He even forwent to build a workshop for himself at the house, reasoning that he would always have the more than suitable workshop at Castle Horeb, during his lifetime appointment as the Magister of Science. Bathsheba was easily upset and starting to show during the construction, but Daedalus would just simply embrace her whenever her temper was short and reassure her that it was only for a little while, that everything was on a trend for the better.

Slowly their temple-goings became more and more awkward. Where once they had gone separately, people began to notice that they arrived together, that their conversations had taken on a note of domesticity, and that Bathsheba was gaining weight. They made speculations, which were mostly accurate. The social pressure they exerted was agitating Bathsheba's already frayed nerves—she and Daedalus were not married, it was a severe transgression that they were having a child—old women frowned and young people would slander them, and Daedalus found Bathsheba sobbing fitfully in their sinful bed one day. All that he could tell her was that he would make it better, somehow. She replied that they wouldn't, just couldn't go to the temple anymore. He told her that changing their lives for a bunch of old women was nonsense.

He practically had to drag her all the way to the temple, the next Sunday. "We're not going to change our ways, just because they're all pretentious hypocrites."

"Let me go, Daed. Please, I need to go back. Please, just let me go."

"Please come. Trust me." There was a further reason he didn't mention, why he refused to bend to the chiding of the white noise, a reason that he kept to himself because he didn't know if he could explain. Already he had become sentimental of the temple for its connection to him and Bathsheba, and he resented every bit of interference that arose against that dominating mood of his.

The sermon that day had acerbic undertones that Daedalus could hear all too clearly, and it was eroding at his cochleae. The preacher was extolling virtues to no end, the pure soul, and his eyes would slide down his left nostril every so often to meet Daedalus' own, and Daedalus knew that he and Bathsheba were the tacit subject of the sermon, the mistake to be learned from. The preacher had just said something about the unsalvageable path of iniquity when Daedalus burst from his pew so violently that the preacher nearly stumbled from his dais, a fall that might have been fatal.

Everyone, especially the preacher, was taken aback when Daedalus hurdled onto the dais, chasing its former occupant down and into the obscurity of the landing that was behind it. He made one more threatening gesture to the preacher, before turning to the congregation.

"*Ich bin verrucht.* I'm speaking today. I don't have anything prepared, but we'll see what I can do." He took a moment to evaluate. Then he said, "Let's be honest with ourselves, just this once. Can we agree to that?" Daedalus subjected as many of the people in the audience as he could to an accusatory glance, which he made in one broad sweep. "Let's hear a sermon about what we *truly* believe in. You've been filling your heads with lies and self-delusion, Sunday after Sunday, and I'm surprised you can still walk with so many blatant contradictions affecting your balance. Here, I present to you your morality: Defame your friends, and praise the enemy and the stranger—you'll always be making friends. Lust after just anyone, but do not act on any of it—or just act quietly if you do, and pray that the God you half-believe in doesn't include the half that has eyes and ears. While you're at it, pray that this same God doesn't mind seeing you only once a week, like some estranged parent you used to have that you keep in some corner room, whose dementia doesn't mind, doesn't notice. Your star shall always be on the rise—and you don't forget that lowering everyone else's star produces the same effect. These hymnals you sing curry favor, the efforts you make at putting on airs aren't meaningless because the neighbors have noticed, and that is the measure of things.

"What I want you to take from this, this introspection we're having, what I want you all to do, so long as you retain the memory, is take something that you fancy you do very well. It doesn't matter what it is, it doesn't matter how good at it you actually are. Then find a history book—you might have to steal it from your child—find where you fit in. Pencil it in the margins. Leave something for posterity to edify itself with. The beauty of this is that you won't have to retain that memory I exhorted of you any longer, after you've done this. You won't need any memory at all, the book will do it for you. Books are holy things.

"You should give alms because you are wealthy. You should give advice because you consider yourselves all so wise. You should give love because you're all so damn loveable. It shouldn't occur to you that there might be other reasons to give these things, that even a poor man can give alms, a simple man can give advice, and an outcast can give love. It's self-evident that it was your superiority that made you kind, and your kindness that made you superior, and so full of gifts! And if anyone refuses to accept these gifts that you bear, you should remember that it's just because you deserve better, you deserve someone that recognizes all the valuable gifts you have to give to the world.

"There. I hope that this was refreshing for you. The rest of what I have to say doesn't come from a preacher, but a fellow sinner: we are both just as obdurate. If you're going to let a preacher say one thing while you believe another, I will do the same. At least someone in this building has to be inconsistent at all times—for this moment it has to be me, the only one left. Now that I've preached your morality, I will believe in another. If you contest—oh, I wish you wouldn't be so dense, but I'm fully aware who I'm talking to—if you contest, all I can hope is that some higher enforcer of consistency exists in the world. Let me amend that—I don't hope he exists, I know he does.

"I have a child on the way," Daedalus continued. Bathsheba blushed deeply. Her face had been one of shocked awe for most of Daedalus' tirade, but finally changed now to scarlet as she turned to bury her head in the pew. "And I'm not going to just let it be a pawn in this game you've made of morality, a pawn to be condescended to. No. Leave me and my family out of it—that's right, I don't need your conventions, and the sanctions of your authority, to dictate who I consider family. *Immer sein Kind.*" With that, he dismounted brusquely from the dais, and quickly took Bathsheba by the hand, which startled her because of how unperceptive her head was, buried in its pew. He escorted her tersely out of the temple, faces of confusion and disdain following his every move. As he left, he shouted back, "You can continue playing now!"

They were walking to their house, and Bathsheba insisted sullenly, "You shouldn't have said that. You shouldn't have said any of that. Now they'll look at us differently."

"You say that as if we liked the way they looked at us before. You're right, it will be differently, but instead of being outright critical, they'll just be… confused, for a while. Probably."

"You shouldn't have done that. You really shouldn't have."

"It was for us."

Then Icarus was born, and finally the two were married. What was stopping them before was the supposed impurity inherent to a living thing growing in another living thing—or something to that effect, but that was the best explanation Daedalus could surmise. Their supposed impurity had precluded the supposed sanctity of holy union, so that holy union could only be had when the impurity was exorcised. Such were the conventions of life. Attendance at the ceremony was low—Daedalus' parents (Bathsheba's refused to partake) and a couple of close friends of each, and that was all.

Daedalus continued to make startling advances at his job, as the Magister of Science, the role of which he heavily adapted to suit his interests. A majority of the Magisters didn't have much to do with the field they represented, beyond to advocate for it, mostly relying on the viewpoints of other people to get their platform right. Daedalus considered advocacy as only of a secondary importance—he wasn't concerned about laws that might be made of scientific truths, or profits to be gained, he only cared for science in its purely exploratory and creative capacity. So he used his clout as the Magister of Science to staff himself with several assistants, and took the progress of the field into his own hands. He would talk about it with Bathsheba while she fed the baby in the kitchen he made for her.

"You really don't want to hear about it? The truth behind disease? But I promise you, I really do, that it's groundbreaking stuff," he would say. "We've been living under a misconception for so long—disease isn't a punishment for misdeeds, or being possessed by evil spirits. None of that. And it isn't having your humors out of balance—we might be overly melancholic people but it doesn't make us sick, not directly at least. There are microorganisms in the world, things that exist even though you can't see them. I know, the thought is dizzying, but it's the truth of the matter. These invade the body and amass in sickening number, wreaking havoc through the delicate balance of the human body—it's always so close to death, but constantly saving itself from the edge. It's absurd."

"I really don't see how this affects me." More than her words, the disinterest of her face spoke to Daedalus.

"You…" Daedalus had to pause a long moment, because he couldn't make sense of her resistance, couldn't understand why the unbridled truth wouldn't interest absolutely everyone. "Well, now that we have a better understanding of the causality of disease, all these preventative measures start suggesting themselves. We're on our way to something. This also has a lot of implications about the Lepers—there's *leprosy*. It's a bacteria, not a curse. We've been looking at things the wrong way for so long, we have a fundamental worldview shift on our hands."

"Well, none of it concerns me."

They had another kid, Ephraim, which meant 'I have been productive in the land of my affliction' in a language that no one in Gibeah spoke anymore. Soon after she gave birth to him was when she had a sort of breakdown, elicited by some apparent provocation that Daedalus had made. "You really don't do anything for me," she complained. "Didn't there used to be a time that you would do things for me? In the beginning? What changed, did I change? Am I no longer the kind of person you want to do things for?"

She was just barely able to stifle an emotional outburst that threatened to interrupt her. "Because I don't know what I'm supposed to do anymore. I've been stuck in this house for eternity, practically, and it's far too familiar to me, nothing new, nothing exciting. Don't I deserve excitement? I don't even own a mirror, you didn't think to put a mirror in this godforsaken place, and I don't even know what I look like anymore. I want to know what I look like, because I'm sure it isn't good."

Daedalus had been sitting in his chair, working restively at calculations and formulas in a notebook of his, trappings all of his work, and was caught entirely off of his guard. "I… you know what, my answer is going to be to show you something. I can't just explain—let me show you."

She was reluctant to follow, but he eventually got her to the temple, their temple, where so much of their courting had taken place. The pews were covered in dust, old articles of worship were in disarray about the place, and there were parts of the building deteriorating for lack of upkeep. The sun worked to highlight the dust floating in streams, in places it could find its way through the dirty windows. He took several quick, large strides ahead of her, so he could turn and face her, to address her grandiloquently as he gestured accusingly with his arms. "Don't you see, there's no one here anymore. They've all moved on to the next big thing, the next eternal truth, whatever that might be. They're lowering bears into this 'Bear Maze' they've devised, they don't show up here anymore. So I can't say all the things I said before, I can't do those things for you again. Yeah, I could say what I did again, but it would be a wasted effort, there'd be no one to listen."

"Are you referring to that one time? When you got up and made a fool of us? What makes you think I want that again? I wasn't asking for that."

Daedalus was at a loss for words, but his mouth ran anyway. "Are you serious? Nothing I've done has been more essentially for *you* than that, not even the house, and I hope you don't mean for me to build another house for you by all this. That would be stupid. So I don't know what you mean, I don't know what else I can do for you." Daedalus was really worked up, furious, but couldn't vent it effectively, so that his face became really agitated. Bathsheba only gave him one more glance before turning and leaving the awkward silence of the temple, after Daedalus had said everything he was going to say.

When she was gone, Daedalus didn't pursue immediately. He was mawkish, he lazed in one pew after another, in the order that they had led to her, thinking desperate and broken thoughts until their weight exhausted his mind. He would watch as spiders crawled across his shoulder, and laugh to himself, a private and unhealthy laugh that only he knew the meaning of. When he'd had enough of that, when it had drained all of his soul, he set about the temple, sifting through its myriad objects until he came away with a mirror.

They would spend long hours in the living room, whose grand window opened into a yard of fauna that were mostly experimental hybrids. Beyond, there were houses and shops in the distance, which Daedalus also liked to think of as experimental hybrids, between life and the inanimate, between consciousness and indifference. He used those kinds of reflections to motivate his erratic temperament. Bathsheba would just sit in her deep languor—where most women would take up sewing, or some such hobby, she did nothing, and her empty hands would just tremble emptily.

At intervals she would strike up a random conversation, and, on one particular occasion, she interpolated into the abysmal quiet of the room: "David is coming over soon. Just so you know."

"What? Who is David?"

"I've told you about David several times—you never listen. Do you need to hear it again? He's someone I met at the market."

"Why is he coming over?"

"Just to visit. I thought it would be nice if the two of you met. You could be friends, I bet. He's a really nice person."

Daedalus' supercilious nature had been getting the best of him lately, and it compelled him to object even when his objections were reproachably inchoate. "I really don't need a friend right now, and that being said I can't see any good reason for him to be around here."

"Me and him get along really well, we're practically the same person," she countered.

"You're practically the same person? And what am I? In

relation to you, that is? Somebody else entirely? Have I become insufficient to you, is my incompatibility insurmountable—when we breathe the same air, when I breathe out, is their not enough oxygen left for you to breathe in? I must be suffocating you, then. What's all of this? What has the past long while been? We're tending in a direction I don't understand, my compass has no bearing whatsoever. Tell me, explain all of that to me."

She just stared at Daedalus blankly.

"Now!"

"I don't understand the things you say. I'm sorry, but I can't answer you, I don't know what you're looking for. I don't know what you like about me, I don't know a lot of things and it's really starting to get to me. You always seem so angry all the time, like nothing I can do can make you happy. We don't see things the same." She paused on those words for a while, as if she was only hearing them herself, and needed time to understand them, and her bottom lip quivered all the time, and Daedalus could only think of how red it was and how much he despised the content of everything that was coming out of it. "And people need to see things the same way to get along," she said. "We just can't get along."

Daedalus burned. "You're ruling out the possibility entirely? As simple as that." He had a conviction which lay, for whatever reason, below expression—that anybody in the world could get along in an appreciable fashion. True, people had bitter dispositions, but any claims that might have been made that bitterness was essential to their identity, Daedalus dismissed as spurious. The historical fact that people have had irreconcilable difference in the past didn't occur to him as having the weight of a necessary truth. And perhaps his belief on the matter wasn't well founded—he had yet to run the sufficient experiments to prove or disprove—but he maintained it anyway. He did not try to bring his sentiment to the surface, for Bathsheba's benefit. He just flailed blindly. "I hope you realize, though I know you never will, just how utterly horrible it is of you to feel that way."

"Well, you don't know how to change my mind. David is coming over. I need people that I can talk to. I'm not just going to sit around and be lonely and bored because you want it that way. I'm a person too."

It took Daedalus a week to have the presence of mind to remember where he was as he traversed the world, so distracted was he by all the thoughts that were prone to enter an oversensitive head and make a home of it. Some heads were more receptive than others to them, pre-furnished, as it were—Daedalus had one of those. In his absentmindedness he'd been spending long hours at his workshop in Castle Horeb, working with wax and feathers. He had been neglecting his duties as a legislator, more than usual, and if anybody came to him looking for an excuse, he would demonstrate to them just how busy he was, 'changing the future', as he would say, and he'd bid them leave him in peace. If anyone still persisted, he'd show them a gun he'd built.

He took an inventory of the things he had left in his life. The list seemed embarrassingly short to him. All the things he valued most were hard-won truths, especially the ones that lay ahead of him, and not behind. And those were difficult to count—perhaps they refused to be numbered, such evanescent things that charmed his soul with all the promise of a succubus. There were a few tangible things that came to his mind, though. There was a book that he adored, an hourglass with many connotations to him, and his son Icarus, who was by then five.

The hourglass reminded him of his inadequacies, and that was what he cherished it for. Before making an hourglass, he had thought that it must have been the simplest of things, just putting sand into a retainer and letting it go. But no matter how many times he tried—he tried different quantities of sand, different types, different apertures in the glass—hour-glasses he made would never count an exact hour. It was always fifty nine minutes and some amount of seconds, or sixty one minutes. Often, the same hourglass would vacillate between both, or the grains would stick, and he ended up throwing a lot of them against walls. It was a bleak day when he finally broke down and acknowledged that he couldn't make one the way he wanted to—and he kept the last instantiation of his failure. Cherished it.

He had another son besides Icarus, Ephraim, a loud and domineering three-year-old, but as much as Daedalus hated to acknowledge the fact, Ephraim didn't mean as much to him. When he had his slight outburst at the temple, Daedalus had promised that his child wouldn't be their pawn. That child had turned out to be Icarus. But it wasn't only that moment that bound them closer—not just a promise made. More than anything else, when Daedalus looked at Icarus, he saw himself. He saw himself and Bathsheba at a happier time, before the parameters of their relationship had decayed. When he looked at Ephraim, the decay was what he saw, not himself. The decay and someone else, someone foreign.

So one day, without the slightest of fanfare, Daedalus gathered the few articles of import to him, his book and his hourglass, and told Bathsheba that he wanted to take Icarus on an errand. She asked what for, his response was nothing in particular, and then he gave her a meaningful kiss on the forehead that he felt ambivalent about for years to come. Then he was on his way.

As they walk, Icarus runs ahead and falls behind and deviates from the path with all the freewheeling spirit of pure youth. To keep him near, Daedalus tries to engage him in conversation. "Tell me about school, Icarus. What have you learned lately?"

"Myshkin is making silly faces in class again, daddy," Icarus shouts from somewhere behind. "And the teacher says, 'I don't much 'ppreciate

it, young sir, them faces you're makin',' but Myshkin doesn't listen 'cos he's not paying attention and the teacher really gets upset and now Myshkin has to do extra work."

"That's interesting, but what did you learn?"

"Don't make silly faces."

The sun is just rising, its weak rays reverberating through the forest. The path is rough but manageable, its disuse obvious in places where overgrowth is creeping in, reclaiming what was lost to it. It is still overcast by the shadows that blanketed it for a long cold night, but everything is waking now. The air is full of the sound of waking.

"Daddy, what kind of errand are we making? There is just nothing out here!"

"It's hard to explain, Icarus."

"But I always have to explain things to you!"

The adolescent plea for fairness rings rich in Daedalus' ear. There was a time when he himself was young, he recalls it vividly even as its vigor was waning from him daily, and he remembers all the life-altering choices that were made for him, over him, without the slightest attempt made at consultation. "Sometimes, things just go awry, and you have to try to fit the pieces back together, Icarus. People... people are unconscientious sometimes, and they break your stuff. You just have to put it back together as best as you can." Something in Daedalus' soul is crying, but he doesn't know how to comfort it.

"What does unconscious mean?"

"Unconscientious." And Daedalus smiles in spite of himself. This is why he loves his child—his child asks questions into the unknown. So many kids don't do the same, they live heedless lives and become heedless adults that Daedalus occasionally has to talk to, and interact with. And when he does, and mentions something unconscientious, he sees the unrecognizing but unquestioning vacancy in their eyes, and there is almost nothing that disgusts him more. "Unconscientious means that they don't care, or they don't know better. Maybe they just don't pay attention, kind of like your friend Myshkin."

"Myshkin isn't my friend. And I saw him unconscientious one time, they had to get him a doctor." Icarus continues to skip along, and then with all of the dawning disappointment of someone who realizes that they've been cheated out of something important to them, he says, "So, we're putting things back together? Why do we have to go all the way out here to do it?"

"I don't know, Icarus. I really don't know."

This answer doesn't fully appease Icarus, but he doesn't vocally object. He finds enough distractions along the way to keep him content—he chases squirrels and throws sticks and all the while they come closer to the northern coast, the ocean.

It blooms in front of them like a flower that could drown the world, if it saw fit. It is melancholy, and if our humors are out of balance maybe it's because we can't join ourselves to the ocean, nor the earth that surrounds it—it will forever be out of us, and we'll forever be lacking. Its waves still beckon invitingly, though, and Daedalus is reminded of a time long before, when he had a good day.

There is a pack strung across Daedalus' back, and he carefully lowers it now, and removes its contents. Two sets of wings he unfurls, white as an angel's, and they make the once-inviting sand that cushions their feet seem dirty and unfeasible in comparison.

"What are those?" Icarus asks in sheer wonder.

"This is how we fix things. We put them on and we go away. You have to turn around." Icarus complies dumbly, the novelty of the wings being overwhelming for his grip on reality. "Here, I just need to attach them in several places," Daedalus says. "This might hurt a little at first, but it will be okay."

Icarus winces, but then they are on, and he gives them a few probing flaps while Daedalus adroitly fastens his own slightly larger wings across his back and arms.

"What are these for?"

"You can fly now."

Like any fledgling, trepidation sets in quickly at the realization of a very large step to be taken, and Icarus' slight frame trembles. "Why can't we go together? I like it better if we went together."

Icarus means that he wants to be carried, Daedalus knows. "We can't, son. I'm almost too heavy by myself for any of this to be possible,

I'm on the very edge, and if I carried you, we would fall. You're going to have to do this on your own. But I'll be right behind you."

Icarus is perhaps unconvinced, but puts on a brave face. Daedalus warns: "These wings are delicate things, Icarus. We're defying nature, and that's hard to do very well for very long. Please, listen carefully. You can't fly too high, and you can't fly too low. Too high and the wax in the wings will melt, too low and the feathers will be weighed down by all the water they pick up. A middle path, son. We have to take a middle path."

"Do you take a middle path, daeddy?"

"… You ask all of the hardest questions, son. Now, let's just try this. And remember that I love you."

Icarus hesitates at first, and rises on diffident wings. But in the air there's a pleasant breeze and the warmth of a tepid sun and it excites him greatly—freedom manifest. The temptation is very large for such a voracious heart, and soon he is soaring among the zephyrs.

"Icarus!" cries Daedalus, who flies the reserved flight of jaded wings. "You are going too fast! Come back to me."

Icarus is deafened by the zealous wind in his ears, and a paternal sun extends the fullness of its warmth with broad arms, and Icarus can't refuse the invitation. Icarus flies higher and higher, and Daedalus, recognizing the danger, speeds after him. But his weight is too great to match the swiftness of his son—in desperation, he abandons everything he thought to take with him, the most sentimental of his possessions, a book and an hourglass, because he reasons that every advantage he can have is necessary now. These articles fall the long distance to the ocean, miles below, and Daedalus can see the weakening integrity of Icarus' wings, still high above him.

"This is folly, boy. Haven't I taught you better? You can't take things to this kind of extreme." But these words are just as futile as the ones before them, they are lost just as quickly in the rushing wind.

And then a fateful moment, when Icarus is silhouetted against the sun to Daedalus. The right wing fails—Daedalus sees it in black—broken clean apart at its main joint. Icarus flails desperately for a few moments, but no amount of flailing can compensate for the lost appendage. He spirals downward.

There is a moment that Daedalus thinks he might have a chance after all, as Icarus is falling to his level. He exerts everything he has to go faster, his lungs already burning from the effort. But even this death-pace is not enough, and Icarus falls past him, into the deep blue below. Daedalus no longer cares to think, he dives right after.

Then there are a few seconds of the purest freefall Daedalus will ever experience in his life, and Daedalus won't remember any of them, because he hits the ocean with such force that he loses consciousness. He had tried to change, right before the impact, but his wings were already too saturated with water. He had fallen too far.

He wakes up on the shore some time later—how long, he doesn't know. His first thought is about a cloud that resembles something he can only vaguely recall, but this is immediately supplanted by concern for Icarus, who his heart insists is somewhere nearby, just has to be. So he combs the shore for hours, days even, almost the entirety of the northern coast he knows by heart before he is through—two of the longer stretches look strikingly similar and he sometimes confuses the one for the other.

He doesn't sleep for any of it, and starts to hallucinate heavily. They might have been welcomed, these phantasmal appearances, if they came in the guise of Icarus, but they are monsters, they are the darkest parts of Daedalus' mind projected out into the world to haunt him.

He does find one thing, a broken hourglass whose sand has all been let from out one of its sides. Unthinkingly, unfeelingly, he fills it up, grain by grain from the sand around him, as he stares out over the broad expanse in front of him and doesn't know what to make of it, can no longer join words to their meanings and thus can't have even the simplest of thoughts as he sits there.

But finally he arises, to address Apollo, sinking slowly into the ocean in the distance. The only thing he had yet to abandon, his God, he speaks to now with clenched fists. "This is what it's come to? I can't even tell my tears apart from the ocean anymore, it's all salt, it's all the same. What would you have me do, Apollo? Just sit around and let all these things happen to me, take it quietly? I wasn't made for that. I can take abuse, but I wasn't made for it. I have these people with the stupidest expectations for me, that everyone expects me to simply tolerate; I have a woman

I dearly love who won't feel the same way back; and I have this hypersensitivity that makes every stomped foot feel like an earthquake. Can you really expect that I just live with it? In all fairness, I don't think you can. But when I try to make a change, when I try to salvage what little I have left, you strike me down. Can you be this cruel, Apollo? I can't think of one single thing my son didn't mean to me, it was everything…" and Daedalus can't speak again for nearly an hour, but finally resumes again, "It's hard to believe in you, Apollo. Sometimes. It's hard to do a lot of things. I hope it's enjoyable for you, when I can't rise to the occasion. I hope you're getting use out of one simple man's misery." And with a final blunt lucidity: "I hope you understand if I don't want to talk to you for a while." So he doesn't talk. He just sits in silence as the sun sets on him.

He has to go back. His wings are damaged, and furthermore his son is lost—he has nothing to escape with. The distant shore of a foreign country is only taunting him, he has to turn his back on it and face all the people he tried to run away from again.

At first nobody knows any better. Daedalus has just been three days gone, and Icarus too, and everyone who noticed it was only mildly worried. Bathsheba had suspected some eccentric idiocy out of Daedalus, and that it was just taking longer to actualize itself, but that he would be back.

So when he comes back, nearly everyone is unconditionally sympathetic, until he explains what happened, upon their insistence. Because he doesn't lie. He has the opportunity, but instead he chooses to put an honest face on a disastrous event.

On account of his actions, since he thought to permanently neglect his office as the Magister of Science by running away, he is permanently banished from it. The King considers it treason that Daedalus acted the way he did, and won't have anything to do with him, even after the surprisingly close friendship they had nurtured in the previous five years.

Apollo won't answer the prayers that Daedalus won't offer.

And there's a long while where hanging his head in shame, when nobody else is watching, is the best thing that Daedalus can manage.

But the hardest moment is before any of this. It's the moment he stands in front of his own front door, before going in for the first time since running away. Before anybody knows what has happened yet. And *he could avoid that moment for a while, he can walk aimlessly through coasts and forests and streets and darkness, but eventually he has to come back. He hasn't slept for days and his face is still red from crying. He will have to find the words to tell his wife that he has killed their first child. He stares at the handle to the door for a while, trying to understand how a person was supposed to use it at times like these. A handle on things. Yet it has to be opened, so he opens it.*

Three years later, he was in the process of lifting his head again. But the ocean made it hard.

DER DRITTE TEIL: DIE AUFLÖSUNG

KAPITEL ELF: BEAR FACTS

"TELL ME A little about König Scherzeherz," Daedalus said to Sofia.

"Oh, well there's just so much to say, I wouldn't know where to start. I may need some time to think it over before I answer—no, never mind, I'm answering you now.

"He's a great... animal. I really wish that the beautiful things he says didn't sound like just so much noise to you, I think you would have an appreciation. As far as bear orators go, he's probably the best there ever was, although without a written record of bear history that's a fairly baseless claim I'm making. They do have a rather rich oral tradition, but you'd be surprised by how little oral tradition praises great orators.

"He takes exceptional care of me, I could go on at great lengths about all of that, but I'm fairly sure that whatever you're looking to hear, that isn't it. You want great deeds, don't you, the feats of strength and wit that make him a worthwhile addition to your repertoire of persons—I get the feeling that the fact that we know so few people, in the grand scheme of things, doesn't bother us because we've convinced ourselves that we've found and harnessed the top tier of them to ourselves. I'll try to put him in that tier for you, I wouldn't want to waste your time. There are a million things I could tell you about Scherzeherz, a million things I love about him, but they would almost all be boring to you, because they're all everyday things.

"So the highlights: Scherzeherz is of noble birth—this is something people still make a big deal about, right? Like, when I am remembered by posterity, it'll most likely be on account of my royal heritage, and the essential quality that that lends me. Anyway, Scherzeherz is royalty too, but he's a disenfranchised royalty, which is almost a more noteworthy tale than if he were in power—people expect dominance by kings, so that long, prosperous and effective rule becomes synonymous with a boring rule. When a king loses the reins—his sovereignty is gone, his throne is usurped, he is beheaded—this is the kind of story we tell as people, to whittle time.

"I simplified the war between the Niederbears and the Höherbears when I told you of it earlier, for time's sake. Allow me to lay out a few more details—there was a time when the two lived apart, harmoniously. Then there was a time when harmonious wasn't enough, and the Höherbear subjugated the Niederbear—that was the world that Scherzeherz was born into, the son of a king who had lost his kingdom.

"This is where his oratory prowess comes into play—the Höherbears, complacent in their victory, let him live. They were so confident in the thoroughness of their dominance that they let the strongest figure of a possible rebellion live, because they wanted to prove that the Niederbears would still be helpless.

"Scherzeherz took advantage of their hubris. By day Scherzeherz would endure the humiliation that the Höherbears orchestrated for him—this was before they had developed their dependency on Gibeahn food, mind you. They would make him gather salmon in the Tiber River, with all of the other vulgar bears. But by night, and long nights they were, the Höherbears would neglect the Niederbears, because they thought they could afford to. And that's when Scherzeherz would be organizing the resistance.

"Scherzeherz was subtle at first, amassing numbers and resources, biding his time. Then he brought about a time of flagrant sabotage, an incident of which involved a vital bear corn mill, and another that involved a slave uprising that had casualties for both parties. These activities nearly cost Scherzeherz his life, if not for the unconditional loyalty of some of his fellow Niederbears, who helped him avoid that fate. He realized the nature of his position—a crossroads. He could no longer proceed from the underground, or he would be killed for sure, and for naught. He either had to proceed no further or to surface, and proceed overtly. My brave Scherzeherz chose to wage open war with the Höherbears, even knowing how unsuccessful this had been the last time it was attempted—it had cost him his father, something he remembers well. He did it anyway—I think this displays most clearly his character, and is something I love dearly about him.

"Of course, he lost massively. Bloodier, and with more casualties than the first war. Scherzeherz himself fought valiantly, killing even more Höherbears than a recent epidemic that had been considered tragic beforehand, which is why one of Scherzeherz's titles is the Schwarzetöter, which roughly translates to 'more plague-like than the plague.' These are all facts that I paraphrased to you before. Ironically enough, after the battle was resolved in favor of the Höherbear, they let Scherzeherz live again, by the same rationale as before. Where it ends up is this, here, with him and the very few that survived the ordeal. And if you've seen how they still choose to follow him, through all the hell they've been, I hope you realize how indicative that is of his character," she finally concluded.

"The only thing that would make that a better story would be some romance, a little bear maiden caught in the midst of it all," Daedalus replied.

"No."

King Richard had been making all the appeals he knew how to make as a king, and inventing ones that he didn't. Either it was the longest night he'd ever experienced—and he'd experienced some long nights—or the morning had come and gone, but the sun had never deigned to dawn. If he were to guess, it should have been mid-afternoon as he sat in his Throne Room, fretting over the darkness that surrounded him. But he didn't know for sure—without the sun, his sense of time was useless. If it truly was just night, he was far too agitated to even think about sleeping.

He had a sinking suspicion that he was completely delusional, but his instinct was to ignore that suspicion and act in his capacity as king, which meant to protect the populace. At least that sounded like a good idea for his current situation. If the sun had disappeared, it was likely that humanity was in at least some amount of jeopardy.

Even though all the Magisters were gone, there were still servants that he could call on to do his bidding. Not that he trusted any of them. He expected that underneath their fair complexions they were all housing leprosy, they were spies sent to subvert his every whim, which was tragic because he was very fond of the proper fulfillment of his whim. He called them anyway, and hoped that some sense of honor or respect amongst even the Lepers would obey his command, which was the will of Apollo. The fact that the Lepers were diametrically opposed to the will of Apollo didn't cross his mind.

"Perfidaes!" he called into a vacuous silence, then waited the sufficient amount of time that even a traitor would take to respond. As his need became dire, he was realizing a few fundamental flaws in the structure of Castle Horeb. Namely that without any Magisters, the servants were hard to get a hold of, because they were housed deep in the bowels of Horeb, where they belonged. King in the head, servants in the bowels—the proper order of things, he always said. Ordinarily, he could have sent any one of his Magisters to retrieve them, but without a messenger they were far removed, with no easy means of communication. Horeb was like a man that needed to defecate, but had his spine entirely severed. At least that was the analogy that occurred to Richard, who was distracted for a while from the exigency of eternal night, as he considered how it was that paralytics realized that they had to do their natural duties. If he could ever reach someone again, he would tell them to have his scientists investigate that point, instead of the useless tranquilizers that cost him every useful peasant he once had at his disposal. He'd heard of people being paralyzed on account of horses, but he never thought he would be the victim. Years later, a Gibeahn scientist did in fact solve paralysis, because of arrangements originally made by King Richard. And so, as it often happened, another of life's greatest afflictions was only solved when it directly affected the comfort of a person in power. The trend was soon noticed, whence came the Gibeahn expression, "If you want a cure to your disease, go give it to the King."

Whether because he wanted to save his populace, or solve the mysteries of paralysis, Richard resolved for the first time in a very long time to leave his Throne Room through the front door. The thought that Perfidaes would hear him from three stories and numerous passages away soon occurred to him as unreasonable, although that recognition did not stop him from feeling a significant amount of resentment towards the man. When he left, when he violated so many years' worth of strident principle, it was with that resentment as the driving force.

Until that point, three rooms had comprised his life—the advent of a fourth room confused him to no end, and it was his anteroom, of all places. The long and twisting passage that he was accustomed to, the one that linked his Throne Room to the Augury Room and his bedroom, went to great lengths to avoid all interface with all other rooms, and the implications they contained—he had made an architectural commitment to his agoraphobia, like mortar over the windows of his life.

It was an intense experience, his anteroom—he had to re-conceive the entire world, which had been hard enough for him to birth the first time, the world being as large as it was. He had to grow a new compass. Vague recollections of what he had asked his architect to build him slowly entered his head. He didn't even remember that architect's name, much less the childhood fantasy of a castle that Richard had scribbled on a piece of paper to serve as the architect's guidance.

It was like becoming reacquainted with his childhood fantasies. Amid Penrose staircases, and internal flying buttresses, and so much other superfluity, he saw unicorns and honey and other sweet memories from his childhood, and knew all the while that he was insane, that he was seeing things wrong. But it had been so long since he'd seen anything new that he didn't know how to see things anymore, and there was nothing he could do about it. The only reason that he knew the basic direction of the servant's quarters was because of how he'd eavesdropped on Magisters complaining about the route they had to take to get there, and he usually let them carry on for a while before he castigated them for insubordination.

It wasn't long before he was completely lost. He even tried to retrace his steps, but that only disoriented him further. He began to panic, and in his despair he plaintively cried out, "Perfidaes!"

To his great surprise, Perfidaes answered. "Your Majesty? What are you doing so far from your Throne?" Perfidaes' voice was tinged not so much with worry—as it perhaps should have been—as with confusion.

"I think I'm trying to save Gibeah. Hypothetically, if I thought that the sun hadn't risen when it should have—not just tardy, but entirely unaccounted for—how crazy would I seem?"

"Not crazy at all, your Majesty. We actually noticed a while ago."

"Then why didn't you tell me? As ruler of the kingdom, my kingdom, I need to know when the sun is missing."

"Well…" The servant racked his brain for an excuse as if his life depended on it, because it probably did, with how erratic and irritable Richard was of late. Secretly the servants had hoped, with good reason, that they would just never hear from the King again, but Perfidaes knew well enough not to mention those hopes. "We were going to look into it on our own, and not concern you with it. We were under the impression… that you wouldn't notice, is all, and we didn't want to cause you any undue stress."

"You really thought I wouldn't notice? As if I've lost touch entirely with my kingdom?" The real reason that Richard kept referring to 'his' kingdom was not because it strengthened his argument to claim ownership, but because it comforted him to imagine that there was a kingdom that he had a personal connection to, and that he wasn't lonely, that he had something left to his name and that it happened to be an entire nation in his servitude. "Don't answer that. I don't even want to know what kinds of things go through your lowly vermin heads. Just… continue your investigations, but get everyone else in Gibeah, to the last man, inside this Castle. I feel a storm coming, and it's imperative, absolutely imperative, that the people are sheltered from it. And if you would provide me with a… an escort, to accompany my kingly presence, it would only be appropriate."

"Yes, your Majesty. Right away, your Majesty."

The night air was unseasonably cold, and even the bears were huddled together to preserve their meager warmth. If the bears were concerned by the curiosity of a missing sun, Daedalus couldn't perceive it. For his own part, it was a discomforting thing, but he felt that it had been a long time coming and he shouldn't be surprised.

The moon was far into the process of waning, the scant

light that it projected selectively illuminating the startled trees—not even the deepest of winters had denied them sunlight altogether—and the unkempt fur of the bears around him, the rough texture of which inexplicably awed Daedalus. If he had to make a guess, extrapolating from their behavior, like the disgruntled shuffling of their feet, the bears seemed restless. He had a strong urge to return to his precarious dwelling, but Sofia had requested his presence at a sort of meeting that was to be held.

His curiosity was extreme, as to the purpose of the meeting, but the cold was overwhelming and he couldn't come to terms with the thought of huddling with a bunch of bears, who were still massive for being of a smaller variety. He had nearly given in to the instinct of self-preservation, of running away, when Sofia appeared from around a grove of trees, accompanied closely by Scherzeherz. They made straight to the group, and were greeted as warmly as the frozen mammals could contrive. The women of the tribe were nowhere to be seen, and Daedalus could only assume they were hard at work on some custodial duties, or something to that effect.

Sofia gestured encouragingly to Scherzeherz, who only hesitated momentarily before descending into a plethora of guttural vocalisms. Either there was a somatic component to the bear language, or Scherzeherz had a hard time keeping still as he spoke. Daedalus was disappointed by the gradual realization that he still didn't know why he was out there in the cold, and Sofia wasn't giving any indication that she would help his confusion. She just looked off vacantly into some dark recess of the sky, avoiding Daedalus' imploring stare.

Whatever was being said, it must have been in the fabled Scherzeherz style, because the bears became uproarious, gnashing and prancing all over the place. Then they began moving, which was entirely unexpected by Daedalus. He had thought that maybe they were just dispersing to go home, but found out better when he was ushered by several of the bears to accompany them.

They had travelled nearly a half mile before Daedalus could finally get Sofia's attention, so he could learn the reason for the excursion. Sofia sounded as if she would be vehemently intractable at first, but finally conceded in a sigh: "Fine, I will tell you, but surely you've realized that I would rather keep the details of what we're doing secret, so it's unconscionable of you to insist like that."

"Secret? Obviously all the bears here know something I don't, unless that was all just a bunch of noise at the camp. Why is it that I'm the only one left in the dark?" Daedalus was genuinely indignant, and it was forcing its way into the tone of his voice.

"Because you're the only one who isn't trustworthy. But since you insist, here you go, just for you, just how you want it. We're going to invade Gibeah."

"Invade Gibeah? But you already have plenty of women, is that really necessary? And I don't really want to participate in the violent separation of women from their society, which I hope you can understand."

"Pay better attention to my choice of words. I said invade, not raid."

"Invade… for what?"

"To conquer. The Niederbear's star is on the rise, it's a new era, and the first step in this new era is to conquer the Gibeahnites."

"What changed? Because the sun is gone? Because that's the only change I've seen, and a star gone missing is not a star on the rise, sorry to say. I fail to understand why any of this is warranted or advisable. You said yourself that needlessly risking lives was out of the question for the Niederbears, that they only make necessary risks and ensure their survival."

"That was before," she said.

"Before what?"

"Before the bear suit."

Daedalus didn't respond on account of how emotional he

was, and instead just seethed in his own thoughts. So that was how it was. Their women weren't even a week pregnant, had yet to miss a period, and already the confidence of the Niederbear was manifoldly multiplied. Daedalus found a sickening amount of audacity in their decision, and since he couldn't induce himself to vomit and get it out of his system, he had to just suffer through it. Finally, he spoke: "And what makes you think that I'd like to take part in this? I'm not the type to happily comply while you conquer the city I know and love so well, the place I was born. I'm a little more patriotic than that, a little more loyal."

"You'll comply, whether it is happily or not. You could prove useful to us again. And don't make me laugh with your talk of being loyal, I'm not in the mood for humor."

"You mock my loyalty? Is this about three years ago? You said that you didn't blame me, that you could empathize. Could that have really been disingenuous? Is the truth finally coming out?"

"I just feel differently today. Today you are a treacherous coward, and you are coming with us to Gibeah whether you like it or not."

"I can't believe I pitied you back there," Daedalus said coldly. "I made you that suit because I saw that you were miserable and despairing, and I thought that I could help you out. Solely from the compassion of my heart—how misdirected it must have been, I didn't realize I was tossing a rope to a jackal."

"That's quite enough from you on that topic, unless you prefer to die. Your pity is the last thing I would ever want—you did something unforgiveable, when you abandoned Gibeah, and killed Bathsheba's son. The bond between a mother and child is just something unfathomable to you, you can't begin to understand its depth, its complexity, its importance—and you severed it from her. What you did to Gibeah is in the same vein, she is a mother that you disavowed. Your masculine shallowness has no sense for such things, so while I don't expect you to realize the gravity of your misdeeds, I won't ever forgive you for them either."

There wasn't much that could be said after that. The possibility of levity was far past, and Daedalus wasn't in the mood to provoke Sofia further. He shivered, whether from the cold or the abrupt, scathing way that Sofia had dealt with him. Fleeting desires to run away entered his mind, but he knew that the bears would be sent after him, and as bitterly self-righteous as he felt at that moment, he really didn't want to die for it. But the thought entered his mind.

Thus they made their silent way through the Cretan wilderness to Gibeah, with a reluctant Daedalus in tow.

"Can this really be all of them?" Richard was skeptical of the still sizeable crowd of Gibeahnites that was crowded into his Castle, a crowd that he had expected to be much larger. He had expected to have to give out salvation by lots, with some unfortunate souls on the wrong side of the moat, cursing their poor luck. He would have been a dealer of fate, one house he would spare and the other he would condemn, in the true fashion of the arbiter. He was partly disappointed that everyone got to be spared, partly disappointed that so few people were left under his reign. It seemed like a mistake.

"Are you sure you didn't miss a neighborhood? Or half of the city? I know that it's been a while since I've had the whole city over to the Castle, but I could have sworn that there were quite a few more peasants."

He was beginning to suspect that the problem was a faulty method of gathering them all—he really didn't know how it was done, but knew that it must have been wrong. Once again he imagined a bodily analogy, with himself as the head—he was always a disembodied head, free from the corruptibility of the body. Just like a head, he didn't know how to actually digest food, he only knew when the body was hungry, and when he should feed it. That was how he operated. It wasn't his job to digest food. But when the stomach started doing a slip-shod job of it, sending half-digested food in the wrong directions, a head had to step in. Even his impoverished knowledge of digestion had a few basic recommendations—he had given many suggestions on how to gather Gibeahnites in times of need, years before. One very good idea of his had involved a bell tower that was at the very pinnacle of Castle Horeb, and how it was to be rung in a particular fashion in states of emergencies. At least he thought he had a bell tower. Regardless, he doubted it had been rung.

"We assure you, your Majesty, this is everyone. Most of everyone, at least. There were a few dead people we found in their houses while summoning everyone, and we weren't sure if you wanted them too. We decided to err on the side of leaving dead people where they lie."

"How many dead people? Never mind, I don't want to know," King Richard said, deciding that for the moment he didn't wish to inflate his numbers with dead corpses. "So be it. If everyone's here, then I want Mars Magnate Wallace and Sezurus Magnate Stairwell at my side. Immediately."

In short time the King's bidding was done, and both Wallace and Stairwell were accounted for. They both looked a little haggard, because normally it would have been the middle of the night. But day or night was a distinction that Richard didn't consider anymore, because with the sun gone he felt and acted as if time didn't apply, save for the impending doom he felt in his heart.

The King said to his Magnates, "Good, good, the both of you are here. I'm going to address everyone, but I wanted to speak to the both of you first. We're going against great forces, evil forces, we're in a dire strait, and the two of you need to be on the top of your game."

"What are we going up against?" asked Stairwell, disinterestedly.

"I have no idea. But it's huge. We need to hole ourselves up in here as best as we can, we need sufficient provisions to survive this. It's a veritable draught, we have to open up the stores. There's a lot of tasks that need overseen, and you two are the ones for the job. Can I trust you?"

Wallace and Stairwell's reply was as vague as the question they were presented with. "Sure."

"I have to address the people now. But I want to see a mirror first. Somebody show me a mirror."

Chiron, a servant that had been appointed to the King to guide him through Horeb, knew that 'somebody' meant himself. "Right this way, your Highness."

Wallace and Stairwell followed along, since the details of their duties were none too specific. They knew that they might be called on at any second, if only to be yelled at for not clairvoyantly knowing their duties, and they wanted to be on hand whenever that happened. It was a considerable trek before the party came upon a bathroom, a wall of which was lined entirely by a crystalline mirror, worked ornately at its edges. Chiron showed Richard in, while the remainder of the group stayed outside.

In a few moments Richard had rushed out again, face flushed and eyes wide with terror. "Everybody, come with me. I command you to accompany me."

They obeyed, and followed into a bathroom whose volume was greater than nearly any house in Gibeah. Huge marble tiles were dissembling walls, and to their right were porcelain lavatories that shined brilliantly white. The room was perfect in its disuse—their intrusion was perhaps the first time the room had been entered since it was constructed. For whatever reason, dust collected nowhere, and spiders built no webs. Richard indicated the mirror. "This! This is what I've been looking for. I knew I looked like this."

Richard's reflection was ghastly pale, and every hair from his scalp was gone. Because of the red, irritated skin that was left behind, it looked as if every strand had been removed by hammer and chisel, rather than any natural cause. What hair was left on his face formed a sprawling, ragged beard, and his eyes were sunken deep into his skull, at the apogee of their orbits, with dark pouches marking their recession. Richard stared at all of his decrepit features like they were a possession he knew he always had, but couldn't find through years of searching—until just then, hidden in the guard of a friend once trusted. "What's different about this mirror from the mirror in my Throne Room? Are there different kinds of mirrors?"

Wallace, who was uninitiated in the daily dealings of the Castle, responded before anybody else could. "You don't have a mirror in your Throne Room."

"Of course I do, it's on the… eastern wall," Richard said. His hesitation before giving the cardinal direction of the wall was on account of so many years not considering the room in relation with the rest of the world.

"Your Majesty," said Chiron, who was taking it upon himself to resolve the King's confusion, his delusion. "What you have in your Throne Room is a portrait of yourself, which is in fact a different kind of mirror." This misconception of the King's was common knowledge amongst the Magisters, but they didn't disabuse the King because they were aware of the potential severity of his reaction. Whereas the servants that Richard rarely associated with, such as Chiron, were largely unaware of the danger, which alone could explain Chiron's tactlessness.

"I'll teach you, you insolent prick," said Richard.

"Teach me what?" Chiron asked, honestly confused.

"To respect a higher order!" With those words, Richard fell upon Chiron. Chiron was too unsuspecting to react, and Richard, who would have killed the servant if he had a lethal weapon at his disposal, tried to make do with his bare hands. The result was an impotently flailing mass on the ground, with Wallace and Stairwell just awkwardly standing around because they knew that interference would be stringently punished.

Eventually Chiron was able to worm his way loose, and chose to run away before the King could get a hold of him again. "You're lucky!" The King yelled after him. "If I can remember, you'll have quite the reward waiting for you when you get back!" The King turned to the mirror once more, adjusted his disheveled clothing, and, seeming satisfied, said, "Take me back to my people. Whichever one of you knows the way back."

As they made their way, Stairwell taking the lead, the King was obviously impressed by the scale and elegance of his Castle. "If I had only known," he would say. "Well, I don't know what I would have done, but I would have known. Is this place very large? Are there many places people can defend themselves from? These are all things that need to be kept in mind."

"No idea. I think the last person that would have known all that has fled," said Stairwell, referring to Chiron.

"Well I want people sent to scout it out, find out the lay of the land. There's no use being home if you don't get the home field advantage." They had finally reached the large Hall where all of Gibeah was milling about, and only after a few wrong turns. "Time is short. I must speak to them now."

In his education, lessons of rhetoric and public speaking were the most salient of memories that he had. His educators had known the task at hand, with Richard—they were shaping a future king. They would gather any drunkard they could find off the street, put them in a room, and make Richard expound a wide variety of topics at length. Meanwhile, his rhetoric tutor would sit in the front row with a large wooden stick, and correct him when he went astray, whether in form, content, or poise. As a result of the education he had received, Richard was the man he was that day—feeble, neurotic and confused, with blemishes pocking his body. And the people he spoke to best, and was most confident in dealing with, were alcoholics. But even at his most confident he had an ever-present fear of the switch, of wooden pain, in the back of his mind.

"Ladies and gentlemen!" he yelled.

The crowd continued as it was, largely oblivious, murmuring to itself. Richard was elevated by way of a floating staircase, where he found a potted plant, which he used to get their attention by throwing at the nearest person he could find. His aim was true, and as the man lay bleeding on the floor, he had everyone's attention.

"Ladies and gentlemen." Richard's eyes instantly became vitreous, and, just by the sight of them, anyone who had a deep understanding of the human psyche would have anticipated that he was about to make some very personal statements. "First and foremost, you're all drunk. I can only help you if you're drunk. From there I can make a long list of pathetic appeals that you will find irresistible. I'm actively forgetting right now the face that I saw in the mirror. I'm also forgetting my inability to tell the difference between a mirror and a picture—I'm suppressing all of those thoughts that would seem to detract from my right to stand in front of a crowd and demand its absolute attention.

"There's all of these lines, that I knew were cleaving their way through my forehead, and nothing would verify it for me until now. I don't know what I saw back there, I'm still making sense of it. It looked a lot like my father before he died, just consumption and the waste of a human face. Sallow eyes and a dead soul—the most vivid memory I have of his face is when I studied it for a long time after his beheading, back when I was still a child. Maybe that's the only memory I have of it, since it kind of replaced all the memories I had before it. I don't remember my father's love, his compassion, his fatherly concern, because I saw his severed head. I'm suppressing all of this, because these kinds of thoughts would just get in the way of effective rhetoric.

"But shouldn't I be worried? Are there health concerns associated with whatever is going on with my face? And my body? I haven't been comfortable in weeks. Just existing pains me. It's not a sharp pain, nothing honorable, nothing to be proud of, just a slow, dull annoyance that I can't escape for the life of me. Grinding me into nothing. There was a time I was leaning from my Throne to pick up something that I had dropped. And halfway down, of a sudden, I felt entirely well, the dull pain subsided. It was euphoric. I was deathly afraid that if I moved again, all the pain would come back. So I stayed that way, for days. By the end of it, my back was so horribly disjointed that I couldn't walk for more than three steps at a time. Just physically incapable. And that's one of my better memories of the past few years." After taking a moment to breathe, Richard visibly cringed. It was because he felt he had made a mistake with his rhetoric, and had been conditioned to expect the sting of a lash at such times. No one noticed but him.

When the pain never came, he diffidently continued, "I assure you, you dissolute drunkards, that you know nothing of the weight of responsibility of a king, of being in possession of a kingdom. Everyone is always wanting to defer things to a higher authority, it's a natural human impulse. When there's a discrepancy over the meaning of a word, it is resolved by turning to a dictionary. Why is this? A dictionary can be just as mendacious as all your drunken friends, and might arbitrarily take their side, defining *abulia* as 'the proper technique to castrate a bull. Etymology: *a-* away from, *bul-* bull, *-ia* having to do with balls.' And then your friend will all be like, 'That's right, because mania just means a man with balls, like me and you, we're manic, told you so.' And you'll just believe it all, because a dictionary told you to. I have to be everyone's dictionary. I can't follow that natural impulse of turning to a higher power, it ends with me. I have to deny my humanity, for all intents and purposes. Therefore, I am divinity. But between you and me, I don't know what abulia is. I'm only confiding in you because I doubt you'll remember when you sober up. But I honestly don't know—what do you think of that? Better yet, don't answer, because I'm suppressing all this.

"I am now the most convincing man ever. Watch this, watch this tact, it's nearly manipulation, I won't deceive you because it isn't worth the effort. You're drunk, yes, but there's a basic human element in you that wants to do better for itself, wants to do good. Most people take it to their grave unused, but it's there, its power can be pulled from. You're ashamed of yourself—half of the time you won't admit it, your pride interferes with announcing your shame. I know it doesn't make sense, but that's humanity for you. So listen closely as I make you an offer, or, more nearly, as I take advantage of this 'higher' impulse of yours. Yesterday your family was disappointed in you to no end—you used to be an upright man, people would turn to you in their times of need, and you had just the right clout to pull them out of it. But then one day you lost your grip on things, your footing, you fell to drinking, fell further to beating your family, and that bright future you had, the bright future that every strapping young fellow supposedly has when he emerges into the world, is lying in some corner of what used to be a respectable home. Broken now. What happened yesterday was that some stimulus—a smell from the past, a name that hasn't been heard in a while, something found in the bottom of a drawer—reminds your loved ones of happier days, and that is worse than forgetting them altogether. They get this look in their eyes—you're still mostly unreachable in your despondency, but you recognize this look, this broken manifestation of human expression, which nonetheless conveys its meaning in just *how broken it is*. Recognizing this look has sent you into the deepest low you've ever known. What I'm offering you today is a return, varnish for your tarnished image. I can make you stand again, I can fix your broken expression, I have all of the mysteries of paralysis solved and you need only hearken to me. What it's going to take is your compliance.

"The path back to righteousness isn't easy. There are imperious forces out there in the world that only serve to knock people over, to make beggars out of Apollo's disciples, and to take advantage of a man when he is down. Show me some courage—for the rest of this speech at least, I'm insisting that you have it in you. We're going to take every piece of material we can spare to fortify our defenses, and weather this storm. When it's passed, the sun will be shining again—yes, I know the sun's missing now, but don't dwell too long on such things—and we'll emerge free people, into rosemary fields that were promised long ago, the birthright of humanity. Am I understood?"

The response was resounding, and satisfied Richard in that it was the sound of a crowd twice as large as the one truly present. "Then please, you lowly drunkards, put down your bottles and start gathering everything you can find. Let's get organized."

They were outside the city wall, and Daedalus had a private laugh once more about its height. It was about the size with which a private man would try to unsuccessfully discomfit a prying neighbor. He finally saw firsthand how it was surmounted, the bears making only a few very simple but well-executed maneuvers, and then they were in the city proper. He was hauled bodily by Scherzeherz, along with Sofia, because their humanity was otherwise inadequate to keep up.

The streets were otherworldly dark. Daedalus had never seen them at night without a single lamp lit—his eyes had mostly adjusted to the dearth of light, but still the darkness was so present that it shifted liquidly in his vision. It seemed like large amorphous things were always moving about him, because his eyes were incapable of making a normal amount of sense of their environment. He felt like he was lying in his bed, eyes closed, drifting to sleep. And a soft breeze was blowing.

They arrived at the Castle without incident, the formidable stealth of the bears most likely being severe overkill for the impossibility of being spotted. The Castle alone emitted light, which had made it visible from miles away as the bears advanced, silent except for the sounds of exertion, rapid releases of breath that crystallized instantly on their muzzles.

When they drew up to the Castle's towering form, the bears paused, as if awaiting further command. Daedalus listened expectantly, and could only just hear Sofia whispering fervently into Scherzeherz's ear. Scherzeherz issued a terse command, and the bears made one concise circling of the Castle. When they were back at the start, Scherzeherz said something bestial to Sofia, to which she only warily agreed. Then, with one great leap, Scherzeherz was scaling the Castle, with Sofia and Daedalus clinging on for dear life. It was only after the ground was gone that Sofia turned to Daedalus, to speak for the first time since their conversation of loyalty earlier. "You're going to want to hold on tightly. Don't worry, it won't hurt him."

Scherzeherz was grunting deeply, and the city fell quickly beneath them, or at least the ephemeral pieces of it that were visible. Daedalus felt like it was his soul that was lifting, that his body had been left somewhere down below, blending in with the rest of the black, and that wherever it was it was fine, it was peaceful. The weight that he had to support by clinging melted away, there was just solace and weightlessness and an exhilarating ascension, though he only felt its exhilaration as if through a filter, a viscous substance, somewhere deep and below.

He had never felt so elated, not even the pig compared. Sofia's pressing warmth to his side was fine—she was a misguided, *acceptable person*, who deserved a lot of things from the world, and the world was listening, it would provide for her if it could. The bear was a channel. The stars had never appeared to him so bright. Maybe they *were* rising, all of them. In absolute darkness the stars fared the best, they were shining for all they were worth, and Daedalus had the thought that even though they were innumerable, the darkness still encompassed them all, the darkness was somehow *more than* innumerable, and in its absolute superiority it cushioned everything, an un-discriminating ether for everyone.

And then all of that ended when Scherzeherz burst through a window of the Castle, dragging his charges along behind him. The light rushed back in and whatever clarity Daedalus had before was lost, his body came back to him and it strongly desired the center of the earth. It was taking him with, sub-verting him with its base desires.

Only then did Daedalus realize that Sofia had been talking to him the whole time—her words entered him all at once with the light. She had been saying that it was all strange. The bears had to improvise, because the Castle had never been fortified before. Something was amiss. Scherzeherz was the only one who had the physical wherewithal to make the climb, and he did it with the two of them as burdens, no less. Everyone else was a mass of lassitude—Scherzeherz would have to open the Castle gate from the inside, if he wanted any support from his fellow Niederbears. Daedalus was fully expected to help with-out objection.

Although the King made a lot of noise about gathering ma-terials to defend the Castle, and was asking questions about the best places to defend from, he didn't do much besides talk about those things, and didn't seem to care if anything je said was actually acted upon. The main gate had been closed, and that was really the only precaution taken.

The Gibeahnites were giving Richard a wide berth, as he was acting exceptionally peculiar. A large percentage of the population had never seen the King before, just heard that he was prone to peculiar behavior, but those that knew him knew that he was being a very different kind of peculiar that day—not frenetic and senile, like he usually was, but walking around as if in a trance, and unleashing loud and raw utterances, be-fore falling prostrate to the ground in prayer, and then more utterances. As a result of his behavior, the Gibeahnites were actually listening to him with rapt attention, as he would go on and on.

"The divinity has departed this land. It was the result of ignoble, human impulses, an old crime committed once more, an eternal crime. The divinity was cast down by human hands. The darkness is upon us. Do not despair—the divinity that departed from us then is imparted once more to me, it will make a last stand here, so long as your faith buffers it. Have faith."

People were beginning to notice the bird shit that covered large portions of his body, and the entailed stench. "Our Mars Magnate, our god of war, to us, please!" he yelled.

Wallace had been reclining against one of the statues that lined the wings of the Hall, trying to distance himself as much as he could from the present, but the present beckoned him to the center of the Hall, to the King, surrounded by a throng of Gibeahnites.

"Times without number, our Mars Magnate has proven that no force could best him—if there's one thing that wizened features should connote, it is a perseverance that the world could not defeat. Age is not feebleness. He is a model citizen, fastidious, as shown by his exemplary service as a gate sentry. All those peaceful nights that you found sleep are owed to him, though he would not take the credit, for he is modest, as shown by the unassuming way that his name has not dispersed to the four corners of the world—no, some of the greatest people you will never hear a single word about, because inherent in greatness is humility. He is courageous— twice he dared venture into Samsonbear territory, to retrieve flowers, and twice he was the sole survivor." Stairwell was leaning against a statue of his own. "Twice he carried out what no other man could, which is the mark of Providence. Fortune smiles on this man. And for all these reasons and more, I present to you your champion, your model citizen, who will see us through these dark times.

"Stand your guard, Mars Magnate, for our trials and tribulations are descending the stairs now. This is our proving ground."

For all of these things that he said, and that he seemed to be communing with divinity, the people whispered amongst themselves, "Is Richard also among the prophets?" Whence came the expression.

Everyone's attention was turned to the staircase, the presence of which was the dominant feature of the Hall. With no consideration at all it passed over floor after floor, not deigning to lead to any of them, until it disappeared into the altitude, like it connected to heaven and the road to heaven was too sacred for any deviation. It was forebodingly empty when they all turned to it, but as they listened the sounds of movement seemed to issue from it, faintly at first, but gradually accumulating along with the anxiousness of the Gibeahnites, until it was veritably roaring. Richard produced a sword—from where, nobody knew, because their attention was diverted. He bestowed it on Wallace, who responded as if startled awake. "Your weapon, our last hope. You have to make us proud, Wallace."

In a flourish, Scherzeherz entered view, bounding over the entire last flight of steps. He thudded resonantly on the marble floor, ushering in a silence that would last until panic would flood its banks, some time later. The King continued to speak, but it seemed to be a part of the silence, not a violation of it. "We have produced our champion, enemy, and if I'm not mistaken, you've produced yours. And here it is. This will be the resolution of everything between us. I pray for you, enemy, I really do, because divinity is on our side. But of course you'll want proof." With those words he presented Wallace, who by then had the space of nearly the whole Hall constricting around him. The Gibeahnites had universally pressed themselves against the four walls, to watch but to otherwise be unaffiliated with the spectacle.

Sofia and Daedalus dismounted from Scherzeherz and surreptitiously joined the crowd, which was receptive in its dumb fixation on the apparition of a bear and Wallace. These are the thoughts of Wallace, arms weighed down by the weight of the dastardly sword, as Scherzeherz barreled toward him at the speed of nil recurring:

"Was it ten years ago or twenty, that I lost my vision? Will I ever know? Everything blurs together, things become impossible to sort. Sundays are a blessing. It's hard living with a mauled family. My son won't take after me, not with all those bite marks, not with such mutilation. He doesn't have my nose, not anymore. He used to. My wife, self-conscious about missing half of her face. I don't think I've slept for a very long time, not since Sunday. Sundays are a blessing. Day of rest. The week was made wrong, there should be more days like Sunday in it. Which means that the world was made wrong, since the way the week was made was based on the way the world was made. Prunes. I'm no longer capable of digesting any of the foods that I love. Wasn't I three when my mother came back from the market, sunlight haloing her hair, and she hadn't bought a thing at all? Three whole hours at the market, didn't buy a thing. Please tell me that I was three, I don't want to be losing my grip on things. And Jamal. Or was it Marcus? Was it Marcus or Jamal that stole the turkey from the Grand Feast, without anybody noticing? How do I know the story if no one noticed? If anyone asks, it was Marcus. I'll tell them Marcus. And it must have been on a Sunday that it happened, I wouldn't know the unknowable if it wasn't a Sunday that it happened. Sundays are a blessing."

As these thoughts went through his mind, his body was dead still, even as moment by moment Scherzeherz was getting closer. To the crowd it looked like the purist display of courage they had ever seen, to be so unmoving in the face of imminent danger, and their hopes grew splendidly, expecting something epic to be nearly occurring.

He didn't even raise his sword an inch in defense, Scherzeherz just swung, unimpeded, and took Wallace's head clean off, with one of his great paws. Scherzeherz was surprised by the facility at which it came off. The humans had made such a big deal out of that one man in particular, so he had expected something more.

Then everyone panicked, fleeing in every direction, pressing people even closer to the walls, until those closest to the perimeter were suffocating from the pressure. Amidst all the chaos Scherzeherz was able to lunge through the large doorway that was opposite the staircase, splintering it apart, to continue to the place that he knew the gate-release to be.

When the bear was gone, everyone had thought that their luck had come through after all, that their death was not the object of all these bear-happenings, like they had suspected it to be. They collectively sighed, in great relief. Until Scherzeherz returned with the whole Niederbear tribe, amplifying the pandemonium to a theretofore unheard of level.

The bears made quick work of blockading all channels of escape, including the door they had come from, the staircase, and several other side-passages that led to other parts of the Castle. The humans were too unorganized to present a challenge to their moves, with most people only concentrating on how loudly they could scream. Stairwell was sitting atop one of the bears, but there were still a score of others that nobody dared challenge. When everything was in place, Sofia resurfaced from the crowd and apparently took control once more. Richard hadn't moved from where he stood prophesying just moments before, so was easy to locate by Scherzeherz. The bear king placed the human king in the very center of the Hall, which was still vacant, save Wallace's limp form and blood. Daedalus timidly came forth too, since he felt out of place with the delirious Gibeahnites.

A thick gauze of incredulity covered Richard's face. "Sofia, could it really be you, come back to me after so long? I can't believe it, that you've really returned. Captive by the bears, they've put you up to this." All vestiges of the confident voice with which he had been prophesying had left him.

Sofia's laugh was so cold that it made all of Daedalus' hair stand on end. "No, Richard. I've come back to Gibeah, not to you."

"What... what do you mean?" Richard's face was all confused tenderness, as it probed the stolid expression of Sofia. "I've been dreaming day and night of your return, devising ways to get you back. Surely, you've felt the same?"

Sofia turned to address someone else, a bear, who was making fearful waves of the crowd by circumnavigating the walls. "You've found the winch by now, haven't you Gregor?" The bear grunted something in reply. Then there was a rattling sound from above, and as Daedalus looked up he saw a platform lowering steadily to their level, suspended by chains.

"What on earth is this contraption?" Richard asked.

"It's a guillotine that you had installed yourself, to make public spectacles, dear. We're about to have one ourselves."

Richard in no way recollected having a guillotine installed in his Great Hall. If he had known about it, he surely would have used it—he could think of hundreds of times from his past when a guillotine would have been useful to him. Its advent just furthered his confusion.

The King adopted a patriarchal tone, seemingly out of nowhere. "You won't harm the people of Gibeah. We command that they go unharmed." The Royal We appeared from nowhere.

Sofia wasn't impressed. "We're not here to harm the Gibeahnites, we're here to rule them. They're perfectly safe, except for the harm they do themselves avoiding imagined harm. We're here for you, Richard, to rectify your misdeeds of the past. This guillotine is for you alone." As she spoke, it finally came to rest, its minimalist simplicity at a stark contrast with the ornateness of the room around it. It was just a block with a groove, crowned by a long, wooden frame, garnished with a triangular blade, atop a platform.

Richard turned his confusion to Daedalus. "Surely this is your treachery, Daedalus. This guillotine should have been your fate, if there was any justice in the world. You have one last chance to redeem yourself, by sparing our Majesty."

Daedalus' face was horribly contorted. He was looking from Sofia, defiant, to Richard, suppliant, to Scherzeherz, licking something from his feet disinterestedly. Since it seemed that Sofia would allow him a response, he proffered one that he knew was most likely out of line, though he no longer cared: "First of all, that you would expect fealty from someone that you've treated like you've treated me, Richard, is just something I don't understand. But I don't blame you—you're in a difficult place, you're lashing out. I assure you that I'm not in any position to save you—I'm more of a prisoner than your wife. For Sofia, though, I reserve a great quantity of blame."

She instantly became indignant, and began to stalk after him, but she did it slowly, with great affected dignity, which allowed Daedalus to continue as he retreated. "Did you say that you're rectifying some misdeed or another, Sofia? It's a fine way that you've figured out to do that, here. Replacing one tyrant with another. I very nearly can't believe that you've come here to do this, to kill Richard, but from what I've recently come to learn of you, I don't know what else I should have expected. You just scathingly accused me, it couldn't have been more than two hours ago, of disloyalty to the kingdom, and to my son. What is it that you imagine you're doing now? What sort of contrivance of logic allows you to live with yourself? Is it because you imagine yourself as the future of your kingdom, that you do not think that you are betraying it? Is that how I'm disloyal, that I didn't have the audacity to supplant the government that I defied? I'll keep that in mind—I'm just finally learning the proper way to live in this world, even after all my years. And Richard is, by all rights, as close to you as Icarus was to me. That same look in Richard's eyes," and Daedalus pointed to a scared, confused Richard, even though he didn't want to, "is nearly the same look my son made while falling through the air. The only difference I can see is that it broke my heart so see those eyes, from Icarus—it still breaks my heart, whenever I can't manage to sufficiently distract myself by keeping busy. When I'm idle, my heart is broken. I will forever be busy, then. Your heart, on the other hand, seems well. Let me conclude, then, by saying that you are a conscienceless hypocrite—but do whatever you want. I just want no part in it. I shouldn't have been dragged here. I would have done better spending more time with the ocean."

When Sofia was quite sure that Daedalus was done speaking, she let off stalking him, and returned to Richard. "Get him into place," she commanded several nearby bears. As they wrestled him to the guillotine, Richard was pleading, and most likely would have been crying if all the moisture of his body hadn't been dried out of him through the desert of his skin. "Please, Sofia, I don't know what I've done for you to be this way towards me. I love you, it's always been you. I made a Queen out of you. Anything you asked for, I could have done for you. I would have made you a city. Sofia? Please?"

Sofia refused to respond, she just stood quietly, arms crossed, while Richard was situated by bears. And when it was all arranged, she said, "Everyone! Everyone, you have to watch now. This is a public spectacle." And on her signal, Scherzeherz let the blade fall.

KAPITEL ZWÖLF: HUMAN RESOLVE

"HEAR YE, HEAR ye," cried a commoner into the desolate streets of Gibeah. "I am here today to speak of the abuses of our government.

"There has been much ado lately about the coup against our King, just days ago. There has been celebration for a tyrant being deposed, and for the new reign of promises that has been showered on our heads ever since. Our new leaders talk about equality, opportunity, happiness. But keep in mind, brethren, that all reign comes from above—so long as there is both a firmament and an earth, a high and a low, the poor and the rich, equality does not exist. Heaven must first be subsumed by the world.

"I imagine that I will be censored tomorrow, that I will end up dead in a gutter somewhere, if I say what I mean to say. I feel that it needs to be said anyway—though it is most likely in vain, I will give my life for something, for just the possibility that some truth might be heard. Freedom of expression means everything. And it will be a long fight, by expression itself, through which that freedom is obtained. Expect it to be hindered at every step, my brothers.

"There is no difference between our old ruler and our new.

The ursine addition to our sovereign is not a return to nature, but a nearly equivalent substitution of brutality for bestiality.

"You say that the transgressions of the past would make any change a welcome one. Transgressions like the Pact of 458, which prevents the marriage of nobility to commoners. Love has to know bounds. Transgressions like the Atrocious Acts, which introduced exorbitant taxes on both alcohol and tea, nearly the only sanitary means of sustenance that we can reasonably afford. Starvation and sickness are our lot. And the Flower Draft, which cost us the lives of many sons. We have no future. These are all substantial names, these laws, with substantial consequences. Names that we can invoke whenever we wish to lament our deplorable state.

"But I assure you, brothers, that none of these are the cause of our woes. They are identifiable faces, yes, but the faces of phantoms. A phantom has never been the cause of the injustice leveled against us poor commoners. I repeat, they are not causes, but symptoms. What the true cause is, it is hard to say. It is a mess of convoluted wires above our heads, seemingly inaccessible to all but the most heinous of people, those that utilize it to keep us in our place, subjugated.

"It is not important, though, to make sense of it. We do not need to know *why* we are miserable to know *that* we are miserable. Whatever its cause may be, dying in the streets of starvation, of cold, of dehumanization, cannot be justified. When my son can't get a proper education, when my father can't get proper medical attention, something has gone awry.

"I am with you, in the respect that I don't know the answers. I can't make sense of any of this intractable confusion called life. There are many of you, too many of you, that will *claim* to know the answers, but this is often the most telling indication of cluelessness, of a shamelessly ignored aporia.

"Take a second to revel in the aporia with me.

"Apollo's fate is of the greatest import. We still need to make sense of it. I want you to make a pact with me, right here, right now, that we will try harder. A pact that, whenever we see oppression, we will do what is in our power to over-throw it. A pact that, whenever we encounter the impover-ished and defamed, we will lend a hand to those that are down. A pact that we will never just be content with the answers we have, but will always try harder to further our understanding of things. I don't think I exaggerate when I say that compla-cency is our worst enemy.

"Not ourselves. I always mentally gag when I hear the ex-pression 'my own worst enemy.' Not just because I have dif-ficulty swallowing every platitude, but this one in particular. Love yourself. Whatever it takes. Have some self-respect, and have some ambition. Then, and only then, will we possibly have our answers someday. And we'll be fine."

A small crowd had drawn around the eulogizer, but a ma-jority of the people would rush by, on their way to some er-rand or another. For the moment, the streets of Gibeah were pitch black, because the normal lamp schedule had been main-tained. Even in the absence of the sun, the lamps were lit sometime after vespers and extinguished around dawn, or at least the best approximations of both. Thus it was only really possible for the Gibeahnites to see where they were going at night. And since they had a predisposition to see where they were going, at least when they were sober, a large portion had adapted to becoming active at 'night,' though they still had to do their jobs at 'day.' It was a confusing time.

One of the new excuses for shirking duties plaguing Gi-beah lately was to feign deafness. In the absence of the sun, the Niederreign—so the Niederbear's new government was called—had instated a bell system to wake people up at the right hours, but it was exceedingly easy to claim to have slept through all of their pleasant jingling. At least much easier than claiming temporary blindness, back in the days of the sun. Not to say it wasn't often done, pretending to be blind—it was just much more difficult to provide plausible explanations, in those days.

In the Castle, tensions were high. Richard had bled a lot more than anyone had expected, and left a dark stain in the Great Hall that nothing could get out, alongside the smaller but still morbid stain of Wallace. The Niederbears were experiencing, for the first time in a long time, the difficulties of ruling a bunch of unruly people. Furthermore, although König Scherzeherz was technically the paragon of rule, all of his decrees had to be translated by Sofia, who willfully took liberty with their contents. Scherzeherz must not have been entirely ignorant of her sway, because the two of them were beginning to feud. In the inchoate form of their growing disagreements, it seemed as if Sofia was attempting to speak the bear language herself, the way she barked.

Daedalus had been moping about, haunting the Castle because he wasn't allowed to leave it. He was constantly objecting to Sofia that his presence was pointless—the whole reason he had been forced to partake in the invasion of the Castle was that he might 'prove useful,' and he hadn't been called on for anything at all. He told Sofia that it would always be the case, that she could keep him around all she wanted, but unless there was some other animal she suddenly had the desire to copulate with, he didn't see any good reason to be there. He was mostly ignored. What burned him the most was that ever since he had resolved to take control of his life, when the bears had liberated him from Horeb, nothing had changed. He was still just as imprisoned. Ironically, by the same bears, in Horeb.

He had taken to reading old documents in the Horeb records, so that he was largely oblivious to the developments of the outside world, both environmentally and politically. The fact that no sun existed was beginning to concern some farmers, who were sowing their fields to the light of a lamp. Only after all the seeds were cast did it occur to them that they might not fare so well. And the stores of the previous harvest were near depleted. The rampant communicability of the fear of a shortage led to ruinous speculation, with the price of wheat quadrupling in a matter of days. The Lepers were blamed.

While all of that was happening, as if to exacerbate the situation, the city was parceled out to the Niederbears—who wanted to be referred to as 'Overlords'—into fifty demesnes, drawn up by one of the Niederbear woman. Shortly after the Niederreign had established itself, it sent after all the women it had left behind in its old territory, which they entirely abandoned. All that remained was the vacuous shells of ill-conceived houses and the telltale signs of bygone ravenous feasts.

The Gibeahnites weren't taking kindly to their Overlords. It wasn't really the concept of the Overlord that bothered them, since it was a concept which was long familiar in Gibeah. Rather, it was the title itself, which had two instances of superiority in one word, first *over*, then *lord*. One or the other would have been tolerable, but the conjunction was provocative to the sensibilities of the Gibeahnites.

One Gibeahnite would sardonically say to another, while blindly sowing his field by lamplight, "So, I hear Lord-Over-Highness-Grand-Beacon of Hope Hansel is raising the tithe to twenty percent of our crop. The outrage, wouldn't you say, Aeneas? Leave it to a bear to not understand that tithe means tenth. Now, I know I'm not supposed to be gainsaying[1] any of the royalty or anything, but if I can't grow no crops whatsoever, how am I supposed to be able to afford twenty percent? It's because these damned bears eat so much, they need more of our food. I thought the old Magister of Public Safety, our old lord, was a lard-ass, but these bears could eat him under a table. Out of my pocket. And how, pray tell, are we supposed to worship anymore? You can't very well go throwing bears into the Bear Maze in a world ruled by bears, can you. They probably wouldn't take kindly to it. But where does that leave us? Has no one told the Niederreign that we need a new way of

[1]   Probably meant 'speaking badly of.'

showin' the gods we're still thinking about them, since the old way's become so awkward? Man, I don't have a mind for such things, I'm just a farmer that most likely has nothing left to his life but to starve, lucky me."

The sentiment was widespread. The bears did eat a lot. So when the Höherbear announced that it was to invade Gibeah, the Gibeahnites were only far too willing to provide for their ease of conquer. The Niederreign had tried to prevent the diffusion of the announcement—the Höherbear had the kind of audacity that, instead of invading silently after the disappearance of the sun like the Niederbear, preferred to announce its plans of invasion to its victims two weeks in advance, followed by a reminder when two days remained, and one last reminder at two hours, so that no mistake was made about when they would arrive. The content of the announcements proved hard to suppress by the Niederreign, and through some unknown fissure in their seaworthiness the Gibeahnites knew, with certainty, when they should expect their new rulers.

The Niederbears were not the type to go down without a fight. They employed nearly the entirety of the Gibeahn population to shore up the city walls—at least that was how they attempted to employ the Gibeahnites, but as the following conversation between a Gibeahn commoner and another illustrates, as they 'labored' on the wall, obedience couldn't be expected from even the most rightfully subjugated of people.

They were two elderly men, whose seniority allowed them to avoid the Flower Draft but did not prevent them from being enlisted to fortify the wall. They had been assigned a hundred-foot section, just like hundreds of other groups like them, and within their section fell ten houses that were propped up shabbily against the wall, even leaning outside of the city where their heights exceeded the wall's height. They had to haul enormous stones through people's homes, up their dilapidated staircases, and out the window, where they could be deposited at the top. While they were dragging one of those large stones, one said to the other, "I was listening the other day to some curbside prophet, who was talking about how the Niederreign is just as bad as Ol' King Dick was. I absolutely agree. In all my life I've never had to build a wall, and I almost made it all the way through, but just look at me now, building what's supposed to be the largest wall this city's ever seen. If we'll ever actually see it—I'm still kinda fretting about the sun. Where did these stones come from, anyway? I didn't think Gibeah could afford this kind of renovating. Anyway, I think I agree with that prophet, all these leaders we got now are bad news— the Höherbears, on the other hand, sound like the real deal. I don't know how you feel on the subject, perhaps I should have asked first, but my loyalty doesn't lie with the Niederbears. You can sell me out, if you want. I don't care anymore."

"I'm not about to sell out nobody, don't you fret. I agree with you about agreeing with that prophet. You've heard talk, then, of the resistance?"

"Oh, watch out, Martin, there's something you might trip on."

"I can't see around this damned rock. My neck isn't what it used to be. You're going to have to direct me to avoid it."

"Just a little to your left."

"Whoa! I thought you told me a little to my left?"

"No, I meant that it was sitting a little to your left. Are you alright?"

"I'm fine. What is it, what did I trip on?"

"I don't know. But whatever it is, it's starting to cry, so we should move on quickly. These people really should keep their houses tidier, you never know when someone's going to need to build a wall outside your upstairs window."

"No truer words have ever been said. Now, I was saying about the resistance…"

"Oh, right. I've heard about it. A lot of talk about how we should band together, use our combined strength to overthrow oppression, and all of that highfalutin jargon. There's always that kind of talk, but at the end of the day nobody follows through, they just do what they're told, out of fear. I mean, look what we're doing here, and it's not like we're getting anything out of it."

"What's keeping us, then? That bear they have watching over us, he's got some forty other groups to watch over besides us. Is there really any way he can do an effective job of it? I mean, I feel like he's watching my every move, I can see his giant claws tearing me apart something fierce, but is any of that realistic? You don't even have to answer, I've been feeling that way my whole life, like there's someone always over my shoulder, and it just can't be shaken. Doesn't matter whether it's realistic or not."

"So what does that mean? Are we just going to wall the Höherbears out? We might as well be walling ourselves in."

"Here, just set this down over there, on whatever that is, so it's easier to pick up when we pick it back up again. Yeah, right there."

"Why are we putting it down? You tired?"

"I'm tired, yeah, but tired as I've always been. That ain't the reason. I just can't think while I'm toiling away like that, and I want to do some deliberating. You wanted to know if we were just going to wall those Höherbears out… I don't know. I think so. Probably. We're just two people. If everyone was in on it, well I'd feel like we could do it, be a resistance and all, but there will always be those people that chicken out, and the whole thing will fall through. So we don't want to participate, lest we fall with them."

"Let's pick our rock up."

"You just hold on there! I'm not done thinking. Accompany me to our window, over here. Let's see if we can discover what our laboring neighbor is up to. It's darkness, pure darkness out here. This is probably what being born in reverse would be like, as I lean out the window like this. Or perhaps the opposite holds, maybe this is what being born is like. It's hard to say which would be light and which would be dark, between the world and the womb, don't you think? Never mind. I can see light, coming out of yonder window, but it's empty... no, wait. I see shadows, I see movement... there he is, out the window! And he's looking out at us, he's waving! Actually, I can't really tell, truth be told. But it feels like he's waving at us. Oh, I could just paint this, there's something so subtly poignant in the array of it all."

"You started talking different, Monad."

"Just go with it. I've been living too long not to go where the wind takes me, does that make sense? And the wind is taking me to a place that I want to draw our laboring neighbor, leaning out into the midnight air at some unknown hour of the day waving at nothing more than a general direction, because there's no way that we're any more perceptible to him than he is to us, yet he waves anyway—the brazenness, the wistfulness! The humanity. I feel like there's a lot of humanity in what he's doing now, and nothing fills a canvas better, in my opinion. Do these people have utensils I could paint with?"

"I don't see anything. Unless... whatever we set the rock on is leaking out something black, will that do for you?"

"That's pretty much the only color I need to depict this world, so it will do fine. And since it is so close to our stone anyway, I will use the stone as my canvas. And since nothing better presents itself as a brush, I will use my hands."

"What on earth could you be painting? That's just a bunch of scribbles, what are you doing? You must see things in a strange way. I didn't see anything like that when I followed you to look out the window. Are you sure you even know how to paint?"

"I take liberties every now and then. You'll have to forgive me my abstruseness, but I assure you that what I'm doing here is far more real, far more what I saw, than the light that entered our window, journeying from his. That light is a vagabond and a fraud, compared to this."

"You've truly lost it."

"Lost it or not, I'm done. There you have it. And we've wasted a considerable amount of time, while I've been painting and you've been criticizing my skills of representation. Grab the other end."

"Where are you taking it? Wait, we're using this, after you've spent so much time on it?"

"It's fine. It's how I wanted it all along—there's actually something I find very appealing in the idea. I once heard someone say that the work done for another, for the Niederreign or whoever might be importuning our labor, is entirely foreign to us, that we put nothing of ourselves into it. We are nothing but estranged. I'd like to think I am refuting that in my own little way, just now."

"Whatever you say."

"Just lower it gently out the window, now... whoa! What have you done? What did you set it on, on your end?"

"I couldn't tell. Everything out here looks the same."

"Did you hear that crash? It fell all the way to the bottom, didn't it."

"What should we do?"

"... Go get another one."

Needless to say, when the Höherbears arrived, at a time that everybody expected, there was no resistance. At least none that could be reasonably attributed to the Gibeahnites. The wall, even after being labored on for a full week, was the same manageable height as when the work had started. The dropped bricks of many incompetent builders even facilitated their climb, acting as a makeshift ramp. The Höherbears poured into Gibeah in their excessive numbers, as simple as that.

The Niederbear chose to defend the Castle, so that circumstances were harshly similar to just a month prior, except that this time the Gibeahnites were left in their houses to fend for themselves. This ended up being inconsequential for the Gibeahnites, because the Höherbear was an extremely goal-oriented tribe that recognized who was a threat and who wasn't, so made their way straight to the Castle.

Also in stark contrast to the Niederbear methodology was how the Höherbear took the Castle. Instead of scaling it and accessing it from some obscure entry point, they chose to ram the main gate, without even checking to see if it was barricaded first. To that end, they brought an enormous battering ram, fashioned from the oldest tree in the Cretan forest, which had acted as a gondola for the entire Höherbear nobility until they arrived at the gate. At that point, the nobility was deferentially assisted from its perch atop the ram, and then the Höherbears lifted it once more to commence. A slight complication arose when the diameter of the tree proved to be larger than the width of the gate, but it was quickly resolved and the gate split shatteringly into many metal and wooden fractions.

Leroy was a noted fisherman amongst the Gibeahn population. A large quantity of the food that was stolen during Bear Raids came from his wares, but he was a longsuffering fellow who would return to the river to restore his depleted inventory, without complaint. The fisherman's way of life had entered deeply into his mentality—he was apt to, whenever he wanted something, stop and stare unblinkingly at some remote thing in his vision, for sometimes an hour at a time. Patiently, ever patiently. It didn't matter what it was—if his friend had a delicious-looking wedge of cheese as they sat together for lunch, or if there was some comely maiden that piqued his heavily enduring virginity—he would stop and stare. It was how he was conditioned. Also, whenever he saw an opportunity, he would snap to attention, as if he had some snaring hook at the far end of some extremity of his, and he would make sudden and struggling grasps at things. Because of that proclivity of his, what little friends stuck by him only tolerated his presence when they felt capable of managing his startling nature. Thus he wasn't invited to any weddings, or funerals, nor to any occasion on days when his friends were feeling exceptionally vulnerable. For that reason he never dealt with people in poor moods, so never developed a capacity for consoling.

In the week prior to the Höherbear invasion, Leroy had been having a golden age. The eternal night was just as confusing to the fish as to their human counterparts, and as a result they were always biting. It was thought that as many as seven species of fish were harvested to extinction in the Golden Age Week of Leroy, a natural tragedy perhaps only morally offset by the fact that his contribution likely singlehandedly prevented the starvation of the Gibeahn populace, on account of its massively failed harvest of crops.

So, the day of the Höherbear invasion, he had been drifting in his boat down a wide Cretan river that he had special permission to be on. Gibeahnites leaving the city was even more strictly prohibited by the Niederreign than it had been by King Richard, but the bears were more than willing to make exceptions for fishermen. He had been assiduously hauling in catch after catch, of what he could only assume were fish. The size and the kind were impossible to verify with no light to see with, so everything was tossed indiscriminately into a writhing pile. It was a grand old time until he heard strange noises issuing from one of the banks, some twenty yards in the distance. Looking in that direction achieved him nothing, so he listened intently—it was by the way the still-flopping fish collectively went into paroxysms of fear that Leroy knew that there were bears coming toward him, in a very large quantity. His long dealings with fish taught him those sorts of things. He frantically grabbed for the oars, which slipped out of his hands multiple times, as much from his fearful shaking as from the fish mucus that made his fingers practically useless for gripping. When he finally had them secured, it was with more profanities than strokes that he crossed the river to the opposite bank, agitating the river into a frenzied wake that seemed to invigorate the invisible bears, who began roaring.

As he drew up on the bank, and stumbled over the boat's

siding, there were a few moments that he thought to drag the boat along after him. He finally had a firm grip on the prow of his vessel, and even moved it a few cubits up the steep embankment, but the boat was digging deeper and deeper into the soil with every inch, because of the couple hundred pounds of fish that resided within it, pushing it down. He hesitated irrationally at the thought of leaving such a valuable load there, for the bears to despoil. Ire filled his every pore. But then he heard the bears reach his shore, splashing flagrantly, and decided that it perhaps wasn't worth his life. So he ran.

His greatest surprise was when the bears did not stop for the fish, but continued to pursue him as he ran through the forest. Before that terrible realization, Leroy's plan had been to stop a good quarter of a mile away, catch his breath, and slowly return to his river, to assess the damage that may have been done. But that plan shattered instantly—apparently the bears wanted nothing at all of the fish, and that boded horribly for Leroy.

In spite of not being a particularly fit man, Leroy was more evasive than even he had thought himself to be. The bears were dementedly swift, something he also hadn't expected, but even as they surrounded him and commenced to close in around him, he found a way to escape, squirming on his hands and knees and slipping through the unwitting gaps between bear claws and jaws, to be free to run again. The bears were furious—at the beginning, they seemed to think of it as great sport, gaining up on a lowly human fisherman. But when they couldn't subdue him after many failed attempts, they started unleashing unearthly guttural sounds that would aurally permeate Leroy's mind even when the bears had to stop to breathe, so that he felt as if they were ever-present, ever-pressing. The sound fueled his desperate attempts at escape, it *was* his consciousness.

Somehow he managed to get to the city walls. Tactlessly he had come to a place where there was no gate for some distance, and he silently cursed his idiotic ways, thinking himself to be done for. But his conventional way of thinking, that he needed a gate to get through a wall, was vanquished when he saw the convenient ramp of bricks and stones surrounding the whole circumference of Gibeah. He was exuberant—he bounded up one of those piles and jumped from its pinnacle, without giving a thought as to where he might land, or how high he might be jumping from.

The answer was that he landed in the middle of a street, some fifteen feet lower, most of the fall being absorbed by his face. And as he lay there, bleeding profusely, his thoughts were that he surely was done for, that the bears were right behind him and they'd have their devilish bear-ways with his person. But the ending never came. Eventually he propped himself up to survey his surroundings, but they were just the comfortable black that he'd come to associate with the world, nothing of bears. And he felt his luck very strongly.

Then he heard another strident roar, and the fear it inspired in him carried him all of the way to Castle Horeb.

An hour later, then, when the Höherbears came crashing through the gates of Horeb, Leroy was there on the other side, wondering what sort of moral crimes he possibly could have committed to deserve his misfortune. It should have occurred to him that the Höherbear invasion, an inevitability he was well aware of, would have the Castle as its goal. He was just incapable of thinking straight, with so many bears around all the time. When the gate came careening inward in all its shards, he was right there, prostrate body and supine heart, praying to whichever gods there were left in the sky that things might improve for him.

When the bears filed into the Castle they did overlook Leroy, which might have been a blessing, but it was mostly because he was obscured by a very large piece of wood that had fallen on top of him as he prayed, which had been slightly less than a blessing.

From his suffocating sanctuary he watched the proceedings. The bears that entered seemed to observe a decidedly strict decorum in everything they did—they marched in tempo, maintained lines, and looked to have some of the finest grooming afforded by the Cretan wilderness. Once through the gate they advanced steadily, and trailing this first contingent were bears of a slightly different demeanor than the rest. They stood upright while the former were on all fours, and they were covered in what must have been a bear's rendition of beautification. To Leroy they appeared fancy bears.

Suddenly a flash of light overtook everything, a dazzling and invasive light. The world hadn't seen such a brightness since the lost luster of the sun, which had left a month for the world's eyes to adjust to nearly total darkness. Leroy felt as if his eyes were being stabbed, until he retreated into the confines of his wreckage. From there he could just barely make out the figures of stunned bears, stumbling and pawing at their faces from the excruciating pain of the light. Only seconds later, ursine figures that looked to be far more composed blurred through their ranks, and blows and lashings were exchanged in a confusing jumble of light, accompanied by sounds of agony and surprise. Then the one set of bears disappeared into the seared edges of Leroy's vision, leaving only the first set of bears.

One of the bears that remained, who Leroy could make out better and better as time went on, roared explosively. He was a model specimen of a bear, a towering figure covered in scars where no fur would grow. Leroy only had specious blotches of color from the moment before to extrapolate from, but the transient bears were more the size of Cardinal sharks, whereas most of the remaining bears recalled to Leroy the size of an Emporium whale. The Cardinal sharks were Niederbears, and the Emporium whales were Höherbears, if he had to guess. The scarred bear was larger than his brethren, at least a foot longer than an Emporium whale, the largest bear Leroy had ever seen. It was this bear that seemed to be in charge of the Höherbears, at least of the non-fancy sub-category.

When the scintillating had at last completely cleared from Leroy's eyes, so that he could finally see the source of light, he saw that it was a magnificent chandelier that adorned the center of the atrium. And, counter to his expectations, there was nothing otherwise excessive about the lighting of the chandelier, aside from its luxuriousness. It had simply been lighted as it normally might, and a normal amount of lighting had become blinding to all living Cretan things. He had expected some sort of domesticated sun, conjured magically by the impressive means of the Niederbear. He'd been wrong before.

The eyes of the Emporium whale bears had adjusted with his own, and the terrible moment came when the bears became active, splitting into different schools and dispersing through the many corridors of Horeb. If they had all dispersed, Leroy would have possibly found solace. But the fancy bears had stayed, along with a couple of the homely sort, who began to root through the pervasive debris of the room, coming closer and closer to where he was situated.

There had been people that Leroy was with, in the moments before the bear's entry—it wasn't just a habit of Leroy's to stand alone by imploding gates. Some of them were desperate types that didn't trust the permeability of their houses, who suddenly repented for the poor work they did of building a wall when the Höherbears finally advanced. They had all crowded around the outside of Horeb, until the Niederbears had reluctantly conceded to let them in. The peasants weren't allowed any further into the Castle than Leroy himself had been standing—some well-dressed, 'cultured' woman had told them all that it was a 'benediction' to be where they were, before she departed for elsewhere. Leroy had lost all of those kindred spirits of his, after the explosion, until he witnessed as one by one his comrades were exhumed by the large bears, and collected into a fearful mass. When his time had come, and it was undeniable that his crushing barrier was about to be lifted from him, he did what came natural to him—he preemptively wriggled his way out of the wreckage, and weaved his way between all the bears and debris in furious, random motions.

The bears seemed impassive at first, stolid, indifferent figures, but then a primitive response was triggered deep in their heads, and they tore after him, plowing through and sometimes throwing aside the large pieces of wood and metal that blocked their path. Leroy's instinct was to find a narrow place, somewhere he could wedge himself and rest easy, but the Castle was infuriatingly lacking in that respect. Every bit of it, down to the minutest of parts, was lavishly enlarged so that no such narrow place existed. He darted through passage after passage, but none of them were of a size that would impede the bears, who tenaciously followed after him.

His recourse, then, was to endurance. Actually, it was quite possible that it never entered his consciousness that he was taking recourse to anything. The accessible portions of his brain were a complete void. But something subterranean demanded that he moved forward unwaveringly, that he survived. That impulse took him upwards, through spiral staircases, long tracts of aimless passageways, followed by more flights of stairs. It happened that along one of those passages he found a bear, stationed in between himself and his only prospective course. Animalistic fear possessed every piece of him—he was surrounded. Yet he flowed through the close quarters of the bear, without hesitation. Fortunate to his cause, the bear had been caught entirely by surprise—first by his presence, then by his alacrity to go right by, although Leroy didn't know either of those things.

Then he heard snarls and exchanged blows behind him, though he never turned to discover what their explanation might have been. The next stretch of passage he took didn't have a wall on one side. Instead, it had a short railing, beyond which was a huge expanse of a room, with the floor far below.

There was a scene, that great distance removed, of bears fighting bears and the screeching, chiding voices of women, but Leroy couldn't make sense of any of it. It was like some strange
dream that Leroy had dreamed as a child, and complained to
his mother about for its incoherence and pointlessness. He
wanted better dreams, he had told his mother. His current situation was certainly an atavism of those old dreams, incoherent
and pointless, senseless and deranged. Still running, he had an
impulsive urge to find his mother to complain to her. But then
the scene faded behind the imposition of a wall, and Leroy noticed that, once more, nothing was following him. It was like
that glorious and free moment he'd had jumping from the city
wall, the blood from which had finally hardened into a crust
over his face. His final instinct was to turn into an unobtrusive
room, in the middle of a long hallway that heavily resembled
all the hallways preceding it. He was breathing so heavily, in
loud, gasping breaths that he couldn't stifle, that he didn't notice the man in the room with him for some time.

The man, for his part, did nothing to help himself be noticed. He stood in silence. His clothing was conspicuously disused, as if it had suffered much more from time than the work
it had done, with faded colors and all the soft age of an oracle on her deathbed. His clothing was in stark contrast to the
clothing of most other Gibeahnites, Leroy included—it was
not the cloth of the common man, which had blithe, raw fi-
bers that were nonetheless torn and abused, like a man cut
down in his youth. The face of the man gave the opposite impression of his clothes, the impression of unnatural, recent ag-
ing, so that the man looked as if he should have been forty, but
had all of the blemishes and impurities of a far more advanced
age. Those were all observations that Leroy would eventually
make, as soon as his human faculties returned to him.

When the man spoke, and first made his presence known
to Leroy, it was a voice that was strangely musical but decidedly piano, like an orchestra that wished not to disturb its slum-

bering companions. "What are you running from, exactly?" he asked.

"Bears!" was Leroy's reply.

The man took a long moment to laugh to himself, although his gaze was downcast and he was scuffing his shoes, which were the same faded, disused material as practically the whole essence of the man, save for his face. "Running from the bears? When you were just heralding them in, yesterday? I honestly can't believe the mutability of you people."

"They're just down the hall. I don't know why they stopped, they had me surrounded, a bear was just lying in wait for me up here. But I got by and they stopped."

The man laughed again, the man laughed so much that Leroy was beginning to wonder if the man's face had dissolved from overexposure to caustic laughter. "The one already in the hallway wasn't waiting for you, to surround you. He was making sure I stayed here. He was a Niederbear. It's just the point that I was making, that you can't tell one bear from another, yet you protest against the one while you welcome the other. And tomorrow you'll probably switch sides again. But I apologize," and the laughter immediately left the man's voice. "I don't mean to be derisive, not with you. When I consider humanity as a whole, it is only for me to become sardonic and bitingly sententious. But whenever I am confronted by one of you, the individual, it's hard for me to feel anything but an affectionate sympathy, a sickness to my stomach that I caress lovingly. Come to the window, I want to show you something."

Leroy was hesitant—first of all, he didn't trust the man, not with his strange words, his maniacal shifting of mood, and his crazed eyes; and also, he didn't expect anything to be visible out the window. Windows had seized to serve any purpose at all, in Gibeah, and Leroy was rapidly losing any sentimentality he used to have for the holes. But he fearfully obliged— then he became transfixed, by something he saw shimmering out the window. He became entirely immobile, as if waiting in ambush. The man joined him there and said, "That, that constant glimmer of light you see, is the Chamber of Divine Justice. And notice," and he switched tones again, to something bitterly vindictive, "how serene it looks. The picture of serenity. No bears are attacking it, no bears defending. I can attest to the reason for this—it's how impregnable that place shows itself to be. Not the inviting kind of impregnable—some impregnable things seem almost invitingly so, as if to say, 'Just come and try to impregnate me.' So people do. But on the other hand is a dismissive impregnable, the kind that one doesn't even bother with the thought. I petitioned that we all move to it, before the Höherbears arrived, so that we would perhaps weather the invasion—the Niederbears have a long history of not being able to weather things—but nobody would listen. Then I petitioned that at least I myself be allowed to go there, and then they put me in this room. In full view of the Chamber, no less. These bears and their women all have a marvelous sense of humor, take my word for it."

Leroy was silent and impassive, his eyes were still inextricably fixated on the shining Chamber in the distance, and although he had heard every word spoken he assimilated none of it, his attention was elsewhere. The man continued the conversation unabashed. "That's them, making noise in the hallway. Perhaps the Niederbear would have had a chance, but the overwhelming number of Höherbears will be the deciding factor. Everybody thinks a castle is always the best place to defend from, it's ridiculous. Come, we're not safe here. The bear's sense of smell will find us in any room that we linger too long in. The only option is to keep moving."

He veritably had to wrench Leroy from the window, but once Leroy's view was interrupted he was compliant, and let himself be led out into the hallway, then in the opposite direction of a still-persistent noise in the distance. The man's pace was nonchalant, which Leroy thought was curious until the man explained without prompting, as if he knew by intuition any and all questions that were in the minds around him and selectively answered a few of them—although Leroy wasn't entirely sure, nor entirely impressed, since he was the only mind around. "There isn't a life-threatening ordeal compulsive enough to make me run. I will, at most, deliberately walk away from such things, and if they catch me anyway, so be it. At least I won't be out of breath when they do."

The passage once more let out into the upper reaches of the large, expansive room. The scene that Leroy had witnessed before was still playing out, but they were at a slightly different juncture than before. The battle was winding down—there were still animals savagely trying to pry each other's heads off, by the look of it, but it was with a readily apparent lethargy, like the intensity of battle wasn't strong enough to prevent the bears from falling asleep.

The man found in his larynx the force to laugh again. "They skipped hibernation this year, so everything they do must be through the lens of a wakefully dreaming nightmare, constantly on its way to, but discomfited from, falling asleep. There's probably a better way to put it—there are so many chemicals in the head that don't respond well to the tempestuous flux of life, and this is the result. One day you say to yourself, 'It is of absolute necessity that I don't go to sleep right now, things must be done and can't be put off,' but your body doesn't follow, can't do the chemistry right, and this is what you get." The man turned to continue down the hall, only to find that they were at the end of it. No other path existed besides the one that Leroy had taken to get there, behind them, through the bears.

"Of course, Newton *would* build a pointless balcony, overlooking his pointless creation. He's the one who designed this pathetic excuse of a castle, if you didn't know. And when he was done with his pointless work, he probably stood right here to admire it, right at this dead-end he so cleverly constructed." The man surveyed everything around him sweepingly. "This is Newton's theater. Let's enjoy the show while we can. I will introduce the cast. Those," and he pointed to the fancy bears, "are the Höherbear royalty. They spectate every single battle of the Höherbears, which is intended to be somewhere between a privilege and an insult for the enemy. They can be seen in all of their noble glory, and have sacrificed their valuable time to watch the enemy die—privileges, both. The insult is that the entire Höherbear force is not employed, their most 'powerful' figures just sit it out, but they will still be triumphant in the end. They laugh at all of the underdeveloped societies in which everyone must labor to get by. Beautiful stuff. And over there," he pointed to a few bears that were seemingly flanked on all sides by the enemy bears, although Leroy couldn't differentiate between any of them because they all looked like the enemy, "that's one of those 'underdeveloped societies', that's König Scherzeherz, the kind of nobility that still has to fight, has to labor. And it looks like he's about to lose. His wife, or whatever you'd call it, must be down there somewhere—she's long since stopped deigning to speak to the likes of me. Too many stupid forces. Although what do I know, I'm a scientist. It is likely that the finer points of all of this just escape me, I'm missing by oversight all of the things that make this purposeful and worthwhile. And decent, don't forget decent."

The noise down the hall had meanwhile been crescendoing and crescendoing, a counterpart to his soft piano, and its source finally broke into view. "Best just surrender," the man said. Leroy couldn't help but squirm uncontrollably anyway, as the bears closed in around them.

In short time, Leroy and a select group of others were in the Chamber of Divine Justice. Leroy had struggled at first against his captors, but as soon as it became apparent that the Chamber was their destination, the Chamber and its effulgent light, Leroy had immediately been placated. It had been a very long time since he had crossed the threshold of the imposing building—it was an Emergency Council. He had been implicated by way of fish that had been stolen during a Raid, and his expertise had been desired. At several points his ordination to 'Magister of the Fish' had been discussed, but his overweening smell had repulsed the Court's idea to do so, and he had remained naught but a Gibeahn commoner. He still found occasion to smile anyway—fish were his passion, not politics.

The mystery of the light was never answered for him. It was an ephemeral light. From a distance it had seemed perfect and willing, like it would disclose all the secrets of life—but it was a will-o'-the-wisp, he lost sight of it when the colonnades of the Chamber interceded, and it never reappeared. Leroy had willed with the whole of his heart that it would be inside waiting for him, but the inside of the Chamber was—although satisfactorily lit—disappointingly lit, as far as Leroy was concerned. Because his light was unaccounted for.

So he was familiar enough with the building, and furthermore he was experiencing an intimate, involved little episode with it, with the light, which felt scandalous, but he didn't recognize any of the beings in the place. There was the man that he'd been talking with—that he'd been talked to by, rather—when the bears had overtaken them, but it was an obvious point that he'd recognize someone he'd just met. Everyone else was bears and unfamiliar faces, the greater portion of them feminine. The Emporium whale bear obviously had the upper hand, escorting a very ashamed-looking assortment of Cardinal shark bears. The Emporium considerably outnumbered the Cardinal, and used that advantage to bodily surround the Cardinal wherever and whenever possible, in a way that felt like gloating to Leroy, who admittedly knew nothing of the tendencies and behavior of bears. But he could extrapolate, he could imagine what it might mean if fish were to behave in such a fashion, and then transpose what then became easy knowledge for him. Gloating. Fish loved to gloat too, whence he derived a lot of pleasure from tearing them out of the water. Deep down he had an affinity for humbling things.

He spent less time trying to make sense of his circumstances and more time trying still to solve the mystery of the light, which mattered much more to him. Often, with his obsessive impulses towards shiny things, he was healed of it as soon as the stimulus was removed—he could just forget instantaneously and move on with his life, with further stimuli. But that light had been different, it had left an imprint in his head and it was constantly demanding his attention, even when it was gone.

Nevertheless he paid fleeting attention as an Emporium made a lot of noise, and everyone settled into seats or on the ground. Then it made a lot of other noise, and Leroy noticed that the old man from before was sitting next to a woman, whose face struck Leroy as familiar but yet one he couldn't place. The man was asking her to help him out, and she replied in a whisper that Leroy was close enough to hear, "You really don't want to know. It's a bunch of temerity, is what it is. They've already defeated us, but they brought us here to try us for war crimes on top of that. That's the way they are, they can't just be content with their martial superiority, they have to invoke their ideals, and systems, and make it sound as if this is justice, that our losing was the objectively justifiable order of things."

"What's he saying now?"

"He's saying that all of the leaders of the Niederreign have been arraigned, to rightfully be tried in a court of law, the obvious outcome of which being that we'll be found guilty of nearly every atrocity imaginable."

"The leaders of the Niederreign? Then I wonder why he's here," he said, indicating some man to his right. "But don't tell me, because I don't want to know. And who is this to my left? I tried speaking to him in the Castle, but he never said a word in return."

"To the best of my understanding, he's just a mistake. In

Höherbear culture, a master fisherman is one of the most prestigious positions that can be held, at least among the working class. So it's a misinterpretation, a mistake they made in translating their values to the workings of our society. They think he's important. You'll find, or at least you would if we aren't all executed for this, that the Höherbears make a lot of fallacious translations, assumptions like that. It's because they're always running errant around the world, proving their dominance, but they don't have the attention span to appreciate anyone else's culture, anyone else's concerns. I want to strangle every last one of them."

"In their defense, I wouldn't call what you and the Niederbears have a culture."

"I'm fairly certain that, as much as I want to strangle the Höherbears, I want to strangle you more."

The man reacted strangely, he let his eyes drift down to the woman's hips, and exclaimed, "I think you're starting to show."

Her reaction wasn't offended—her eyes lit up and she grasped her abdomen. "Really?"

"Oh, certainly. Almost definitely."

His response pacified the woman for some time, and she didn't translate or explain anything, she just sat there with a pleased, complacent face as she stroked her belly. "I'm going to call him Jasper," she finally said, after much introspection.

At that moment one of the Cardinal bears was led to the dais. The Emporium bears were there waiting for him, where the Council used to sit before they were all killed by a horse. Leroy and the other prisoners of war had been put where the Witnesses used to gather, and many Emporium bears loitered around the old Audience seating. All the Emporium bears began jeering loudly, and the escorted Cardinal bear was deposited in the center of all the Emporium bears, on the dais. Leroy was finally focusing enough to notice that the bears on the dais were the fancy bears. The lone Cardinal bear began to talk, surrounded by all those Emporiums, and Leroy was struck with the funny idea of the sea's analogue—a lone, defiant shark, surrounded by a bunch of whales. The shark would be brave and assertive, but the whales would massacre him.

The old man said once more, "Help me understand."

"He's making his case for his actions, to be acquitted. It's mostly a formality. He says, 'I hate you, Höherbears. I've always hated you. I was born with this bitter taste in my mouth, and I grew up to learn that it was your filth, the residue of your stinking oppression that inextricably covered my tongue. Whenever I would catch a fish, it would already taste rotten, because I couldn't taste it without the intercession of my tongue and its concomitant foulness that you gave it. You pollute the rivers, you pollute everything that nature has to give, and you do it through the conduit of my tongue. I will never forgive you for the bad taste you leave in my mouth.

"'So what should I do with that tongue that you so defiled, but make sure that it gives you no end of trouble? I used it to gather unrest against you in Thalia, I used it to...' No, no, that's vulgar," said the woman, suddenly breaking from her translation. "I can't repeat that."

The old man replied, "You can't always hide things from me that you don't want me to hear. I'm starting to pick up on key words, or didn't you know that I was capable of learning? He said something about a woman."

"It's vulgar, she reiterated. "Anyway, 'And even if it is its final use, I use it here to denounce you. I don't presume to be persuading any of you, but I feel that if I hold up a clear enough (he says river, but mirror would make more sense to us) mirror, you'll at least cringe at what you see, even if you don't understand that it's you on the other side of that mirror. It's a sickened creature, fat off of the tartufferies of life. It can't love anything, because it always sees itself in everything, and even though it's obsessed with itself, it doesn't love itself. It makes kings of jesters and lackeys of gods.

"'I'm a poor bear, I have nothing to give but my life. I've

been made poor by serving you for so long. So then, this is what I propose—that I not only be acquitted, but also rewarded for my contributions.'" There was more jeering from the audience, and also there was another Cardinal bear in the audience, detained by the Emporiums, that vocalized something in response. The lone bear then added, translated by the woman, "'It seems that my friend Gregor is willing to contribute twenty pounds of fish—it's a modest sum, but it's what I have.'"

He was then unceremoniously led off the stage. An immediate reply was given by one of the fancy bears, and the Emporium crowd roared in approval. The old man pestered the woman once more, "What did he say?"

"It's not as bad as I thought."

"What is it?"

"Life in prison."

"For who?"

"All of us."

A week went by, and nobody had talked much in their cells at Castle Horeb. Leroy had been floating around the restricting confines of his prison, constantly running into walls as if he couldn't make sense of them. He had a persistent feeling of deprivation that was gradually working its way from his stomach up his spine, and he felt that when it made it to his head he would throw up, or explode, or the gods only knew what he would do.

He shared a cell with the old man, who seemed to be just basking in the pleasantness of the situation. Except for once in a while when his face became contorted, and Leroy feared for his own life. Across the hall was the woman from the Chamber, and the Cardinal bear that Leroy would always see as lonely, after he'd seen the humiliating way all of the whales had made him futilely fend for his life in front of all his subjugated shark friends, just to put him in prison afterwards. The Lone Cardinal shark bear. And there were more beings adjacent to the both of them, but they couldn't be seen, except for the occasional outstretched hand or paw through the gratings, visible whenever Leroy desperately pressed his face against the bars. There were times he felt small and insignificant enough to slip right through, but for some reason he was never successful.

A week after they had been shamefully dumped there, the woman finally spoke to the old man from across the hall. For the entire week she'd only spoken to the guard bears as they patrolled their ward, and intermittently to the Lone Cardinal she was enshrined with, but the former was unintelligible and the latter inaudible, so that when she finally said words, human words, it nearly dazzled Leroy from its unexpectedness. She said, "I promised myself I would never talk to you again, Daedalus, but I feel like circumstances force me to. Because if we escape, I get the feeling I'll need your help, and if we're here forever, I feel like I'm bound to give in and talk to you anyway. So here I am." She cleared her throat.

The old man had been reclining on his back for hours, staring at the ceiling, oblivious to the world. She seemed to expect him not to answer, and had something else she intended to say, but before she could continue with her empty throat, the old man interrupted. "Yes, there you are. And you wouldn't be there, had you listened to me at any point. I told you it was overextension, an outright stupid idea to conquer Gibeah just because you felt an upswing in courage after you thought yourself capable to reproduce. Continuing to live as if you were the last of your kind, like you had been for so long, was always an advisable course of action. And you didn't listen when I told you that killing Richard was the act of an inconsiderate hypocrite. Not that this is why I believe you should have spared him, but if you had, it might have been him in these cells instead of us. Unless the Höherbear goal was solely to humiliate you. But if that was their intention, you gave them the opportunity of bringing you low by placing yourself so high. And you didn't listen when I said that the Chamber would have safely harbored us all. Instead, you let the Höherbears take advantage of it." His voice was almost distractingly raspy from a week's disuse.

"Shut up," she said, "and listen. There's a lot of things I've discovered, this past week. The Höherbears have been sharing a lot of secrets with me—they've been taunting me with truth, because they're under the belief that I'll never be able to act on it. What they've been telling me is of exceptional interest to you, since you're a Gibeahnite.

"As you know, we're all important people." She said 'important people,' but she said it ever so wearily. She was a beaten and broken individual, by her voice, and she was on the verge of not being able to say 'important people' anymore, at least not in reference to herself. "All of the commoners, on the other hand, have been put in the Bear Maze."

All the Gibeahnites within earshot gasped—most had loved ones that they thought were still thriving on the surface. That was not the case for any of the recent prisoners, who were mostly Cardinal bears and the women that accompanied them, but there were prisoners that were there from before, who still had tenuous links to the outside world. Leroy was among those that gasped, although he had no loved ones. She continued, "No need for concern. It seems that being dropped into the Bear Maze isn't fatal. They're enslaved there. It has been a recent revelation to me that the Bear Maze is not considered a deathtrap, at least not by the Höherbears. Quite the opposite—the Bear Maze is the capital of the Höherbear Empire. The humans have been sent down to serve them.

"This explains why none of the Niederbears have returned from being placed into the Bear Maze by you sniveling Gibeahnites. I've just been mockingly informed that they too, the Niederbears I knew and loved, are in servitude. In the Bear Maze."

Her face was vindictive rage, but then it lightened. She smiled. "But not everything is all and well in the Höherbear world. It seems like they lost communication with their capital. The reason that they came here was not solely to humiliate us, as you insightfully offered, Daedalus, but rather to investigate and recover their lost capital. They say that, about three months ago, something happened to sever their communication, and they still can't figure it out. The Bear Maze, the maze itself, is different than it was two months ago."

The old man had a long, gleeful laugh to himself, and he had a look on his face that his whole life had been validated, the same look a salmon always had on its face after surmounting a waterfall. Leroy would know.

"What's so funny about that?" she asked.

"Nothing, nothing," said the old man, dismissively.

"Anyway, they can communicate again with their capital, through the entrance of the Bear Maze. So they learned about the troublesome alterations, but they can't overcome the physical gap between the portal and the ground below, and they can't start at the end either, like typical maze-solving methodology. Apparently from the entrance to the ground is some great height that can be survived by a fall, since the Höherbears have cushioned the landing, but nothing they can easily construct can get bears out of it, out of the Maze. Bears can't climb rope, can't climb ladders. They need something a bit more substantial. So they have begun devising their solution, devising something far more substantial, with the Gibeahn graveyard as its construction site. But it will be seven years until it is complete, they say."

The woman gave the old man a long time to consider her words. He resumed staring at the ceiling. The woman was waiting impatiently against the grating of her cell, and when he didn't seem like he would ever return to the conversation, she shouted angrily at him, "Well! What do you have to say to all of that?"

The old man smiled. "I didn't hear a question, in anything you said."

"You know, I've been watching you closely, this past week,

and it's sickening. You're trying to convince yourself that you're happy here. I can see it in your demeanor. Half the time you're all smiles, you're miles below the surface for the rest of your life but you still find the gall to smile. You strut about your cell like you own the place and it's the greatest windfall that ever could have landed your way. But the other half of the time some ghostly thought possesses you, you sulk and you're despondent. I'd like to venture a guess as to what it is that makes you sulk—it's your rationality returning to you, it's you realizing that humans weren't meant to live like this, and that no amount of trying to convince yourself otherwise will change your mind. Am I right? Is half of you sane? Does half of you want to get out of here, like I do? You must know things about this prison that I don't—you built it. Help me out. The sane half of you, help me out. And we'll get out of here."

"Oh, so many points to address," the old man sighed quietly to himself, like explanation would be the greatest of burdens to him. "We'll start with where you're unequivocally wrong. Sound good to you, Sofia? I..." He hesitated for a moment, as if saying anything about himself was outside of his forte. "If I really wanted to get out of here, if half of me wanted out, I would be free to do so. I 'sulk', I'm agitated sometimes, because I know that I could escape if I wanted to. This is something that really upsets me—I take the time to build something for someone, something with superbly refined details for its use, and they use it like a monkey would use a dictionary.

"I'll illustrate my point. Sometimes, in politics, it's expedient to put a person into jail that you don't, as a ruler, really want to put there. It's a public display, though, to appeal to the masses. For our example we're going to say that this hypothetical prisoner is really your friend, something like that. Let's say he got drunk one night and crapped on the statue of Prometheus that we have over there by the old brook. You know, the kind of thing that really upsets people, that everyone calls for justice about. They demand it. So you put him in prison, but he escapes. People are dissatisfied that he escaped, but in their eyes you still did right as a ruler, you still dealt justice. So you win. As a ruler, you win. You've done right by your friend, who is free, and you've done right by your people."

The woman was still exceedingly impatient. "I can't believe that you would see fit to explain politics to a queen. And how is that relevant? At all?"

"I'm in one of those cells. Made specially so that a prisoner can get out. I go through all of the trouble of creating a political device, a very useful one at that, to help in those kinds of situations. And its use has been completely forgotten, otherwise I wouldn't have been put here. I'm not some drunk friend that crapped on a statue. It's that kind of lack of appreciation that really—"

"Are you serious? You could just get out, right now?"

"Yes. And it bothers me to no end. At least half the time, as you so ineptly noted. So—what were my other points? Oh yes. I wanted to say that your psychological insight is fatally lacking at best. I wanted to say that I don't think you're in any position to evaluate my sanity, even if I help you out by providing the true details as to my disposition. And I wanted to say that I can see no reason why escape would be a good idea. The Höherbears rule Gibeah. We wouldn't have anywhere to go. What could you possibly accomplish by escape?"

The woman's face became quintessentially maternal, an effect that was surprising for Leroy—he had entirely forgotten about his mother. She said, "Maybe you don't have a reason to want to escape. You don't seem to care much for the amenities of life. I, on the other hand, have Niederbears inside of the Bear Maze that I must liberate. This is a shared life's passion that I have with Scherzeherz—we have people that we tend to, to the end. I wouldn't expect your commoner's sensibilities to be able to relate, at least not to that. But you do have a wife, don't you, Daedalus? I honestly can't remember her name, but I know you have one. She must be slaving away, this very minute, to the pleasure of some Höherbear."

The old man's face took on a quality that defied Leroy's interpreting. Because no one called on his friendship when they were feeling vulnerable, Leroy had no experience with whatever emotion the man was experiencing. "Fine," he said. "I will escape. What's the plan?"

"Once you escape, could you let the rest of us out?"

"Your cells require a key to open, and I'm not one for stealth. I could never steal the keys from the Höherbears, not the way they safeguard them. Nor am I strong enough to lift the grating from its hinges—but that's something I've seen bears do, before. Can't Scherzeherz just lift these off? I know the force necessary to do it, I know the physics of all of that, but I have no idea how strong a bear is. Do I even need to be involved?"

"I've talked to Scherzeherz about that. He's been trying it out, and he's decided that at least four bears are required to make it work. And only three bears are down here—you can't tell, from where you're situated, but we took inventory from here. Three bears—the rest were dropped into the Maze with the Gibeahnites. I told Scherzeherz that three should be close enough to four, but he insists that it just isn't possible. You really have no other ideas about how these can be opened? Is your cell the only one built the way it is?"

"Yes, it is." The old man took a while to contemplate to himself. Finally, he said, "Listen, there's a stash of my old weapons just down the hall. If they've forgotten about the purpose of this cell, they've forgotten about the stash. All the other stashes were destroyed, along with the old Castle, but I can guarantee that this one still exists—it's a holdout from the past, just like this dungeon was."

"Which weapons?"

"The sun weapons."

"Surely those don't still work."

"Why wouldn't they? You don't know anything about how

they work, so don't assume."

"Fine. And those could get us out of here?" the woman asked. She was looking hopeful.

"They're strong enough to decimate these bars. I promise."

"And you can get to them?"

"Absolutely."

There were still quite a few hours that separated them from the moment it would be possible to do what they intended. The woman asked, very simply, "How do they work, anyway? Your sun weapons."

"I suppose that would be helpful to go over, before the time comes," the old man answered. "I want to start by saying that I thought it would be hilarious if the pinnacle of technological achievement, like my weapons have been called, was really just an act of faith. I suppose there's slightly more to it than that, but that was a large part of it. At its core it is nothing more than a few of Apollo's hairs, in every gun."

"Apollo's hairs?" was her startled response.

"Yeah, I got a hold of some. They were entrusted to me— but that's a different story. They're powerful. And if you say a sincere prayer in their presence, they will activate, so to speak. Some complicated things happen, but basically what it comes down to is that matter can store and release energy, and that's all that really needs to be said. If the energy is released without proper channeling, it will go in all directions. A large part of what my weapon does is to focus that energy into a single direction, and you'd be surprised how devastating that can be. It's really just light, but more intense than you've ever experienced in your life."

"What do you mean by a sincere prayer?"

"Pray like you would to Apollo. Have you ever done that? Do you have any piety in you? My all-too-youthful thought had been that if I made piety a necessary step before destruction, I could vastly control the occurrence off reckless violence. But it didn't take me long to learn that even pious, otherwise well-intentioned people are prone to do stupid things with powerful weapons."

"Interesting."

They waited for what they deemed to be the perfect moment. It was 'night', and the bear-guard only patrolled their area every half hour. As soon as the bear had gone by on one of its rounds, and was out of sight again, Daedalus pulled on some obscure lever in the corner of his cell and his door swung open, as simple as that. "You stay here," he advised Leroy. Then he went in the opposite direction from the guard, disappeared around a corner, and everyone was left to wait with bated breath.

In five minutes, he returned. In his hands there was a complex-looking mechanism, with wires and panels and a trigger and a barrel. It looked as if not much consideration had been taken for its aesthetic appeal, but the end result was still sightly and awe-inspiring on account of how foreign and strange it looked. He had another one across his back.

The woman was beaming. "You found them?"

"Right where they were left." He didn't waste any time with gallantries and superfluities, he just whispered a quiet prayer, aimed the barrel at the juncture of lock and door, and pulled the trigger. The effect was reminiscent of when the Niederbears lit the chandelier—it let out a searing beam of light that scarred Leroy's vision for hours. The efficacy was undeniable—the lock entirely melted, leaving the door to swing freely. The Lone Cardinal and the woman were free.

It was already decided that the two other bears, locked together in another cell, would be the next to be released. The old man made short work of getting them out. Leroy just trailed along, free merely because he had been fortunate enough to be coupled with the old man in a cell. Even if the other people didn't like the fact that he was with them, they were courteous enough not to tell him to go and wait in an unlocked cell, to resume his life sentence for being a fisherman.

When all three bears were free, the woman made them demonstrate that they weren't capable of lifting gratings, on a cell of two women who were apparently dear to her. After they strained for a full minute at the task, she desisted, and allowed that the old man use his sun weapon. Then the old man paced the hall, looking one by one into the dank cells. It had been decided that he could select among the remaining prisoners whoever else was worthy of salvation, their utility being the major factor.

"Stairwell," the old man said. "I didn't even know you were here—I didn't see you at the trial. Why haven't you said anything all this time?" The man referred to as Stairwell, an overwhelmingly stocky man with a resolute face, didn't reply to the question. The old man expended another shot to free him anyway. "I don't know why you'd want to go with us," the old man said, "but I'd like to have you along."

He went further down the hall. Halfway past the cell of some inconsequential lunatic, the old man's leg was abruptly seized by the occupant. The old man turned the weapon on him. "Let go," he demanded.

"You… you're the one that talked to Apollo. You are! I'm not crazy. They didn't believe me. They told me that gods don't talk to mortals. You have to tell them I was right."

The old man looked as if he didn't know what to do. "That—that's all you want? For me to tell them you were right? You don't want to be free?"

"Free?"

"Alright, I'll tell them. But you have to let go first."

"Thank you, thank you," he mumbled, and let go.

The old man proceeded down the hall. The next cell he looked into was a man lying in a pool of blood, a golden arrow shaft sticking out of his chest. "Korah, is that you?" The old man had the resigned look of someone who didn't think there would be an answer, probably assuming that the other was dead. The scene was too morbid to assume otherwise. Everyone was surprised when the pathetic figure moaned. "… Yeah."

"Are you in any condition to move? What happened to you?"

"I don't want to talk about it. And I can move."

"Wait," the woman said, and drew the old man aside. "Of what practical use could this man be to us? He's half dead. He'll just slow us down."

"He'd probably be of more use than any of the bears you have there. And especially of more use than your women. Half dead or not, I've seen amazing things out of this man."

"So be it," she said. And Korah was freed.

At the last cell, the old man gave a cursory glance in and walked on. The woman had to rush forward and pull the old man back. "Just hold on, there," she said. "We need this man."

"I'd rather not."

"Daedalus, is that you?" came a voice from inside.

"Hi, David," he said to the man in the cell. "Listen," he whispered to the woman. "We only have so much ammo here, we're on a limited supply, and I think it would be best if we just conserve the shot."

"No, I won't have any of that," she said, loud enough for everyone to hear. "That man is the single most lethal man I've ever seen."

"What do you mean?"

"He's killed at least ten bears that I'm aware of, with his bare hands. We're the ones that put him down here. But if we could convince him to be on our side, he would be invaluable. And it seems like he knows you. If I'm not mistaken, even a little affectionate for you, so it shouldn't be too hard."

"If he killed that many bears, how come I didn't hear about it?"

"We stifled the spread of the information. We didn't want anybody to know we had any kind of weakness."

"I can't believe I'm doing this. This is just one more thing I'll never forgive you for." And he freed David. "That will be all of us," he said. "And it's on to the next stage of the plan."

There were three other people added to their group, the prisoners who had formerly shared cells with David, Stairwell, and Korah. Their names weren't asked. The one that had been paired with Korah looked to be traumatized from long exposure to the sight of blood, and probably hadn't expected himself that Korah was alive, even after a week of close proximity.

Quietly the old man led them down several passages, and then very cautiously to the end of one more. He alone peered around the final corner, to survey what was on the other side. Then he gestured for them to return, and they retreated those several passages to discuss.

"It's pretty much as bad as I thought," the old man said. "When I built the dungeon, I thought it was a good idea, for convenience's sake, to make all paths go through the kitchen. The bears have picked up on this convenience—they use the kitchen as a dormitory. We were able to circumvent the actual dormitory, and I hoped against hope that they had a respect for conventions. But really I knew better."

The woman reasserted herself as the plan-maker. "Do they have guards?"

"Two."

"David, Stairwell, König darling, and you other bears—we need to incapacitate these two guard bears, first thing. We don't want to use the sun weapon except as a last resort, which Daedalus will continue to be in charge of. Actually, Daedalus, give your spare weapon to our fisherman friend, here. I'm sure he's developed quite an aim, through his career. The rest of you need to await your opportunity for crossing. If we do it right, we'll be able to walk through. König will take the lead," she said, and continued on into further details.

From the moment Leroy had been handed a weapon, his eyes began to glaze over, and he became deathly still. The old man noticed, and came to him with concern. "Perhaps he wasn't the best choice to give a weapon to, Sofia. I've been spending a lot of time with him lately, and he's... devoid. I'm not sure anything really goes on behind those bug-eyes of his, it's like he sees everything but processes none of it."

"That's no way to speak about a person. In their presence, no less."

"But that's just the point. I'm not sure he's a person."

At that minute, it happened. "*ICH BIN VERRUCHT. IMMER SEIN KIND!*" Leroy suddenly spouted, much too loud to go unnoticed by anything in the prison. He failed to insert any actual content between the two holy phrases, like a normal person would have done. Bears immediately began to stir in the distance. Then Leroy charged off in their direction, without a single ounce of reservation.

"Is this really happening?"

"We have no choice now, we have to follow him."

Everything was chaos. They caught up with Leroy as he was charging through the kitchen/dormitory, shooting at everything that moved. "Apparently even that counted as a prayer," Daedalus had the presence of mind to say. "Almost impressive in its efficiency, even. 'Dear God, Amen'. That's the kind of thing that passes for piety these days."

There were at least fifty bears packed into an only moderately sized room, and most of them, those that Leroy hadn't killed, were awake and furious. They closed in on the party. Daedalus watched as David punched a bear clear through the face. Stairwell had changed tactics, apparently deciding that spending the kind of individual attention he was used to on one bear would get him killed by forty others. He parried incoming claws and used his wide girth to shove away bears that impeded their path.

"Help me!" shouted one of the people that nobody knew the name of, as a bear had latched on to his leg and began dragging him off.

"Not worth it," Daedalus said to the others, and they forged ahead through the violence. Scherzeherz was valiant, Daedalus had to admit. The fluidity and grace with which he eviscerated his distant cousin bears was truly astounding. He easily moved from one to the next of the Höherbears, and it made Daedalus wonder what had ever held Scherzeherz back in his quest for the liberation of the Niederbear.

They made it through the kitchen, but they were still being pursued. So they ran like hell.

"This wasn't how it was supposed to be," Sofia bemoaned, as an emergency alarm began ringing through the space of the Castle. They had scaled many stairs and were finally in the regal setting of the Castle, which Daedalus thought to be significantly improved by all of the recent destruction and blood that covered its every surface. They ran through it all, and Höherbears came from every direction to join the pursuit. The sight presented behind them would have been enough to make any of the party faint, if they had the nerve to turn and see it. Hundreds of angry bears.

As they approached the main gate, which had been fortified once more by the Höherbears, Daedalus shot it from a distance. The true potency of the weapon was finally demonstrated, as the ray widened considerably from the barrel until it connected with the gate, disintegrating it instantaneously. The party climbed through the rubble.

The air was as fresh and dark as ever. Daedalus turned to Korah as they ran, to make sure he was okay. He was in disbelief that even though the Leper was obviously impaled by a devious-looking arrow, he was faring fine. Daedalus himself felt like he was going to die from running, he was breathing so heavily. "I haven't had this much exercise since the day my son died," Daedalus gasped to Korah.

And things were going alright, and it seemed that they might arrive at the Bear Maze without incident, or at least as much as their circumstances could be said to be 'without incident'. They somehow outpaced all of the bears behind them. But Daedalus had a sinking suspicion that all was not well, despite appearances, and his doubt was validated when suddenly they were cut off.

There was no warning. No one anticipated it. The Höherbears had cleverly hid themselves in a hedge, about a half-mile distant from the Maze. A brief moment transpired when Daedalus thought that he was going to die. One second everything was fine—the next, a bear was gripping him by the shoulders and was preparing to devour him whole, judging by the extent he opened his jaws.

Daedalus almost didn't react well enough. The functionality of his mind completely disintegrated, thoughts wouldn't follow other thoughts in the proper order, there was no system and the weapon in his hands made absolutely no sense to him. The trepidation was all, the look inside the bear's eyes, the background of the terribly foregrounded jaws—but he pulled the trigger anyway. He didn't know why. And the bear melted.

In a continuation of not being able to think, or just not wanting to, he ran on without a second glance backwards to verify the wellbeing of his comrades. He was all the way to the Maze by the time it entered his mind that waiting for them would be a considerate thing to do. Sofia was already there, she was looking at something in the east. "I can't believe it," she said.

He turned to see what she was referring to. He couldn't believe it either. In the place of the old Gibeahn cemetery was a massive structure, surrounded by torches. It disappeared into the pervasive darkness above, so that its true height was inestimable. The Höherbear's solution to the Maze. What could be seen had the look of a work in progress, with unrefined edges and huge stacks of raw materials lying everywhere, giving the impression that it would be even that much larger. And, if it was to be believed, it would still be another seven years before it was finished. Sofia and Daedalus looked at it as they would have looked into abyss.

Stairwell reached them, König reached them, and finally a lagging Korah. "Where's Leroy" Daedalus asked.

"No idea," said Sofia.

"Are we waiting for anyone else?"

"No, best we don't."

"Are we just going to jump?"

"Yes."

They each experienced the kind of hesitation that accompanies the moment before jumping into a bottomless pit. One by one, though, they overcame it. And darkness opened up below them.

KAPITEL DREIZEHN: BEAR MAZE!

AS HE FELL, Daedalus was reminded once more of Icarus, of falling futilely after his lost child. He was more than reminded—he was reliving it. He imagined the sun once more in its radiant glory, with the power to melt human aspiration, the wax in the wings that were his escape. The reality as Daedalus fell into the Bear Maze couldn't have been more different—it was darkness manifest, but he saw a sun. In his reenactment, though, in his longing, he caught up with Icarus on the descent. He clasped his child with three years' worth of repressed paternal anxiety, and the child was screaming something, perhaps an objection to Daedalus' strangulation, but it was lost in the rushing wind. Still a mile below Daedalus saw waves, and he wondered if he'd be able to hold on to his son through the force of impact.

Then he hit something far more solid than water, far sooner than he expected, and the illusion imploded. He thought at first that the darkness he was experiencing must have meant he was unconscious, but then he had misgivings about being conscious of unconsciousness, and realized that he was wide awake with eyes wide open—it was just the world that made it seem otherwise.

He couldn't breathe for a while. All the thoughts he was having were drawing their vitality from the breath he had taken before jumping, some time before. His diaphragm was being disobedient, or unresponsive, or something. He tried to operate his lungs with his hands, pressing underneath his ribcage, and that seemed to help. Eventually it seemed that he might not die, and he was relieved.

Then he vividly relapsed into concern for Icarus. He remembered the life, the warmth he'd contained in his arms as they had fallen. He turned to his side, and groped into the darkness for whatever might be there. As soon as his hand came into contact with someone, they spoke: "Why did you grab on to me while we were falling? Is that you, Daedalus? We could have died, had one of us landed on the other. That was dangerous."

"Sorry, Sofia," Daedalus said, and rolled back over in disgust. The disparity between her and Icarus was too much for him to handle, and he nearly vomited onto the surface pressing hard against his cheek. But his stomach remembered that it had no contents, and only heaved drily.

"When I heard," she continued, "that the fall into the Bear Maze was survivable, I was expecting something a little more pleasant. I've never fallen so far before." Daedalus was thinking about how much he disagreed, about how she had too harshly beheaded her own estranged husband for the love of a bear, but he said nothing. "And these are hardly cushions," she added.

The latter point, he agreed with. The 'cushions' weren't too far removed from solid ground—they felt like a thin layer of turf against his cheek, a sheen at best, nothing more. But they had served their purpose. For him and Sofia, at least. He didn't hear the movements of anyone else, and was worried. "Who else is there? Speak if you can hear me," he said.

He shouldn't have brought Korah. Korah had an arrow through his chest, and such a jarring impact could never be alright. So few things had been thought out well in the dungeons, Daedalus was beginning to feel.

Then Korah was the first to answer. "I'm still here. Korah, that is."

Daedalus crawled toward the sound, and was simultaneously disappointed by the functionality of his body. Crawling was hard. He made a vapid attempt anyway, and despised his age.

"Korah, you're over here?"

"Over here."

Meanwhile, David, Stairwell, and König had all responded, but Daedalus didn't acknowledge their responses, didn't even really hear them. "Korah, I've been meaning to talk to you, for a while now. But things have been hectic. How are you?"

"Is now the time?" came from Sofia's direction, in her indignant voice.

"Daedalus," Korah said. "I think this is my fault. It's pretty much all my fault. I caused the darkness. Well, I caused Gibeahnites to cause the darkness, I should say. I Suggested some things, and they threw Apollo off a cliff. But that practically makes it my fault, I own it, and because of all that we're here, and it's looking kind of grim, and you have my sincerest apologies. It's your wife that you're here for, isn't it? It's my fault she's here." He was delirious, he was spouting words as if he had no idea how to control them, and behind it all was genuine sorrow for whatever he may have done to Daedalus.

Sofia interfered once more with their conversation. "Wait, is Korah the leader of the Lepers? It's starting to kind of come back to me. How dare you have the audacity to bring the leader of the Lepers on a rescue mission, Daedalus? Are you out of your mind, or just stupid?"

With Scherzeherz being the only bear around to corroborate her, Daedalus was quickly losing his fear for Sofia, and had long since lost his pity. "You didn't even recognize him, Sofia. Not even when you were given a name, when we freed him. I was never disingenuous about who he was. If you're such an incompetent ruler that you can't recognize the most threatening enemy your state had, then you don't deserve a say in whether it's prudent or not to have him around. Only if you recognized his personhood would I even consider your advice, but you don't." Daedalus turned back to Korah, or at least he thought he did. There wasn't enough light to tell. "I'm not blaming you, Korah. I know enough about what the Lepers do, what the Lepers are, to know that it's the Gibeahnites at fault. They knowingly disposed of their own God, I have no illusions. But none of that is what I asked. I asked how you are."

Sofia interrupted again, was always interrupting. She didn't seem daunted by the disdain in Daedalus' voice, or was perhaps motivated by it all the more. "I hear bears. Bears are coming. The sun weapon broke on the way down, didn't it. We're helpless."

"No, it didn't break," Daedalus responded. He had verified its state by running his fingers up and down its length, and nothing felt out of place. "But it doesn't have any more energy, any more shots. This is what I meant when I said conserving shots would have been wise. And there's no recharging it, the hairs are permanently expended when they're broken."

"Why would you make a weapon that relied so heavily on pieces of godforsaken hair?" she asked derisively.

"No reason." The bears were closing in, he could hear them as well. Daedalus was upset, because there was so much that he wanted to say to Korah, and so much he wanted to hear in return. "We'll have to finish our conversation later," Daedalus said to Korah. "I'm sure that there'll be plenty of opportunities to talk, in the life of servitude we have ahead of us."

"Aren't we going to resist?" pleaded Sofia.

"I don't feel up to it, do you?" None of the other survivors, David, Stairwell, or Scherzeherz, sounded up to the task either.

A light suddenly filled Daedalus' vision, like the sun he'd just imagined, exposing the cavern for what it really was with its illumination. In the extreme distance above, he could make out a dark portal to the outside world. Running down from it was rough-hewn stone, with moss growing in its crevices through the long descent it made to the cavern floor. Daedalus finally got a good look at his cushion, and it was much to his expectation. Not an incremental gore-hill of dead carcasses, but a thin layer of turf. In his rampant imagination's defense, there were spots of blood here and there that stained the landing. Korah didn't even land on the cushion, it turned out, but on the raw stone of the cavern.

The light was a lantern carried by a Höherbear. There was a small party of them, very nonchalant as they approached the group. Daedalus noted that even though they were similar in appearance to their above-ground counterparts, with their dignity, there was an obvious subterranean quality to them. Their eyes were slightly glazed over, and they always seemed to be distracted, looking at nothing in particular. Dust worked subtleties in all of the crevices of their garb.

Daedalus readily submitted as one of them easily lifted him from the floor and slung him across its shoulder. He could stand to be carried for a while, he thought. Which was probably counter to that other resolution he had while being carried by bears. Something about taking absolute control of his life.

Halfway to wherever he was being transported, it occurred to Daedalus that he could understand the Höherbears as they spoke amongst themselves. Daedalus hadn't felt more directly connected to the world, with the exception of a few highly absorbed creative lapses, than the moment he realized that the bears were talking about him and he knew exactly what they meant.

As he'd mentioned to Sofia during the trial, he'd been gradually garnering a vocabulary, but that did nothing to explain the proficiency he had at that moment—every aspect of the language was disclosed to him, with not just the blundering sufficiency of a foreigner, but even the incisiveness of a native.

They were saying, "It confuses me that the Colonials would drop more servants at a time like this. Why weren't they dropped with the rest?"

Another bear, the largest of the lot, who wore a heavily embroidered chemise and didn't seem to think anything of it, said, "These were holdouts. Hiding in dark corners like the vermin they are. But our brethren smelled them out, and here they are." His explanation was deemed perfectly adequate by the rest.

Sofia's plaintive voice arose from somewhere behind Daedalus. It sounded like she was talking to herself, but her concern was too great to remain in the confines of her head. "I don't get what they're saying."

Daedalus, confident that the Höherbears didn't understand the Gibeahn language, said to Sofia, "They're just confused. They don't know who we really are."

Something about what he said proved to be extremely surprising to the Höherbears. They immediately deposited him on the ground and thoroughly inspected him for the first time, as if expecting some revelation in Daedalus' appearance that they'd missed before, in the perfunctory gathering of slaves.

Sofia continued talking all the while. "No, I mean I can't understand the words they say."

"Maybe they speak a different dialect than the Höherbears we're used to?" Daedalus offered, but knew that if that were the case, his sudden understanding of the language would be that much harder to explain.

"I can understand them fine," said König Scherzeherz. Daedalus found it strange, and even a little exciting, to really hear the celebrated orator for the first time.

"I can't understand him either!" Sofia exclaimed. "My König darling, I can't understand any of it!" and she descended into tears.

"I can understand them too," said Korah.

The Höherbears had the same initial reaction to Korah as

they had had to Daedalus. They placed them together, and began an interrogation. "Where did you learn the Holy Tongue from?"

"No idea," Daedalus answered for the two.

The Höherbears were obviously offended that someone would have no idea where they learned their Holy Tongue from. "And why have you said that we don't know who you really are?" continued the bear in the chemise.

Daedalus hesitated before answering, to consider tact. He knew why he had really said it—they were special prisoners, the deposed leaders of Gibeah, in a way. To be kept separate from the masses for that very reason, that they were leaders. But if he explained that, then it was likely the same fate as before would await them, a special prison or a special execution. So instead, he opted for a tactic which he didn't know the prospects of. "We are gods."

He wanted to consult Korah before conferring godship on him, but had neither the opportunity nor safe language to do it with, the bears ostensibly understanding his every word. It seemed to Daedalus like an inappropriate thing to do without consent.

"Gods?" The bears also wanted to privately consult each other on the matter, and unlike Daedalus they were in a position to do so. They bid Daedalus and the rest to stay put, while they withdrew a fair distance and exchanged hushed whispers. The distance was unnecessary, or at least Daedalus could surmise the exact nature of their conversation—they were slave-gatherers, and didn't know the proper etiquette for finding gods. They didn't rightly know how to proceed. While they were most likely talking about such things, Daedalus said to Korah, "I'm sorry."

"Do you know how this is going to turn out?"

"Not really."

The bears returned. The result of Daedalus' claim and the Höherbears' deliberation was that he and Korah were allowed to walk, while everyone else was carried like before. And so they proceeded.

Free then to observe as he pleased, Daedalus took in his surroundings. The layout and look of the Maze were much as he had imagined them to be—from the blueprints he had of the place, and knowing the exterior distance from the entrance to the exit, Daedalus had already conjectured the scale of the Maze. The Maze began with large, open segments, conveying a feeling of freedom and wantonness, but the further along toward a solution, the more constricting it became. Daedalus enjoyed the kind of psychological impetus that such a technique employed—it caused the prospective solver to subconsciously choose freer passages, and therefore the wrong passages. But the concern that led him to add to the Maze, all those months before, was that one trick was not enough.

Ever since he had learned that an entire Höherbear Empire existed down in the Maze, he'd been puzzling over how it might fit. His best guess, what seemed most logical, was that the larger areas would be used. But the entrance *was* the largest of areas, and yet was entirely vacant, as if in deference to the fall. If there was any appreciable population of bears, they were crammed into the claustrophobic constraints of the narrower passages.

Sofia was disconsolate the whole way there. She kept making pleading implorations that Scherzeherz be able to understand her, but apparently the incomprehension went both ways—Scherzeherz could make nothing of her noise, he would say, but she would keep making it anyway. Scherzeherz didn't seem to take it as harshly as Sofia. Or if he did, it was with a laudable equanimity.

"Daedalus, you have to translate for us," she said.

"No thank you."

They began to see Höherbears coming and going, making their way through the dismal passages. The closer they came to their destination, the lighter their surroundings were. It piqued

Daedalus' curiosity mercilessly. Where they were, the light was wan. But it had to be a marvel, wherever it came from, since it must have been lighting miles of maze, turns and walls and dead ends all, and with such constancy. The lantern that was held by one of their escorts didn't compare—it flickered and stretched out effetely. A few more passages and it wouldn't even be necessary.

Eventually came a divergence of passages, at which Daedalus and Korah were to go one way and the remainder the other. Daedalus waved goodbye to a sobbing Sofia, to König, and to Stairwell. Korah waved to David.

"Where are you taking us?" Daedalus asked his captors. Secretly he was nervous and full of misgivings, but he did his best to maintain a godlike clarity and fullness of voice.

"To the King," he was answered.

"And they?"

"To the farms."

Everything in the Maze was built unforgivingly in compliance to the parameters of a maze. The path to the King was uninterrupted, but all of the offshoots along the way were brimming with lattice structures. The lattices added two or three levels, whereon bedding was situated, and places for eating, for natural duties, for market. Monumental architecture. It was all supported by wooden structures, tenoned into the stone walls of the Maze. The bears circumvented their inability to use ladders by making large piles of dirt, piles that could be mounted to get from one level to the next, usually against the wall of a dead-end. All of it was covered in a thin layer of dust, ubiquitous in the Maze, from what Daedalus could tell.

The Royal Room was no exception. It was the only place Daedalus had seen that was physically separated from the rest of the Maze, by a large wooden door that took up the whole width of the passage, some six cubits. A large brass knocker adorned its center, and a bear used it to tap out a pattern while the rest waited. Shortly after, the door swung inward slowly, revealing the lavish living quarters of the Höherbear King.

Dust covered everything. The King had a throne adapted to the form of a bear, in that it had no proper seat, yet signified by way of other chair-like features, namely arms and a back in regal style, that it was indeed a throne. By the look of it, it was never used. Daedalus was actually disoriented by its vacancy, because his long acquaintance with King Richard had strongly associated the concepts of *throne* and *occupied* in his mind. His conceptual disorientation led him to assume that something was terribly amiss until he spotted what must have been the Höherbear King, in the far corner of the room, nestled in a bed of straw. That corner of the room, upon further inspection, seemed far more to have the trappings of use than any other part. Daedalus and Korah were led past the throne to an obese mound of fur that expanded and contracted in slow, rhythmic breathing. A much smaller bear stood guard to the King, and it was he that spoke when they neared. "Your business?"

The bears that had brought them there briefly explained the details of the 'new prisoners,' as they called them, making special note of the two that spoke the Holy Tongue, Korah and Daedalus. They expressed their uncertainty of how to handle the two, as best they could without actually admitting uncertainty. Finally, the King's guard spoke: "Allow a moment for the King to speak."

Then everyone stood silently, Korah and Daedalus awkwardly, as the guard watched the King sleep for a solid three hours. The two humans quickly grew bored and tried to move about, but every time they did they were poked and prodded until they stood still. Then, without any apparent instigation, the guard turned back to the wakeful and said, "It is interpreted from the snoring of the King that the two are to be put to death, for the abasement of the Holy Tongue."

If Korah and Daedalus had been reasonably indoctrinated into Höherbear culture, they would have known that the length of their wait was due to the fact that the King had to be in a state of REM before he was to be interpreted, and they had just arrived at a bad time.

Korah and Daedalus were obviously disconcerted, but it was Korah that finally said, "Can't we actually speak to the King? I don't like how his snoring was interpreted. Perhaps it is just me, but I heard something entirely different. Like the early signs of sleep apnea."

"The King cannot be woken!" shouted the guard in petulant response.

"Is that a normative or descriptive statement?" asked Daedalus.

The guard was preparing an even more vitriolic response when the King stirred. It started with the sounds of virulent trembling, like the initial stages of an earthquake. The sounds emanated from somewhere deep within the mound of fur, but pervaded the whole room. Then the mound began to amorphously shift, finally exposing the bloated but otherwise typical features of a bear.

"Where am I?" were the first words of the somnambulant King.

Daedalus was later to discover that the King wasn't supposed to wake up. The King never woke up. There wasn't a single Höherbear that remembered the last time the King was awake. He nonetheless remained the King—an elaborate art of snore-interpretation had been developed to ensure that the King wasn't ineffectual in his eternal slumber. Legend had it that in times long ago, the King had internalized such an impressive store of food that divinity was conferred on him by that merit alone, and the kingship along with it, right before the resultant bodily dedication of blood to his stomach guaranteed in its thoroughness that he wouldn't have enough blood in his head to achieve consciousness for an effectual eternity—or so it was thought, until that fateful day when the two Abased Gods woke him with infernal perfidy.

But Daedalus had none of the relevant historical context

when the King spoke, and so he didn't quite know how to understand anything that was going on, including the cluelessness of the King and the sheer surprise of all the other bears.

The King was not immediately answered, because the proper decorum of speaking to the King wasn't known. But then the King was very insistent that he wanted to know where he was, so the guard fearfully said, "Home, you are home."

That answer didn't do much to placate the King. He was inconsolably irritable in his every dealing with his surroundings, surely the result of sleeping his way into being unaccustomed to the world. Like a newborn baby he acted, as irritable and unaccustomed to the world as a newborn baby. The King's next question was, "And I am King?"

"Yes, your Majesty."

And even though the King was blatantly unaware of anything that had happened in the Bear Maze ever, he was informed of the basic identity of Korah and Daedalus and asked what he would have of them, as per Korah's request.

"These two? These two here speak the Holy Tongue?"

"Yes, your Majesty."

"Proof. I require proof."

"You heard the King," said the guard to the two. "Proof, he requires proof. Say something."

They both hesitated, before Korah said, "You know, that kind of prompt is the worst kind. People always ask you to say 'just anything,' when they hear that you speak a foreign language. 'Say something, anything,' they say. And you can botch it all and they never know the difference, they think it's wonderful all the same. You can make it all up, for all they know. I want to express my distaste for that. Think of something you want said, before you ask that a foreign language is spoken for you. Please."

"So, it is true," said the King. "Come forth, you," he said, pointing to Korah. Korah obliged, and the King continued, "And this arrow that sticks out of your chest, this is surely the work of Apollo? I recognize the make, the luster in the feathers."

"Yes, it is."

"How is it that your path has crossed with the Sun-God, child?"

The guard interrupted, "Actually, your Majesty, as peculiar as it may sound that he has interacted with Apollo, it's quite commonplace now, for the simple reason that we're lighting the Bear Maze with his radiance. We put him by the farms."

"What is this Bear Maze you speak of?" asked the Höherbear King.

"Home. The Bear Maze is home. It's the capital of your Empire."

The King looked like he wanted to know more on the subject, but proceeded with other questions. "And what is it that keeps Apollo where you put him?"

"He doesn't move at all. His sleep is as imperturbable as yours is. As yours was. The two of you are often compared—a lot of theories were developed about the passive neglect of divinity, but those are going to need serious revising now, I imagine."

"He doesn't move? Very well," the King said, before returning to Korah and his arrow. "You've done something to provoke the wrath of a sleeping God? You wear a stigma, I can see it. You've been marked. For the rest of your days, then, you must be a symbol." To the guard again, he said, "Take him to the place of the Sun-God, and bind him to a pole, for all to learn humility and submission to divinity."

Korah protested but was dragged away, after the unassailable word of the King had been heard. At least as soon as it was agreed upon by the other bears that the King's word was unassailable—the finer details were all still in the process of being decided. Daedalus awaited a fate similar to Korah's.

"As for you, my wizened friend, you also speak the Holy Tongue?"

"Yes, your Majesty."

"Come closer." From how close the King made him stand, Daedalus could see the exorbitant sleep in the King's eyes, and he could feel that the King was still somewhere else in spirit, not in the Bear Maze at all but on some other plain where dreams and hallucinations crowded his mind. "You," the bear said. "You are a son of Dionysus."

Everyone present gasped, except Daedalus, who only felt uneasy and overwhelmed by the pungent smell of sleep, of so much sleep. The King still prophesied, unabashed: "How is it that your path has crossed with the Drunken-God, my child?"

"It hasn't."

The King ignored him. "This man cannot be touched. There is no pole that the stigma of Dionysus can be bound to, no boundary that can contain his disciples. I have become intricately familiar with the work of Dionysus in my night's slumber—let this man free."

"As you say, your Majesty," a bear replied.

So while everyone else that Daedalus knew was bound in servitude, he walked a free man. Word of who he was, and what he was, found its way quickly through the Maze, and everyone looked at him with wary eyes. He used his liberty to talk to the inhabitants of the Maze, but his stigma interfered on numerous occasions with his will—he was avoided almost universally by the Höherbears, and also by the more superstitious of the Gibeahnites. Still, he wanted to learn about his situation, so he persisted in his endeavor.

Daedalus couldn't quite figure it out—earlier the size of the Maze had seemed logical to him, matching his expectations for it. But then as he walked it, and gradually familiarized himself with its customs, inhabitants, and infrastructure, it became the size of a city. Yet it was implausible that it would be the size of a city, since it fit entirely within the confines of a city itself—in the graveyard of that city, no less. But somehow,

underneath the land of the dead, life prospered in all its fullness. He would walk the passages of the market, for instance,
and it would be thriving with activity, with bears hawking their
wares, bears buying, bears leisurely making their way around it
all, and the occasional Gibeahnite that was compelled to haul
loads to and from the farms, used in place of a horse. All the
trappings of a city, of *life*.

The Gibeahnite horses would be tethered to troughs,
whenever their owner wanted to run errands about the market, and Daedalus would sheepishly wave at them. He knew
full well that they would recognize him, with the amount of
notoriety he'd been incessantly accruing for nearly five years.
They would furtively wave him over to them, and mostly out
of curiosity he obliged.

"Yes?" he would ask.

"You need to get us out of here."

"That's what I originally came to the Bear Maze for. But
I'm not so sure it's going to happen, now. You might never
leave the Maze—sorry."

"No, we don't mean the Maze. The Maze is fine. We mean
the market—you need to free us from the market."

Daedalus would always then examine their bonds, hoping
for their sakes that they were actually securely fastened in a
way that warranted a plea to extraneous forces, but every time
it was a simple knot that a real horse could have undone without effort. "Do it yourself," he would say. "It makes me irrationally proud how many things my son Ephraim could solve in
this Maze, but no one else here seems capable of."

"No, sir. See, if we do it ourselves, we're to blame, and we'd
be liable for punishment. But if you do it, we're in no way to
blame, you see."

"I'm going to look past the fact that if you advise me to do
something, you are complicit in the act, and therefore still liable to blame. That's all difficult to understand, I get it. But, I
ask you, if you wouldn't want to be to blame for freeing your-

selves, why would I want to be to blame?"

"No, sir." They would only say 'sir' because he had something they wanted—he hadn't been called 'sir' since he had a large amount of affluence in his favor as the Magister of Science. "They wouldn't blame you, because you can't be blamed. You are Dionysus, you are chaos, and chaos can't rightly be blamed for anything."

"I'm not Dionysus."

"They say you are."

"Well, I'm going to be a disappointing chaos, then. I'm going to walk away now, and leave you to enjoy your trough. Best of wishes."

Eventually he found a Höherbear that would talk to him, something he sought in particular because he knew that if he never discovered the ways of the Höherbear, he would never discover the way *from* the Höherbear. Just like in Gibeah, only the old and senile would deign to talk to him, because they weren't fully cognizant of his identity and its ramifications. He hated how his life seemed to follow him everywhere—Wallace had been his only willing compatriot in Gibeah, because Wallace had been too engaged in the past to know anything of the present, anything of Daedalus. Daedalus had been subtly devastated by watching Wallace beheaded by a bear. By Scherzeherz, no less. And now Daedalus found himself a Höherbear Wallace, a hoary relic of a bear that made a living of being a beggar on the main passage of the Bear Maze, a job eerily similar to Wallace's. Daedalus sat down next to him.

After spending several minutes convincing the bear that he had nothing to offer it by way of food or coin, Daedalus was finally able to sway the conversation in the direction he wanted it. It was an incremental swaying though, as the bear wouldn't directly leave the subject of food and coin, so instead of fighting the grain Daedalus embraced it. "How is it that a fine bear like yourself is allowed to starve in such a prosperous Maze?"

"It's because I can't change with the times, is what it is, and they hold it against me. I come from an era where starving and poverty were the norm, but then times change so quickly and now the trend is to be sated and wealthy, and none of the young fellows are considerate enough to show an old bear how it's done."

"I wouldn't think that a time existed when the Höherbears were ever poor, or anything comparable. They seem to be the striving, successful type," Daedalus said.

"Well, normally that would be the case. But a long time ago the way out of the Maze got closed, and the light here got so dismal. We had been importing food from our Colonies, all of it. It was foolish to be so dependent—I probably said so, at the time. When our Colonies were cut off, so was our lifeblood. We nearly starved, we were getting by on practically nothing. I shouldn't say we nearly starved, since most of us really did. But then there was a miracle, a sign from the gods—the sun was dropped down into the Maze, just the thing we needed, and we were able to grow our own crops. *They* were all able to, I should say. I think I was left out. I should also say that it wasn't really just a sign from the gods, it really *was* a god. Slightly more than a sign. I don't know—the world is confusing."

"They're using Apollo to grow their crops? I had heard something on the subject, but I didn't quite believe it. How did they get him to assume such a menial function?"

"You're going to have to go easy on me with the words there, young bear. But I think I get your gist—he's sleeping, just like our King. It's the mark of divinity, to be completely unconscious and oblivious to the world."

"The Apollo I know wouldn't just sleep the day away. Something happened. And the King's awake now, too."

"No he isn't. They took care of that. And when he was awake, he wasn't the King. Don't act like I'm completely oblivious to the world, now—I'm no god. I hear things. Bears would rather give me useless bits of information than anything to live on."

"Where are the farms?" Daedalus asked.

"Right, right, straight, left, straight, right, right."

Daedalus couldn't make sense of the chronology presented by the beggar—the bear said it was a long time ago that the Colonies were blocked off, but Daedalus had thought that it was his alterations to the Maze that caused the severance, which only would have been several months before. He decided to visit the farms, and from there to get directions to the end of the Maze.

The whole northern side of the Maze was dedicated to farming—Daedalus didn't think that it truly was northern, it felt eastern, but it was referred to as northern because nobody knew better. True directions weren't really important anyway, only consensus. At the junction before the farms began was a barrier the width of the passage, though it could be seen over.

Daedalus discovered that the gate easily swing open, and once he did he found himself confronted by two lounging bears nearby. One immediately spoke. "A free human? How'd he get past us? This is unheard of! Better yet, a free human returned to slavery! In all my days, I've never seen it."

"It's still not unheard of," said the other. "That's Dionysus, not a human at all. If he was human, surely he'd be a slave, because that's the way of things. But he's a god."

The first bear tried again. "If he's a god, why's he awake? Doesn't seem like god material to me."

Daedalus inserted himself into the conversation. "While our one friend here used some horrendously wrong premises to get there, his conclusion is right. I'm not a god. You've heard something wrong—supposedly I have the stigma of Dionysus, or am the son of Dionysus, but that's something else entirely than being a god."

"Well, we're not talking to you regardless."

The one very disappointing thing about absolute freedom was that beings could still refuse to talk to him, Daedalus found. They were all constantly assuring him that he could do anything he wanted, but their first reaction to him was always to distance themselves from him as much as they could, as if with such freedom he became the most imminent of dangers. Daedalus felt more impotent than immanent as he wandered the Maze.

He couldn't get the guards to talk anymore, but he figured that not much more from them needed knowing anyway—their purpose was already stated by the first bear. They were there to keep the servants in, to keep the humans on the farms. And most likely they also monitored the traffic from the farms to the market, when the humans became horses.

So he found nearly the entire population of Gibeah. Each Gibeahnite was allotted a plot/passage of land that they were bound to tend, and in return they received enough food to ensure that they could work the next day. He would edge up to a turn in the Maze, so that he could hear the tender of the next farm but couldn't be seen, and he would just listen. This is what he heard: "These Höherbears are the worst thing that ever happened to us. I almost preferred farming without a sun, because at least then I was a free man. Sure, I had an Overlord that promised to take the majority of my produce, but at least it was *my* produce that they were taking. And the Magisters! What agreeable fellows they were in comparison!"

Just then an old Magister would always show up, and say, "You really think so? We could go back to the way it was. I have some truly marvelous ideas for governance. Just a few easy steps would get us there—strikes, and so on. By my estimation we could achieve autonomy in no time at all. It warms my heart that you've been keeping the faith."

Then the first farmer, the old commoner, would always say that he had just been talking to himself and didn't mean to be overheard, and if he could just be left in solitude again to continue his work that would be great. The Magister would sulk away.

Finally Daedalus approached a farmer. He needed to know the sentiment of the people he thought to save, and eavesdropping, though fertile, was not enough.

"How goes it, farmer?" he said.

"Why aren't you on your own farm?" was the farmer's immediate question, offended that someone else might be receiving a benefit that he equally deserved but wasn't getting. He didn't seem to know who Daedalus was.

Daedalus preferred to allow the farmer to keep his indignation, rather than clarify his identity, because he had seen being recognized go awry so many times before. He said, "I just don't have to farm right now. Special arrangement."

The farmer nodded, but was still decidedly jealous towards Daedalus. Daedalus asked, "Going to be a good harvest?" As he did he looked down the rows, which happened to be ears of corn nearly halfway to maturity, about waist-high. Only six rows could fit on account of the width of the passage, and Daedalus thought to himself how curious it was—a true-to-form farm being grown inside a maze, the sunlight natural but without a visible source, like a narrow farm overshadowed by an omnipresent cloud. It was simply curious.

The farmer couldn't see why a human, therefore a slave/farmer, wouldn't know all about the prospects of the harvest, but he answered anyway. "Not as good as last season. My field should have been fallowed this time around, but the Höherbears don't care about such things. This field will be permanently barren in no time at all, at the rate they're going."

"Not as good as last season? And how many seasons have there been before that?"

"More than I can count."

Daedalus didn't know if the man had answered his question or not. He wanted to know how many harvests the man had personally taken part in, in the Maze, but may instead have just heard the obvious fact that many seasons had preceded the current. It was also possible that the man didn't understand numbers. Daedalus didn't pursue his clear answer, he said, "Huh."

They stood in silence for a while. Thinking to lighten the mood from barren fields, Daedalus said, "It's a nice setup you have here." A cottage in miniature was situated at the very end of the passage, a dead-end. It didn't look like it could fit anything in it, but was nevertheless picturesque, a pure and wonderful distillation of pastoral simplicity. Daedalus meant what he said, but was once more trying to elicit the farmer's feelings, not to convince the farmer of his own.

The farmer said, "As if! The Magisters took the best of land to themselves, they even got flowers growing there. All I got was what was already picked over. That's just my luck, always my lot."

"Why were the Magisters given first choice? I didn't think the Höherbears recognized any difference in status of the humans. I hear Queen Sofia is just a couple acres over."

"Oh yes, that harlot."

"Excuse me," said Daedalus. "How did the Magisters get first choice?"

"Because they were here first."

"Oh really?"

"Yeah, we didn't know either, that they'd been here a while. We asked them how, and they say they were blessed by the noblest horse they'd ever set eyes on. They say they think it was an angel, a saddled angel."

"I have no idea what that means."

"I don't neither."

"So are you happy with your circumstances, then? Would you like to leave the Maze?"

"Don't speak like that!"

"Why not?"

"Get off! Get off my farm!"

Next, Daedalus visited a Magister as the one-time legislator worked his own farm. The man was wary to have Daedalus around, but couldn't avoid it, because he was too unctuous to turn a visitor away, too self-righteous to quit his work, and too untrusting to leave his farm. Begrudgingly he warmed up to Daedalus, never friendly but forthcoming nonetheless. Daedalus said, "It's... interesting to see you again, Simon."

"Hi, Daedalus."

"I hear you're playing as a farmer, these days."

"I hear you're the God of Chaos and Debauchery."

"You can't believe everything you hear."

"You can't, but I have an easy time believing that one."

Daedalus fumbled for conversation. He chose levity. "Being a god isn't as empowering as I thought it would be. Nor as entertaining. I feel like mortality added a very valuable perspective to life."

"I, for one," said Simon, "am learning a lot, from the life of a farmer. Things that I wish I would have known sooner. Had I known half the things I know now, about farming, the materials and labor required, the methods and so on, I would have been a much more effective leader, especially being the Magister of Resources as I was. This is all extremely pertinent to the absolute, arbitrary power I had over farming, and yet I knew nothing of it."

"That's..." Daedalus was honestly surprised. "I think I'm actually proud of you. That's not right. I respect you now. That's not right either."

Simon's face made an expression that Daedalus didn't know the meaning of.

Daedalus decided to get to the point. He feared a response similar to the Gibeahn commoner's, for the question he wanted to ask, but knew that his long acquaintanceship with Simon changed things somehow. "Are you happy then, to stay and learn the ways of farming? Or do you want out of the Maze?"

Simon looked long and probingly into Daedalus' eyes, full

of suspicion. Then he said, "I'm going to show you some-thing. I shouldn't, I don't trust you, but I will." He led Dae-dalus to one of the walls, an indeterminate distance down its length. He led him to a spot and pointed, and Daedalus fol-lowed his gesture to an inconspicuous patch of flowers that was growing under the shelter of the wheat that rose above it.

"What is it?" Daedalus asked.

"A flower. You don't recognize it? All of us Magisters are growing them."

"That sounds… lovely. I'm glad the Magisters can still find diversion in servitude. This must be the source of the com-moner's continued jealousy of you, though they speak lovingly of the past they lived under you. The best of land. A couple of flowers. I can't make sense of their inconsistencies. Sorry, I'm very distracted of late."

"It's okay. I don't understand a bit of what you just said, but it's okay. And I should have known better than to think that you would recognize it. I forgot that we kind of made sure you would never know about things like this ever again, when we blacklisted you. The flower is the key component in a sedative that was formulated under our careful guidance. In time, we'll have enough to get out of here. So, to answer your question about if we want out, it's on the agenda. And we don't need your help, if that's why you're asking."

"You have it all worked out? How do you intend to do it? Perhaps I am slow, but I see no way that a sedative will get you out of here, unless your only plan is a prolonged mental es-cape."

Simon said, though it sounded like an admission that was hard to swallow, "We wait seven years, until the Höherbears above bridge the gap between there and here. Then we tran-quilize everyone, and walk out."

"What if it doesn't work like that? You have no idea what the thing up there that they're building looks like, much less how it works. Maybe it will only work for bears, or only work for those that they allow up? Have you thought of that?"

"What could a bear possibly do that we couldn't? And what right do you have to introduce doubt into our plans?"

"I've seen what they're building, and it's strange."

Simon just stood quietly, then. Daedalus spoke again. "And there's no thought of going the traditional way, of solving the Maze?"

"No, nothing of that."

"Why not?"

"Have you seen the way out?"

"Not recently. Will you take me?"

"I can't. I have to work my land."

"I'm the God of Chaos. Don't resist."

They were nearly there, according to Simon, when a group of Höherbears rounded the corner behind them and shouted for the two to wait up. Simon instantaneously bolted, the last Daedalus would see of him for a while, and so he waited alone as the bears caught up. When they had, Daedalus said, "I didn't see which direction he went. But he has my commendations as a good worker, it was me that tore him away from his duties to guide me somewhere. If you could forgive him, or at least go easy on him. He's a delicate man."

One of their party said, "Who is it that you're even talking about? We came here for you."

"For me? I didn't think you wanted anything to do with me. I've been trying for weeks now to talk to you individually, and I've had no appreciable success. What changed?"

"It's the King. We're worried about him, and we wanted you to have a look at him."

Daedalus smiled, but he didn't mean it. He said, "I don't know what you've heard of me, but I'm a scientist, not a doctor. There are small but all-important differences between the two that make your request infeasible. And even if I were a doctor, I would still know nothing about bears."

"You make far too many assumptions," said the spokes-bear. "Stop trying to anticipate the conversation and just listen. Or better yet, follow us and we'll show you."

"Do I have to go?"

It seemed that the bears had anticipated the question, but had no answer. They scuffed their paws and waited in silence. Daedalus said, "I'm going to assume, all apologies, that your silence means to say that I needn't accompany you. I'm going to have to make an assumption or two if everyone refuses to talk to me, that's the way it goes. But don't worry, I'll go with you."

"You will?" a bear asked, perking up.

"I want to see what you've done to your King," Daedalus said. He also wanted to know what kind of assistance bears would ever ask of him.

Once more he found himself in the Royal Room, and the Höherbear King was right where Daedalus had left him. This time, though, the dust seemed stifling to Daedalus. It caked everything, it obfuscated the carefully wrought heirlooms of the room until nothing could be made of them, until it seemed that it was the dust that was proudly on display, and so many years of ostentation were buried in the past. It engrained itself deeply into the fur of the King, changing his color and making him blend with the rest of the room. Daedalus hardly dared breathe, because he felt that if he did he would stir it all up and choke to death on the resultant cloud. He stopped breathing, so that his breathing wasn't stopped.

The bears that accompanied him weren't as careful, or weren't as observant, or had gotten used to it, or were braver than Daedalus. Daedalus refused to decide which it was, because they had made him very self-conscious about the assumptions he made about the world. He said, "You've shown me. And I still don't understand what it is I'm to do."

"We're not sure he's alive," said the bear that was still the only one that had spoken to Daedalus that whole time. The rest were perfectly mute, as if they had collectively decided that a concession had to be made to speak to Daedalus, but they wanted to minimize their casualties to just the one bear. Daedalus felt like a man with a terminal disease, talking to his healthy but quarantined comrade.

"Why would he be dead? What happened to him?"

"Well," started the bear, who first gathered the explanation on his tongue before expounding, "after lengthy theological dialectic, we decided that divinity should be asleep. Well, to be more specific, we decided that we needed to either revise our theories of divinity and kings, or revise our divinity, our King. The second option just sounded easier. More practical, I mean. We tried persuading the King first, let me assure you, that he needed to go permanently back to bed. But he insisted that he was quite awake and didn't intend to go to any eternal sleep, for quite some time at least. So we weren't left with a choice."

When the bear stopped resolutely there, Daedalus asked, "And? What did you do?"

"The specifics aren't important."

"Yes they are. What do you have me here for, if the specifics aren't important?"

"We're not telling you how—it's the King's business."

"The King's business? Just because it involves the King doesn't mean that treason is the King's business. That's right, I said treason—whatever you've done to him was very obviously against the King's will. And you won't tell me what you've done? I honestly don't know why I'm here. This is what I do, I ask questions. If you didn't want questions asked, you shouldn't have invited me."

"All we wanted," said the bear, "was for you to look into his head and see if he's still dreaming. If he's still dreaming, then he's still the King. He's not showing any external signs of dreaming, though. We need you to look inside. And here's your personal stake—if he's dead, you'd be guilty of deicide.

We wouldn't punish you for it, since you're a god yourself, but it would probably weigh on your conscience."

"I'm not a god!" Daedalus yelled, forgetting himself and consequently gagging on the dust he created. "And why would I be the one guilty of deicide?"

"You would be guilty because you were the one that woke him up. And you are most certainly a god, that's why we brought you here. Dionysus, God of Dreams. He said, when he was ignoble and awake, that he knew you well from his dreams. Visit him again as you've done before, and discover his wellbeing."

On the inside, Daedalus was in hysterics. But to humor them all, he leaned in closely to the massive King.

And suddenly he was alone. He hadn't moved, he was standing in the same place as before. The King was also in front of him, but Daedalus hardly counted him as a presence, although his chest imperceptibly rose and fell as it had before. No one else. They were alone.

Also different was that the dust was gone—Daedalus was finally struck by the sincere regality of the room. Richard's Throne Room had been a massacre of affectation, shoving affluence down the throat of the eye until the observer was either coerced into the belief of regality or went blind. The Bear King's room flowed smoothly into Daedalus, he took it willingly, and was impressed by the artifacts and tapestries that lined the walls, completely covering the stone of the Maze so that it was believable that they were in a domicile hallway of sorts, which led to pleasant, grand places. He noted for the first time a large map of Crete that had many miles of land shaded, bordered by long, winding territorial lines, and in their center was 'Bear Maze' in bold letters.

Then Daedalus woke up. Or everyone and the dust came back, he couldn't tell. The bear guard said, "You did it, didn't you? Was the King well?"

"Whatever you did to him," said Daedalus, "the King is

sleeping even in his dreams. But he is dreaming. I want cleared of all charges of deicide."

Months went by, and Daedalus never could make complete sense of what happened to him in the Royal Room. He wasn't Dionysus, but something had indeed happened in there. And since that seemed to legitimize his identity in everyone else's eyes, that he had demonstrated the ability to enter the dreams of another, he was looked at differently—fearfully, by beings he could only presume thought of dreams as their last bastion, and suspiciously, by beings he could only presume thought they had valuable secrets stashed in their subconscious.

There was once that he had woken up in a cot provided by the King's men to find himself completely surrounded by bears. When they realized that he was awake and aware of their presence, they all acted like nothing was going on, but he knew better. He didn't sleep very well after that—he knew their views on divinity. At any moment they could get it into their heads to do to him what they did to their King, and he would never wake up again.

The Magisters made a new Court, because it was the only way they knew how to interact with themselves on a social level. Eerily, Oliver, the Magister of the King, presided over their Court. He wore a crown of wheat, and sat on a wheelbarrow throne. The Magisters thronged about him, and resumed all of the petty conversations that had been interrupted by their horse.

Daedalus wasn't invited to attend, but, as the representative of Dionysus, no one told him that he couldn't. He sat with his back against the Maze, and listened as they tried to work through their difficulties with the flowers they were growing. Oliver, fulfilling both the office of the King and the Magister of the King, announced a speaker. He said, "To assist us in our current dilemma, the Magister of Science would like to grace us with his presentation, 'On the Beauty of Flowers'."

The Magister of Science took his position to the right of the Royal Wheelbarrow, and said, "Esteemed members of the Court—I've been asked by many of you to assist in extracting the sedative from the flowers we've harvested. And you've come to the right person—as the Magister of Science, I have a certain expertise in the principles of separating materials.

"When it is desired to separate alcohol from water, it is expedient to boil the mixture. When it is desired to separate wheat from the chaff, the mixture requires threshing. Certain differences in physical properties, such as boiling point or density, allow us to manipulate the materials in a way that separates them. So when it is desired to separate a sedative from a flower, we first have to ask ourselves the nature of their difference. To understand the nature of their difference, first we must understand the nature of flowers and the nature of sedation.

"The true nature of a substance is usually a complicated matter that can only be resolved through hours of deep, insightful reflection. But, at least in this instance, one of our answers is easy—the true nature of a flower is beauty.

"The truth of this assertion is easily proven—the colorful growths of plants are not called flowers, if they are ugly. A red leaf is not a flower—it does not have the beauty of form, or the beauty of composition, that would otherwise elevate its status to flowerhood. A leaf is just a flat sheet of paper, really. Boring, coarse, useless—their sole purpose is to provide shade to the world, and, for such a menial purpose, beauty would be out of place. Flowers, on the other hand, are meant entirely for human aesthetic enjoyment. With what else should a man adorn his garden, but with flowers? They are pleasing to the eye, they are soft, supple—like a young girl, emerging into womanhood.

"In fact, the similarities between women and flowers don't end there. Beauty is the essence of both, and therefore, from a scientific standpoint, they are technically identical. They both thrive for a certain season, and then wither into obscurity. The season of a woman is longer, but not by much. They are both at their most attractive when they are rosy, and full-bodied, but many other colors and shapes exist for both. And both are at their best when they are cultivated by men, men who have a greater sense of aesthetic, of composition and arrangement. Most pertinently, both are extremely dangerous. It is no coincidence that these flowers are the most dangerous weapon that we as a society have discovered—women are the most dangerous weapon that we've always had. But because it would seem more practicable to weaponize the flower than it would be to weaponize our women, we will focus on the flower.

"That is the nature of a flower. The nature of sedation is a little more tricky. Some would say that the essence of sedation is sleep, but that would be defining a word with its synonym—a common mistake, for the unscientific. It would be like defining light as brightness, or time as duration—correct in a way, but perfectly uninformative. What I would like to propose, as my professional opinion as a Magister, is that the essence of sedation is submission. To be sedated, therefore, is to submit, which requires that another force is submitted to. A dominant force, naturally. Already, this should make some sense to the better-informed members of the audience—it is often that we say we have 'submitted to sleep', submitted to a sort of divine force that dictates our daily cycles.

"For those that need more convincing, my theory draws from the correlation I've already made between women and flowers—it is very often a case that solutions already found in one field are perfectly suitable for their analogues in other fields. When a woman is being unruly, she requires that a man reassert his dominance over her. In that way she becomes sedate again, she becomes compliant, she becomes manageable.

"What these self-evident truths would seem to suggest would be exactly what we are looking for—a way to separate a flower from a sedative, a way to separate beauty from submission, a way to separate a woman from obedience. All three of these things are equivalent. One of them, we know very much about. We take our knowledge from the lattermost category, women and obedience, and apply it to the flowers.

"What is required, then, to get our sedative, is to be more lenient with our flowers. To be less strict about where they grow, to allow them more promiscuity with the insects that wish to defile them, to not hold them to the standard that we know, by natural order, they should adhere to. If we do those things, it is my scientific belief that the sedative would quickly come right out, in the very same way that a woman without a firm hand keeping her in line quickly loses her beauty.

"This, I am confident, is a solution to our current predicament, and one that could easily be implemented, even if it feels unnatural. Thank you."

General applause.

Daedalus couldn't help himself. He asked the Magister of Science, after waiting in the line of men congratulating him, "How was the sedative extracted before? I am having a very hard time imagining your method being successful."

The Magister of Science was offended, but answered him anyway. "I am confident that that was the way they did it."

"Who is 'they'?"

"The men who were in charge of the flower program before. A bunch of intern-level type fellows, commissioned by the Court a few years ago."

"Why don't you just ask them how they did it?" Daedalus was exasperated with all of the Magisters, but they had a monopoly on the flowers, which they guarded with their lives. He wanted to help them through their ignorance, if at all possible. What hurt Daedalus the most was that the irrational man he was talking to was the one that had replaced him as Magister of Science, three years before. It took everything he had not to strangle the idiot.

"The King had them all killed. The old King. After the second failure of the flower expedition. They knowingly withheld information about the Samsonbear's immunity to the sedative, which was treason."

"So everyone that knew anything about it was killed. Brilliant."

Not wanting to deal with the Magister of Science anymore, Daedalus turned to the whole inadequate congregation. In a raspy, old voice, he said, "You all can try it his way, if you want, but I suggest that you maybe try it in some other ways as well. You know, on the off-chance that his method fails. And if it isn't too unsettling for all of you, I would like to help with finding those other methods."

To his surprise, it was Simon that said, "I second that motion. And I'll personally watch over him, to make sure he doesn't commit any acts of treason."

Oliver looked at everyone in turn, at the Magister of Science, at Daedalus, at Simon. "Very well. Make it so. The sooner we solve this problem, the sooner all of us can return home."

Another day, Daedalus had been nervously fidgeting with the sun weapon that he still carried around with him, for the comfort it provided, when it nearly melted his leg off. Without a single strand of hair in it, it worked. It very directly defied the way he had made it, and the way he had understood it to work. But he had never understood it completely to begin with, he had just taken advantage of a few observations made, those years ago when he was credited with developing the sun weapons.

Almost more than he wanted the insanity of so many recent events explained, he wanted to see the end of the Maze. Many things waited there for him—his additions to the Maze, and an end to the mystery of how well they did their job; Apollo, who was putatively nearby, to light the farms—the humans and their farms had been put between the end and the rest of the Maze to keep them from wandering; and finally Korah, who from what Daedalus heard was staked in close vicinity to the God, as 'a lesson,' the King had said.

For the longest time he had been far too busy to even consider making the trek—multiple times he had been summoned
to the King, to update everyone on his coma. The Magisters
had eventually fully enlisted Daedalus' help, and solicited his
advice, and asked him to help with the compound of the tranquilizer because they honestly didn't know how it worked after all. Even more bizarre was the influx of Höherbears that
wanted him to do miracles for them. They brought him their
sick, their broken, and their dead, for him to fix. No matter
how many of them he turned down, still more came.

But eventually he broke away from all of his distractions
and set out once more towards the end. His thoughts were of
Korah, and the conversation that he had promised after their
fall. He was passing through the farms when suddenly he began to stumble. His vision blurred, and he wiped furiously at
his eyes, thinking that he might have been going blind. Still
he proceeded, but when a choice of left or right opened up
in the Maze before him, and he knew the right choice to be
the correct one, he took the left anyway. He couldn't understand why—he was conscious of his error even as he made it.
His heart began beating louder and louder, until he could hear
nothing over its rhythm flowing in his veins. As he came up to
the dead-end of the path he had chosen he collapsed, trying
as he fell to catch himself on the wall, but it was of no avail.
There he lay.

"I hear that you've been going around impersonating me."

Daedalus dazedly turned over to see the person addressing
him. It was a boy, who had laurel tangled between the thick lay-
ers of his hair.

"You're not doing a very good job," the boy said.

"Are you…" Daedalus started, but trailed off.

"I am Dionysus."

"I tell them that they're mistaken," Daedalus stuttered as an
excuse. His head was throbbing and he couldn't comfort it. He

tried to put his hand up to offer it help, but he was distracted as it made its way across his vision by the lines in his palm,
which he then paused to inspect.

"That's what you tell them half of the time. It's not important. What I came here to say is important. I've decided to help
your people."

"What made you decide that?"

The boy smiled. "That's also not important. Listen to me.
You will threaten the Höherbear King with seven plagues, one
by one, unless he lets your people free. I've hardened his heart
against you, so he will not take your threats seriously. All seven
plagues will be fulfilled, and the world will know my power."

"He's…incapacitated. He's asleep. He can't be threatened."

"That's what I meant."

"Why would I threaten a sleeping bear?"

"It's the only way you'll be free. By the end of it, I promise
that you and your people will be let out of the Maze. But you
must start now."

"What do I do?" Daedalus didn't even feel like it was himself asking the questions, he felt like he was a corn stalk, being
crushed by an old man that inconsiderately fell on top of him.

"Go to the King. Say that if you are not freed, wild animals
will be let loose on the city. Can you do this?"

"Yes, of course."

"Good," the boy said, and cheerily walked away. Daedalus
thought that he fainted.

The next day, since he didn't feel well enough on the day he
met Dionysus, Daedalus knocked on the door to the Royal
Room. He'd never come uninvited before, and was nervous
about how he would be received. The door swung inward just
as promptly as ever, and the lone guard that watched over the
King said, "I humbly prefer that you weren't here, Dionysus."

"I have a message to deliver to the King," responded Daedalus.

"He's sleeping right now."

"… I know." Daedalus brushed past the bear and made his way to the King. Instantly he fell into the bear's dreams, just as unintentionally as before. Daedalus was in the room that impressed him so much once more, alone with the ever-slumbering King.

He didn't do as he was told, not right away. He felt stupid, making threats to something that wouldn't respond to them—he felt like it was an empty, disingenuous gesture to no avail. Moreover, he felt too pleasant in the room, too at home, to speak anything of violence, of plagues. The King had such a mythical, calming presence, and Daedalus was breathing easy and feeling relaxed for the first time in a while. Before he said anything at all he sat with his back against the soft mass of the King and rested, calmly taking in his surroundings and not thinking about much in particular. Finally, when he felt like his peace couldn't go on any longer, he said from his seated position, "I am to tell you that unless you let the Gibeahnites go, there is to be a plague of wild animals, let loose on your city. You probably can't hear me so you probably don't care, which is probably why I've been told to do this. But that's the way it goes, I guess. I'll return to threaten you again, rest assured." And Daedalus woke.

His resolve to visit Korah was renewed, after he had done Dionysus' bidding. He was already well on his way when he was caught up with by a Höherbear that couldn't speak for panting. An entire minute went by, as Daedalus waited. He was impatient. "What is it?" he asked.

"Dionysus! We need your help. We heard the noise of things dropping into the Maze, so we sent the Gathering Party, thinking that we had more slaves to help out on the farms. They were jaguars, an exorbitant amount of jaguars. Almost the entire Party was mauled, there was one that escaped to warn us. Jaguars are slowly solving the Maze. If they get any better at it, they'll be in the city in no time."

"So what's the problem?"

"I sense that you don't care, but I plead that you take the matter seriously. There are a lot of problems. Jaguars in the city would mean jaguars in the farms eventually, and I've heard how you've taken a special interest in the humans. Also, I think that the fact that our Colonial brothers would throw jaguars into the Maze proves that they're going insane. Which wouldn't bother me so much, if they weren't in charge of building the Exit Apparatus. I fear that we won't ever get out of here, with insanity at the helm. Plenty to worry about."

"I myself don't worry that the jaguars will attack the Gibeahnites, and I don't worry that the Exit Apparatus might be a failed endeavor. You're going to have to figure things out on your own. Or wake your King. If you knew what was good for you, you would wake your King. I must be going."

Daedalus had to be firmer with the bear than he wanted to be. He honestly did want to help, to make amends for the consequences of the threats he'd made, of the plague he delivered, but he wanted even firmer not to be distracted anymore, wanted to see Korah and the end. So he persevered, though he felt no end of guilt for it.

He left the bear behind and made his way farther into the farms, into the Maze, than he ever had before. He warily passed the intersection that Dionysus had overtaken him on. Nothing happened. It was looking like he might make it, and he was feeling relatively happy, until he felt something familiar in his surroundings.

Familiarity concerned him. A greatly disproportionate amount, his faculties of reason insisted. Familiar feelings with places one has never been are bound to happen, it said, and shouldn't be heeded strongly. But then something deeper in him insisted that something was horribly amiss, and it brought bile to his stomach.

It wasn't just that the current farm he was crossing looked like all the farms before it. That seemed the reasonable, plausible explanation. It was something else that Daedalus couldn't put his finger on. And he wanted so badly to get past it, to get through, that he picked up his pace.

He felt it the strongest, the worst, as he passed a cottage that extended itself three stories high. A voice answered his fears, it said, "Who's out there? Is that you, David?" It was Bathsheba.

He seriously considered running away. He had been thinking about Bathsheba a lot more than usual of late, and had been intentionally avoiding her ever since he got there. What prevented him from running was that he couldn't decide between forward and backward. So he stood absolutely still as she edged the door open, peering through it to finally meet his eyes. "Daedalus!" she exclaimed. She rushed out and flung herself on him, and he stumbled backward from the unexpected weight, but managed to keep upright.

"Baths…"

"It's been so long. What have you been doing?"

"I don't know," he said. It was the first time in a very long that he'd been prompted to reflect on his actions, those long months since he'd last seen his wife, since before he was imprisoned for violating the sanctity of the Maze. If only those that had accused him of violating its sanctity could see the Maze now, he thought to himself. But then he remembered that they could, they were a couple farms over doing forced labor.

What had he been doing? It seemed like a dream, among bears and wars and gods. The feeling of a dream reminded him of the latest absurdity of his life, and then he didn't want to reflect anymore. So he said flatly, "Nothing much. What about you?"

"I've just been here. Farming with David and a girl named Miriam. You should really say hello to David. And you should meet Miriam." She had already begun to walk towards the far end of the farm, where two figures were hunched over, working in the soil. "You have to be careful with Miriam, she's really easy to upset. But she's very sweet once you get to know her."

Daedalus couldn't protest, his emotions were all drained and he didn't have anything left to speak with. Miriam spotted them as they approached, and she said something to David that made him look up. When he recognized Daedalus, he rose and walked forth to greet him. In the few seconds before the two parties met, Bathsheba said, about the farm, "It really is a pleasant place. And I'm even lucky enough to have company! The Höherbears put the women on larger farms, but they put them in pairs with a man, and look how well it worked out!"

Daedalus could just almost smell his wife, over the formidable smell of barley that hung over the fields.

"Daedalus, good to see you again!" David exclaimed. "I was wondering what happened to you, after we were all separated. I was worried that you and that Leper would meet an ill fate. Glad to see you alive."

"Glad to see you anything." Daedalus was spent, plainly and simply spent, and Bathsheba was already getting cross because she suspected that he was treating David poorly. He could see it in her eyes, but he couldn't do anything about it. "And who is this fair lady?" he asked of Miriam, who truthfully had the fairest complexion he'd ever seen.

She was timid and shaking, and tearstains marred her face, but she answered, "Miriam. My name is Miriam."

"Pleasure to meet you, Miriam."

Just then the roar of a jaguar interpolated itself into their awkward silence, and Bathsheba and Miriam were startled, especially Miriam. Daedalus said, "I hope you can excuse me, but that's something I have to attend to." He made to leave, but paused one more time before doing so. "Where are the kids, Bathsheba?"

"They're in the cottage, sleeping."

"Okay," he said. "I'll be back. Sometime."

Minutes later, at the gate separating farm and city, Daedalus met a jaguar. On its back was Dionysus, using its ears as make-shift reins. Daedalus choked, Daedalus said, "That jaguar isn't meant for the Gibeahnites, is it?"

"No," Dionysus said. "It is for you."

Daedalus didn't respond because Daedalus didn't know how.

"You did well," Dionysus said, "with my first charge. The second plague is the fires of the sun. I want you to go to the King once more, and threaten him with the fires of the sun, unless he frees your people."

"And he won't listen again?"

"And he won't listen again."

Daedalus found himself reclined once more against the mass of the King. He had lingered longer than before, thinking about his wife and the Maze and why he liked that room so much. He didn't know why. The furniture had been rearranged since his last visit, by a ghost or something as unreal, and he didn't know if it meant anything. He was no interpreter of dreams, just an observer. The map of Crete had been taken down, the King's throne had been rotated around so that it faced the back of the room, and several pieces of furniture had travelled short distances. An hourglass sat on the table counting time. Half of its sand was in the upper portion, the grains falling steadily into the pile below. Daedalus watched it for a while, watched time.

"I told one of your own that if they knew what was best for them, they would wake you up," Daedalus told his back-rest. "I'm sorry they're so delusional, but I don't think it's my fault. The next plague is the fires of the sun. Unless you free the Gibeahnites, that is." And Daedalus sat there for half an hour more, quietly, as if he were trying to console a trage-dy-stricken friend by just his presence. At last he rose. "Sleep well."

Again Daedalus attempted to solve the Maze. The fires of the sun surely had something to do with Apollo, he reasoned, and it only further upset him that he had yet to discover the exact circumstances of Apollo's being at the end of the Maze. To minimize the chances of intercepting his wife again, and becoming distracted from the goal, he chose to go at night.

The Maze was the exact opposite of the world above. There, it was eternal night and everyone always felt they should be sleeping or on their way to it. In the Maze it was always day, imparting the feeling that everyone should be up and active, that things needed done. It was hard to remember to go to bed. Once, Daedalus had stayed awake for what amounted to three days straight because he didn't realize the time, and only fell asleep because his body had decided to shut down without warning him. He had woken the next day, very confused on the floor.

If he went during 'night', and if Bathsheba adhered to the prescribed times of the Maze, he could slip past unnoticed, he thought. He could make it to the end.

And it was very nearly a successful idea. But as he snuck past their cottage, and he could hear the muffled snores of its occupants, it occurred to him that he could slip into the dreams of others. He wanted to continue to the end, but he dearly wanted to know what his wife was dreaming of.

So he quietly turned the knob of the door, like a thief. He thought it was funny that his intentions belonged to the dead of night, and yet there he was in broad daylight. His hope was that Bathsheba occupied the main floor and it would be as simple as that.

It wasn't Bathsheba, it was David. Daedalus had to strongly resist the urge to bash the man's head in with anything he could get his hands on. Daedalus found the ladder before he dwelt too long on such thoughts.

The next floor was Miriam. The last was Bathsheba. For the first time in what might have been ages, Daedalus got into bed with his wife. And then, for the first time ever, he slipped into her mind.

They were sitting in a church. Their church. The windows were much brighter then when he had left them, the sun streaking through and making the hair of the congregation translucent as they sat in their pews, and it illuminated half of the dais in a downward stroke. No, the windows were *larger*, the windows were impossibly large, too much for the structural integrity of the building, but Daedalus didn't think much of it because he had Icarus on his lap and had a hard time thinking of anything else—he hugged his son tightly to his chest, and thanked the gods that be for his gift. Icarus protested, saying he couldn't breathe.

Ephraim and Manasseh were there, Wallace was there, David was there but Daedalus didn't mind, Miriam was there, and an old set of neighbors that he hadn't seen in a long time. Daedalus' parents were there, a few rows behind them, who he hadn't seen since the two of them died within a month of each other, and Daedalus turned to wave, and they waved smilingly back. There were so many people there that Daedalus recognized. There was an impossible amount of people, in an impossible amount of sunlight.

While he was turned away the preacher began to speak— Daedalus faced forward again, to meet the eyes and left nostril of the preacher. He said, "We've been through a lot, I know we have. But we're still standing. I want you to think of all the times you didn't think you could stand anymore." Daedalus thought about the last time he'd been in church, thought about the day his son in his arms had died, he thought about losing his mind adding to the Bear Maze when his wife had sold him out, about the times he'd been in prison and the times he'd been used. "You made it. They didn't bring you down. And since you made it, you can be here on a day like this when the sun is shining and there's no reason not to be happy. I want you to remember that there will always be days like this. You can count on them. The next time you're down and nearly broken, I want you to count on this, trade on this, on a day like this. It will save you, because it needs you just as much as you need it."

Daedalus looked at his wife and she looked at him and she smiled and he smiled back and he could feel the pressure of a grip on his right hand and it was Ephraim, who had taken it to his own. He brought his second son closer to his side, because he knew that he should.

"I want to take a minute to talk about love. I bet that half of you hate or fear this word, and the other half of you don't know what all of the hate and fear is for. It *is* an infeasible sounding thought, that people might be *meant* for each other. How does the expression go? How does the sentiment go? 'You're born alone, you die alone?' Well, that might be true, and might be convincing, but you surely don't *live* alone. I once expressed my exasperation to a friend about how people are so hard to reach. I have a job of reaching people, you see—most of you do it out of charity, of philanthropy. Love of people. Bless your souls that you do for free what I do for a living. My friend said, 'that's the way it is.' Born alone die alone.

"My belief is that every one of the moments that you feel like you can't stand anymore, all those moments I told you to recall, have this difficulty as their root—people are hard to reach. Reflect for yourself and see if you agree. And if this is true, that all of the hardships of life arise out of the difficulties of community, then a truism like 'born alone, die alone' can't be the simple truth, can't be 'just the way it is'. Something inside of us, something inalienable, was built to overcome this difficulty. To confront it, to know its hardship, but to eventually overcome it. If it was a thankless hardship we would have set it aside by now.

"Take a look around you. Appreciate the efforts of these people as best as you can. Especially when it's hard. And we'll keep showing up Sunday after Sunday, and we'll make a worthwhile life for you. Because I'm convinced that this is what it looks like to overcome the difficulty of reaching people, a day like this. Sundays are a blessing."

Daedalus couldn't stay, Daedalus had to keep going forward, and forward meant away. Daedalus woke up, Daedalus kissed his wife on the forehead without waking her, and Daedalus took the ladder out.

He hadn't thought he could traumatize himself witnessing the dreams of others. But he was feeling horrible and mawkish again, and every step was difficult, and he was farther than he'd ever been before.

A few hours later he heard crying from the cottage of one of the farmers he had to go by. It was, by convention, very late at night and no one had any business being up. He was determined to see the end but he was curious, always curious, so he peered through the window into the darkened interior of the house, to see a woman with her head buried in her arms sitting at a kitchen table, sobbing to herself. It was Sofia, he recognized her immediately.

Softly he knocked on the door. He could hear her, first surprised by the sound, then composing herself for a minute before she cautiously went to the door and asked, feebly, "Who is it?"

"It's Daedalus," he said. "Would you let me in?"

He had never loved the woman. His feelings for her had ranged from indifference to pity to contempt. But as they exchanged only silence and sat in her kitchen, Daedalus comforted her in his arms because he couldn't think of anything better to be done. She was soft and pathetic again, Daedalus was repenting of all the hatred he had of her, even though he still couldn't make sense of the strong drive that had led her to kill her husband.

They did have one conversation. Her hand strayed to his back, where he had his sun weapon like he always did. She said,

"You still carry this around?"

"I don't trust anyone around here."

"So it actually works still? You said it didn't."

"I didn't lie. It really was used up. But the nature of the weapon changed."

"That doesn't make sense. Scientific things don't do that."

"Why not? I already told you that the weapon was an act of faith. That much is still the same," he said.

And eventually she was asleep, and either because he couldn't help himself or he wanted to, he entered her dreams with her.

It was much different than any of the dreams he had been in before. In the King's dreams and in Bathsheba's he had been a part, possessing his body and moving as he pleased, or at least had the sensation of such. Sofia didn't dream of Daedalus, perhaps refused to, so he was a disembodied consciousness, only observing it all.

The other dreams had been static, as well. Sofia's dream quickly demonstrated how erratic it was. It was more concerned with a story than a feeling—if there was anything Daedalus took away from the first two dreamers, it was a feeling. Now he had a story.

It started in Castle Horeb, though the nature of the rooms and passages betrayed that it was the Maze underneath, with Horeb superimposed over it. Daedalus didn't recognize the room they were in, but he recognized the architectural idiocy that still unsettled him every time he saw it. It was slightly misrepresented, but he knew the tendency of Sofia's rendering.

She was in front of a mirror, cradling her jutting belly with her hands, lovingly. On the other side of the mirror was Scherzeherz urgently saying something, but it was all nonsense and she gave him a bemused look in response. She was more concerned with her growing baby than whatever he might be trying to say. The mirror shattered violently, but she was nonchalant, she walked away to the orchard. At the orchard men were at work, and Daedalus recognized them all as Magisters. Oliver, the Magister of the King, eagerly greeted her. She was reluctant, she tried to turn back, but the way back was closed to her and she had to be in the orchard.

"My dear wife," Oliver said to Sofia.

"I'm not your wife."

"Nonsense," he said. "I am King Richard, and you are my loving wife."

"You're lying, you're lying!" she screamed and cried and tore at her hair.

None of her actions deterred Oliver from his conversation. "We've decided, the Gibeahnites and, more importantly, the Magisters and I, to get things back to the way they were, the natural order of things, here in the orchard. It's different, certainly, but we think we can make do."

Daedalus noticed that every now and then the foliage of the trees coalesced into walls, a maze, and every now and then Oliver's face flickered to Richard's.

"You're not him. You're not him. I killed him," she said over and over to herself. She sat in a corner of the orchard and wouldn't let anyone come near her. The Magisters, and other Gibeahn commoners that came seemingly from the ether, did try to come near her. They shouted reproaches that she was denying the conjugal rights of her husband, and that she was being generally unprincipled and uncouth. They threw things at her, fruit from the orchard, and she didn't tend to her appearance, she had a broken mirror, so soon she was slovenly and trembling alone.

There, amongst her filth and sorrow, she delivered her baby alone. The only people she had were the people that reproached her, and when they saw the awkward, horrendous process she was undergoing they finally left her alone, but only because they were disgusted. The baby was a strange amalgam of bear and human.

Scherzeherz was never there. He seemed to be floating

along the edges of the dream, as if he was always in Sofia's thoughts but otherwise absent. And she cried and nursed her monstrous baby and the Gibeahnites cursed her, accusing her of adultery and whoredom.

And then it faded into nothing.

He had actually fallen asleep. When Daedalus awoke, he noticed that Sofia had awoken before him. And she had taken his sun weapon.

At first he didn't panic, he didn't think anything too serious was happening. He went forward, to the end of the Maze, with a deliberate walk, confident that there couldn't possibly be any distractions left in his life to stop him on that final march.

And he was right. The Maze became brighter and brighter—the correct directions were always obvious, because every correct turn brought a blinding brightness. Even though his eyes slowly adapted to its intensity, it was always renewed by the next turn, so that Daedalus was constantly dazed by the light. To his surprise, the Maze finally widened considerably. Several of the walls had been demolished, and after so much time in the narrow confines of the Maze it felt practically like being outside to Daedalus, especially since the sun was out.

There was a line at the sun. Peasants, the Gibeahn commoners, lined up at the deity to pay tribute. In their hands they held their meager allowance, for all intents and purposes their *livelihood*, and one by one they laid it next to Apollo on an already massive pile of tributes. They kneeled and spoke a few words softly and then deferentially walked away, their skin reddened by such close exposure to the sun. As Daedalus drew up on the scene, Sofia was next in line. He watched from a stone's throw away—with her left hand she carried her monstrous baby, and with her right hand she pointed the sun weapon at the God.

KAPITEL VIERZEHN:
HUMAN MAZE!

THE SUN WEAPON took all of the radiance of Apollo, and gave it back. It was the plague of the fires of the sun, Daedalus realized, it was Sofia at the end of her wits with the most powerful weapon the world had ever known, with the source of its power as present as it was possible to be—the weapon seemed to derive even more intensity from Apollo's proximity.

The beam actually seared the fabric of existence—it was hard to think of what that might have meant, it was hard to look at it, and it was hard to be anywhere near it. Things just didn't exist the same in the path that it travelled.

Apollo was sent flying. He crashed into a wall and fell into the resultant pile of rubble. Next she turned the weapon on the Maze itself. The beams weren't nearly as intense, since Apollo was some distance off, but still they tore through all of the passages and annihilated everything in their path. Daedalus looked down one of the newly formed shortcut passages and could see the cottage of a farm nearly a mile away, missing its top portion and the rest smoldering.

Daedalus didn't have any good ideas about where to go. After seeing the wreckage of the weapon of his own creation, and appreciating very thoroughly its potential, he knew that there wasn't a single safe place he could go. Still, some places had to be safer than others, he thought.

He briefly considered trying to placate Sofia. He imagined there were a few words that he could say to convince her to stop, but then he looked at her, destroying everything, and he was fairly confident that he just wouldn't make it close enough to say them to her. Besides, he didn't know where her anger lay, if it was with the bears, the Maze, the Gibeahnites, the world—with him.

To his dismay, through the new, wide vista of a very simple Maze, he saw the Höherbears mounting a resistance. They were gathering at the gate before the farms, they were deathly scared but they were desperate. Daedalus could see it all. Already Sofia had been going for a solid ten minutes, he judged, and she didn't show any signs of stopping.

Daedalus hid behind a rock, a large portion of the ceiling that had fallen on an unsuspecting group of Gibeahn commoners. Not because he felt any less prone to being evaporated there, if a beam came his way, but because he thought that not being visible to Sofia would be wise.

He felt an honest pang of guilt, shame, and pity, a combination of every negative emotion he was capable of, when the first wave of Höherbears tried to overtake Sofia to save their Maze, their home. He couldn't see Sofia, he couldn't see the expression on her face as she did it, but he could see the beam as it swept across the field and erased them.

The ceiling began to show signs of instability, it was quaking and Daedalus began to say his last words, repenting of all the wrongs he'd ever done. He missed Bathsheba.

Then he saw Apollo stir. It was the second time he'd seen divinity awaken—seen divinity become mundane, as the Höherbears would have it—and he feared the consequences of the second wakening far more than the first.

Apollo wasn't terribly fazed by the beam that had been capable of destroying existence. He was made of something sturdier than existence. There was a slight blemish on his armor, and normally that would have distraught Apollo, but it was one of the rare occasions that the vain deity didn't care much for appearances. Daedalus was watching him rise, and the swift gathering fury on the deity's face, when he was startled by a tap on his shoulder. It was Dionysus.

"Are you enjoying the second plague?" he asked.

"This is more than a plague," Daedalus said. "This is the end of everything."

"Don't exaggerate," said Dionysus. "This might be more intense than you are used to, but it's a *plague*. I don't make hollow threats. There has to be weight in them, there has to be casualties. My power must be known."

"There isn't going to be anyone around to know it."

"Sure there will be. It will all be over soon. Apollo will take Sofia, and it will be the end of it. The next plague is darkness. It is on its way, as soon as Apollo leaves."

"When he takes Sofia? You promised the freedom of the Gibeahnites, not their death. I won't accept death as a plausible form of freedom."

"Sofia isn't really a Gibeahnite. She ran away. If you asked her, she would identify herself as a Nicderbear. Besides, I know that you only have contempt in your heart for her."

"I just don't think this is what I agreed to," Daedalus stated.

He made a very poor decision. He left Dionysus where he was standing, to charge after Sofia. Besides the first few steps, wherein a beam nearly decapitated him as it careened over his boulder, it was a fairly uneventful sprint to where Sofia was radiating death, to where Sofia was being a plague.

"Sofia!" he said. "You shouldn't have done this."

"I know," she said. She stopped. Tears were streaming down her face. Her arm with the weapon slumped to her side, letting it fall. Through it all she had kept cradling her baby with her left arm, and it still slept soundly.

"No, no," he said. "Now's not the time to give up, now

that it's started. Pick the weapon back up. But we need a better plan than the one you have." When she didn't respond, he picked it up for her and put it back into her hand. "This can't overcome Apollo. But it can slow him down. Listen, I need to go get something. And I'm bringing the Gibeahnites with me. You've got to promise me to be more careful with your aim. Hold them off. Let us through." He could see that she was in shock, and she only nodded dumbly to his words, but he hoped enough had sunken in that things would work out. Daedalus began to run away. Apollo chose that moment to speak.

"The sun is mine!" was all he said. He notched an arrow and shot it directly into the sun weapon. Daedalus stopped to hold his breath. He thought to himself that it might already be over—the God had recovered too quickly. But to his surprise the weapon absorbed the arrow, consumed it and shot it back with all of its power, knocking Apollo from his feet again. Daedalus took the opportunity to run.

Past a corner of a wall that was only barely standing, he saw that more Höherbears were waiting for an opportune moment of their own. Sofia was being more sparing with her destruction, and it looked like they might have considered it a sign of weariness—they were organizing themselves for a move. Daedalus ran past all of them and to the farms of the Magisters.

He found Simon crouched behind the ruin of his cottage, talking to himself. Simon didn't acknowledge him at first—Daedalus had to lightly kick the Magister to get his attention. Only then did he look up and say, "Oh, hi, Daedalus. How are you today?"

"Not the time for that," Daedalus said. "Simon, where do you keep the tranquilizers that we made? It's important that you tell me."

"Why do you want to know?"

"I have a feeling that they work on Apollo, and Apollo is over there about to massacre everything alive. Please, just tell me."

"Second shelf of the wardrobe," he said, pointing to his demolished house.

Daedalus left him to wade through the wreckage, frantically shifting pieces of rubble until he finally unearthed a wardrobe, upended but otherwise intact. He had to flip it over to open the drawer, but it was none too difficult. Then he had it all, he had the darts and the blowguns they'd made out of hollowed vegetable stalks.

"Come with me, Simon," he said. "We're all leaving." The Magister didn't object, although he was slow to follow as Daedalus made his way to the beginning of the farms. When Daedalus reached the gate that marked the beginning of the bear's homes, he turned around and started back.

On his way back to chaos he told everyone he came across, all through the farms, "If you want to survive, you need to come with me. Bring only what's necessary, and tell all your neighbors. Hurry. We're leaving." Some would protest, saying that there was no way out the way that he was going, but he firmly told them that they were in a time of crisis and their opinions didn't matter. Soon, he had almost all of Gibeah behind him. At least what was left of it.

Back on the battlefield, things weren't going so well. Apollo had simply left, taking his radiance with him. Daedalus was almost disappointed, because he never got to test the validity of his theory with the tranquilizers. There was still light, so the god wasn't so far away, but it was waning quickly. His departure might have seemed like a blessing, but it did not bode well for Sofia—her weapon relied entirely on the presence of Apollo. He must have realized that, the nature of the weapon, and bowed out while Daedalus was gathering Gibeahnites. The energy of her weapon was depleted, and in the absence of its terror the Höherbears were finally making their advance.

All the Gibeahnites that had been there the whole while, as they had been paying devotion to Apollo—no small number of them—were huddled fearfully around Sofia, who must have won their confidence somehow. And Scherzeherz. Scherzeherz was impeding the march of the Höherbears, alone. The Höherbears were between Daedalus and the exit, attacking Sofia. He had no choice but to deal with them.

"Pass the blowguns out," he told Simon, and handed the bundle of weapons to him. Daedalus considered the amount of munitions they had, as compared to the Höherbears they were up against. They had actually accrued a decent amount, over only a couple months—plants grew fast when the sun was always out. "Tell them to be ready to shoot when I command them to."

He marveled at the creature, at Scherzeherz as he took on a hundred bears that were every one his superior in size. Had they all attacked him at once they would have overwhelmed him easily, but their difficulty was that they didn't want to deviate the larger group, which was always moving forward, so they only committed five Höherbears at a time. What they hadn't realized yet was that five Höherbears at a time didn't stand a chance against Scherzeherz, and thus he whittled the group, little by little, as they trekked the still considerable distance to Sofia and the Gibeahnites. Every now and then she would unload a shot, but it was feeble, and even if it did make contact it wasn't lethal.

Daedalus ran out to half the distance between his party of Gibeahnites and the advancing Höherbears. "Scherzeherz!" he called. Scherzeherz turned to him. When Daedalus had his gaze, he gestured the bear back to where he was standing. He feared that Scherzeherz wouldn't understand, or wouldn't listen. But to his great relief the bear bounded toward him, breaking through the current of Höherbears. In no time at all, the Niederbear King was at his side.

He shouted back up to Simon, "Do it!" and they unleashed the first volley, which fell with general success among the ranks of the Höherbears. His fear had been that their poor aim, combined with the intractable inaccuracy of vegetable stalks, would have claimed Scherzeherz as a victim. But he and the bear stood at a safe distance as the second volley was launched, and nearly half the Höherbears were felled. Still they deliberately advanced, and they were moving out of range.

Daedalus asked Scherzeherz, "Why don't they run? I'm not complaining that they're walking, but if they ran they would reach Sofia in no time."

"They're a proud animal," Scherzeherz replied. "They keep straight lines when they march, at all costs."

"This can't be all the Höherbears," he said. "There are thousands more in the city."

"This is only the advance troop," said Scherzeherz. "They won't mobilize the full army until they have all the nobility and the King on the Spectating Ram. Fortunately for us, the King might be too hard to lift, so the army will never come. They won't fight a full battle without their King."

"This is so easy," Daedalus said.

"It always has been."

They moved forward and shot again. And again. And soon there was only five Höherbears left, but they persisted like a spider that had lost seven of its legs. Daedalus even took his group of Gibeahnites, along with Scherzeherz, and ran around them to join Sofia and everyone with her. There, they waited patiently until the five were in range again, and shot. Only one of those darts made contact, so Daedalus told them to hold fire until they were at pointblank range. From ten feet away the Gibeahnites unloaded twenty darts on the remaining four bears. But only three of them fell.

"Did every one of those shots honestly miss that bear?" Daedalus yelled at his conscripted artillery. But then one of the Gibeahnites, who had keener eyes than Daedalus, pointed out that there were already four darts sticking out of the bear at various places, and yet he persisted. "We've already hit him?" Daedalus asked no one in particular. "How is he still moving?"

One of the nearby Gibeahnites erupted, "It's a fucking Samsonbear!" before fainting in a spray of vomit.

Pandemonium broke loose. No one even stopped to consider if the bear at hand fit the description of a Samsonbear. Myths of the Samsonbear had guaranteed from the cradle onward that none of the Gibeahnites possessed the resolve to stand up to one, neither physically nor rationally. Even though many people were screaming and making other human noises, there was a brief halcyon while the bear stood stock-still, seemingly basking in the terror he inspired, like he lived for it. Or at least it was a halcyon relative to the moments thereafter, during which, among other things, Daedalus watched the Samsonbear dismember Simon with the most disturbing of ease.

Since the Samsonbear stood between the Gibeahnites and the rest of the Maze, the Gibeahnites chose what was left them—the end. They ran en masse, and the bear jovially tagged along, killing who he could on the way, which proved to be everyone he got within five feet of. The victims were mostly of the slower variety, the elderly and the children, who the bear killed indiscriminately, reveling in their blood. Daedalus fell into that group. Once again he was easily winded, he was lagging behind everyone, even though he was giving it the best effort of his life.

Daedalus tripped. He didn't even know how it happened— he was fairly certain that he had tripped on his own foot, and so he felt, as he fell, that he deserved to die for such a poor display. He heard the sounds of screams mutilated mid-utterance rapidly catch up to where he lay, and once more he repented for all the sins he'd committed since the last time he'd repented, some thirty minutes prior. He squeezed his eyes shut in preparation for the end, then had a change of heart and opened them, just in time to see the Samsonbear hurtle over him. It was magnificent. The bear brushed by so closely that its hair imparted a good stroke of the blood it had been absorbing from countless hapless victims, like some morbid brush on a human canvas. When Daedalus finally recovered from his shock, it was with a vibrant red stripe across his entire body.

Daedalus struggled to his knees. He was a battered man, and even a trivial fall like the one he'd just experienced was enough to keep him out of sorts for a very long time. But he needed to help the Gibeahnites. He felt it a cruel irony of life that he, the one with the answers, would be left in the dust while the healthy but otherwise daft remainder would be absolutely helpless when they did arrive at the end, the same end that had discomfited the Höherbears ever since Daedalus had put it there. He was sure then that it was his work that bottled the Maze. He couldn't even stand up to help them, and in the meantime they would all be killed by a demonically bloodthirsty bear. He hated it. He watched it all.

Stairwell was making a stand. He had a deep wound that crossed his chest, so large that Daedalus could make it out even with his poor vision from hundreds of cubits away, but still he made defiant advances at the Samsonbear. Without any weapon to speak of he was doomed to failure—the Samsonbear was an unholy kind of strong, and agile. But Stairwell was tactful, he would wait until the bear turned his attention on some doomed person—by that point all the Gibeahnites were backed up against some obstacle that Daedalus couldn't see from his perspective, with nowhere to go—and then he would tackle it from behind. Several minutes of flailing by the bear would ensue, as Stairwell slowly and deliberately tried to pin limbs and work his way into a chokehold, with all the artful constricting of a python. But eventually the bear would overpower him before he could succeed, and it would cast him off, leaving him to try again.

After a few repetitions, the Samsonbear realized that Stairwell would just continue to be a problem unless definitively dealt with, so it turned its full attention on the man. The man didn't stand a chance, but put on a brave face and assumed a fighting stance. The bear lashed out with an arm and Stairwell was only barely able to deflect it with his own, catching it just an inch below the fatal claws. His block felt the overwhelming impact of the bear's strength, it sent him stumbling back, and he was only weakly able to resume the same stance he had been in before as the bear came after him again. But he did.

Then Scherzeherz stepped in. The Niederbear King was perhaps more weary than anyone, for having singlehandedly killed fifteen Höherbears, among other things, yet he threw himself on the Samsonbear and together they became a blur of rolling and thrashing and deafening roars that were the most primordial of sounds Daedalus had ever heard. It was obvious by the sounds alone that the Samsonbear had never been presented with such a challenge before.

Daedalus couldn't really make out any of the details. Truthfully, from the distance he was at, the bears looked identical to him. The only reason he could tell them apart before was that one was dismembering the entire Gibeahn population and the other wasn't. Normally, the length of the Samsonbear's fur would have given it away, but for some reason, though it was surely a Samsonbear, it lacked their most obvious trait. Its fur was of the same length as Scherzeherz's.

So when one bear harshly batted the face of the other, or pranced on the other's undefended back after tossing it down, Daedalus had no idea how to feel, like he was a spectator at a sport he'd never seen before. But when one of the bears actually ripped the entire arm off of the other, he strongly hoped that Scherzeherz was on the winning end. Judging by the sound of the audience, his hope was wrong, but they could also have just been squeamish at the sickening display.

Out of nowhere came a man, a large pole trailing him and the shaft of an arrow preceding. It only seemed that he came out of nowhere because all attention had been paid to the bears. There was no doubt about his identity, even from Daedalus' blind distance. The man said a few words to the fighting bears, and then the one that still carried the arm of the other in its mouth slowly followed him. Daedalus couldn't hear any of it from his distance.

Those excruciatingly present could hear it all. The man, bound to a stake that still bore the visible evidence of being recently uprooted, had casually dragged himself and his burden to the fighting bears and asked, "Would you please identify yourselves?" To the audience it sounded like normal words, but it was more than that, since it was intelligible to the bears—it was the Holy Tongue.

"Scherzeherz," said the one-armed bear being sat on.

"Thomas," said the other, around the arm in its mouth.

"Thomas," Korah said. "A strong sounding name. I've been told that the quality of a man, or should I say bear, can be inferred from their name. It's a strange theory—names are usually chosen by the parents, after all, and who is already themselves as a child anyway? But I think there's some truth to it. I think we slowly become who everyone thinks we are. So when you are a Thomas, and we have presumptions about Thomases, you slowly become one with our presumptions." Korah's features quickly went from pensive to levity. "But maybe that's all just a bunch of nonsense. It's not important. What my point was, is that I feel like I know a lot about you, even after only a brief appraisal. Would you like to hear it?" Korah began to back up slowly and the bear followed, its ears pricked and facing forward, alert.

"I've just watched you kill a considerable amount of people. From where they've had me posted for months, just over yonder, I've been able to see a lot of things, I've been like a monk—all solitude and meditation, perhaps even insightfulness, and I've been considering a lot of things. I've been a martyr, I've been an example not to follow, I've been in Coventry and I've seen so many people, making obeisance to Apollo and being themselves. I didn't come down for any of them. My energy has been lacking, I've been tired, I've been bleeding out a hole in my chest for longer than I can remember. But I came

down for you, because I have something to say to you in particular—I feel that you especially need talking to, that to you
in particular I am meant to relate. Please excuse me if at any
point I'm not fully making sense, I've been delirious.

"A lot of people dead, and you did it. Most anyone would
take this to be very indicative of character—'Oh, he's killed
a lot of people, he's a murderer.' As if the term 'murderer'
circumscribed your character perfectly, as if it sufficiently explained *you*. But a lot of people have killed a lot of people. I
think *I've* killed a lot of people. So yeah, maybe we're all murderers, but to leave it at that would be to do a mediocre job of
defining us—there are plenty of *ways* to be a murderer. Cold-
blooded, passionate, heroic, bored, ignorant—I've known a lot
of ignorant murderers, I think that this category captures a
lot of them—let me do a better job of defining you, because
surely everyone you've ever known has only done the mediocre job, and everyone deserves to be well defined at least once
in their lives.

"You are *Thomas*. You said so yourself. And I think it's only
appropriate that you said it around an arm in your mouth, and
I'll tell you why. Thomas. A dignified name, a righteous name.
Conceited, and quite easily the name of a murderer. It has a lot
of tradition to it, and thus derives its dignity, I would wager. It
is in opposition to a myriad of colloquial truncations—Thom,
Tommy, Tomkin, so on. And the opposite of colloquial is of-
ficial, established, *dominant*.

"And so I bet my life that for all of yours you've been proving yourself, proving yourself dominant. You only believe in
relative value, in a stronger and a weaker, and so to find yourself you've always been fighting, pitting yourself against opposing forces to see where you stand. To fill the dignity of
your name you've always been finding victories for yourself,
always been the stronger force. I bet it's addictive. I bet that
there's a lot of issues in self-esteem inherent to this game, a
precarious arrangement whereby you constantly redefine 'vic-

tory' to ensure that you've always been having it, and also whereby every redefining you commit you doubt more and more that you have the right definition, since it's proven itself mutable to your indecisiveness, and nothing mutable is trustworthy, nothing you can rest your hat on. And everyone wants firm reassurance that they can find their hat when they need it, isn't that right, bear?" Korah had drawn up to the very edge of an abyss. His left foot nearly strayed over the edge from his negligence, but he recovered and stared into its darkness, something he found himself doing a lot, lately. He then turned back to the Samsonbear with a final resolve.

"Once in everyone's life they'll do the easiest thing they've ever done. In every Thomas the Murderer's life, it will be done intentionally. More often than not, they'll do it immediately following the hardest thing they've ever done, and you just had a substantial difficulty with that base bear, didn't you? Every Thomas the Murderer will get so pathetically diffident that they will seek out the weakest force in existence, because, relative to it, they are at their strongest. Old people and children will no longer suffice, you'll find yourself a man that's been dead for months, bound to a pole, at the edge of an abyss, that isn't even offering you a fight. But you'll find a reason to consider it a fight, you'll find some spurious provocation in my conduct by reaching into that deep well of self-delusion you've dug yourself, in all your redefining. And the easiest thing that this Thomas the Murderer does will also be the last."

The bear had been seething anger from Korah's first words. Something in the broken way the man hobbled infuriated Thomas until it was intoxicating, it was poisonous and he was fully under its influence, deranged by its adverse effects. By the end of Korah's tirade, he'd had all he could stand of the man's presence, and in an act of consumption, in an act of deferral, he blindly tackled the man. And together they fell into the abyss.

There was a sound of shattering.

All the while Daedalus had been dragging himself along the ground, to where man and animal had been confronting each other in their tendentious ways. Moments after Korah and the Samsonbear had gone over the edge, and all the witnesses were somewhere between absolute shock and relief, Daedalus painfully lowered himself into the abyss after the two.

Everyone else was fearfully confused.

Three cubits lower, the tip of Daedalus' right foot found solid ground. Nearby were Korah and Thomas, both gasping for life. Shards of glass fatally perforated the body of each. Daedalus tried to lower himself carefully, but his strength gave out on him halfway and he collapsed into the pit, a shard of glass piercing his leg, but not life-threateningly. Daedalus made his way to Korah in spite of it all. The lunatic was trying to whistle, even as he was dying.

"Was that supposed to be a Subversion?" Daedalus laughed with no humor. "Did it turn out the way you thought it would?"

"I've never had a talent for it," Korah responded.

"Never mind that. I was thinking we could finally have our conversation that I promised," Daedalus said.

"It wasn't an abyss at all," Korah said.

"The illusion of an abyss is just as effective as a real abyss. Until people are desperate enough to jump into it, that is."

"You say that like you put it here yourself."

"I did."

"H-how?"

"Wasn't too difficult. Just a small amount of digging and a household mirror. And a couple of other modifications, but none of them were too laborious."

"A household mirror. How did you think of this? And why?" Korah said, deference leaking into his voice.

"I was trying to protect the Gibeahnites from bears, the only way I knew how. Other people were using walls, tranquilizers, proscriptions. I am a puzzle maker, a deceiver. I take the everyday and put it out of context, because that's what works best. Mirrors into abysses. To answer your question, I thought of it because it is what I do."

Daedalus could see by Korah's expression that he didn't really want to talk about the trivial things of Daedalus' life, he had personal concerns of his own that were to be resolved then or never. In a shallow abyss, it wasn't that hard to see. Actually, there was more to it than that, Daedalus realized as his eyes adjusted to the darkness of the pit—Korah was lying in a pool of his own blood, as usual, but his headdress had become unsettled, and underneath, in its absence, was exposed a perfectly normal scalp.

"Korah, your head…"

"My wife, Miriam. Did Miriam find the opportunity she was looking for? She's my wife. Did you know, she was a Leper once? But she was healed. She left me for a city. Gibeah. All this time that I've spent watching all the Gibeahnites come to Apollo, and I haven't seen her. I was always watching, just for her, but she never came. Did she die? She couldn't have died, could she have? You probably don't know."

Daedalus hesitated. "No, she didn't die. I've seen her."

Korah's eyes lightened back up away from death. "You have? How is she?"

Daedalus thought of the timid, easily upset creature that his wife had become, and he thought about the utility of telling the truth to a dying man. "She's doing great," he said.

"Great? She's doing great without me?" Korah's eyes darkened again, death came back. "That's entirely a surprise to me. It seemed to me like you had to be a bear these days to be well situated. And you can't help the way you're born. I couldn't help the way that I was born, a man of meager talents."

"I wouldn't say meager—"

"Meager," Korah insisted. "It's why you've never heard of me, until I decided to join the Lepers. I am the epitome of average, just look at me," Korah said as he wiped away all of the makeup that covered his face, revealing in patches an admittedly nondescript face in all the places extrusions had been carefully arranged to cover it. "I was a talentless man, destined to never have a word I said be heard. So you know what I did, in my pathetic state? I convinced myself that the Lepers were lesser people, that among them I would be like a deity."

Korah was not a Leper. "It's impressive, really, to be such a consummate deceiver, even among deceivers," said Daedalus, trying in any way he could to console the dying man.

"All that time I spent with them, and I never became one. I was told time and time again that all I had to do was look at them. I didn't think I would always have to be a deceiver." Korah paused. "Bring them here," he said, motioning to all of the people above, the Gibeahnites still unsure about the precipice. "They need to hear all of this."

"No," said Daedalus, deciding to be firm rather than obliging on that point. "They don't have anything to do with you. If I brought them here, even though you saved them all, they would deride you." Daedalus could see the top of Sofia's head from where he lay, and reassured himself of the truth of what he was saying. "Just talk to me. You don't deserve anything but to be respected, and that is what I have for you."

"Respected?" said Korah deliriously. "Did you hear what I just said? I thought they were lesser people. I made the mistake of my life. I thought that, even though I was so average, I had all the right ideas. Like I knew the purpose of life, the valuable from the worthless. And when I came to the Lepers, it was with the intention of convincing them of all those things, of my stupid convictions."

"Korah—"

"Listen to me! I believed in historicity, morality, justice. And when I couldn't make any of them appreciate those things as I did, I held it against them. I've only recently discovered how immodest I've been. How sickeningly, unforgivably immodest. I love the Lepers now. I didn't deserve to be among them either. Every single one of them was a better person than I've ever been. How ironic is that? I hope this makes up for it."

"Can I talk now?"

"Yes, sorry. I didn't mean to be irritable at you. I want to hear the things you have to say. I've been waiting a long time to hear the things that you have to say. Do you know that the Lepers look up to you? All of them. They would never dream of interfering with you. There is a tacit rule that you aren't to be Subverted. If you went to the Leper Colony yourself, they would welcome you with open arms."

"Why?"

"Respect. You're such the romantic, and the things you've brought to this world are an undeniable testament to human ingenuity, to the human spirit."

"I can't make sense of that. A large majority of my inventions were used as weapons against the Lepers themselves."

"That may be, but did you know how your weapons would be used? You've never had a personal agenda against the Lepers, have you? The myth of Daedalus, that has made its way all the way to the Leper Colony, is of a man unaffiliated with the daily happenings of the world—a man locked in his study, at the limits of human intelligence, just for the sake of it."

"I think we distort each other," said Daedalus to Korah, thinking of all the mistakes and petty decisions he'd made in his life. Unlike Korah, though, he didn't want to confess any of them, didn't want to come clean of any of them. "Do you know why it is that the Gibeahnites hate me so much? I figured it out."

"Tell me."

"It's not because I killed Icarus. I always pretended like that's the reason, because it's what the reason should be. I deserve all the reproach in the world for what happened to Icarus. But when I'm thinking clearly, the reason is this—it's because of the wings. The wings are the greatest weapon I ever made, more destructive than any sun weapon, or anything like that. They despise me because I only made it for myself, I refused to make it for them. I made my most desirable, my most destructive weapon for only myself."

Daedalus looked deeply into Korah's eyes, to see what kind of judgment was reserved for him there. All he saw was waning life. So he added, "If you were just a Gibeahnite all along, why didn't you follow Miriam? You could have done it easily. You could have lived a normal life together."

From the death in his eyes was produced a single tear. "Could you bring her here to me?" he asked. Then he died.

Daedalus emerged from the pit a changed man. Not for the better, not for the worse. He just trusted people less, and was a substantial amount more jaded. He pulled the glass out of his leg and cast it aside. He stood up, and all of Gibeah was thronged about him.

To the nearest able-bodied-looking people he said, "All of you—yes, you—clear out the pit. There's glass and bodies. Be careful, but clear it all out."

"Why should we?"

"If you want to get out of here, you'll shut up and do it." Thus Daedalus quickly took command of everyone. No one else questioned him, no one proffered themselves as another candidate to save everyone from their sorry circumstances. They just obeyed.

He took the sun weapon from a despondent Sofia, and shot himself in the leg. He didn't even gauge the intensity of the shot before he did, he just blindly trusted fate as he held the barrel to the gaping wound where the glass had been. Once cauterized, he took the weapon to the empty socket of Scherzeherz. He thought to himself how any human would be ghastly pale from the amount of blood-loss the bear had sustained, but, on account of his fur, Scherzeherz looked exactly the same, just a little asymmetrical. Bears were so different from humans. The bear growled weakly as Daedalus pulled the trigger.

Then Daedalus waved the gun at everyone, telling them to listen to what he had to say. "It is quite possible that a Höherbear army is raising itself, even as we speak, back in the Maze. Or maybe it isn't happening at all. But what is safest, what is best, is that we avoid the possibility altogether by proceeding forward. Unless you like slavery. I'm open to intelligent objections to the plan. I know the way forward, through all these obstructions, because I'm the one that put them there. To protect you from bears. I know that they ended up encapsulating you with the bears... regardless, I know the way out. Follow me. Let's go."

They allowed time for the pit to be cleared of all its glass and bodies, then Daedalus had dirt piled at both ends to allow for ease of access for the old and the weary. Thus did the Gibeahnites cross the Eternal Abyss, an optical illusion accredited with the dissolution of the Höherbear Empire.

Daedalus explained, as they proceeded through more passages, that there was still much to be done. He had spared no effort to ensure that the end of the Maze was unsolvable by anyone except its creator.

The walls exuded confusion as if it were the mortar that held them together. People often had to be dragged away from them, because they had become paralytically mesmerized. More than one person asked Daedalus, "How did you even do this?"

"It's what I do," he would say. "You would remember the kinds of things I do, had I not been absolutely disenfranchised."

Others would ask, "How long did this take?"

"Two weeks," he would say. "Or maybe three. I lost track of time, among other things."

There was once when they had gone a few passages without Daedalus saying a word—he had been explaining all the reasons why they had to proceed just so, so his silence was strange—when he then told everyone, "We must turn around now, and go back the way we came. For a while."

"You were leading us the wrong way?" they would complain. "We thought you knew what you were doing."

To which he would respond, "No, that way was the right way."

Confusion was the Gibeahnites' response. "If that was the right way, why are we turning around?"

"Exactly," Daedalus would say. "Who would think that, if they were going the right way, they should turn around and consciously go the wrong way? That is exactly the kind of logic I must counter-employ, as a maze-builder. The only way to get through this stretch of the Maze is to go the right way, then turn back and go wrong."

"That doesn't make sense," people would keep saying.

"Exactly," he would always reply back.

There was one fork at which Daedalus told the Gibeahnites, "One group must go that way, while the other goes this. It's the only way to get through." At that point people were largely incredulous of Daedalus, but listened nonetheless, because he somehow seemed to be right in everything he did. "David," he said. "You take a party and go that way. I'll lead a party that goes this way, and we'll meet up at the end."

"Will the way be obvious?" David asked.

"Yes, you won't need my guidance to find where I'm sending you, I promise. If you'd believe it, I had you in mind when I built this portion."

Bathsheba interceded, "I'll go with David's party."

"Best not," Daedalus told his wife. She listened, and the two parties went the two different directions. Still further they continued until one passage where Daedalus told his followers, "We must wait here a while."

He had known from the beginning that their current passage would present a problem to him, being on the wrong side of it, but he had hoped he could resolve it when he got there. A Gibeahnite asked him, as everyone else became settled, "How long do you expect we'll be here?"

"Best you prepare to stay the night," Daedalus said. The sunlight was getting gradually dimmer, until it was almost entirely gone, as if the Maze was experiencing its first natural progression of time in ages. The Gibeahnite was content and returned to his people. Daedalus sat with Scherzeherz.

"How is the arm?" he asked the warrior.

"Better than I thought it would be. I felt like it was all over, like I wouldn't be able to live for shame, after losing to that Samsonbear," Scherzeherz said.

"Why is everyone so hard on themselves?" Daedalus asked, not looking for an answer.

The warrior didn't answer anyway, he said instead, after the two just stared into the dark passage ahead of them for a while, "What is it we're waiting for this time, exactly?"

"Interesting thing," Daedalus said. "We're waiting for divine approval. This is literally the last obstacle between us and the world outside, but I fear that we won't be able to get past it after how much we've been ingratiating ourselves with all of the gods, lately."

"Divine approval?" Scherzeherz asked. "Why would you make that an obstacle in a maze?"

"It seemed like a good idea at the time," Daedalus responded. "This is the point in the Maze that people's spirits would be so broken that they would start cursing the gods. It's a natural phenomenon. After surviving so many hardships, people start asking the higher powers how any of it came to pass under their watch, and accuse them of many similar injustices. And the deities are bound not to take any such indictment lightly. And if this is the case, the hardest maze to solve is the one that demands that people be in harmony with the gods at its end. I made it too hard. Even I, its maker, didn't have the resolve to make it to the end without bitterness. I've angered all the gods. No Apollo will come. No Dionysus."

"I thought you *were* Dionysus," Scherzeherz said. "And even if that was an exaggeration, it is at least the case that you've been in league with him. Why won't he come to your aid?"

"I didn't submit myself to carry out his plagues. I couldn't tolerate the inhumanity of it, I walked away with his will unfulfilled. He wanted the world to know his power, he said. But he asked for cruel things, he asked for more than I thought it was reasonable for me to give. So I disobeyed him."

Scherzeherz bore no resentment. "What do we do now, then?"

"We wait," Daedalus said. "We let the world sort it out."

Everyone had been asleep for hours when Daedalus woke up. He didn't know why he had become awakened, and he couldn't fall back asleep, so he sat up. Nearby, Scherzeherz still lay, snoring heavily. Daedalus considered the bear—he wanted to know what kind of thoughts filled that wide, proud, ursine head, and he also wanted to know if his affinity with Dionysus still existed. So he attempted to enter the dreams of the bear.

He was standing in a river, and it was the most refreshing feeling of Daedalus' life. Every other dreamer he'd followed had enclosed themselves with walls, even Sofia's orchard had really just been the Maze in disguise. Only Scherzeherz dreamed of the outdoors, and Daedalus took in the early morning sky with the most welcome of hearts he had. He watched the sun dawn for the first time since the Gibeahnites had built the city walls. To think that, of all the dreams he'd had or seen, it would be a bear's that he was jealous of, made him laugh.

He couldn't just enjoy himself, though. He was there to learn, and Scherzeherz was just visible around a bend in the river, though Daedalus couldn't make out what he was doing.

To get to Scherzeherz, Daedalus relinquished himself to the current. The waters splashed over his face, they tempered his irritable mood. He just drifted until he had arrived to Scherzeherz, and could make everything out.

Scherzeherz was already dreaming himself with only one

arm, but he was jovial, he was splashing around and uninhibited by the sacrifice he had made. There were other bears along the bank, and Daedalus could see that they were fearful of the waters. Scherzeherz employed all types of imploring—he demonstrated how fun it was, how free and liberating, he spoke words, which once again were nothing but the guttural sounds of the bears to Daedalus. But the bears wouldn't join him. Daedalus could see the reason for their hesitation in their eyes—they were afraid of sacrifice, they were pedantic, they were deaf. Scherzeherz was making the most convincing animalistic noises that Daedalus ever heard, and yet none of them would budge. And so Scherzeherz enjoyed the river alone.

Daedalus let himself drift again, away from the dreamer, because he couldn't stand the sight of the bear being ignored. He lay on his back and watched the foliage drift by, its branches and leaves playing with the streaming sunlight. He could hear birds in the distance, but he wasn't haunted by them.

Dionysus was drifting alongside him. "I thought you'd abandoned me," Daedalus said.

"You abandoned me," Dionysus said back.

"Will you let us through the Maze?" Daedalus asked, only half curious of the answer, because he was perfectly calm.

"I will let your people through," Dionysus said. "But not you. Your people are still my own. I have a Promised Land for them. I want you to tell them that. But you disobeyed my will. I will let you see the Promised Land, but you shall never enter it."

Daedalus considered those words, considered the sky. "Yeah, I'll tell them all that," Daedalus said, and drifted into dreams of his own, where there were no gods, no bears—just peace.

When everyone awoke, he gathered them to say his goodbyes.

He didn't have anything to say to Sofia.

He said to his wife, "I love you. There's a world ahead of you out there, always has been, and you'll be happy. I promise. You'll find a way."

"David will be there?" she asked.

"Yes," he said. He kissed her on the cheek. He took his son Ephraim by the hand and led him away from everyone else. He said to his second son, "Ephraim, I wish I had gotten to know you better. I'm sure you will grow to be a fine man, and I'm sorry I won't get to see it happen. I haven't been fair with you. You deserved every bit as much attention as I gave Icarus. I promise that someday the world won't put all of its hopes and dreams into firstborns. It may still be a long time to come, but we're on our way. Take care of your brother Manasseh for me." The kid ran off back to his mother, with a childish stride, and that was that.

He then said to everyone, "You are all permitted to go. Dionysus allows it. And he wants you to know that a Promised Land awaits you."

"You'll show us the way, won't you Daedalus?" came a voice from the crowd.

"No, I've been forbidden, by Dionysus."

"That isn't fair!" said another voice from the crowd.

"Don't," said Daedalus, "go against the will of Dionysus. It is only by his good graces that you can go forward. If you accuse him of unfairness now, then the way is lost for all of us."

"But it isn't fair," said the same voice.

Daedalus had had more than he could stand. "You know what?" he said. "If this 'Promised Land' that Dionysus speaks of is full of people like you, I don't want to have any part in it anyway, even if it were just on the other end of this passage. But it's not just at the other end of this passage—there might be a Promised Land ahead of you, but it's still a long time in the making. Out there, in your city, it is still the bears that rule, and there's a large amount of work to be done before they are overcome. I've seen too many good people mistreated, and too many incompetent fools with power. Putting a Promised Land under people's feet doesn't make them any less people. The best man I ever knew wandered from place to place, people to people, never feeling at home until it killed him. I had a friend that was an obliging fellow, and so more and more responsibility was deferred to him by the lazy and the inconsiderate until the weight of it all killed him as well. And I had a son… what happened to him was me. People like me. I don't want to go to a Promised Land that has people like me. Because no matter what, love won't work, friendship won't salvage anything, and every 'meaningful' purpose in life imaginable won't be enough to console the wayward spirit. I hope it's enough for you. I hope you're all ignorant enough that the shortcomings of paradise won't ever occur to you, you'll just be happy, live long, thrive. But it's not for me. Don't argue my case that I should be able to go with you. I don't want any part in it."

The Gibeahnites shamefully ambled their way out of the Maze with Daedalus escorting them from behind, like a host that stopped his own party just as it was getting started, to make everyone get out. He walked them all to the exit, and took in the view that Dionysus had told him to, a paradise in the distance, though he didn't absorb any of its details because he didn't care. Then he turned around.

He had heard about many creators becoming the victim of their own creation. There was a man that built a brass bull, a torture device that was lowered, complete with a person inside, over a fire until the person boiled. It even had a clever device that transformed their screams into the sound of a bull snorting. The creator was the first of its victims—the king he had made it for wanted to see how it worked, and the nearest person was put into it. The creator. Simple as that.

The sun was at Daedalus' back when he turned around, Apollo was behind him, so that his shadow stretched out before him. It occurred to him then how nondescript he himself was, something Korah had been talking about. His silhouette could have housed anyone imaginable—in it he saw Wallace, Korah, Stairwell, David, Bathsheba, Richard, Simon, Sofia, Miriam, the preacher, even Scherzeherz. He lifted his arm parallel with the sun, so that its shadow became truncated, and saw in himself the magnificent bear. He saw in himself Icarus, Icarus three years later, a newly grown man, full of the potential of life.

But those were other people. In the shadow of infinite possibility, Daedalus could only do one thing that was truly his own—he spread the wings that would always be his downfall.

NACHWORT

Korah,

I solved the Bear Maze today. I don't know exactly what inspired ev-eryone to try again, but we reached the end. Finally. There was so much that happened in that Maze. I'd like to write to you about it sometime in detail, but for now, I guess, I want to focus on what happened at the end. Daedalus yelled at us all, and sent us away. His family, his friends. Ev-eryone was there, we all saw it. I guess I wanted to write you to tell you that I hope your next journey in life is full of happiness, and that everyone there is able to reach the people they love in time, and not cover themselves in mud and die in optical illusions instead of returning to health. I hope that you can tell your lover that you love them in the way you can, and that she can understand it and reciprocate it in a way you can understand. And I hope, far more than any of that, that time has done good things to you, and that it keeps doing good things to you, and that you are happy.

Miriam